TY
[...]S OF YORK
~ BOOK TWO ~

MONSTERS
AT THE
GATE

Published in paperback in 2023 by Sixth Element Publishing
on behalf of Ben Sawyer

Sixth Element Publishing
Arthur Robinson House
13-14 The Green
Billingham TS23 1EU
www.6epublishing.net

ISBN 978-1-914170-49-2

British Library Cataloguing in Publication Data. A catalogue record for this book is
available from the British Library.

This is a work of fiction. Names, characters, businesses, places, events and incidents
are either the products of the author's imagination or used in a fictitious manner.
Any resemblance to actual persons, living or dead, or actual events and places is
purely coincidental.

Ben Sawyer asserts the moral right to be identified as the author of this work.

Printed in Great Britain.

HOLLY TRINITY
AND THE GHOSTS OF YORK
~ BOOK TWO ~

MONSTERS AT THE GATE

BEN SAWYER

CHAPTER 1
1604

The men came for her just after dawn, and she did not stop to tell anyone where she was going. They led her silently through the recovering city to a small tumbledown barn, still showing signs of damage from the recent terrors. She knew this place. The last time she was here, monsters had been at the gate.

Now the nightmare had passed, and it was where the strangers were.

Inside, a man and a woman were hard at work behind a long table, surrounded by what looked like the tools of an apothecary. The men directed her to a small wooden stool in front of the strangers, then scurried away in awed silence.

She bowed her head and wrung her fingers, but her fascinated eyes constantly flicked up to the pair, who joked and bickered in a language she did not understand. Nevertheless, she recognised the simple ease of a long marriage.

The woman was grinding herbs with a mortar and pestle, while the man poured the contents of assorted ornate bottles into a battered metal pot. A chunk of vivid pink sandstone sat on the table between them, which he picked up, humming gently as he allowed the contents of a bottle to trickle over its surface into his mixture. It was like something from one of her father's stories.

"Your father taught you to read."

The sudden switch to English made her start. It was the wife who had spoken, and was regarding her with curious eyes.

"You must forgive me, I have not had time to learn much about you," she said. "But that detail interested me. My father

1

taught me to read as well. A long time ago, when it was an even more daring act than it is now. Never underestimate the terror a woman with a book can inspire."

She smiled nervously, and bowed her head again. When she looked up, she saw the husband grinning broadly at her through his thick, curly beard. His eyes were kind and gentle.

"My father used to say 'there is a reason for everything'," the wife continued, as she added the contents of her stone bowl to her companion's iron vessel. "This is a sentiment you have no doubt heard expressed by others. Churchmen will say it is God's plan. Philosophers look for patterns and an order to the world. I know that what you have seen must make it hard to believe such a thing can be true."

The wife came out from behind the table and almost glided across the room towards her, so graceful was she. "I am truly sorry for what has happened here. When I was told of you, I assumed you had lost everything, but the townsfolk tell me your father lives. And you have a sister, I believe. This troubles me. It must have occurred to you that by going down this path you may never see them again."

The wife knelt before her, taking hold of both her hands. "I do not believe that everything happens for a reason. Sometimes, things merely happen, and so often, this is a cruelty. You know this more than most. But people – people always have reasons. Always. They do not always know them or understand them, but the reasons are there, and drive them to whatever ends."

The stranger touched her face, holding her head up and staring deep into her eyes.

"You will be the King in the Mountain. Your life will be longer and stranger than you can possibly imagine. The world will grow and change around you, becoming something none of us can foresee, but you will learn to live in it. You will hold a light against the shadows and you will not fear them. And you will be alone. But you must know why. If you are to be strong enough, you must know why."

She gave a nod to indicate her understanding of the stranger's point. And she told them the reasons that, centuries later, she would forget.

THE McALLISTER
INVESTIGATION I
SOMETIME IN THE 1980s...

"Treasurer's House was bought by York industrialist Frank Green in 1897, to showcase his collections of objets d'art and antique furniture. He commissioned a series of 'period rooms', each in the style of a different era, seeking a more comprehensive approach to the preservation of history than maintaining the building as it had appeared at any particular time."

•

The large brass pendulum at the edge of the Great Hall gave a dull tick as it swung back and forth. Amid the apparatus on the table, a smaller arm moved in a similar manner, but merely squeaked ever so slightly. The towering emptiness of the space amplified their duet until it echoed off the surrounding stone, wood and plaster. Dylan did not hear it, however; his attention was entirely elsewhere.

His work station sat in front of the fireplace, cables snaking away from it across the black and white pattern of the marble floor. A bank of bulky monitors displayed grainy monochrome footage from various parts of Treasurer's House. The small metal armature left a trail of zig-zagging patterns across the paper below it as it squealed back and forth, measurements folding into a neat pile beside the table. Vivid green sine waves pulsed across the tiny screens of three boxy, battered oscilloscopes while needles twitched in simple white gauges.

It was an incongruously modern set-up in an incongruously ancient room. If Dylan had stepped away from his desk, he'd also have vacated the 1980s. Beyond the hall's three internal doorways lay a stately home decorated Georgian style. If he left by the double doors immediately behind him, tranquil gardens with a view of York Minster's north side would surround him. But a flash of inspiration in the distant past had compelled the owner of Treasurer's House to get all medieval on this hall.

Not that Dylan was paying any attention to the decor – his mind was focused on the sounds he was listening to, sounds that felt to him like the product of some distant other world.

The most striking thing about the hall was its height, the ceiling a staggering three storeys up from the floor. Chunky wooden rafters stretched beneath it, and a three-tiered chandelier dangled on a long chain from the middle of the centremost beam. Paintings of assorted vintages lined the walls and, more anachronistic still, a row of Roman columns stood alongside the dark wooden staircase to Dylan's right, near where the long pendulum hung, suspended from a clock located several floors above.

Dylan was oblivious to its sonorous tick. His head was encased in a pair of domed headphones that blotted out all other noise, so he did not hear the footsteps as someone approached him from behind. With one swift yank, the jack of the headphones was free of its socket. The entire hall reverberated to the music, which soared in the open air.

Dylan nearly fell out of his seat as he tore the headphones from his ears. He looked up to see the sharp features of Professor McAllister, staring at him disapprovingly over her glasses, and mumbled an apology as he plucked the needle from the record and silenced Freddie Mercury in the middle of his eight-minute magnum opus.

"Damn," she said, tapping the side of the rightmost monitor, which displayed nothing but static. "How long has this one been… oh, never mind."

Dylan looked sheepish as the professor examined the patterns on the mound of paper and compared the chunky brass thermometer on the table with a smaller one produced from the pocket of her cardigan.

"Is everything okay? I heard something." Brian was leaning out of a window of the minstrel's gallery above them. A row of stags' skulls underneath the casement stared down along with him. A clacking and rustling came from the left-hand doorway as Sophie tottered in on heels Professor McAllister had sworn off rolling her eyes at, while Brian emerged down the staircase that creaked under his burly frame.

"Everything's fine," the professor said. "Just another little musical interlude from Mr Kitson. Brian, could you go to the drawing room, camera three is on the blink again. Sophie, see where Richard's got to. I've been waiting over an hour for my coffee."

"Um, I know how the cameras work too," said Sophie indignantly.

"Yes, but Brian snogging his boyfriend for five minutes isn't going to get my coffee here any quicker," Professor McAllister retorted, taking a moment to flick a wink at Brian's stunned expression. "We've been here two weeks. Did you honestly think no one had noticed?"

"I hadn't noticed," said Dylan, and no one listened. At eighteen, he was only a few years younger than the rest of McAllister's team, but right now he felt every minute of it.

Brian sprinted for the entrance Sophie had emerged from with unusual swiftness for his size.

"Is there something else?" Professor McAllister did not look up from the instruments as Sophie waited expectantly, fingers working the irregular surfaces of the chunky orange necklace that dangled loosely around her neck.

"I'm not just here to make you coffee, you know," Sophie said, with a modicum of defiance.

"You're not here to make it at all. Richard knows how I like it, while you are merely an excellent researcher. But since he has apparently failed in his task, the terrible burden now falls upon you. Godspeed, brave sister, and make me proud."

Sophie opened her mouth to respond, thought better of it, and clattered away in the opposite direction to Brian, the sharp, plasticky clacking of her heels and jewellery fading as she departed.

Dylan shuffled from foot to foot as Professor McAllister settled into the work station, analysing each instrument in turn with a swift but complete precision.

"Is there anything I can do?" he asked.

"Just stand there and hope you haven't made me swear off involving undergraduates in these little jaunts." She glanced at the record player, and her quiet sternness was momentarily eclipsed by a half-smile. "*Sheer Heart Attack?*"

"*A Night at the Opera,*" he corrected her, his face reddening. "I still should never have let you bring that thing."

Suddenly, all the monitors went dark, followed by the chandelier. The hall was plunged into gloom, until Professor McAllister's torch provided a small burst of illumination.

"Now what?" she grumbled.

Sophie stopped sharp as the lights failed, and steadied herself on the close walls of the steps leading to the basement, or 'below stairs' as she had taken to calling it. Feeling her way along the rough plaster, she moved carefully along the corridor. A tiny, regular noise echoed through the darkness and she could see a line of light in the bottom of a doorway, right where the staff kitchens should be. She breathed a sigh of relief – Richard had a torch. She'd gotten out of the habit of carrying one once she'd discovered how much the designers of the house *really* liked chandeliers.

She followed the light and the noise into the dull, modern kitchen, where the sound came into focus as a dripping tap. A torch lay discarded on the linoleum, casting rings of light across the bottom of the door. Her fingers settled on its rubbery stump, and she let out a sigh of relief when the beam picked out Richard's shaggy mullet and broad shoulders by the sink.

"Where have you been hiding? The prof's gasping for her coffee."

Richard did not move, did not respond in any way. His face remained turned away from her, watching the drips grow and fall. Sophie's torchlight caught the strange green stone that dangled from a leather band at his wrist, and she smiled fondly at the invitation to talk about his travels that she knew it represented.

"I should warn you, she's on to you," she teased. "I told you you'd never get away with it, cooped up like this all this time."

The water continued to drip. Sophie moved closer, placing a hand on his unmoving shoulder. Her eyes caught a flash of red across the back of his hand.

"Did you cut yourself?" she asked, then screamed.

Professor McAllister and Dylan had been following Sophie downstairs in search of a fuse box when they heard the cry, just before the lights flickered back into life. They found Sophie curled up in a corner of the kitchen, a lit torch clutched in her hands. She screamed again as they entered the room and tried to retreat even further, her gaze snapping around her. The tap was dripping, and Dylan, for want of anything useful to do, turned it tighter.

"Richard," wailed Sophie as the professor crouched beside her, discreetly checking for signs of injury. "Richard was... he was here, but he... he..."

"Come on, let's get you back upstairs." Professor McAllister gently slipped the shoes from her feet, deciding that nobody should even attempt to walk in those things in a state of shock.

Between them, they led her back to the Great Hall. Sophie was quickly settled in the work station chair, while the professor made straight for the left-hand exit.

"I'm going to find Brian and Richard. Stay here and look after her."

She passed the house's ornate main staircase and entered a regal green drawing room, where a huge camera sat immobile on its tripod, an alien invader from Planet Eighties. Professor McAllister could hear voices from the adjoining Court Room. She hoped that Brian had managed to find Richard. Anything more complicated than a clandestine gay romance on university time was more than she needed right now. Her hopes of a simple resolution were dashed as soon as she stepped through the door.

The Court Room's main feature was a huge display case on a central table, standing at head height like a miniature glass cathedral. Inside was an intricately carved model of a tall ship, two feet from prow to stern. The professor knew its history well. It had been carved from whalebone by prisoners of war, a grisly detail she used to detect students who might have followed her for the wrong reasons.

Brian stood on one side of the vessel and behind it were two strangers. The first was a woman in a leather bomber jacket coloured a vivid shade of purple, with a vast mass of curly auburn hair sitting atop her head. Beside her was a shorter figure, clad in a tatty green parka. The round, pale face of a teenage girl stared out cynically from the fur-lined hood. The professor slipped off her glasses, the better to fix them with her most commanding stare.

"Would you mind explaining who you are, and what you're doing here?"

"That's not fair. That's what I were gonna say," said Holly Trinity. "I never manage to get mine in first."

CHAPTER 2

"We need to talk," Mira Chaudhri began, but didn't. She paced the empty bedroom, occasionally stopping to study the notebook in her hand. There were a lot of things scrawled on it, a lot of crossing out and rewriting. Parts of the page felt calm, others really didn't. Mira sucked in a long breath and rehearsed telling her boyfriend everything.

"Okay, when we first got together, there were all those murders. But what nobody knows is they weren't committed by a man. It was a monster, but it was also a ghost, it was a sort of monster-ghost…"

She broke off and shook her head at the foolishness of her words.

"We need to talk," she started again. That bit she felt confident with. "About ghosts, because ghosts are real, in fact there's one in this flat that you've never noticed, but don't worry, he's alright, but when we first got together, there was this one ghost, that was also a monster, that was also a serial killer – No, no, no."

"Look, back when we first got together," she said, the notebook trembling in her hands. "There was this thing that was killing people, and I stopped it. Me, I stopped it. I saved the city, I…"

She looked in the mirror, gave it her most important face, and whipped her reading glasses off in a single dramatic flourish. She laughed at herself, but it wasn't getting her anywhere. She tossed the book to the bedside table, where a few pages flipped forward on their own as her ghostly flatmate made his suggestion on where to proceed next.

"Thank you, Joe. We need to talk… about Holly. I haven't told you everything about her. She's not exactly a normal person…"

She stopped in mid-sentence and shook her head. "Just in case you'd somehow got that impression."

Mira confronted the mirror again. She did not like the way it was looking at her.

"Look, we need to talk about me and Holly." She tossed the notepad on the floor and improvised. "You see, Holly isn't a writer, like I told you. What she actually does is protect the city from, well, monsters. I guess you'd have to call them monsters. Because monsters are real. And ghosts, ghosts are real too, and a lot of monsters are also ghosts, but not all ghosts are monsters."

Mira retrieved the notepad, which had been nudging her foot to emphasise that last point, flicked through a few pages, then slapped herself on the forehead with it.

"Sam, we need to talk," she repeated. "About me and Holly. Because Holly is a sort of… I guess you'd have to say hero. Just don't tell her I said that, I'll never hear the end of it. She's hundreds of years old, and all she does is keep this city safe from terrible things. Things you wouldn't believe. Monsters. Real monsters."

Mira was gathering steam now. She stopped pacing and leaned in to tell her story to the woman in the mirror.

"And I've been helping her. So I guess you could call me her sidekick, but I'd really rather you didn't. She needs me, you see. She's supposed to sleep for years between dealing with these things, but there are too many of them now, so she doesn't sleep much, gets exhausted and needs a hand. And all this time I've been hanging out with her, actually I've been helping her save people and protect the city and fight monsters. I've been scared out of my wits and nearly died and seen the most amazing things, you wouldn't believe it. And I'm sorry I didn't tell you any of this sooner, I just couldn't because…"

The woman in the mirror glared accusingly at her.

"Any ideas?" she asked. A bad one leapt to mind.

CHAPTER 3

"I think you should have a boyfriend," Mira said to Holly as they headed to their latest confrontation, then clarified the suggestion when greeted with a puzzled expression. "Or a girlfriend, if you'd rather. Do you have a preference?"

"You can get me one of each, I'm not fussed," said Holly. "Any particular reason?"

Mira laid out the plan she had been concocting for the past week. "I thought it would be a good standing explanation. Every time you need me, I could say you were having problems with him, or her, and needed comforting. Then I'd always have a simple reason to give Sam, but it would always be important. And eventually, you could split up and need even more support."

"Do we have to split up?" said Holly. "Can't we get married instead? I'd love a big wedding."

"You can't get married, they're imaginary."

"Always the bridesmaid, that's me," said Holly. "So this boyfriend-slash-girlfriend, what are they like? Are they a bit gorgeous? Have I done really well for meself?"

"They're imaginary," Mira repeated.

"Yeah, and you're the one who's imagining them, so give me some details!"

"It doesn't matter, they're not real!" Mira felt frustrated at allowing herself to be goaded. "They can look however you want."

"Fair dos." Holly closed her eyes as they walked, a contented smile stretching across her face. "Ooh. Oh wow, I am such a lucky lady."

"Forget I said anything," Mira sighed, refusing to rise to her friend's teasing any further. "Just tell me about tonight."

"Unfinished business," said Holly. "About three hundred years ago, I ran into a bloke by the name of Sir William Crockmoor. Nasty bugger whose wife weren't much better, and each of them were planning to do away with the other. Only Billy's got an ace up his sleeve. He's got a revenant stone."

"What's a revenant stone?" asked Mira, humouring Holly by picking up the question she had pointedly planted when it would have been easier to plough on. "I'm guessing that's where it got magical."

"It's a thing for bringing people back to life." Holly was warming to her story and swung her umbrella in a series of arcs as she spoke. "Billy thinks he can use it as insurance if his wife gets him first. Now these things are not to be bollocked about with, so I messed up his ritual and then his wife stabbed him in the face with a trowel. She were a terrifying woman. The thing is, I left a few loose ends hanging. I weren't able to get me hands on the stone, so they buried it with him, and turns out I didn't stop him coming back to life, just pushed it back to, well, tonight. He'll want to pick up where he left off with his missus no doubt."

Stained glass light dimly shone through the evening shadows, coming from a small church that Mira guessed was their destination.

"But she's dead," Mira said. "Isn't she?"

"The trouble with revenants," Holly continued. "You never know how much of themselves they're gonna bring back. And it's been a while, so there won't be a lot left of him. He might go round killing people at random 'cause he thinks they're his wife. So, we need to put him back in his box for good. Oh, here we are."

They were standing in front of the church now and could hear singing from inside. The sound prompted Mira to grab Holly's arm as she headed for the gate.

"Holly, wait. Is this St Oswald's?" she asked.

"Oh, yes," said Holly. "We'll have to sneak in through the concert, but nobody'll notice."

"But that's Grace's choir," Mira said, afraid in a way simple danger could not provoke. "My boss, from the bookshop? I was supposed to be here tonight, but I said I couldn't come. And I sent Sam in my place!"

"Don't worry, I won't let it hurt them."

"I know you won't, but what if they see me?" Mira said. "What am I supposed to say?"

"You just tell them I were terribly upset because me boyfriend or girlfriend refused to marry me," Holly said matter-of-factly. "So you brought me to the concert to cheer me up. Then I needed a cry, so you took me down into the crypt so I wouldn't bother anyone. Or you tell them the truth, which gets my vote and saves us both a lot of scutting about."

"Crypt?"

"Crypt," said Holly and led Mira to the archway. As she did, she gave her lower lip a theatrical wobble and wailed. "Why don't they love me?"

"Stop that."

"I try so hard, I just don't understa-a-a-and!" Holly moaned, as she rested her head on Mira's shoulder and gripped her sleeve tightly. She gave Mira a cheeky smile as she straightened up. "Okay, I'm done now."

They tiptoed through the vestibule and poked a head around the inner door. The choir were in full flow, voices filling the chapel. The audience was small and scattered, and it didn't take Mira long to spot the back of Sam's head in the nearest pew.

Holly pointed along the church and mouthed 'over there', gesturing to a small door at the far end of the outermost aisle. The space between them and the audience was lined with stone columns and shelves of prayer books. Holly strolled in, utterly casual in her demeanour, planted herself behind the second column along, and gestured for Mira to join her.

Mira took a nervous glance at Sam. He looked half asleep, and she smiled fondly at his willingness to bore himself rigid just for her. Then she scurried to the nearest column and pressed her back hard against it. Holly flashed her a wink and sauntered into the church, remaining completely unnoticed by anyone as, by some strange means, she generally did.

Mira risked one more look in Sam's direction, dropped to her hands and knees and shuffled after her, trying to keep herself lower than the top of the shelves. Soon she had passed behind the choir, and risked a crouching run to the door that, as per usual, had magically unlocked itself at Holly's touch. They ran down the stone steps into the undercroft.

The ceiling was low and the space cluttered with ancient stone tombs and rough supporting columns. They picked their way through the shadows, checking the worn writing carved into each stone, while the muffled sound of Handel drifted from above. The light from their torches swung back and forth, swirling patterns of dust collecting in the beams.

"Anything?" whispered Holly.

"No. It'd be helpful if you had some idea where they buried him," Mira replied as she backed away from a tomb into a mass of cobwebs which she hurriedly brushed from her hair.

"Found it," said Holly, directing her torchlight into the far corner.

Mira was about to ask which tomb it was, when the obvious answer presented itself.

"The one that's open," Mira said, and they both scoured the chamber for signs of not-quite-life. A dull burst of applause came from above, before a new song began.

Out of the corner of her eye, Mira caught a glimpse of another source of light, a dull red glow on the far side of the crypt. She batted at Holly's arm, and together they edged a footstep at a time towards it. The light was emerging from a hunched shape seated perfectly still on the floor.

Holly reached out to prod it with her umbrella, producing a dry tapping noise. Her light fell on the crown of a cracked and ancient skull, and beneath that the rest of the naked skeleton, arranged in a cross-legged position. The source of the light hung from a leather thong around its neck: a round metal ring some three inches in diameter, with a glowing red gem held in the centre by eight radiating arms. Holly handed her torch and umbrella to Mira, and reached forward slowly, her fingers wriggling as they closed in on the amulet.

With unnatural swiftness, the dead thing moved. Its right hand caught Holly's wrist and the head lunged forward to face her. The front of the skull had been caved in by a blow that had removed the upper jaw entirely, leaving only empty eye sockets above a gaping hole, while protruding lower teeth snapped beneath it. Holly shrugged effortlessly out of her purple greatcoat, leaving the skeleton clutching an empty sleeve, and snatched the umbrella from Mira's grip, adopting a fencer's stance.

The skeleton unfolded its limbs like a marionette and rose to its feet in one smooth action, tossing Holly's coat aside. The glow from the gem was fiercer now, making the lines of its ribs stand out in sharp silhouette. A rumbling echoed around the crypt as the light burst forth, streaking towards them like a jet of flame. Holly grabbed Mira by her collar and pulled her behind the nearest tomb as the light dispersed, leaving an acrid smell. They could hear bony feet clicking across the stone floor over the distant singing.

Holly raised a finger to her lips. "I don't think he can find us. No eyes, no ears." The clicking steps persisted, accompanied by a grinding, and Mira visualised the skull turning on ancient bones.

"So, raising the dead and laser beams?" Mira whispered. "Were you going to mention the laser beams?"

"Yes, I forgot, I'm sorry," said Holly. "Look, if he's trying to kill us, that probably means he thinks one of us is his wife, which is good 'cause he'll stay down here and not go after anyone else. And it's bad, 'cause he'll try to kill us again."

Mira tensed as she heard the rumbling rise behind them.

"Like so," said Holly, and they leapt to their feet as another flash erupted forth, smashing the tomb to fragments and scattering the remains of its occupant across the floor. Holly and Mira crouched behind another, as the skeleton resumed its patrol.

"Okay, thinking. Stories with the revenant stone." Holly's face was screwed up in concentration. "The knight wrapped it in his carmine cloak..."

"We don't have a magic cloak!" interrupted Mira.

"Not magic, it just means it's red," Holly explained, as Mira chanced a glance over the top of the tomb. She couldn't see the skeleton, but could hear his sharp footsteps, growing fainter and more distant. It should have been reassuring, but Mira knew what it meant.

"I think he's going for the stairs," she whispered.

"Can't have that," said Holly, gripping her umbrella tightly. "See that tomb over there?"

Mira nodded her understanding, and Holly leapt to her feet.

"Hi, honey, I'm home!" she shouted, as Mira ducked behind the other tomb. The skeleton turned with a jerk, and the amulet pulsed. Holly opened her umbrella in front of her as the thunderous noise filled the air. The light flashed out across the fabric canopy, which burned and shrivelled to nothing as the force unleashed dispersed across it. Holly cast aside the twisted and glowing frame and dived over the tomb to huddle beside Mira.

"Okay, red light, red cloak – maybe it can be blocked by things that are red. That makes sense," Holly said once she was safely in cover.

"So what do we do?" asked Mira, then noticed that Holly wasn't looking at her face but where the torchlight was falling on her chest, illuminating the colour of her top. She gave Holly a look that drew a line in the sand.

"No."

"It'll work, trust me," Holly pleaded.

"Why didn't you bring anything red if you knew we needed it?" Mira asked.

"Because I forgot that and all!"

"I am not stripping off in a church while my boss sings the bloody *Messiah*!"

"Fine. Then it'll kill us, then go and find some other people to kill as well. Happy now?"

17

Suddenly, the skull of Sir William lunged out of the shadows right next to Mira's face. She scurried away with a cry of shock as his fingers grasped ineffectually for her and another burst of light and noise erupted from his chest. Holly and Mira dived behind two pillars, pressing themselves firmly against the stone as the terrible clicking began again. Mira clutched her torch and breathed quickly.

"I need to get close to him," Holly whispered, glancing out to check on the current whereabouts of the skeleton. "Give him summat to aim at. I need a distraction."

"You want me to let him shoot me?" Mira gasped incredulously.

"You're wearing red, you're bulletproof!"

"You don't know that!" Mira hissed. "What if he shoots me in the face?"

"Mira, this will work, I promise," said Holly and flashed a reassuring smile.

Mira responded through gritted teeth, then leapt out from around the pillar with a yell, holding her arms up in front of her face.

Mira heard the noise of the amulet, then felt a warm sensation cascading across her body, like being blasted with a hairdryer. She had to admit, Holly was right. The colour was keeping the energy at bay.

She risked peeking out from between her arms, to see Holly sneaking up behind the skeleton and grabbing for the medallion's thong. The skeleton spun to face her, snatching handfuls of her hair. But it was too late. Holly pulled back and yanked the amulet away. The force of the motion sent the skull tumbling from its neck to roll across the floor and land at Mira's feet, making her jump back a step. The headless skeleton stood frozen for a second as whatever was holding it together left, and the bones fell to the ground with a clatter.

Mira exchanged a triumphant grin with her friend, just before she smelled smoke. She gazed down with wide eyes at the smouldering hole burned through the front of her top, then cast an accusing glare at Holly, who was already casually bundling bones back into Crockmoor's tomb.

"We need to be smarter than this," Mira groaned as she patted out the final embers.

"We beat it, no one got hurt, don't see how we could do better," replied Holly with a dismissive wave of a shin bone.

"Well, first of all, you brought me to a place I couldn't be tonight," Mira began. "Or where I could have been already if you'd told me. Then you didn't actually have a plan. When you came up with one, you needed something we only had with us by chance. If I'd worn blue today, we'd be dead right now."

Holly took a moment to take in the review of her night's activity as Mira tossed a femur onto the pile.

"Shall I stop there?" she asked. "Or do we need to discuss scorch marks on my tits?"

"It's not that simple, alright!" Holly protested. "I wake up, I don't have time to work out a plan, I've just gotta make it up as I go."

"So let me do the planning," Mira offered. "I don't sleep when I'm not needed. You've got all those books about monsters, let me use them! I wrote a dissertation on the British Empire... I know how to research bad guys."

"I suppose that's a thought," Holly agreed. "All you need to do then is explain to Sam why you've brought home Volumes one through twelve of *How to Kill Terrifying Supernatural Beasties That Oh By the Way Are Completely and Absolutely Real*. Since you're so set on not telling him about any of this."

"Can we not do this again?" sighed Mira. "Scorch marks, remember?"

"I'm just saying, you're a little on edge lately," Holly pressed on as they dragged the stone lid back over the crypt. "And maybe the problem isn't anything I'm doing, maybe it's down to the fact that you're spending an awful lot of time lying to your boyfriend."

"No. Right now, I'm going to have to go with this being about you," Mira said, folding her arms defensively.

"Look, I appreciate this is none of my business..." Holly said.

"Agreed."

"And maybe I don't know all that much about modern relationships…"

"You are feeling insightful tonight."

"But it can't be good having secrets is all I'm saying!" Holly blurted out. "You're supposed to be sharing your life with him, and you're hiding a great big chunk of it. That's not gonna work forever. One day, the bit he gets won't look like you anymore. Believe me, I know."

Mira felt her irritation fading, flaking away from the fear and sadness it concealed. "You're right, I know you are. But what am I supposed to say? He's never going to believe the things we do. I barely believe the things we do! Guess what, Sweetie? Tonight, I fought a skeleton with a magic death ray! How was your evening?"

"You see? You're every man's fantasy!" said Holly. "But yeah, it does sound daft, now that I think. Kind of awesome, though."

"Thank you." Mira smiled to herself. "I'm sorry I took it out on you. And I promise, I will think about what you said."

By the time she'd got back to her flat, she had already made up a story.

CHAPTER 4

"A candle?" Sam asked, giving up on a straight face at the sight of the burnt circular hole in the front of Mira's top.

"Yes, I was leaning across the table and whoosh, there it was," she said. "So embarrassing, I could not believe it. It was quiet, so I don't think anyone saw more than they should."

"We can but hope." With a fond smile, his fingers brushed a clump of cobweb from Mira's hair. "You are definitely getting clumsier, by the way."

Mira tried to smile at the thought. She'd always been a little bit accident prone and had never expected to be grateful for the fact. History had provided her with a catalogue of excuses.

"Yeah, this is definitely a new low. Now if you're done enjoying my latest hilarious misadventure, I'd better go and put something else on."

"Don't feel obliged to on my account," Sam deadpanned.

"Really? This is a good look for me, is it?" Mira cocked an eyebrow in his direction, gesturing to her exposed torso as she sidled forward with a smile. She kneeled on the sofa with her legs on either side of him, and lowered herself down to kiss him, while his hands slid the damaged material up as he drew her closer. She pulled back for a second and placed a finger on his lips.

"Curtains," she said, then scurried across to the window. Once she had pulled the curtains shut, she tugged the burned top over her head and flung it in his direction.

"Now then. Where were we?"

If Mira had looked through the window, she may have seen Holly looking back at her from the footbridge just outside the Rowntree

Wharf building. For her part, Holly caught a glimpse of her friend's gleeful smile as she shut out the world. A sleek grey cat strolled past, and she stooped to address it as a confidante.

"Well, someone's gonna have a good night," she said softly. "But not, I suspect, an honest one. She'll not listen till it's all gone wrong, will she?"

The cat paused to listen to her enquiry, before sauntering off into the night.

"Thought not," said Holly mournfully. "In't love grand."

She watched the ripples on the dark water of the River Foss as she pulled the revenant stone from her coat pocket. The faint glimmer from the gem was fading. She was satisfied with her night's work, but something amiss had been scratching away at the back of her mind all evening. A familiar sensation swam into focus and she let out a sigh.

The nearest end of Rowntree Wharf was a tower rising seven storeys up from where she stood. A short metal gantry extended from high on the wall facing her, a preserved relic of the building's industrial past life. A tiny figure could be glimpsed in the moonlight. Holly trudged in the direction of the entrance at the far end of the bridge. Tonight wasn't done with her.

She made her way up the stairwell to the uppermost inhabited floor, and found the hatch in the ceiling leading to the roof. It stood open, and a ladder had been thoughtfully left for her. With a sense of foreboding, she clambered up into the dusty storage space above. Thick concrete steps ran up one wall, leading to an open door.

Holly stepped out onto the roof, pulling her coat tight against the night air. She could see her sister standing near the edge of the gantry, her long ginger hair and the dangling tassels of her bobble hat tossing about in the wind.

"Hello, Trouble," Holly said grimly.

"How do you always know when I'm there?" Erin asked.

"I picked it up bloody quick the day you started crawling," Holly replied, stepping over the short wall surrounding the tower's roof to land with a metallic crash on the gantry. The whole structure shook, but Erin remained unmoved. As Holly came to stand beside her at the precipice, she offered her a sweet from a paper bag clenched in her left hand.

"Piss off," Holly said with impeccable politeness. "What brings you here?"

"I had a gap in my schedule. We were expecting a big flap tonight with that revenant turning up. Bit of a surprise it didn't kill anyone, we were all set to sort out a couple of extra hauntings. Anyway, my evening's freed up so I thought I'd have some family time."

"You were there tonight."

"Official capacity, nothing naughty." Erin giggled to herself as she rocked back and forth on her heels, making the gantry shudder. "You aren't half shameless, you old tufthunter. Ooh, Mira, it's coming to get us, take your clothes off quick."

"And now you're here," Holly said. "I've warned you, if you go near her again…"

"Yes, I know! I'm not allowed inside the building anymore, remember!" Erin spat. "I had to bloody climb the walls to get up here!"

"Why are you up here?" Holly gazed over the edge at the river so far below, then pushed back a cloud of curly hair the wind had thrust into her face.

"So I could make that point, obviously," Erin said with all the contemptuousness of someone who had been a teenager for a very long time. "You and the Death Collectors have both been very clear about it: stay away from Mira-sodding-Chaudhri!"

"And her fella," Holly added.

"And her fella," Erin grumbled. "I'm a good girl, I do as I'm told."

"That you do," Holly whispered. "But you don't listen to me, and you certainly don't listen to them, so I've got to wonder who's doing the telling."

"Not this again," whined Erin. "I thought we'd settled this ages ago."

"No, Erin, we didn't settle owt," said Holly, her voice heavy with almost parental disapproval. "You lied through your teeth about it, as usual, and I couldn't be bothered having another row."

"And you want one now, do you?"

"I want to know what's going on wi' you!" Holly shouted over the whistling wind. "We've been playing silly buggers for so long, but it's different now, can't you see? I need to know, before it's too…"

Holly wavered off balance, her head swimming. She looked down at the amulet and saw the light was gone. Her terrified gaze caught Erin's for a second before she fell backwards, her feet slipping from the gantry into the open air. Pain shot through her arm as a tight grip seized her wrist. She looked up through blurred eyes to see Erin holding on with both hands as her legs flailed uselessly beneath her.

"Oh, dear, have we fallen over?" Erin said, her face all wicked smirk. "Where's your carer got to? Shouldn't she be looking after you? Or is she off getting all besteamed with her fancy man? The revenant stone's all used up. It's time for beddy-byes."

"You can't just drop me, can you?" Holly gasped. "You've sent all kinds of monsters after me, you keep saying you hate me, but I know you're not gonna do this. You know why?"

Erin rolled her eyes. "Because you're my sister and I wuv you."

"Because you've been told not to," hissed Holly through gritted teeth.

Erin's mocking expression slid away, and with a groan of effort, she hauled Holly back onto the gantry. Holly lay slumped on the hard metal floor, breathing heavily as she pushed on through the exhaustion.

"You can feel it, you know you can," gasped Holly. "The spirit world's a bloody mess because summat's coming. I'm awake more often because it's coming, you're able to do what you do so much because it's coming. It's gonna be like 1604 all over again, and *he's* behind it all. He's got a plan, for you, me, all of us. Please, Erin, you have to tell me who he is."

Erin sucked in her bottom lip as Holly spoke, glancing out across the city with a childlike nervousness forming in her eyes.

She swallowed hard, then crouched down to Holly, shaking her head with a disappointed smile.

"Oh Hol, you're getting paranoid in your old age," she said. "There's no him, no grand plan, no evil mastermind. There's just a sad, lonely old woman who wants to think she's something more than pest control. Nobody tells me to do the things I do. I do them for me, because it's fun to watch you scurrying about like your arse is on fire. You should be grateful. The more you're up and about, the more time you get to spend playing with your little friend. You like playing with your little friend, don't you?"

Holly turned her face away, but Erin's small fingers gripped her throat tightly and turned her head to look, drawing out a ragged choke.

"Say it," snarled Erin, her face twisted with monstrous rage.

"I like playing with my little friend," whispered Holly.

"That wasn't so hard, was it?" said Erin in a sing-song voice, as if talking to a wayward child. She helped Holly, trembling, to her feet, the anger instantly sated by victory. "Up we get now."

"You know what else I like?" said Holly in a gravelly choke as she leant up against Erin.

"Do tell."

"Having an indestructible kid sister's brilliant," she said, and grinned. A flash of panic crossed Erin's face before Holly shoved her hard over the edge of the gantry.

Holly collapsed in a heap and waited to hear the wet crunch of something colliding with the concrete below. She stood on wobbly legs and clambered clumsily over the wall to fall on her side on the roof of the tower.

"Oh yeah," she breathed. "That felt good."

She forced herself on, back down the way she had come, stumbling onto the bridge, not stopping to hear the succession of groans from where Erin had landed. It wouldn't take her long to piece herself back together. Holly staggered through the back streets of the city, her vision a blurry mess, heading for Holy Trinity, the tiny hidden church she called home. By the time she made it, her body was aching all over and drenched in sweat. She yanked the trapdoor leading to her hen hole open and prepared to return to her eternal sleep.

THE McALLISTER
INVESTIGATION II
SOMETIME IN THE 1980s...

"When Frank Green gifted Treasurer's House to the National Trust, it was on one condition – nothing should ever change from its current state."

•

Holly and McAllister walked side by side into the Great Hall, flicking suspicious glances at each other with every step. Brian followed while the girl managed to sneak ahead without being noticed. She tossed her coat over the bannister and settled herself on the staircase, adjusting her loosely knotted school tie for maximum rebelliousness.

Sophie was still shaken. She scooted backwards in her seat, recoiling from further surprises, as Holly strode over and tapped experimentally at the equipment. If the stranger had noticed Sophie's distress, she showed no sign of being bothered by it.

"Don't touch anything," scolded the professor. "Mr Kitson, will you please check if any of the phones are working, we may need to call the police. How are you holding up, Sophie?"

The young woman nodded, her composure gradually returning. While Dylan headed for the entrance hall, the professor produced a hip flask from her handbag and passed it to Sophie with a smile. Brian came to her side, placing a reassuringly broad hand on her slight shoulder. McAllister saw the agenda behind his kindness but could not blame him for it. He wanted Sophie calm enough to explain what she had seen.

"Who are you lot? What are you doing here?" asked Holly, scooping up a parabolic microphone and waving the Bakelite dish around erratically.

"I said, don't touch anything." McAllister extracted the fragile and expensive device from untrustworthy hands. "Now, before I call the police…"

"The phone in the office isn't working, Professor," said Dylan as he returned from his errand.

"Professor? So this is a research thing? Sorry, wrong foot, should introduce meself, Holly Trinity. I'm a sort of…" Holly turned to look at the girl, who pointedly did not help. "What did I say I were gonna start calling it? Psychic investigator, that's it. This is my assistant, Erin. Say hello to the nice people, Erin."

The girl raised a two-fingered salute to the room and lay back across the stairs.

"Professor Eilidh McAllister, Department of Parapsychology, University of York. I wasn't informed of any other investigations into this site. May I see your permit?"

Holly stared blankly at her.

"Credentials, then."

Holly shook her head slowly.

"So, you're amateurs and you're trespassing. Mr Kitson, could you check the phone in the staff room? If it's not working, go and find a policeman. I wasn't lying about that, just in case you had anything else to add, Miss Trinity."

"What have you done with Richard?" Brian shouted, moving aggressively towards Holly.

McAllister raised an authoritative hand as she assessed the possibility of him taking a swing at the new arrival.

"Who the scut is Richard?" Unfazed by the possibility of either violence or law enforcement, Holly roamed the hall in an exploratory mood, while Erin broke her silence with an audible groan.

"One of them's missing. That's why they're scared," she called down in a condescending voice. "Now hurry up and get rid of them. I'm bored."

"Oh, pumpernickel," grumbled Holly. "Look, you all need to leave right now. This is going to get very bad very quickly, probably already has. You came here to prove that ghosts exist, is that it? Well, congratulations, they do. Now off you all pop."

The scientists remained where they were, Dylan frozen inches from the exit, looking back for a sign of what to do next.

"Sophie, can you tell me what you saw?" McAllister asked, waving Dylan out of the room as she turned away from Holly, but always watching her from the corner of her eye. "Do you know what happened to Richard?"

"He was... he was in the kitchen," Sophie answered after a long pause as all eyes fell on her. McAllister could feel Brian's concern for her ebbing in the face of his need for answers. "But it was like, he was someone else... he was... I'm sorry, Professor, I don't know what I saw..."

"I think I told people to leave," Holly called out. "I remember saying that."

"He looked like Richard, but it wasn't..."

"Sorry, is this what the 1980s are gonna be like? With no one listening to me?"

"That phone's not working either, Professor," shouted Dylan as he charged back into the hall.

"Then go and get a policeman, quickly now," McAllister instructed him, her voice sharpening as Holly returned to the bank of machines and fiddled with the controls.

Dylan ran to the external double doors, and stopped, baffled by what he saw. He felt ridiculous even mentioning it, so instead scurried off in the direction of the entrance hall.

"It was like there was someone else's eyes..." Sophie continued.

A burst of white noise erupted into the hall, echoing round the vast emptiness. Holly leapt back from the oscilloscopes in shock at what she had unleashed, then took swift advantage of being the centre of attention.

"Now listen to me, the lot of you. There is summat bad here, and you need to leave right the scut now. I promise we'll try and find your friend, but the rest of you, get out. Leave your stuff, it'll be here in the morning, just go. Now."

"She won't leave," said Erin after a moment's silence. "Neither will the big bloke."

"What about the others?" Holly asked.

"Hard to say. Peer pressure's a bastard."

Holly let out a wordless grunt of frustration and held her head in her hands for a moment.

"Fine, how many?" she said in an offhand manner.

"I dunno."

"Yeah, you do too, so don't mess me about, I'm in no mood!" Holly stalked up the stairs to Erin's vantage point. "You need to tell me how many of them are gonna die, how it's gonna happen, when it's gonna happen, and what you're gonna do after."

"I don't know, I told you, we're off the bloody map!" Erin snapped back, louder and shriller. "It's all messed up in here, I can't tell what's going on! Some of them. Maybe the lot, I dunno!"

"Then what's the bloody point in having you?!" yelled Holly, her face flushed.

"Is someone going to die?" whispered Sophie, wide-eyed with terror.

"You see this, this is why I'm so glad we're back on speaking terms, because you're just so scutting useful!" Holly griped at the girl, who shrugged dismissively. "Can you at least tell if their mate's dead?"

"Yeah. No idea what happened to him though."

"Oh, God," gasped Brian. "Richard's dead?"

"Well, duh." Erin fixed him with a look of utter disdain.

"Alright, enough, you're not helping." Holly descended the stairs and crossed to the work station. She rifled furiously through the case of albums beside Dylan's record player, trying to find each title important. An awkward silence descended, as the scientists considered their options while the girl eyed them contemptuously through the bannisters. The stillness was shattered by Dylan's frantic return.

"Professor, I can't get the door open!"

"Oh, for God's sake," said McAllister, secretly grateful for a mundane problem to deal with. "The keys are in my bag."

"No, you gave me your keys when you sent me to the shop," he continued, all breathless panic. "And I tried the spare set in the office. The door won't open!"

"Too late," Erin called out as she leaned over the bannister with a delighted grin. "Nobody gets out of here alive."

The professor looked up at the girl with hands on hips, as if tackling a disruptive student. "I don't know who you are, young lady, or your sister for that matter…"

"Who says we're sisters?" piped up Holly.

"No one, it's just obvious," explained McAllister, maintaining her commanding stare at the girl. "But I'm sure there's nothing to worry about. Mr Kitson has probably broken the lock. We'll try one of the other doors. If need be, we can climb out of a window."

"What, you mean those windows?" said Erin, cocking her head to the right.

McAllister turned to face in the direction Erin had indicated. She should have been looking at a pair of ornate wooden double doors leading into the garden, with shuttered windows on either side. The shutters at least were still there, but the door had vanished and there was only the bare stone of the wall. McAllister looked up, high above her head, where large external casements had been built to catch the afternoon sun, and found them gone. She stepped forward and ran fingers over where the door had been. The stone felt identical to the surrounding blocks that had always been here. She yanked open one set of shutters, then the other, and more stone greeted her eyes where leaded glass used to be. It was a solid wall and looked as if it had never been anything else.

"Yeah, I wasn't sure how to explain that, but the door's sort of gone," Dylan said, as if embarrassed on the house's behalf.

"I don't understand this. What is going on here?" McAllister said, finally allowing her fear to break through the surface of her frustration.

31

"It's not gonna let anybody leave." Holly's declaration carried a weight that drew everyone's gaze, but she affected not to notice and continued to flick through the albums.

"We're all stuck here. And there's a good chance some of you are gonna die. I'll try me best to protect you, but no promises – chances are I won't save all of you. Erin will make sure what happens next is as painless as possible."

"What do you mean, what happens next?" Brian asked, his anger fading away.

"You're studying ghosts. If nowt happens next, it's a bloody daft waste of a student grant," Holly explained. "And if any of you make it through this, you might just find what you're looking for. Right now, I'm gonna need to see the place where your mate vanished. I want to know what you've found out so far, and what all this stuff does in case any of it's useful. But before we get started, I have one question I need answering."

She plucked a record from the case and held it up for them to see. An eye rendered in warm yellow and orange filled the cover, with a woman riding a huge kite swooping in front of it.

"Is this any good?"

CHAPTER 5

Archaeology, Delia Choi had always maintained, was the slow unearthing of existing fact. A cold, hard reality lay buried and it was the archaeologist's job, or indeed duty, to find its true form and record it, without being distracted by the merely possible.

It was a duty that she reminded herself of as she glanced up from the row of numbers on the scrap of paper, screwed her face up and tried to will the fuzzy letters of the menu on the coffee shop wall into becoming something that matched. It refused. The equally blurry face of the barista did at least assume some level of focus, managing to look annoyed at having its time wasted. She blurted out an apology, as the shape turned away from her with a disdainful noise to address the taller shape standing behind her. She slowly shrank as the competent individual rose to the challenge that had eluded her and ordered his coffee.

"Oh, and... sorry, I don't mean to interfere, but you looked like you were having some trouble," said the tall blurry man in Delia's direction.

"Oh, it's..." she began, embarrassed at having her failure noticed. "I'm supposed to be on the coffee run for work, but I've lost my glasses. Can't really see what I'm doing right now. Sorry, I'll get out of your way."

"May I?" he said, and without thinking, she passed across the paper. "How many people are you ordering for?"

"Twelve," she said. "No wait, it's fourteen today. We've got guests."

"And how many hands have you got?"

Delia closed her eyes as she realised she was only getting

started on today's little challenges, while the blurry man quickly matched numbers to menu and assembled the order.

"Do you need a hand with this lot?" he asked.

"Don't worry about me, you've done quite enough..." she said, managing to at least pay for the small army of cups assembled before her.

"Sam."

"Delia."

"And it's no trouble," he said. "Well, depending on where you work, that is."

York is a city with a history. Possibly several. A good portion of topsoil separates the inhabitants from even their most recent ancestors, and there were many more lurking further down. Which was why it was standard practice for building projects to recruit an archaeologist before an architect. You never knew what you were building on top of.

In a shallow hollow, Jonathan scraped with a trowel around the shape that was starting to emerge. Flashes of jade and silver glinted through the dirt of generations as the sun caught the symbols etched on an object long lost to its light. He stroked his beard in contemplation, snapped from his endeavours by the sound of voices. The past could wait forever, he told himself. Coffee got cold.

"Thanks so much for your help, but it's fine, I can manage," Delia said, as they walked through the uneven ground of the site. She neatly dodged around the trenches and pits with practised ease despite her reduced vision.

"No trouble, I live just over..." Sam began, gesturing unhelpfully to where Rowntree Wharf stood on the far side of the river, safely out of Delia's visual range. "Well, quite close."

"Well, thanks again and..." Delia stopped short as she came to the trestle table where her equipment was stored, and where a black figure of eight shape swam into her vision. As she picked the object up, a burst of childish laughter exploded from a nearby trench.

"So, not lost," Sam guessed.

"Hidden." Delia smiled over gritted teeth as she slipped the round lenses over her closed eyes and breathed out slowly.

"What are you doing?" Sam asked.

"Counting to ten," she replied dejectedly.

"I'd stop." A loud voice rang out from across the site, as a man in late middle age clad in tattered but practical clothes strode towards them. His lined face was framed by long grey hair, a thick beard, and gold-rimmed glasses that shone in the light. He leaned into the trench and yelled down at his guffawing young subordinates.

"Mr Scott, Mr French, Mr Harrow. You are a disgrace to the profession – never come between an archaeologist and their glasses. And Ms Choi, never let anyone."

For the first time he noticed an interloper, and regarded Sam as if he'd unearthed something he couldn't explain. "I know you, don't I? Are you from the company? Or the university? No, not the university, they're supposed to be sending one of the top people to waste my time. Sorry, no, gone. Who are you, what are you doing here?"

"I was helping Delia, I live over there," Sam explained. "Sorry, I'm…"

"The lead guitarist with Pre-Cool Systems!" He loudly pre-empted the introduction, thrusting out a hand to shake Sam's furiously. Delia realised she had forgotten to find out what Sam looked like and took a moment to take in the thin face, scruffy hair and kind eyes wide with surprise at being recognised.

"You've heard of us?" he asked.

"I saw you play at the Swan last week! Bloody marvellous. Sorry, Professor Jonathan Fortune. You've met my assistant Ms Choi, and this is the dig."

He gestured across the plain of broken ground that stretched from the edge of the city centre to the River Foss, fenced in on its remaining borders by a grove of towering office blocks.

"Well, it's the dig for now, before long you'll have another of these bloody monstrosities to look at," Jonathan said. "Still, without this lot getting built, we wouldn't have an excuse to tear the place up. Come and have a look at this. Delia, coffee. You know, I play a bit myself, nothing professional, but keeps me sane between projects."

Jonathan led Sam back in the direction he had come, chatting animatedly about music, while Delia followed a few steps behind with a cup clutched in each hand. They came to a shallow pit about four feet deep. A small object protruded from the soil, surrounded by a scattering of tools. Jonathan bounded into the hole and crouched beside his discovery, while Sam and Delia watched from the edge. He reached into the loose earth surrounding the shape and carefully eased it out. Dust and gravel poured over the smooth surface of a green cylinder about two feet in length which Jonathan held up to them. Tiny, silvery symbols were gradually revealed as the debris flowed away. The shape gleamed like metal, and yet the smooth parts of the surface looked more like stone. There were no signs of age upon it.

"What is it?" Sam asked.

"I don't know." Jonathan grinned up at him. "Isn't that the point?"

Sam was distracted from Jonathan's delighted reaction to his find by a buzzing in his pocket. He fished his phone out and looked at the text message that had appeared on the screen. He did not recognise the number, and the meaning eluded him.

Gjallarhorn is sounded.

In the distance, he heard a cacophony of noise, distant buzzing, beeps and ringing. He turned to look around him and everyone he could see, across the dig and beyond, were fishing phones from pockets and staring in bemusement at the screens. A whispered chorus of voices repeated the strange word, confirming the impossible.

"They've all got the same message," Sam said in an amazed whisper.

Delia turned in the direction of the city and could see distant figures stopping to check their phones. Everyone, all at once. In the windows of the office buildings, she could make out people performing the same familiar motion. It took a moment to notice the beeping coming from her own jacket. As she juggled the cups with one hand and fished around in her pocket with the other while keeping her eyes fixed on the nearest tower, her feet drew ever closer to the edge of the pit, and she tumbled backwards. She landed flat on her back, coffee soaking into the soil around her and her phone held aloft in an outstretched hand.

"I've got it too," she said. "Oh, and also, ow."

Elsewhere in the city, a hard, green ball careened through neatly cropped grass, driven by a blow from a wooden mallet. It came to a halt in front of a tiny arch of twisted metal driven into the turf.

"Well played," said Lankin proudly, leaning on his own mallet as Erin cast a glance around the croquet lawn. On the adjoining greens, white-clad players moved in solitary silence, while others remained seated on benches along the edge. She felt compelled to pull a face in their direction.

"They all go around on their own," she noted.

"According to the strict rules of the game," her benefactor explained. "Players take to the green one at a time. Their opponent waits until it is their turn. I find our way of playing more pleasant."

"Can I be red next time?" Erin asked, as he lined up his own shot.

"There are many rules in croquet, as in life," Lankin said, striking the red ball with a precise blow that sent it flying straight across the grass, neatly pushing Erin's aside to pass under the arch. "One of which is that I am always red. Ah, here we are."

He gestured casually across the park with his heavy mallet, to where a jogger had stopped to check her phone. Further away, a man walking a dog was doing the same. As Erin looked around, everyone she could see was fishing phones from their pockets and gazing in confusion at unfamiliar words.

"It appears that things have escalated a little quicker than I anticipated," he said. "Are you clear on what I need you to do?"

"Yes," Erin replied with cold assurance. "I can handle this."

"I knew I could rely on you," Lankin said with a paternal smile. "I always can. Now is there anything else you need before you get started?"

Erin swayed her shoulders from side to side in a childlike manner and flashed a mocking grin. "Can I have an ice cream?"

"If you're good."

"And if I'm bad?" she asked.

"You get to kill some people."

Mira struggled down the corridor, shopping bags dragging at her shoulder while her free hand pressed her phone to her ear. There was still no response, for the fifth time today.

"Hi, Holly. It's me again. I know you're up, an entire city being texted gibberish simultaneously has you all over it. This is the part where you tell me something bad is coming, so hurry up and do it. Bye."

She opened the door to her flat and the first thing she noticed was the skull, or at least the shape of one. A cycling helmet dangled upside down from a hook on the wall. In its inverted position, the three holes on the back, two round and one triangular, brought William Crockmoor's deathly face rushing to mind. An unfamiliar pair of dusty, battered trainers sat beside her own. Laughter and odd words in voices familiar and unfamiliar came from beyond the living room door.

"Oh gosh, I love that…"

"Have you seen…"

"I only got up to series three…"

Mira edged open the door and glimpsed an unfamiliar young woman sitting on the sofa. Black hair was pulled tightly back from a round face behind thick-rimmed glasses, and a foot in a colourful sock was raised up on a stool. Her laughter was instantly sucked into a nervous smile when Mira walked in.

Sam jumped to his feet and took the heavy bags from Mira's faltering grip.

"Mira, this is Delia," he explained. "She's working on the dig across the road."

"Hi," said Mira, shifting her focus from one mystery to another.

"Hello. Sam was telling me all about you," said Delia plummily, limping as she rose. There was discomfort on her face, whether from her ankle or other causes Mira could not tell. "I took a tumble into one of the trenches. Sam said I could rest my foot here for a bit."

"Are you alright walking on it like that?" asked Mira, her instinct for concern kicking in without being asked.

"No, it's fine, but I should be going. Professor Fortune will be wanting my help with his find. Thanks again for everything, Sam. So nice to meet you both." She hobbled to the door and retrieved her shoes.

"Hang on a minute," Sam called out as Delia painfully pulled a trainer over her injured foot. He ran to a shelf holding a row of DVDs and shuffled a methodically searching finger along the spines. Finding what he was looking for, he extracted it and held it out to Delia, whose face lit up at the sight.

"Oh my gosh, thank you. I missed so much of this."

"Streaming is a thing," Mira whispered, the words coming through a little louder than intended.

"It's got commentary tracks," they both said to her at once. Delia smiled bashfully as she strapped on her helmet.

"Should you be riding with that foot?" Mira asked.

"Probably not," she said with a nervous laugh. She waved the DVD as she hobbled into the corridor. "Bye Sam! Bye Mira! Nice to meet you both!"

"You and your waifs and strays," said Mira, once the door had closed and they were alone together.

"You were my waif and stray," Sam pointed out as he pulled her towards him and kissed her softly.

"And don't you forget it," she replied with a grin. "Now, shopping. I take it you got the message too?"

"Gjallarhorn is sounded? Yeah." They unpacked items onto the kitchen counter, finding appropriate homes for them all. "Delia got it too, right when her boss made his big find."

"Delia. So what were you telling Delia about me?" Mira asked, trying to sound as casual as she could.

"Only the good stuff," he said. "And I showed her the CCTV footage of you on YouTube. Three million hits now, well done."

"There are days when you are good at this game," Mira said, swatting him across the shoulder with a bag of celery. "Today is not that day."

"Damn. Must try harder."

"What do you think it is?" Mira tried to initiate a conversation that had never made much progress. She found herself disappointed once again.

"God knows," Sam said. "Viral marketing?"

"I don't know, sounds a bit spooky, doesn't it?" she said, dressing her concerns up in amusement. "Anyway I looked it up. In Norse mythology, Gjallarhorn is the horn carried by Heimdallr, watchman of the gods. It signifies the end of the world… Ragnarök."

"Heimdallr… is he the one played by Idris Elba?"

"I'm serious, Sam. But yes," she confirmed. "And now everyone in the city is getting texted about it. Come on, that is spooky."

"Ghosts have probably got better things to do than send spam messages," he said as he removed a jar of mayonnaise and a bag of potatoes from the bottom of the bag. Without looking, he stood the jar on the very edge of the counter and turned to place the potatoes in a cupboard. The jar tilted inevitably forward for a second, but before it could plummet to the floor, Joe intervened, and it zipped back a few inches to stand securely in the middle of the surface.

"I suppose they do," said Mira.

CHAPTER 6

Jonathan's artefact found a home in the back rooms of the Yorkshire Museum, while at the University's nearby archaeology department, work began on identifying its origins. Three days of intensive study yielded no answers. Even the material it was made of remained a mystery, and that was only the beginning of the questions it posed.

"This is impossible," Delia said as she and Jonathan walked through the courtyard of King's Manor, the fifteenth century building that housed their workspace. After a career spent in portacabins and modern offices, Delia still couldn't help feeling overawed.

"Things are only impossible until they're not," Jonathan said with a delighted smile. "This was a Viking settlement. They may have brought something made by a previously unknown culture from overseas. The question is from where. Which is why our first priority is identifying the materials and the language of the inscription."

"Yes, but we haven't been able to do either," Delia said, before remembering her mantra. "But we will."

"Cheer up, this is the dream," the professor exclaimed to his assistant. "The first step on a larger journey."

"I thought I'd be spending this week cataloguing Roman coins."

Jonathan stopped to gaze at the bronze statue of a calf that stood in the middle of the courtyard, with a wistful smile.

"Ms Choi, give yourself permission to think big."

Theories were still being flung around the city with abandon. Sam's thoughts of viral marketing grew into a general consensus, but then nothing followed. It was still a source of some excitement, but for Mira, three days was long enough to develop a growing sense of dread.

"Are you still worried about that?" asked Sam, noting the familiar phrase on her phone as she lay curled up beside him on the sofa. He could always tell when something was bothering her.

"I'm not worried, I'm curious," Mira said. "Listen to this. In the Norse legends, Heimdallr blows Gjallarhorn to warn the other gods that the end of the world is coming."

"I know," Sam said. "Ragnarök. You're not the only one. I've heard this a couple of times. This is York, there's an expert on Vikings in every pub. I think all of them were at our gig last night."

A beep emerged from where Sam's phone sat on the arm of the sofa. As he checked it, Mira caught a glimpse of emojis. A lot of emojis.

"Delia's up to episode eight," he explained. "She's very excited. But that's probably not a sign of the apocalypse."

Mira swung upright, pulling his attention back to her mythological theme. "Think about it though, how would a warning like that work in the real world? If you were in a small settlement thousands of years ago and you wanted to warn everyone that something bad was coming, blowing a horn would do the job – they'd all hear you. But how would you do that in a modern city? What's the best way to make sure everyone knows they're in danger?"

"You use people's phones," he replied. "Like one of those Government disaster alerts where they take over the mobile masts."

Mira sat up straight at the knowledge he had casually dropped into the conversation. "They do that?"

"It was in the 'what happens in the event of a biohazard' email I got at work," he added. "Do not tell my sister."

Mira smiled to herself. Sam's background in science had always felt like a boundary. It had never occurred to her until now that his world could be as weird as hers.

"You said the message came when Delia's professor found that weird relic, with runes on it, right?" Mira pressed on, seizing the opportunity and scrolling through her growing series of open windows. "Now, listen to this – Runes carved upon objects serve a variety of purposes. The inscription of the Glavendrup stone in Denmark contains a warning that anyone who moved the stone would be cursed. What if there was some kind of warning on this thing?"

And it passed on that warning using whatever was to hand, she stopped herself from saying. Throwing actual magic spells into the mix would be too bold right now, a judgement his reaction confirmed.

"Mira, this is not the endtimes," Sam replied with gentle amusement. "The message was only broadcast to York. If the world was ending, wouldn't you want to let a few more people know? I'm not expecting to see the dead man's ship coming up the Ouse."

Mira looked at him bemused. He was full of surprises tonight. That should have been her department.

"In the final battle at the end of everything, there's a ship made out of human fingernails with a crew of the dead," Sam explained. "I picked that one up last night too. Norse mythology is weird. Anyway, the point is, you are definitely going to live to see twenty-four."

"That gives the world less than a week."

"Then it won't matter if you don't like your present," he quipped back.

"You totally haven't bought it yet!" she laughed. "I don't mind, you don't have to pretend."

"And I can afford to leave it to the last minute because the world isn't going to end on us."

And there was the precipice. The one she had come up to so many times. Mira could steer the conversation in the direction of the supernatural, drop a thousand hints into mundane topics, but sooner or later, you had to commit, to have the courage to say, 'Well, actually…'

"Of course it isn't," she settled on instead. "I don't think the world's going to end."

There came a rapid sequence of three knocks, a pattern Mira knew all too well. It was a signal that she might want to think about getting to the door first, so she bounded to her feet before Sam could react.

Say the world's not going to end. Why didn't I think of that sooner?

"Where have you been?" she demanded, as she pulled open the front door. "It's been three days."

"Asleep, same as always," Holly replied with a wince. "I woke up with a sod of a headache, which usually means summat big is coming, and it's happening tonight, at the museum. Three days since what?"

"You didn't get the message on your phone?"

"Ooh, that were the other thing." She produced her clamshell phone from her coat pocket and unfolded it to display a blank white screen streaked with black. "Is this supposed to happen?"

"You didn't get the magic message? Gjallarhorn is sounded?" Mira asked. "Or any of my voicemails?"

"No, but you can explain it on the way. Come on."

"Is everything alright?"

Mira spun on the spot to see Sam standing behind her. As she grasped for an explanation, Holly leapt into the breach.

"Hi, Sam, good to see you. I hope you don't mind, but I really need to borrow Mira for a bit. Crisis at home." She attached a crack of feigned vulnerability to the last sentence that Mira could almost have believed.

"I'll just get changed," said Mira and flashed a glare in Holly's direction before she headed to the bedroom.

Sam and Holly were left to half-smile at each other in unfamiliar awkwardness.

"Sorry about this," she said. "We're just, you know, all a bit up and downy…"

"It's okay," he replied. "I mean, you're welcome to stay…"

"No, it's fine," Holly interrupted. "It sounds mad, but a bit of a wander and your missus to chat to does me the world of good. And it'll all be right in the end."

"Well, offer stands."

"Thank you, but I'll be fine," she smiled. "And the make-up shag is generally spectacular, so there's that to look forward to."

"Oh, well, that's…"

"I were walking sideways best part of a week last time. It were almost worth the row."

Sam felt a great rush of relief overpowering him when Mira returned.

"Okay, let's go," she said, then noted Sam's startled expression. "Is everything alright?"

"I were just saying how things were…" Holly began.

"Oh, right, with…"

"My girlfriend."

"Your boyfriend."

Silence descended for a second that lasted forever. Mira felt months of lies exploding in her head, detonating one by one like fireworks while she watched helplessly. She'd been so careful, made every little excuse as complete and concise and impenetrable as she could, and now the simplest had tripped her up. Before Sam could react, she leapt to stamp on the match before another display went off.

"Sorry, girlfriend," Mira exclaimed faster, louder and higher than planned. "Yes, so sorry, Holly, force of habit, what must you think, yes, obviously, girlfriend. Don't know why I said that because Holly of course is…"

"Bisexual."

"Bisexual," Mira continued without missing a beat. "Which is probably why I got confused, because of course, her other half…"

"Dorothy."

"Whom I have never met could have been a man, but is in fact a woman."

Silence descended. Mira eyed Sam's expression and saw that this particular rambling panic attack of a sentence hadn't been quite as endearing as usual.

"Can we go please?" whispered Holly in an artfully small voice, her head bowed defensively.

"I'll be back later," said Mira, and hurriedly kissed Sam on the cheek before they beat their retreat. With a titanic effort of will, Holly made it past the front doors of two of Mira's neighbours before letting out a snort of laughter.

"You're breaking up with her," Mira declared. "That was a nightmare, I am not doing that again. Your sister can be the excuse every time, I don't care how it sounds."

It only took a few steps for Mira to realise the implications of what she had said.

"This isn't your sister, is it?"

"I hope not," Holly said. "If this is as bad as it feels, I don't want her anywhere near it."

CHAPTER 7

It was night in the museum, and the artefact moved.

"It could be from a tribal culture whose language was never recorded," Jonathan mused as he bid the security guard at King's Manor farewell. "Regional variations from tribe to tribe would account for nothing exactly like this being found before. Done for the night, have a good one."

"But nothing *remotely* like this has been found before," Delia corrected. "And we're assuming that it is language. It could be anything. Decorative, functional even."

"The repetition of characters makes language the most likely explanation, but good point, Ms Choi, good point indeed. We must not blind ourselves with assumptions. All possibilities are open to us."

"Professor." Delia nervously gave voice to the secret question that had commanded her attention. "You don't think it might be, you know, alien? From another planet?"

"Most possibilities are open to us," Jonathan corrected himself. "Most."

Night in the museum. The artefact turned.

"I can't believe we got caught out like that, I really can't." Mira voiced her frustration as she found her way around the deserted museum by the light on her phone. The shadowed faces of stuffed animals leered with predatory intent out of the darkness.

"Don't blame me," Holly replied, casting her torchlight upwards in the hope of catching anything out of the ordinary. All she found was the skeleton of a sabretooth tiger, suspended by sturdy cables from the ceiling, its limbs arranged in mid-pounce. "You said I could pick. If you wanted me to have a fella you should've said so."

"I know, I just…"

"Just what?" Holly silenced Mira with a look.

"You've only ever told me about men."

"I've only ever told you about one man," Holly corrected her mournfully and turned away, slipping into a light-hearted instructional tone as she continued to explore. "But there were others before him and after, and some of them were blokes and some of them were girls, and some of them were summat else. I'm allowed to like both."

"Holly," Mira interrupted her with feigned sternness. "Of the two of us, which one is from the twenty-first century?"

"Fair dos," Holly said. "I got a bit used to having to explain that one."

"Hell of a time to come out, mind," Mira grumbled.

"I'm not sure I ever went in."

The artefact toppled over, rolling along the table until it fell to the floor. It vibrated softly, and slowly a plume of pale dust poured from a tiny hole at one end as something drilled its way out.

"Why is she Dorothy?" asked Mira.

"First name that came into me head," Holly replied. "Someone I knew. Someone I let down."

Mira felt from her tone that she should not push the matter any further. Holly's gaze had turned to the floor in an empty hall, and she stood enraptured by the image on the marble, a map depicting the full extent of the Roman Empire. After a second's introspection, she turned to face Mira, who instinctively found herself feeling defensive.

"So what's really going on?" Holly asked. "You look worried, and I don't think it's impending doom that's bothering you."

"No, it's just…"

"What?" Holly shone her torch in Mira's face, leaving her flinching and squinting under the beam. With a sigh, she gave in.

"There's this girl."

The artefact was empty.

The thing rolled and scurried along at speed, limbs stretching ahead of itself, pulling its body forward, seeking what it wanted, needed. Its mind was a single impulse, driving its squeaking, grinding form blindly through the night to where shape was waiting.

"Piss off," said Holly, keeping the torch trained on Mira's face for a second before flicking it away. "You're better than this."

"I know, I'm being silly, I accept that," protested Mira, as Holly resumed her search for unknown forces. "But there was this strange woman in my home, and they get on, and there was laughing and geeking, and if Sam thinks I'm hiding something from him…"

"Which you are."

"And tonight, we made it look like something funny is going on…"

"Which there is."

"What if he sees the appeal of a woman without secrets?" Mira blurted out.

Holly shrugged. "Don't keep them then."

Mira let out a groan of frustration and stomped along the hallway.

"Have you ever had a conversation like this before? You are aware that there is a structure to them, and that you have a specific role to play in this exchange?"

"Is it tough love?"

"No."

"I'm good at tough love."

"It's. Not. Tough. Love," Mira snarled.

"Fine, I'll be supportive," Holly grumbled. "So what's she like then, this temptress?"

"Oh you know the type. Academic, historical, likes nerdy things. Accident-prone," said Mira with grim recognition as she slumped against the wall. "Of Asian descent."

Holly came to stand close beside her and leaned in conspiratorially. "There's a kind of banshee that assumes a form married men will go for, so it can lure them away from their wives, mate with them and eat them. So you never know, I might have to behead her."

"See, now you're helping," said Mira with a coaxed smile that quickly vanished. "Hang on, can you hear that?"

The security guard working the night shift at the museum felt a sense of satisfaction as his cryptic crossword slowly took shape. Fifteen down was 'aromatic rice'.

Night in the museum. It was coming.

A high-pitched squeal echoed through the exhibition. Underneath it was a low rattling and rumbling that grew as the louder noise receded, like something was coming into focus. Holly gripped her umbrella tightly, but relaxed as she saw it.

It was made of metal, shaped like a coiled spring about two feet long, ending in sharp prongs at either end. It rolled along the floor, while a series of needle-thin metal armatures extending from the middle pulled it forward in swift spider-like motions.

"Is this it?" Mira asked. "I was expecting something a bit bigger."

"That's it," said Holly. "Dunno what the scut it is, mind."

The thing had paused now and was turning back and forth on the spot in between them with a tiny metallic creak. It appeared aware of their presence and curious. Holly crouched down and reached to pick it up, but Mira grabbed her by the shoulder and yanked her upright.

"Don't."

"I'm just gonna have a look," Holly said.

"Yes, that's how it starts," whispered Mira. "And then it jumps on your face."

"You watch too many films," said Holly, as the object's limbs tensed and propelled it into the air, the long fingers splaying out as it flew. Holly shifted her grip on her umbrella to the end and swung it like a golf club, the curved handle striking the machine and sending it flying into the darkness.

"Or maybe just enough," she conceded. "Now can I have a look?"

They moved quickly in the direction the creature had gone, and a groaning and grinding noise grew louder with each step. Their torchlight slashed across the darkness, and as they drew closer, they realised it was coming from overhead. They cast their beams upwards to catch the fossilised bones of the sabretooth tiger, which swung back and forth as if in a breeze. The cables groaned and a glint of metal was visible along the dead limbs.

The creature had attached itself to the skull, the corkscrew shape extending into a set of curling, ram-like horns. The arms had unravelled into tiny filaments that traced across the prehistoric remains, which now twitched into life. The head swung vigorously from side to side, straining at the cables holding it in place until they broke free with a rasp of tortured metal and a rain of plaster. One cable swung down and sliced through a display case, creating a storm of broken glass, while another whipped across the room over their heads. The cat skeleton dropped, its bones held together by the creature, and landed on all four feet. It raised its head and opened its jaw wide in a silent roar.

"Okay, that's big enough," piped Mira.

"Bloody kids," grumbled the security guard. He put down his paper and headed wearily in the direction of the noise.

Mira and Holly backed up the stairs, the tiger stalking slowly after them. Its movements were the graceful predatory stroll of a cat mixed with something twitchy and unnatural. Mira felt as if the bones contained the knowledge of what it was to be a tiger and the thing was learning, but occasionally fell back into the old habits of its mechanical form.

They were only a few steps from the top now. Holly raised her hand slowly and waved a finger in the direction of the landing to Mira's left. Mira braced herself to flee, as the cat flicked its head to one side, registering the movement. Claws tapped on the marble steps.

Holly leaned forward and roared, a throaty ululating bellow that Mira took as her cue to run. The tiger did as well, leaping forward as Holly swung herself out of its path and over the bannister, getting her feet in between the beams and gripping the rail tightly with both hands. The skeleton slammed hard into the wall at the top of the stairs, dislodging a rattling scattering of bone fragments. The skull was split right down the centre, and dropped to the floor as the creature toppled, its structure too weak to support itself. The two severed halves of the skull flapped up and down in sequence, each pushing toward Mira and using the teeth to pull itself along as the trailing silver cords of the creature wound around it. It sprang into the air and Mira dived aside, leaving it to disappear over the balcony and out of sight.

Holly was already charging down the stairs in pursuit, and Mira followed. They could hear sharp breaths and muffled screams. Mira recognised a human voice and prepared for the worst.

A burly security guard was kneeling on the floor, his body jerking as bursts of agonised breath exploded from his mouth. The great ram horns the creature had formed were now attached to his head, and the snaking metal filaments wound over his face and under the collar of his shirt. The wires pulled at the edges of his mouth, stretching his lips back over his gums. His hands tensed and untensed as the wires emerged from his cuffs, running over his fingers to form sharp points. A central piece of the mechanism was unfolding, bringing a sharp-edged pyramid of metal to cover his nose, as rings of gold that gleamed even in the dark slipped into position over his eyes. The pain appeared to subside and he rose, unfolding to a standing position with an efficient elegance. He gazed at them with wild, uncomprehending eyes and hissed through exposed teeth, a stalactite of drool slipping down from his distended bottom lip. He turned and ran, the sound of broken glass heralding his departure.

Holly and Mira sped through the modern glass doors and antique stone columns making up the front of the building, and into the chilly evening. The blocky Georgian bulk of the museum stood on the edge of a park, a rolling surface of slopes spotted with dark bands of trees, the banks of the River Ouse just visible beyond. They headed through the greenery at a pace, their quarry soon making himself visible. The horned man leapt into the air, catching the top of the park gates with one hand and spinning himself round with gymnastic precision to crouch like a gargoyle atop the black iron arch. Holly was gaining on him now, and Mira was catching up.

The horned man watched them for a moment then backflipped away, landing on the far side of the road, sending a shocked group of passers-by scattering with a medley of cries.

Holly yanked on the locked gate and it opened for her, allowing them to continue the chase.

"By the way, I went to the venue for the presentation today," Jonathan said as he and Delia headed to his car. "I think you might like it. A place with a bit of history to it. Well, that's par for the course around here, but it can tell a story or two. Enough to get your imagination buzzing, I should think."

"That sounds wonderful," Delia replied. "I didn't think you were looking forward to it. Sorry, I thought you said it was a waste of time."

"Well, if it must happen, at least we can do it with some style," Jonathan smiled. "If I had my way, we'd get your new friend's band to play, but I doubt the powers-that-be would be up for that."

A figure entered Delia's field of vision, running towards them, shifting between upright and all fours. Jonathan positioned himself in front of her as he saw it approaching. The shape sprang into the air and landed in a crouch. As it stood, Delia caught a glimpse of curving horns and distorted features.

Jonathan fixed the figure with a hard stare and it recoiled for a moment, then matched his gaze, its head turning from side to side curiously. The eye contact lasted a moment before it gave a reptilian hiss and lashed out with extended fingers. Jonathan sank to his knees with a wail of pain, clutching his shoulder. The thing pulled its arm back and stabbed forward with a flat hand, fingers driving hard into Jonathan's chest. He let out a sucking gasp and dropped hard to the ground. Delia stood petrified, as the horned man turned to regard her, flashes of silver lines visible on his face.

A figure in a long dark coat with a mane of wild hair sprang up behind their attacker and swung an umbrella to catch his ankle. The man fell and his opponent held the umbrella with hands at either end, pulling it tight across his throat. The restrained man thrashed and struggled. He was much larger, and apparently stronger, throwing his enemy over his shoulder to crash to the ground, before bounding off into the night. Delia's rescuer leapt up and for the first time, she saw a woman's face, barely acknowledging her as she scooped up her umbrella and sprinted after her enemy.

Jonathan's groans brought Delia back to the here and now. She fumbled in her pockets for a phone, trying to think as hard as she could about her first aid training and how it hadn't covered how to remember what you were supposed to do when you were panicking. She didn't notice a third figure approaching, until a hand on her shoulder made her scream with surprise. The outburst made her feel better.

"Is he alright?" said Sam's girlfriend as her face came into focus. The sight of someone familiar was all Delia needed to pull her back to what had to be done.

"I think so," she said as she rang for an ambulance.

"I need to find my friend. Stay here!" was all Delia heard before she was alone again.

"Aliens," she whispered.

The Minster loomed nearby, and the horned man was making right for it. Holly and Mira ran, darting out in front of traffic to a chorus of squealing tyres, blaring horns and muffled swearing.

The horned man swiftly circled the Minster, heading towards the stone walls surrounding the grounds of a historic stately home to the north of the cathedral. As he drew level with the house, he came to a halt on all fours, stretched to sniff the air and vaulted over the wall to land in the garden on the far side.

An ironwork gate painted a vivid blue was set into the wall, and Holly already had it open as Mira caught up with her. They could see the horned man standing on the lawn, framed against the pale stone walls and leaded windows of the house. There was something fortress-like about the facade – two great blocky sections on either side stood proud like turrets, while between them the shorter main body of the house was set further back, a steep sloping roof rising above it.

The horned man drew in hissing breaths through his fixed grimace before he turned and jumped again, diving towards the house and scaling the sheer walls in a scuttling motion.

"We'll never catch him now," Mira said breathlessly, but Holly was focused on her umbrella. She slid back the metal edge of the handle to expose a spring-loaded catch and pointed the umbrella one-handed towards the roof. Her thumb flicked gently over the switch and a gleaming spike emerged from the tip with a ring of metal against metal. With a sharp pop, a hiss of escaping gas and a slight judder of her arm, the entire shaft of the umbrella shot through the air, connected to the handle in Holly's grip by a slim line. When it struck the wall, the spike embedded deeply into the brickwork, while the awning sprang open and bent over backwards, hooks driving into the wall. A black dome now sat on the side of the building, with a metal bar protruding from its apex. The line ran from the end of the bar to the hooked handle, which formed a carabiner she attached to her belt.

"Hang on if you're coming," she said, and without a thought Mira wrapped her arms tightly around Holly's waist. Holly flicked the switch back and they were flying, the mechanism inside the umbrella winding the line back in and carrying them rapidly off the ground. Holly reached up as they came to the top and gripped the bar with her free hand. Only when they had stopped moving and she slipped down Holly's body did Mira's exhilaration turn to fear.

"That were brilliant!" Holly laughed with delight. "Oh, grab hold of the roof before you fall."

Mira's hand lashed out in the direction of the house, finally finding a small patch of flat roof. Holly was holding them up with both hands on the bar now as Mira took a breath and managed to get shaky legs on to solid ground. Holly swung herself around to get one leg crooked over the edge, hauled herself up and quickly and efficiently reassembled her umbrella.

They were on a long stretch wide enough to stand on, with the walls of attic rooms rising up on either end. On one long edge was the sharp slope of the roof, and on the other the long drop to the garden.

"Where did you get that thing?" Mira asked in a burst of bewildered laughter.

"Graymalkin knocked it up for me. Good, innit?" said Holly, looking pleased with herself as she locked the handle back into place. "And it'll take both our weight, that's brilliant, that is!"

"That is pretty - what do you mean it'll take both our weight?" said Mira, her mood shifting in an instant. "You didn't know it could take both our weight?"

"Well, you never know until you do."

Mira peered over the edge of the roof and swallowed hard.

"I'm dieting," she said as she stepped back from the long drop. "As of tomorrow, I'm dieting. And I am never going to stop."

Holly wasn't listening. She was already clattering up the roof, balancing with one hand on the tiles, while the other gripped the umbrella. She had not retracted the spike from the end.

Oh, right. Monster.

There was no sign of the horned man. Mira stayed on the flat, hoping to see some clue from her relatively safe position. She winced at the precarious scraping of Holly's boots against the tiles as she neared the apex of the roof.

"Be careful," Mira whispered. "He must have gone down the other side."

Holly slowly rose upwards, pointing forward with her umbrella, when there he was. He swung his body up with one hand over the peak, both legs clasped firmly together to strike Holly and push her back. He must have been gripping the other side of the roof, lying in wait. The horned man moved so quickly, but Mira felt like she could see every graceful motion.

The umbrella fell from Holly's grasp and clattered to Mira's feet. Mira saw Holly's arm lash out and grab for the edge of the attic wall, leaving her dangling in space. The horned man landed on all fours in front of Mira. He lunged forward and she snatched up the umbrella to block him, his hands grasping the shaft with formidable strength. Mira could feel the handle being twisted from her grip and in the few seconds she had, she did the only thing she could. She pressed the trigger.

Mira was knocked flat on her back by the release of the shaft. The horned man was still gripping it, and was carried off his feet, away from the roof and into the air, before plummeting to the ground. Holly dropped down to stand beside Mira, and they peered at the figure lying motionless on the lawn two storeys below.

"What is it?" Mira asked.

"I don't know."

"Say that again," Mira said in a burst of nervous laughter, but Holly was already on the move, finding a far from secure looking drainpipe to shin down. Mira followed her, dreading with every motion that her hands would slide from the metal, that the metal would slide from the wall, or that the man below would awake before she got there. She still never knew whether a normal fear was more terrifying than a supernatural one. Either way, the crunch of gravel beneath her trainers was unbelievably welcome.

Holly crept cautiously to where the horned man lay. His eyes were closed within those heavy gold rings, and his chest rose and fell rapidly. His body showed no sign of injury from the fall. Mira lightly touched his chest, feeling the network of filaments under his clothes, then hastily drew her hand back in case she disturbed his sleep.

"It's possession," Holly said. "That's no problem, I can do possession. Done it loads of times. But possession's usually stuff that gets in your head, this is…"

"Physical."

"It's like a… a machine."

Mira smiled at the emphasis. Holly said the word machine the way normal people would say ghost. She decided to make it feel more familiar.

"So, you know how to do an exorcism. But we have to remove the physical components as well."

"And I have no idea how we do that," Holly said, lying on the grass to study the horned man's face up close. "Exorcism's easy if you follow the ritual exactly. Getting it wrong usually makes things worse. I've got a nasty feeling if we try and take this thing off…"

"It'll kill him."

"I should say so, yeah," Holly said. "It wants a body. It settled for the tiger until it could do better, but now it's got a real one, I don't see it letting go without a hell of a fight."

Holly was edging closer to the prone figure, studying the delicate filigree on his face. Mira took in the curving horns and exposed teeth, and a memory plucked at the back of her mind.

"I've seen that face before somewhere, I know I have," she began before the horned man's left hand twitched and made her prioritise. "Holly, what do we do when he wakes up?"

Holly snapped up into a sitting position and scooted across the grass away from him. "I think we're gonna need to call in some help on this one. Have you got your phone?"

"Twenty-first century?" Mira fished it from her pocket and tossed it across. Holly whispered under her breath as she tapped intermittently at the screen. Mira could see her trying to recall numbers from memory.

"It was coming here," Mira realised, as she looked up at the great house. "It wasn't just running away from us, it wanted to be here. Why? What's so special about Treasurer's House?"

Mira looked and saw that Holly had stopped dialling. Her eyes were fixed on the nearest window, and there was something in them that Mira did not like. Fear, but something else. Recognition. Mira realised that the house scared her friend in a way that no monster ever had.

"Holly, what's wrong?" she asked. "What happened here?"

THE McALLISTER
INVESTIGATION III
SOMETIME IN THE 1980s....

"Of all the ghosts in Treasurer's House, the most frequently sighted is the Grey Lady. The rooms she is believed to haunt have been noted for producing an unusual sense of unease, particularly in men."

•

"You're sure?" McAllister asked, though she knew the answer.

"Definitely," Sophie replied. "It wasn't like this before."

McAllister's fingertips brushed along the immaculate green wall, her torch casting a halo of white around her hand. The drawing room was one of the few rooms not illuminated by a chandelier. Why would one be needed, with so many large windows overlooking the grounds? But right now, the only light came from a few small lamps scattered about the place. She closed her eyes and tried to remember this room yesterday, in daylight, the sun streaming through, motes of dust swirling in the tiny gold rays. All she had was a constructed vision of light and dust made from every window she had ever seen.

They had not found a single window on their wanderings so far. If they had, it might have felt more significant that the furniture in this room had been rearranged since they were last here. Only the camera remained in its former position.

McAllister knew this was an external wall, but it was becoming harder to tell. She pressed her head against the smooth veneer, hoping she might hear something on the other side. There was nothing. But there was something on this side, a distant singing coming from somewhere in the house.

"How long have we been doing this for?" she asked her assistants.

"I don't know," replied Brian dourly.

"My watch has stopped," Sophie added.

Brian glanced at his wrist and nodded, confirming the same diagnosis.

"I feel like we've been wandering around for hours," McAllister grumbled as they left the room for the bottom of the house's grand staircase, the walls lined with large paintings whose subjects lurked in perpetual gloom. They'd come around in a circle. Past the stairs was the Great Hall, where the singing was coming from.

"What is that?" she said.

"I think it's our guest," Sophie replied.

"It's high time I had another chat with her," said McAllister. She tossed her torch to Sophie who caught it in both hands. "Have a look round upstairs, see if you can find… anything. Come to the Great Hall as soon as you do, mind. And stay together, don't go wandering off. Alright?"

"Yes, Professor," said Sophie with a vigorous nod. She nudged Brian with her shoulder and led him up the staircase.

McAllister strode off in the direction of the singing.

Holly danced. Her motions flowed with the music blasting from the speakers, filling the hall and drowning out all other concerns. She swung her arm in a sweeping arc and leapt, twirling as she landed, booted feet stomping across the hard floor. The heavy tread undermined the lightness of her movement, but she didn't care. Erin sat on the foot of the stairs, with her face rested on the knuckles of her left hand and her eyes singularly unimpressed.

"You look a right naffhead," she said.

"Shut up, Erin, you can't spoil this for me," grinned Holly, striking a dynamic pose in the centre of the room.

"This is what it's normally like doing this, is it?" Erin asked. "With all the dancing."

"No, today is special," Holly replied, her body swaying back and forth. "Today I have heard the greatest song of all time."

"Oh," said Erin, pausing to listen for a moment. "Is that what this is?"

"Damn near four hundred years, Erin, and all worth it. All to hear this."

"I don't think this song is meant to be danced to," Erin sneered.

"Oh, it is," Dylan chipped in from his vantage point by the record player. "You should see the music video."

"What's a music video?" they both asked at once, when the final chorus kicked in, and Holly wasn't interested in hearing an answer. She spun and arched and threw herself into the air, only for the music to be silenced with a squealing scrape as the needle was dislodged from the groove. She landed bottom-first with a bump, and Erin snorted derisively at the tumbling climax of her performance. Dylan couldn't help but laugh, and Erin was taken aback not to be alone – but as she caught his eyes, she gave in to an urge to pool their mirth. McAllister stood by the record player and transfixed Holly with expectation.

"We've had a look round. All the windows and exits appear to be blocked, and no sign of our missing colleague. I was hoping you might have something to add besides natural grace."

"I do, as it happens," said Holly, wiggling her feet back and forth as she sat on the floor. She cast a glance to Erin, who closed her eyes for a second, then nodded in response.

"Well then, would you mind sharing the details of your plan?" McAllister asked testily. "And the precise role Catherine Earnshaw has to play in it?"

"Earnshaw? I thought you said her name were…"

"No, she's a character in the book," Dylan began, before Holly leapt to her feet, flapping her hands in a flash of realisation.

McAllister crossed the hall to the dangling pendulum, noting its stubborn stillness.

"Oh, that 'Wuthering Heights'! It's about that?" Holly shouted, and Dylan nodded in confirmation. "I like this song even more now. It feels like it's meant for me, you know, what with…"

"Oh, God," moaned Erin, eying the ceiling.

"I'm just saying, those notes I gave…"

"Do not let her tell this story." Erin stood and jabbed pointed fingers in the direction of both McAllister and Dylan. "I will kill anyone who encourages her. She knows I'm not joking."

"Mind you, I do regret doing the funny voices when we read it aloud."

"If we could get back to the matter at hand." McAllister silenced the room in an instant. She ran an explorative hand down the immobile pendulum before returning to the group. "You have some sort of plan."

"We're sealed off from the outside world," said Holly.

"I just told you that."

"Not physically, spiritually," Holly corrected her. "Richard's dead and his soul went God doesn't know where. Whatever we're dealing with, it's isolating this house from the spirit world, so things should start to get a bit restless. This is the most haunted house in the city, and all the ghosts are gonna be wondering why the air don't smell right. It's like waking up in a strange place. They might feel like helping us out."

"We've been here for two weeks. We've recorded no evidence to back up any of the stories."

"You're about to," Holly said. "The oldest'll feel it first. Who's the oldest ghost in the place?"

"Well, the first recorded story…"

"No, not who were seen first," Holly interrupted. "I'm talking historically. What's the earliest time with a ghost story in this house?"

"The Romans," McAllister said.

"Right, let's go talk to the Romans." Holly swept a hand to indicate the assortment of exits. "Lead the way. Oh, and bring your parabollocks thingy. Might come in handy if someone's feeling chatty."

McAllister shook her head, but nevertheless scooped up the

parabolic microphone before leading Holly out of the room. Dylan marvelled at the sight of the professor taking orders. For a moment, he forgot he had company. He and the strange girl stood in awkward silence on opposite sides of the hall, Erin fumbling in the pocket of her school blazer until she produced a tattered paper bag.

"I think they've forgotten about us," she said.

"Yeah, they have," Dylan said, avoiding her gaze. The space felt oppressively huge without the distraction of the music. "That's been happening to me a lot lately."

"Tell me about it." Erin half-smiled as she fished a vivid yellow and red sweet from her bag. "So, I think I've had about all I can take of Warbling Heights. What else have you got?"

"I never thought I could get bored of chandeliers," Sophie said. This particular light fitting was made of curving glass tubes and spheres. Besides her torch, it was the only thing illuminating the bedroom, and against the deep green decor, it looked like some weird undersea creature. Behind the curtains was a wall that had not been there before.

Brian only grunted in response. Sophie tried to read something in his fixed jaw and roaming eyes. He hadn't spoken since they'd left the professor.

"Brian, are you alright?" she said. "Maybe we should go back."

"I'm fine."

"Brian, we've only got that weird kid's word he's…" she continued, stumbling over the prospect at the end of the sentence.

Brian nodded in the way men always did when they wanted her to shut up. Recognising the signal was a handy skill, Sophie had found, but obeying it rarely was.

"Let's go back. We're not going to find anything."

"I'm gonna check in here," Brian mumbled.

In the corner, a small set of double doors were fitted into a single frame, which he shoved roughly open and stepped through.

"Brian!" Sophie called out. She sat down on the coarse velvet cover of the bed. Once he was safely gone, she ran her hand over the bedspread and said the last words she would ever say.

"What a waste."

The room was dark, even compared to the rest of the house. Of course, Sophie had the torch, and Brian cursed himself for storming off. Still, he was here now, coming straight back out would look foolish. And besides, he needed to get out from under everyone, just for a moment.

A cloying scent of lavender hung over everything, which he could not remember coming across before. A switch fell beneath fumbling fingers and lights sparked into life, revealing a small chamber of dark wood with decorative hangings on the walls. Brian was not pleased to see the Tapestry Room - he had felt strange in here even when it still had windows, as if he was being constantly watched.

A clock hung beside the door, and it was no surprise to discover that it had stopped. A low, faded armchair stood in one corner, facing into the wall, and Brian could make out a figure seated there. He drew closer and the shadowy shape of a woman came steadily into focus, neither moving nor speaking.

"Professor?" he said, but no reply came. He thought it must be that mouthy kid, but an unfamiliar voice rang out, crisp, well-spoken, wavering with suppressed feeling.

"Is that you?"

"Who are you?" Brian tried to make out her features. It was as if the room grew darker the closer he drew to her.

"It is you, isn't it? I missed you."

Brian could make out the profile of her face, but nothing more. The lights flickered and faded, and he heard a scraping of wood upon wood. Out of the corner of his eye, he thought he saw the clock slowly sliding down the wall.

"Listen, it's dangerous here. We need to leave."

"I missed you," she continued, as if she hadn't heard. "And I waited. You made me so angry, my dearest, but I waited. I knew we could put things right. You wouldn't need all those other women, not anymore. But you never came and I waited."

"Who are you waiting for?" Brian asked, with mounting horror.

"I love you," she said, ignoring the question.

Brian bit down hard on the hurt the words brought bubbling up inside him.

"But today, everything felt so different. So bright and alive, and I knew you were coming back to me. I knew everything would be alright. It is alright, isn't it, dearest?"

Brian reached out, his breath held tight in his chest.

"Oh, dear," she said. "I do fear I've killed us both."

Brian pulled on the chair to find it empty. He ran back to the bedroom, where the curling chandelier was extinguished, and the only light came from Sophie's torch lying discarded on the floor. It took him a moment to recover enough of his wits to realise what that meant.

"Sophie?" he called out. "Sophie, where are you?"

"The Romans are only a recent sighting. They were first documented in 1953," McAllister explained as she led Holly below stairs. "A workman went into the cellar and claimed he'd seen an entire Roman army walking past. Now, he could describe them in great detail, but it didn't match what we knew about Romans at the time, so nobody believed him. But a few years on, new archaeological finds proved that the Roman soldiers based in Yorkshire may have looked a bit more like the ones he saw than the popular image. Of course, we've been here two weeks and not had a whiff of a legionnaire."

"There used to be an old Roman road near the Minster. Is that here?" Holly asked.

"Top of the class." The professor was warming to her theme. "The road runs under the part of the house where they were seen. And in all sightings, they only appear from the knees up, which is consistent with how far down the remains of the road are. The common theory is that these are the ghosts of the Ninth Legion returning home."

"Ninth Legion?"

"They were based around these parts, built the city back when it was Eboracum," she explained. "Then, around 120AD, they went off to Scotland and were never seen again."

"What happened to them?" Holly asked as the professor led her into a long chamber. The ceilings were low compared to the upper house, and the white walls and wooden floors were lit from modern strip lighting. A damp smell permeated the space.

"The Roman Empire marched halfway across the globe, sweeping aside everything in its path. But when they got to my neck of the woods, they built a bloody great wall and stayed on the other side of it." McAllister turned to fix Holly with a loaded glare. "You don't mess around with our lot."

"Fair enough. This it?" Holly indicated an ominous green door in the corner of the room.

"Down there is the cellar where all the Roman sightings have been recorded," McAllister said. "But as I've said, we've not seen anything since we got here, not that that's a surprise."

"Bit pointless coming here if you don't expect to see ghosts."

"Bit pointless being a scientist if you expect the world to put all the work in."

"Yeah, that makes sense," Holly smiled. "Come on then, let's go lend them our ears."

"Shakespeare as well as Bronte. Lovely," McAllister sighed sarcastically. "Did you meet him too? Give him a few famous lines when you were knocking around four hundred years ago? I heard all that nonsense you were saying upstairs."

"I never said I met Emily Bronte," said Holly. "That would be impossible."

"Thank you."

"I mean, she barely poked a head outside her front door, never mind come all the way out here," Holly said as she pushed open the stiff, aged door and stepped through, before turning back and raising two crossed fingers. "But me and Chas – like that."

The stairs descended into a dark, low-ceilinged cellar, where the smell was much stronger. A deep trench cut along the floor and there was no light save for the torch Holly produced from a pocket and swept around the room. Her boot brushed against a small object that went clattering down the steps with a series of hollow cracks that echoed against the enclosed space. She stooped to pick up a smooth tube, made of stiff hide, which she rolled around in her fingers before stuffing it into a jacket pocket.

"So, there you have it," McAllister chipped in as she came to stand beside Holly. "Not a trace of... Over there!"

She batted at Holly's shoulder and gestured into the shadows. A hunched shape could be made out in the middle of the trench. Short and squat, but even in the darkness, a recognisably human outline.

"Richard, is that you?" whispered McAllister as Holly pointed the torch in its direction.

The light caught old and battered leather and a weather-beaten, bearded face staring at them with hooded eyes. Holly moved the light down his body to find it stopped abruptly, like he was kneeling on the rough stone of the floor. There was nothing particularly spectral about his appearance – he was all too real and solid. He looked over his shoulder and mouthed words, but no noise came. Then he turned and rushed away, slightly more or less of his legs becoming visible with each step before he reached the far wall and vanished altogether.

"What was..." began McAllister, before a soft noise echoed off the walls.

"What is that? I can't make it out," asked Holly. "Can you hear it? Hello? Prof?"

"Yes, yes, sorry," McAllister said, recovering swiftly. She pressed one of the headphones looped around her neck to her ear as she panned the dish of the microphone around the walls. "I can hear something, very faint. It sounds like... intruder? Intruder. Sorry, wasn't expecting that."

"What were you expecting?" Holly asked, knocking with her closed fist on the wall where the figure had vanished.

"Unexplained temperature drops, static electricity, recordings of sounds only dogs can hear… or sod all, really. That would be a typical day at the office, but…"

"No actual ghosts on your ghost hunts?" Holly responded with gentle amusement.

"This is the sort of thing I tell students not to expect when I'm weeding out timewasters," McAllister said with a hollow chuckle as she sat shaking on the steps. "He's consistent with the accounts, I'll give him that. I don't think there's any mention of them speaking before, or turning up individually. Am I going to regret saying that?"

A dull thudding reverberated around the cellar, rhythmical and repetitive. It rose to a resounding cacophony, small noises in perfect time. Not unlike a hundred pairs of booted feet marching along a stone road. The sound of a horn boomed out, drowning the stamping for a moment.

INTRUDER INTRUDER INTRUDER echoed off the walls. Holly scuttled back to stand beside McAllister as a line of ten men in mismatched armour and battered helmets emerged from the wall, clutching spears and round shields, their legs invisible below the knees, like they were wading through a river. As they came forward, ten more followed behind in formation. Then ten more. The noise grew louder with each rank, and a horse whinnied somewhere in the shadows. Holly took a vantage point on the steps as the room filled up, and McAllister jumped up to join her.

"Intruder… would that mean us, do you think?" McAllister asked.

"They stay at the level of the road, yeah?" Holly responded.

"Apparently not," McAllister said as the figures rose through the floor with no apparent interaction with the surface. Once their feet appeared, they thrust their spears forward.

INTRUDER INTRUDER INTRUDER was repeated around the mass of soldiery, somehow audible over the clatter of metal and leather, and not matching to the mouth movements beneath the matted beards of the men.

"It's alright! We don't mean you any harm," shouted Holly. "We just need to know what's happening here!"

INTRUDER INTRUDER INTRUDER

"They look a bit more corporeal than most recorded sightings of ghosts," McAllister said, trying to restrain her terror. "Again, consistent with the original accounts…"

"Your point?" Holly asked.

"How corporeal?"

A spear thrust forward and slammed with a metallic scraping against the wall, tearing through the sleeve of McAllister's cardigan.

"That corporeal," said Holly, as a tall figure split off from the ranks, drawing a short sword from his belt.

He swung his blade through the air, and McAllister raised the microphone to defend herself, the dish shattering under the force of the blow. The soldier pulled his arm back for a second strike, as Holly grabbed the professor's arm and pulled her up the stairs, slamming the door shut behind her. McAllister collapsed in a shuddering heap on the floor.

"Tell me they've never left the cellar!" Holly shouted.

"They've never left the cellar," McAllister replied, fingering the rip in her sleeve. "But they've never attacked anyone either."

"Yeah, this has got them riled up," Holly said, backing away from the cellar door in the direction of the exit. "It must be worse than I thought."

She pulled open the door, and Sophie's dead body fell into the room.

"Some days I should just not say owt."

CHAPTER 8

"That'll do you," said Graymalkin. "Don't see him getting out of that in a hurry."

The horned man was still unconscious, but now his wrists and ankles were securely bound in thick manacles of black metal. Chains comprised of dark angular links connected the bonds to each other, while additional lengths curled loose across the grass, ending in heavy clasps. He had not moved while being put in the restraints, but Mira had not felt safe throughout the procedure and still didn't.

"You're sure?" asked Holly, looking down at the purveyor of magical artefacts.

Graymalkin stretched out his short arms, grasped a length of gently twitching chain, and yanked hard, sending the horned man's body jerking back and forth.

"Nowt gets out of those, I told you," Graymalkin said, his demonstration complete. "Don't question my craftsmanship, especially when you've dragged me out in the middle of the night."

"Oh, stop griping. You know you love it when I give you a chance to show off," Holly snapped back.

Mira felt more at ease, enjoying Holly's odd-couple bickering with the small whiskery man.

"Fine. What're you gonna do with him?" Graymalkin asked. "He can't stay here, and I'm not dragging him back to mine."

"Already taken care of." Holly gestured to beyond the gate, where a battered old panel van was pulling up.

The driver sounded the horn as it rumbled to a halt alongside the house, then two silhouetted figures emerged. One moved towards them at pace, with the other ambling a few studied steps behind.

"Hail the King in the Mountain!" Angie said with great ceremony. The old woman raised her hands in greeting and bobbed slightly in lieu of a kneel she did not feel able to attempt. "We give thanks for your protection and humbly place ourselves in your service, until death claims us. Oh hullo, Mira love. How's life treating you?"

Chloe nodded in Holly's general direction, the teenager refusing to engage with her grandmother's theatrics until prompted by a hard stare. She rolled her eyes, adopted the hand gesture, but also did not kneel.

"It weren't my idea to have them do that," Holly protested, looking embarrassed by the whole spectacle.

Getting the horned man into the back of the van proved a far from discreet affair, with Holly, Mira and Chloe half carrying and half dragging the burly figure, watching every second for the slightest sign of consciousness. Angie and Graymalkin kept a safe distance, the former enraptured at the sight, shifting from foot to foot with childlike excitement while the latter gripped the cattle prod he had brought with him should the prisoner recover. The bound figure was unceremoniously dumped into the back of the van, and the loose chains connected to eyelets around the edge of the bodywork, hauling him up into a kneeling position. His head lolled forward, and Mira racked her brains as to what it reminded her of.

The van pulled away from the city centre, Mira wedged into the front alongside Chloe while Holly and Graymalkin stayed in the back to watch over the other passenger. Every bump in the road or creak of the bodywork felt like he was stirring, ready to tear his way out of confinement. It was a relief, but almost a disappointment, when they reached their destination without incident.

They stopped outside a bungalow in the far corner of a cul-de-sac, surrounded on all sides by a waist-high fence of weathered wood. A willow dangled its branches over the small front garden, and a coat of arms depicting a similar tree was carved into the gate.

Between them they lugged the sleeping horned man from the van and carried his dead weight around the far side of the house. The garden at the rear was illuminated by an assortment of light fixtures, casting patches of delicate amber under the grim sky. Beds of flowers bloomed on all sides and a stone buddha grinned from the bushes, his gaze landing on the curving features of a leaping salmon sculpture atop a weathered plinth. And then there was the shed.

At first glance, it appeared to be a normal wooden shed, but as they drew closer, Mira realised it looked more like a bomb shelter. It was crafted from sturdy cement blocks, with a roof and door of metal. She felt a tension in the horned man's arm, and she saw eyelids flickering. The look on Holly and Chloe's faces told her that they had seen it too and they hurried towards the outbuilding.

"Quick, get him in the shelter!" Angie cried as she unlocked the door.

The horned man was unceremoniously dumped on the concrete floor, and Holly and Chloe worked quickly to attach his chains to iron rings embedded where the wall met the ceiling. They leapt back as the horned man jolted awake, lunging forward with a roar. The chains rattled but remained firm, and Holly slammed the door shut in front of him.

Holly, Mira, Graymalkin and Chloe sat in silence on Angie's lawn chairs, all eyes fixed on the shed. The thick walls were doing a remarkable job of muffling any noise from its furious occupant.

"What's that you've got?" Holly asked, noting the object Mira had her gaze fixed on.

She held up the ID badge that had fallen from the Horned Man's uniform in the struggle. Horned Man. Mira realised she was already capitalising the phrase in her head.

"Malcolm," she said. "His name is Malcolm. You know, I'd

almost forgotten how we got here. Do you think we can help him?"

"We'll give it our best," Holly replied, her voice less assured than it needed to be. "Gray, you ever seen owt like this?"

"Not in all my puff," Graymalkin replied, running his whiskers through his fingers thoughtfully. "I've got stuff for removing enchanted parasites. But they're not normally mechanical."

"Tea's ready," said Angie with scarcely concealed delight as she bustled out from the kitchen.

The tray she carried rattled with delicate china cups Mira could tell were her best, and a plate housing a tottering mound of biscuits.

Angie was seized with an idea as she placed it on the round wooden table. "Hang on, I'll see if I've got some apple cake left. Help yourself everyone."

"Thank you, Angie," Mira said, suspecting that Holly would forget. "Do you mind if I steal your wifi?"

"Yes, of course, dear, the password's, um…" Angie turned back from the kitchen door to answer the request, her body pulling itself in as many different directions as possible. "Chloe love, you know the password, don't you?"

"RYCBAR711," said Chloe as Angie scurried back indoors.

Mira smiled. In the time she had known them, she had hardly ever heard Chloe speak.

"She's so excited to have you here," Mira said fondly as her fingers danced over her phone.

Holly returned a thin smile and bit down hard on a biscuit, her eyes drifting back towards the shed as Mira pursued her hunch across the internet.

"Here we are," said Angie proudly on her return, and placed a dense-looking cake on the table with great ceremony. "Ooh, plates," she added, then was gone again.

"That woman has sponge bathed me," said Holly, with a shudder. "Frequently."

"Yeah, I'm not looking forward to the day I have to do that bit," Chloe chipped in.

Graymalkin helped himself to a wedge of cake and chewed with a grimace of effort.

"We could feed him this," he said through a shower of crumbs. "That might work."

"Never turn down cake," Holly said, taking a slice for herself and nibbling a corner with uncharacteristic caution. "And this isn't terrible."

"Got it!" Mira shouted as Angie returned bearing plates.

They gathered around to see the image of a medieval helmet on her phone. The face plate was sculpted with human features. Its nose was sharp and pointed, while its mouth was formed into a gormlessly toothy smile. What appeared to be a set of oversized gold pince-nez extended from a fixture on the forehead to sit in front of the eyes. But it was the non-human feature that stood out the most – a set of curling ram's horns fixed to the crown.

"Well I'll go to…" began Graymalkin, swallowing an expletive in deference to Angie's company. "It's him."

"What is it?" Holly asked.

"Henry VIII's helmet." Chloe dived into the gap before Mira could speak. She breathed out a world-weary sigh as everyone turned to look at her. "Saw it on a school trip to the museum in Leeds. Dead boring." She returned to her seat, leaving Mira to finish the story.

"This helmet was a gift from the Holy Roman Emperor to Henry VIII," Mira explained. "There used to be a whole suit of armour, but only the helmet has survived. And nobody knows why it looks so…"

"Daft?" suggested Holly.

"Exactly!" Mira continued. "I mean, you'd want a king to look dignified, wouldn't you? Why would he wear something like that? For years, historians didn't believe it was really his. They thought it belonged to his jester because it looks so silly."

"But if you've seen a bloke get possessed like Malcolm, it'd be proper scary," Holly realised.

"There were helmets made to look like animals or monsters," Mira proposed. "And deities with horns as a symbol of power

75

crop up in all sorts of cultures. Yeah, maybe the people who made this had encountered one of these... horned men. Or maybe..."

"Maybe what?" said Holly, catching sight of something worse ghosting across Mira's face.

"This creature is mechanical," Mira said, piecing her theory together. "Which suggests somebody made it."

"The helmet's based on this," Graymalkin pulled on the thread. "Maybe this was based on something else."

"And maybe that something is coming." Mira felt an involuntary chill descend.

"A horned beast." Holly downed her tea in one motion. "Tell me again about this text message."

CHAPTER 9

Graymalkin had called a taxi back to town and proposed splitting the fare, but Holly wanted to walk home and think, so Mira elected to join her. A year ago, she would never have entertained the idea of walking home at this time of night, but when she was with Holly, they could go unnoticed and she knew she would be safe. It occurred to her that they were going for a walk together and talking about Holly's latest problem. A lie had been made true, which took some of the sting of her guilt away.

"It was making for Treasurer's House." Mira stacked up the things they knew about their new enemy. "Maybe there's something about the house."

"I wouldn't get carried away with that," said Holly, dismissing the suggestion in a way that surprised Mira. "It were just running away from us."

"No, it was ignoring us," Mira said. "It wanted to be there, we just followed it."

"This one's not a thinker like that. Anyway, first thing is get it off Malcolm's head."

"Malcolm's just one man," Mira said.

"Dark road, that."

"You know I didn't mean it like that, of course I didn't," Mira protested. "Of course we're going to save Malcolm. But I guess you'll be around until we do?"

"Looks like."

"I mean, I'm not suggesting we leave him like that just so you'll stay awake and around." Mira hurriedly reinforced her moral position, but could not resist letting selfishness creep in. "Although it is my birthday in a few days if you felt like coming to a party."

Holly did not respond, and Mira felt obliged to get back to business. She could sense something bad brewing in her friend's demeanour.

"Look, you said this was going to be big and it was happening at the museum, so obviously it is to do with Malcolm, it's just…"

"It's not what it is, it's what it's gonna do."

"And it hasn't really done anything." Mira pressed on with her theory. "If I was a monster that wanted to destroy the world, and I had the power to do it, I'd just get on with it, I wouldn't waste time getting into fights in museums. So what's keeping him?"

"Maybe it has to happen at the right time, like a solstice or summat…"

"Or in the right place." Mira circled back to where all her instincts were leading her. "Holly, what if there's something in that house that it needs to fulfil its purpose."

Holly squirmed under the line of questioning, and Mira knew there was something she had no intention of sharing.

"Well, if it is, it's nowt to bother 'cause he's locked up," she said, making it clear she was done with this subject.

Mira decided to try another avenue. "Sam said the message happened right after this archaeologist, Delia's boss, unearthed some weird object," she considered. "If it was taken to the museum, maybe that's got something to do with it. Oh, my God, that was probably him it attacked."

"Wait, that lass with the glasses were Delia?" Holly asked, revitalised by the scent of drama. "I think I might have saved her life."

"I refuse to wish you hadn't done that," Mira said. "But we should look into this professor. He may know more than we do."

"Maybe," Holly said, a grim conviction in her voice. "This does feel big, Mira. Really big. I can't help wondering if this is Him."

Him. Capitals again. Mira could *hear* the weight of them. Holly's belief in a power behind her sister still made Mira uncomfortable. She'd thought it through, considered whether she was convinced or not. Both answers left her feeling like a bad friend.

"Maybe," said Mira. "But you said Erin wasn't involved."

"It's alright, Mira, you don't have to believe me. It's not like anyone else does."

Mira felt stung, as if she'd been accused of betrayal. Erin was not a frequent topic of conversation between them, and Mira knew not to push too hard.

"It's not that I don't believe you."

"Cheers for that."

"Don't be like that," Mira said in a placating tone. "I get that I can never know Erin the way you do. I've barely met her and I don't really want to again. It's just, from what I've seen of her, and I'm sorry if this is unfair, but she did spend most of that time trying to kill me…"

"Speak your piece," Holly said flatly.

"I don't see Erin as the big picture type," Mira concluded. "I don't see her serving some higher purpose. I'm sorry. She likes hurting you, and I know that must be awful, but I think that's all it is, she's just… chaotic evil."

"She's what?" Holly said, bewildered at the terminology.

"My sixth-form boyfriend was massively into D&D. I can't believe I remember that," Mira cringed. "And I probably shouldn't call your sister evil, but I'm really having a hard time not seeing her that way after all the attempted murder. It's just, I worry about you. I worry that you need to believe in this… Dark Lord. Because if he exists, Erin's a victim and you can save her. Holly, what if you can't? What if this is how she is?"

Holly did not respond, so they trudged in uncomfortable silence. They were close to home, but it was not late enough for the streets to be empty. There were enough people to put Mira on her guard, but she needed an escape from the tension and had no worries about brandishing her phone openly while by Holly's side. She dived into the internet on the trail of the mystery that had gripped her.

"I'm not angry with you." Holly eventually spoke. "I know you're looking out for me."

"It's okay," Mira said. "As far as we know, this isn't anything to

79

do with Erin or… well. Let's concentrate on what we do know, alright?"

"Righty-ho."

Mira sought out a lighter topic as she waited for technology to catch up with her. "So that greeting Angie does…"

"I said I never told her to do that," Holly interrupted.

"Have you ever told her not to?"

"Yes, as it happens. Sort of," Holly said. "I mean not to her, obviously. We've not met properly till tonight. Look, I met Angie's family during the Civil War… What's funny?"

Mira shook her head as Holly registered an amused smirk creeping across her face. "Sorry, it's just a lot of your stories start like that. 'During the Civil War'. You're the classic old soldier."

"Sorry, is this have-a-pop-at-Holly night?" Holly teased back. "It were a very important time in me life, thank you very much. And how many of your stories start at university? Anyway, I met Angie's ancestors back then and they helped me out. They wanted to keep on helping, but weren't too keen on the dangerous stuff, so they decided to handle, you know, the housekeeping."

"And sponge bathing."

"In the 1960s, they installed a bathroom," Holly said, as if making a vitally important point about herself. "God knows how, but there it were. Mind you, sometimes I need to go straight to bed even if I'm covered in entrails, so Chloe's not dodged that bullet yet."

"Civil War," Mira reminded.

"I don't have much proper dealing with them, as you know." Holly continued her tale, while Mira gazed at her phone, eyes flitting occasionally to where she was walking. "But every once in a while, clean-up gets a bit tricky, like tonight, and I need to call on them. First time I do, and it's a fair way on so I'm dealing with a whole other generation, she goes and does *that*. I nearly did meself a mischief laughing."

Mira's eyes were enraptured by her phone, Holly's story barely registering.

"So I says to her, I don't want you putting on airs. I'm not a god, I'm just a lass. Fair enough. Time passes, I need help from the next lot, I get them out – same bloody nonsense! It'd crept back in, and I have no idea where they got it from in the first place! So I just let them have it. Seems to make them happy. Mira, are you listening to me?"

"The helmet's here," Mira said. "In York, right now."

"I thought it were in Leeds?"

"The university is hosting an exhibition," Mira explained with mounting unease. "Historical artefacts from all over the country are on loan. God, I saw this, I was going to drag Sam around it. But it's there on the list, the helmet of Henry VIII. That can't be a coincidence."

"Well, that's handy. Should we steal it?" Holly said, half-jokingly, but could see more to come. "Come on, what's the bad bit?"

"Professor Fortune is hosting an event to showcase his big find," Mira explained. "And some of the items from the exhibition will be on display there to promote it. Guess where they're holding it?"

Holly's eyes closed for a moment, and Mira felt even more scared.

"Scut," she said. "You think we should go to the party, don't you?"

"I don't know why, but everything comes back to Treasurer's House," Mira said. "The creature wanted to be there. The helmet is going to be there. This artefact, whatever it is, is going to be there. And you are terrified of that house. I'm not stupid, Holly, what is it about Treasurer's House?"

"There's nothing. It's safe now," Holly said in a resigned whisper. "You'll be safe. But it's bad. Bad for me."

They stood in silence in the street, people walking past them as if they weren't there. Holly ran a nervous hand through her mess of curls as she contemplated their options.

"Fine," she said, tapping the pavement firmly with her umbrella's tip. "We'll go. Chance to wear a nice dress, I suppose."

"You?"

"I can posh up," Holly protested. "Give me legs a strim.

Anyway, nowt we can do tonight. And you've got some explaining to do, no doubt."

Mira noticed the time gleaming in the corner of her phone's screen and warnings of numerous unread messages. "Oh my God, he's going to think I've been murdered! I'll go and talk to the professor. He sort of knows me... well, knows Sam. And then we'll go to the party, and figure everything out and save Malcolm and..."

"'Night, Mira," said Holly. "Tell Sam I'm considering seeing other people."

Mira walked briskly in the direction of home and considered what it meant. Home. Usually, a night like this would be just her and Holly. Of all the strange things that had taken place, the night ending in tea and cake and the company of friends was the strangest. She imagined a sixth seat at Angie's table. Sam joining the fold. No more secrets, no fear, no lies.

When she reached the flat, she opened and closed the door as quietly as possible. Out of habit, she had taken to checking her reflection in the mirror as soon as she came home, in case of some visible sign of her activities. Twigs in her hair, damage to her clothes, a tell-tale trace of demonic viscera on her collar. Tonight, she walked straight past it, trying to breathe as calmly as she could.

I've got something to tell you and it's awesome, and quite frankly so am I.

The living room stood empty and dark. She looked at her phone and read the most recent text, which indicated that Sam had already gone to bed.

I've got something to tell you tomorrow. When I will be slightly less awesome.

Feeling the confidence drain away, she tiptoed into the bedroom, undressed quickly in the dark and slid into bed beside the apparently sleeping Sam.

"Hey," he said in a half-awake slur. "Everything okay?"

"Yeah, it's fine," she said, shuffling closer in the dark. "Sorry it's so late. I lost track of time."

"Okay." He rolled over to face her. "Is Holly alright?"

"Yeah, she went home to her girlfriend. I think they're going to be fine."

"Until next time," he murmured. His eyes drew open and he took in her face. "Are you alright?"

Mira saw the opening, she knew what she had to do, what she'd always had to do. The future stood before her, as clear as day. One step forward would take her to where she knew she needed to be. In that instant, she made her choice. She took a deep breath and turned her back on it.

"It'll keep. Go back to sleep. I love you."

He nodded gently and drifted away. Mira realised with some misgivings that she felt relief.

CHAPTER 10

"Hi. Can we talk?" Sam asked.

The lecture hall disgorged its content of students out into the summery glow of the courtyard, an excited gabble warbling across the crowd as it dispersed. Abi was left standing alone, fleetingly acknowledging friends as she analysed her brother's expression.

"I've got another lecture in twenty minutes," she said, breaking into a cheeky smirk with a hint of concern lingering in her eyes. "But fortunately for that face, I haven't done the reading, so yeah, we're good. Is this a coffee talk or a day-drinking talk?"

"I don't know," Sam said. "No, coffee. You're here to learn things."

"Shame," Abi replied. "I've missed a lot of reading lately."

Once she was settled in the cafeteria, Abi watched Sam acquiring coffee and steadied herself for a bad one. She could see him furiously composing his opening sentence as he crossed to their table, which was never a good sign. He sat in silence for a moment, staring into his cup as he formed his conclusion.

"I'm worried," he said finally. "About Mira."

"Why, what's happened?" she asked.

"I think she might be…" he began. "That there might be…"

"Ooooh," said Abi as she remembered the precise history of the look on his face. She replaced her cup on the table, extended her arm, and slapped Sam across the side of his head.

"Ow, what was that for?"

"You're being an idiot, and you know you're being an idiot, and you know why you're being an idiot," Abi said matter-of-factly. "If that didn't help, further prescriptions are available from Doctor Abi should symptoms of idiocy continue."

"It's not like that."

"Sam, your last girlfriend cheated on you with your mate and buggered off," Abi said. "It'd be a miracle if you weren't paranoid, but that's all this is. This is Mira, for God's sake, she wouldn't do that. You're just looking for monsters under the bed."

"What if there really are monsters?" he said after a moment, a dark tone catching his voice.

"I'm listening," said Abi with sceptical reserve. "Convince me."

"You remember at Christmas? Mira brought a friend home with her?"

"The mad one," Abi recalled. "White girl afro. She was nice, sort of. Bit weird."

"They've been spending a lot of time together lately," Sam explained. "Always sudden, and usually all night. And something doesn't add up."

"I'm warning you now," Abi said. "If you turn into one of those arseholes who won't let his girlfriend have any mates, I will exploit my status as Mum's favourite and get you disowned."

"I'd never do that, you know I wouldn't," Sam replied. "And Mum doesn't have a favourite."

"Keep telling yourself that."

"It's always on the spur of the moment, right?" Sam pressed on. "There's never 'drinks with Holly' on the calendar. That's not like Mira. She plans. And in the beginning, Holly was writing a book, but she always changes the subject when you ask her about it. Then she was having problems with her sister or her partner, but she's never that upset. And she never comes in when you invite her, she always wants Mira to go somewhere with her. Then Mira doesn't come back till the early hours of the morning. Last time, I found out Holly's bi."

"Mum's. Favourite. Tread carefully."

"She was talking about having a fight with her partner," Sam continued. "But she said girlfriend and Mira said boyfriend."

For the first time in the conversation, Abi looked less than secure in her position. "She might just have got it wrong."

"Remember when we went to Pride?" Sam asked. "Mira

checked online for new non-binary pronouns. That's not the sort of mistake she would make."

"'S'pose not," Abi said with a breath. "Still not sure I buy this, though. Even if Mira is attracted to people with bad hair."

"She came home with this big hole in her top," Sam whispered conspiratorially, making Abi suppress a laugh. "Told me some story about a candle."

"When we went on the red boats," Abi countered. "My mate Leanne got her dress caught on the jetty and her heel stuck in the edge of the boat. Which meant she had to make a decision pretty sharpish. Sometimes life comes with a laugh track, sometimes an audience of leery blokes. But you're imagining Holly tearing the clothes from her body in a fit of passion, aren't you?"

"I don't know," Sam said sheepishly. He felt exposed, treacherous even as Abi settled into the role of his conscience, inquisitive eyes probing his every response. "Probably not…"

"Okay, answer me this," Abi said. "I only met her the one time, you know her better. What do you make of Holly?"

Sam pondered for a moment, and said the words as they pushed each other out of the way in his head, leaving one quiet and unspoken at the back. "I don't know, she's odd, she's hard to read, she's a dominant personality…"

"One word. What's the most important thing? The thing that defines her in your eyes."

"Liar," Sam said in a heartbeat.

Abi closed her eyes and nodded. "Yeah. Actually, I think that's what I would have picked too. Shit."

"And what if it's even worse than that?" Sam said. "They met when those murders were happening…"

"Didn't they catch a bloke for that?"

"Supposedly, but the police questioned me about Holly." Sam's voice had taken on a slight undertone of panic. "Mira too. Then suddenly it's all over, and the guy who did it got killed in a fight with the arresting officer."

"Now that's an alarm bell," Abi said, her face hardening as her interest piqued. "Someone ends up dead in police custody, there's a story there. Still don't see Mira going for a serial killer though. Even one with bad hair."

The joke failed utterly to lighten the mood. The intensity of Sam's unrest was visibly growing, his hands shaking as he reinforced his points with nervy gestures.

"Unless she doesn't know, or she's been, I don't know, manipulated."

"Okay, stop, really stop," Abi said, seizing Sam's hand. "Just answer me one thing, do you trust Mira?"

"Yes," he said without need for reflection. "I mean, I don't want to not."

"Well, I trust her too. And I wouldn't leave you with just anyone."

"Emma took you by surprise too," Sam warned.

"True, but I never liked her. I always liked Mira," Abi corrected. "I still count as being infallible, whereas any time you mention Emma's name, I know you're not seeing straight. The point is, I don't think Mira would do anything to hurt you. And if you screw things up with her, you're an even bigger numpty than I thought."

"I know."

"Holly's another matter," Abi said, staring across the room as she wrangled the thought. "I think you're right. She's hiding something, maybe something bad. Which means either Mira doesn't know, which is not great, or she's hiding it too, which is even worse."

"So what do we do?" Sam asked.

"If we were sensible grown-ups," Abi said, "I'd tell you to have an open and truthful conversation with Mira about your concerns and you'd come out of it with a relationship made stronger by honesty and a feeling that a weight had been lifted."

"If we were sensible grown-ups," Sam pointed out. "I probably wouldn't be seeking relationship advice from my little sister in the first place."

"Well in that case, it's time to go and play on the swings," she said grimly. "And dig up some dirt on Holly."

THE McALLISTER INVESTIGATION IV
SOMETIME IN THE 1980s...

"Visitors to the house have often reported seeing a reflection of a figure in a silver mirror, only to discover that there is no one there. A more troubling experience is caused by the condition known as 'foxing' – the mirror can become misty, until you can only see your own reflection from certain angles. When looking straight on, you simply disappear."

•

"So they hated each other?" Erin asked, confusion creasing her face.

"Loved each other, hated each other, it was all over the place," Dylan explained. Erin studied the album cover in her hands, taking in the image of the slender bearded man, and the wafting gown of the woman who danced around him. She let out a snort of disbelief.

"I'd've told them all to piss off," she said, with a tone that stopped just short of ridicule. "Hardly worth the bother."

"But that was the whole point." Dylan was becoming unusually animated as his enthusiasm grew. "Out of all that love and hate and passion and craziness, you get this amazing music! They had to go through all of that to come out the other side with something special. It's like chaos somehow breeds creativity!"

Erin shook her head as if to dismiss the nonsense. "I'm all for a bit of chaos, but if people do your head in, get rid. Make your own bloody music if that's what you're into."

"Is that what you do?" Dylan asked impulsively and felt a swell of pride for having dropped a personal question into the conversation.

"Most everyone does my head in, so yeah."

"Even your sister?"

"Especially my sister."

"So why are you here?" Dylan asked, and feared he'd overstepped his bounds. But if he had, she showed no objection.

She smiled softly as she returned *Rumours* to the table and fixed him with startling eyes of gold and green.

"That's different," she said with a practiced cynicism. "We're trying something out. I'll let you know if I decide it's worth it."

Dylan grinned at the parallel and pressed his point further. "But that's just it, don't you see? You love each other, you make each other crazy, but you have to be together because what you're doing is…"

"Fine, fine, we're just like Fleetwood Mac," Erin scowled, shifting uncomfortably. "Look, the thing you've gotta know about me and her…"

"Wait, wait you've got to hear this bit!" Dylan interrupted, miming along to the deep notes of the bass guitar solo, his head swaying back and forth with an expression that plucked a laugh from her throat despite herself.

"You're as daft as she is!" she said, and he pulled himself out from his reverie, looking embarrassed at his private enthusiasms made public.

"Erin."

They looked up to see Holly at the far side of the hall, her face dark and threatening. Dylan instinctively silenced the music as she crossed the floor to loom over them.

"Sophie's dead," she said without a trace of concern. "We found her in the room by the cellar. Take a look, see if you can work out what happened."

"Yeah, I should be able to manage that," Erin said casually, looking away to flick through the box of records. "Actually, we were just talking about you…"

"Now, please."

Erin looked up with a cutting remark brewing in her eyes, but it stayed there when they met her sister's icy stare. She swallowed a hollow laugh and stomped out of the room. Holly's eyes didn't leave her until she was gone.

"Sophie's dead?" Dylan asked.

"Yeah," was all the horrified query warranted. After a moment, Holly realised more was expected of her. "You alright?"

"I don't know, I just… can't believe it."

"Well, that's to be expected, I suppose," Holly responded, content her duty was done. "You two seem to be getting on."

"Yeah, she's really cool," Dylan said with a smile, his focus turning away from the grim circumstances so quickly it didn't occur to him to reflect on his choice of words.

"Oh, I don't mean…" he added in a fluster of contextualisation. "Because I wouldn't, obviously, she's only a kid, and that's not what I…"

"Calm down, this is not that conversation."

"Okay." He felt a rush of relief, but his discomfort appeared to have crossed over to Holly with a noticeable shudder.

"I am so glad I never had to have that conversation," she muttered to herself. "I wouldn't have wanted to have that conversation when it would've been that conversation, I am bloody well not having it now, alright?"

Dylan nodded. He wanted to leave the room as quickly as possible, but Holly's attention had been seized by the bag of sweets Erin had left on the table and an odd urgency had overcome her.

"Did you eat any of these?" she demanded.

"I'm diabetic."

"Thank Christ for that," she whispered, snatching the bag up.

Dylan decided it was up to him to seize the initiative if he was going to be stuck in this encounter.

"Is there anything I can do?"

"Probably, but I can't be arsed to think what right now." Holly didn't look at him, her mind clearly elsewhere. "Look…"

"Dylan."

"Dylan. What I'm trying to say, Dylan, is, about me sister…"

Dylan awaited a lengthy outpouring of the complex relationship Erin had alluded to.

"Don't trust her."

"What?"

"You heard me," Holly said as she walked away. "Don't ever trust her."

The five of them gathered in the Great Hall, and Dylan could scarcely believe what he was hearing. The professor recounted her experience in the cellar with the same detachment she used to describe temperature fluctuations. She was treating these things like cold hard facts, which scared him more than anything. He looked to Brian for support, but none of this seemed to be a surprise to him. Maybe he just wanted it all to be true.

Holly took a step back, her tendency to dominate proceedings kept in check. Erin lurked on the edge of the room, deliberately apart. Any chinks in her armour were now utterly closed up. Sophie's body had yielded her no clues.

"We should get some rest," McAllister concluded. "I have no idea how long we've been doing this for, but it feels like too long. But nobody is to leave this room, and somebody needs to stay awake in case of further disturbances."

"I'm not planning on sleeping," Holly said.

"Not one of you, one of us," the professor corrected her. "We still have a job to do. If we are experiencing unusual levels of paranormal activity, then it is our duty to document them thoroughly. I'll take the first shift. Brian, if you could take over in… well, since we can't keep track of time, I'll wake you up when I'm starting to drop."

McAllister sipped the coffee she had obtained with a quick and terrifying dash to the kitchen, and studied the monitors, where nothing out of the ordinary was to be seen. The screen on the right was still blank. Fixing it had been the most important task in front of her earlier tonight, assuming it was still tonight. She half wanted to catch a ghostly face reflected in the screen so she could turn around to see nothing behind her, because if her job was going to conform to cliché, they may as well do all the classics. She felt certain she'd heard children laughing and a low clicking of glass on glass somewhere in the room. The other cameras were fine, although the tapes had long since run out. The time codes would just be numbers by now.

Dylan and Brian lay huddled in sleeping bags on one side of the hall and Holly was roaming the room like a sentry. Every once in a while, she tried to place where Erin was, and it usually took a little time and effort to find her. She was never in the same place twice and McAllister never saw her move.

"Nowt's happening," whispered Holly as she drew a second chair over and flopped into it.

"Same here," McAllister responded. The hip flask sat on the edge of the table, and McAllister poured a measure into her coffee before passing it across.

"Is this a typical day for you, then?" the professor asked.

"Pretty much."

"I was afraid of that." McAllister turned her chair to face Holly and slipped her glasses off, placing them securely folded on the desk. "Let's have a little talk about something we need to clear up. For the sake of my own well-being, you understand."

"Yeah, I kind of glossed over the details, didn't I?" Holly admitted. "The thing is, I'm…"

"Two people are dead." McAllister moved straight past Holly's belated introductions without a second thought. "You seem fairly confident in Richard's demise and I don't see a reason to question you. I don't know who you are or why you're doing this, I don't feel particularly inclined to care. But two people are dead. And I would like to know if that bothers you in any way."

Holly shrank under her searing gaze and studied her hands thoroughly.

"What do you want me to say?"

"Well, I was hoping you might answer my question," McAllister pressed on mercilessly. "Dylan and Brian are here with me. Their safety is my first priority. Also my own, of course. So if that isn't a factor in your decision-making, I'd rather know now. I'm not judging you or pleading for sympathy. But I don't want to start relying on you if it's unwise to do so. Is that fair?"

"Oh, scut," sighed Holly, knocking back a slug of whisky. "You had to make it hard, didn't you?"

"I try."

"You have no idea," Holly said. "Right now, there's two of you dead and three alive. You have no idea how tempting it is to say I'm still winning on points."

"If that's how it is, I won't ask for more."

"You see, this is where it becomes a bit of a bastard," Holly confessed, and leaned back in her chair, watching the ceiling as her voice drifted away. "If I don't care about you, any result other than me dying is a win. I mean, it's not like we're gonna see each other again, once this is over. It's how I'm meant to be. I've been known to lean in that direction from time to time, and it is a lot easier. But you don't half end up hating yourself. And at the end of the day, yourself is all you've got."

"And how does dragging your little sister around with you fit into this dilemma?"

"Oh, well, that's an experiment," Holly said with a sad smile that infected her glib tone. "We've been apart. More than we haven't. And there's a lot of bad we're both carrying around. But came a point, I thought maybe we're all each other's got. She finds living with herself a lot easier than I do."

"Are you hoping to become a bit more like her?" McAllister asked. "Or that she'll become a bit more like you?"

"Fat chance of the second, and God knows I've tried," Holly said with a forced laugh. "But the other one, yeah maybe. I feel like I've stopped liking things lately. Maybe she can make me feel okay with it."

"You seem to like Mr Kitson's music," McAllister offered, and Holly broke into a broad grin.

"I do, don't I? Actually, that were good. Not felt like that in a while."

McAllister upended the flask and noted the absence of a downpour. "You also quite like my whisky."

"Sorry about that," Holly said sheepishly but couldn't put the smile away.

"Don't apologise, I think you're making excellent progress," McAllister said with warmth in her eyes. "Maybe she doesn't have to be all you've got."

Erin stopped listening and sloped away unnoticed, her hands thrust deep into her blazer pockets. She left the hall and stopped at the bottom of the main staircase, where a large bronze carving of an eagle stood on the floor. Its wings supported a marble shelf that was home to a small carriage clock, with hands as dead as all the others. Behind that was a shadowy silver mirror, and a dark and distorted image of Erin stared back accusingly at her real self.

Fingers slipped into a blazer pocket and produced a slim blade, which she tapped thoughtfully against her palm as she approached the glass. She rested her elbows on the marble and sank down in front of the clock, waiting for the movement that would never come. The girl in the mirror continued to gaze at her, a sadness in her eyes that she resisted looking at. Erin pulled herself upright and punched at the silver with the pommel of her knife. The mirror girl still looked sad.

The man behind her did not.

Erin turned to regard the staircase, saw the life-size figures in the paintings lurking in the shadows, and the one solid figure standing among them.

"You must be Richard," she said, peering at what she saw in those eyes. "Or maybe you're not."

CHAPTER 11

"I don't know you, do I?"

Jonathan sat up in the hospital bed and retrieved a set of heavy-rimmed black glasses from the bedside table. He scrutinised the choppy hair and nervously smiling face peering out from behind the bunch of flowers, and winced as his bound wounds stabbed at him.

"Not as such, although we have sort of met. I'm…"

"Mira," Jonathan interrupted. "Sam's girlfriend. Delia told me you were there."

Mira nodded with relief as Jonathan waved her into the room with a lazy gesture.

"I believe you're on the list of people I have to thank for still being here," he said with a broad smile. "There also appears to have been an intervention by Wonder Woman, at least according to Delia."

"My friend," Mira said, her mood relaxing in an instant. "She's impulsive."

"I'm bloody glad she is." Jonathan laughed as he shifted, then grumped at the agony. "Do thank her for me, won't you?"

Mira deposited her burden and pulled up a chair, while Jonathan settled himself back with another grimace that he blended into philosophical serenity.

"Morphine on tap, but I can't be doing with it. Still, not in here for much longer, thank God."

"Oh, good," Mira said. "I read in the *Press* about your big presentation. Shame to miss it."

"Oh, that. Well. Not quite that quick a recovery, I'm afraid. Not sorry to have an excuse, to be honest. Nice house, but the other things I can't be doing with either. Mind you, I'm going to have to break it to Delia that she's hosting. I'm not sure how she'll cope with that."

The image of Delia professionally tending to Jonathan's wounds competed in Mira's head with her putting on a bike helmet when she was going home by bus. Mira did not like the juxtaposition. It was too much like looking in a mirror.

"I'm sure she'll manage." Mira half-swallowed her response.

"Are you alright?"

"Yes, yes, fine," Mira said hurriedly.

"Three daughters. I'm used to people being fine."

"Lot on my mind at the moment, that's all," Mira said, as a buzzing emerged from her pocket. She fished out her phone and saw an unfamiliar number, which she decided could go to voicemail hell. "Such as."

"I reckon the moment you don't have a lot on your mind is the time to worry," Jonathan said with a sage grin. "That's when life's getting boring."

"I remember when life was boring," Mira said wistfully.

"Do you miss it?"

"Not in the slightest." Mira laughed and felt a little exposed. "Are your daughters here?"

"No. Sometimes I'm fine too."

Mira felt the gap in the conversation descend, and decided to exploit it. She had come to realise that a downpour of English discomfort was a useful tool in gaining information, since people will gratefully accept you changing the subject to literally anything.

"What have you found?" she asked.

"No idea," he said. "Which is something to look forward to. Knowing there's stuff to find out, that's an incentive. How did you and Sam meet?"

"Am I a discovery too?" she said, taken aback by the sudden swing in the conversation.

"Oh, yes. Everyone is."

"Well, it's complicated…"

"You see?"

"We were at uni together," Mira said, pausing her explanation at that point.

"That doesn't sound complicated," Jonathan mused, his kindly demeanour eclipsing any sense of intrusion. "I suppose complicated must have come later. And now you help your friend rescue injured professors in the dead of night. You see, you are a discovery. And I wouldn't worry about Delia."

"Excuse me?" Mira was alarmed at her apparent transparency. She wondered how many of her secrets were so easy to pluck out. Still, if Jonathan could detect any ulterior motive, she could not sense it.

"Unless you know something I don't," he swiftly added. "I managed to be a good father for long enough to learn how to interpret the warning signs on a young woman's face. If you don't mind me saying, the sign I'm seeing right now is one of being hurt in the past and afraid it might happen again. Yours, I assure you, is a very old story."

"You don't know the half of it," Mira whispered under her breath, before confessing more openly. "Delia seems… less complicated than me."

"Even if that were a good thing, which is a discussion for another time," Jonathan said, his voice soothing and gentle. "I can assure you nobody is not complicated. And certainly not Delia."

"We all have our secrets," she said, almost to herself.

"We don't have to. Unless you like it that way. Some people do, don't they?"

"I guess," Mira let out a nervous laugh. "Sorry, how did we get on to this?"

"I've got one of those faces," Jonathan shrugged, painfully regretting the motion. "As a rule, people sometimes need to talk to a stranger. And as a rule, I generally like people, so being that stranger works out quite nicely."

"Well, thank you for your concern," Mira said, drawing a line with her voice. "And here was me coming to make sure you were alright."

"Oh, I only got stabbed by some weirdo in a Halloween mask. It's not like I've got problems."

"He was wearing a mask?" Mira asked, this ignorance being the first real fact she'd mined from the encounter.

"Looked like it," Jonathan said. "Big horned night-of-the-demon-y thing. I went through all this with the police. They were here this morning."

Mira tensed at the word and sprang to her feet.

"I need to be going," she said through an anxious smile. "But it was nice to meet you, and I'm glad you're okay and I'm sure we'll see each other again soon. And thank you for the advice. Bye."

She hurried from the room before he could speak, the single word buzzing around her brain. Of course there would be a police investigation. Mira had forgotten that this was even a possibility. The police hadn't been an issue since her first little adventure with Holly, and that had been a less than pleasant experience. She ducked into a stairwell and huddled in a quiet corner, thumbing frantically through her phone, looking for a number she'd hoped she'd never have to ring.

"Agent Scully's phone," said a sarcastic voice.

"Caroline, can you talk?" Mira whispered, ignoring the wisecrack.

"Yeah, give me a minute," came the reply.

Mira could hear a gentle hubbub of noise in the background slowly fading away, followed by a series of banging doors. She guessed Caroline was looking for a quiet part of the police station where she could say ridiculous things without arousing suspicion.

Last year, DI Caroline James had, not unreasonably, suspected Mira of being a serial killer, or at least connected to one in some way. They'd become unlikely allies once the real murderer had been revealed in all its supernatural glory. That didn't make asking her for help any easier.

"Haven't heard from you in a while," Caroline said, once she had found the necessary solitude. "So, it's either been quiet or you two have been doing a good job."

Mira got straight down to business. "What do you know about Professor Fortune?"

"I thought that was it," Caroline said. "Not my case, but I heard your name mentioned. You can expect a uniform on your door before too long, but I wouldn't worry, you're just a bystander at this point. It sounds like no one saw you and Holly together, so…"

"Shit!" shouted Mira.

"What?"

"I went to see the professor in hospital, I…" Mira paused to inwardly curse herself. "I said she was my friend."

"Oh," Caroline said. "In that case, you're going to be asked for a name and address. I'm guessing that's not going to be convenient."

"God, I'm so stupid!" Mira shouted, flailing an impotent arm around her secluded corner. "Why can't I keep my lies straight!"

"The same night, a security guard went missing from the museum," Caroline said, in what Mira remembered as her interview room voice. "Do you know what happened to him?"

"Yes, he's possessed," Mira replied.

"Possessed? Like in *The Exorcist*?"

"Yes. No. Sort of," Mira rattled through the options with annoyed swiftness. "We've got him locked in a shed until we can… un-possess him. But it'll be fine, we just need some time to… work out how you do that."

There was a doom-laden silence on the end of the line.

"I don't think I can have this conversation," Caroline eventually said.

"Why, what's wrong?"

"You've just told me you've committed a crime."

"No, it's fine…"

"Mira, you are holding someone against their will," Caroline said in a low but serious whisper. Mira visualised her making sure she was alone. "And you're asking me to overlook that."

"If you could see him…"

"No," Caroline said firmly. "I am compromised enough. I don't want to know where he is!"

"So no calling off the search?" Mira asked, half-jokingly.

"I'm going to pretend you didn't say that," Caroline replied. "Mira, there are things you do that aren't covered by the law, and I can help you navigate that, but I am not your pet copper and I will not help you break the law. If there's a man in this city being held captive, the police are going to look for him, and I can't promise they won't find him. Jesus Christ, Mira, this man has..."

"No, don't," Mira said with a rush of discomfort. "Don't tell me what he's got, I don't want to know."

"Then sort this out," Caroline said, her voice noticeably lowering. "I can't let you kidnap people. I don't care if he's possessed by the devil."

"It's not the devil."

"Right. Not the devil," Caroline said as if writing it down. Her tone shifted to a more conversational mood. "Actually, is he real? Just curious."

"Not as far as I know," Mira said. "But speaking as an atheist raised by lapsed Hindus, I'm probably not the best person to ask."

"Anything?" asked Sam, depositing the mug of tea on the table with a thud that produced a tiny dribble over the edge.

Abi reached over without looking as she hurriedly scrolled through the information unfurling on the screen of her laptop. She was stretched out across the whole sofa, exiling Sam to a nearby armchair.

"Well, once you've got past church groups who let God take care of the spellchecking and fewer drag queens than I expected, I'm not finding a lot on Holly Trinity," she said.

"She's not very good with technology," Sam suggested. "It makes sense she'd have no social media."

"Yeah, but isn't she supposed to be a writer?" Abi asked. "If you're a writer, you promote. Everywhere you can, or nobody buys your books. Why isn't she doing that?"

"Because she's not a writer," Sam replied. "That was the first lie."

"I wasn't sure you'd say that out loud," Abi said in her most serious tone. "By the way, ISPs never forget. You sure you want to be doing this at home? Mira will not be happy with you stalking her mate."

"See what you can find," Sam said, as he paced the room.

Abi stopped to take in his troubled demeanour.

"You're twenty-five, Sam," Abi said. "It'll be a good few years before you need a young person to do technology for you, no matter how boring you get. If I'm doing the legwork, it's because you're afraid of what you'll find. Are you sure you want to do this?"

"No," he whispered in a ghost of a voice, his fingers fretting anxiously around each other. "Do it anyway."

A knock on the door snapped them from their bleak thoughts, and Sam hurried off to answer while Abi resumed her fruitless searching. For a moment, he imagined Holly standing on the other side, and what he would say if she was. Confronting her felt impossibly melodramatic. Whether the towering police officer in the doorway was a relief or a cause for greater alarm, he could not say.

"Hello, sir," the man said, his voice deep and resonant. "I'm here to speak to Mira Chaudhri, is this the right address?"

"Yes, yes, it is," Sam replied, his mind reeling with a thousand grim possibilities. "She's not here right now."

"Not to worry, sir," he said with a smile so reassuringly jolly it belonged in a children's book. "We need to check a few things with her about the incident last night. When would be a good time?"

"I... Seven? Seven is good." Sam struggled to keep the question clear in his mind. He had the feeling that he looked like he was hiding something, and for an awful moment, thought the burly figure would ask to be allowed in.

"Are you feeling alright, sir?" came the inevitable question.

"Yes, yes, no, off sick today," Sam said, trying to reign in his panic as he lied. "Not feeling great."

"Well, thank you for your help, an officer will pop by later tonight to speak to Ms Chaudhri."

The policeman practically filled the doorway. His twee choice of verb was so incongruous that Sam felt like laughing out loud. He smiled and nodded, then closed the door behind him. When he returned to the living room, Abi let out a nervous breath.

"Oh, God, that's a relief," she said. "I thought he was gonna come in and search my bag."

"Why would he want to search your bag?" Sam asked.

"See, if you ask, then I have to answer and then you have to tell Mum, so seriously, why would you do that?" Abi glared at him defensively, before spinning the laptop around to face him. "Anyway, last night's incident, apparently. Care to pick one?"

The words 'attacked' and 'missing' were the options Abi had presented him with.

"Graymalkin here. Holly's not answering. Tell her the new brollies are ready, and can she give me some clue when she's gonna pick them up?"

Mira was listening to the surly voicemail when she got home. Feeling blamed for Holly's silence didn't improve her mood. She tugged irritably at her shoelaces and tried to switch off the buzzing swarm of Malcolm and Caroline and Graymalkin and Jonathan and Delia and Henry VIII and the imminent arrival of the police, to no avail. She reminded herself that this was where she was safe, where she could shut everything else out and pretend it wasn't there.

When she came into the living room, Sam was sat with his back to the door, his shoulders tensed in thought, and she knew something else was about to be added to the cacophony.

"The police came today," he said, with no intervening greeting.

Mira's head was immediately silenced. A terrible focus pushed everything else out.

"What did they want?" she felt obliged to say, and knew it was a useless contribution as soon as she said it.

"I'm not going to say, 'I was hoping you could tell me that'. I could, but I'd really rather not," Sam said with a weary sadness.

"Delia's boss got attacked, and you and Holly came to his rescue. You saved his life."

"I didn't really do anything," Mira said, edging further into the room. Sam still wasn't looking at her, his gaze fixed on the far wall.

"I once said it was your choice what you tell me," Sam continued. "But if you trusted me with something, I'd try and help. You didn't trust me with this, and I don't know why."

"I trust you," Mira whispered.

"A man went missing that night. Did you know that?"

Mira nodded. She couldn't be doing with more lies right now.

"When you first met Holly," Sam said, an edge to his voice, "People were dying wherever you went, and now people are disappearing and there's the two of you again."

"You don't think Holly..." Mira began as Sam rose and finally turned to look at her, the shell of self-control cracking over his frustration.

"I don't know. I don't know her!" Sam said, raising his voice for the first time in the exchange. "What is it you do together? You didn't come back until three in the morning! Where were you?"

"We just..." Mira tried to reach for an explanation. "She needs my help sometimes and we hang out. She's my friend, Sam."

"And while you're hanging out with Holly, people just happen to be getting killed or kidnapped?" Sam said, incredulously. "Mira, I shouldn't be hearing these things from the police before I hear them from you!"

"I don't know what's going on, I promise," Mira said, but no matter how much she told herself that was technically true, it still felt like the lie it was. "Holly and I, we... look, why don't you come with us?"

"With you?" Sam said, taken aback.

Mira found herself equally surprised at the plan that had sprung fully formed to mind.

"Yes, Holly's got tickets to the unveiling of Professor Fortune's big find," Mira explained. "She asked me to go with her. Why don't you come too? I can't promise it won't be boring, it'll be a room full of historians and I'll get carried away like I always do, but you can see what a night out with Holly is like and nobody will get killed or kidnapped. What do you think?"

"Yeah, I'll come," Sam said, his irritation fading. He stepped forward to her and she dropped into his arms with a sigh of relief.

"I'm sorry," he said after a moment. "It just freaked me out having the police here."

"I understand," she replied. "And I should have said something. It was just all a bit weird. Like you said, happening all over again. Where Mira goes, death follows."

"We'll go to this thing," Sam said gently. "And everything will be normal."

Mira nestled against his chest, seemingly at peace. Her face was turned away where he couldn't see the look of terror in her eyes.

Oh, my God. I just put Sam in a room with Holly.

And Delia.

CHAPTER 12

They waited in silence on a street corner by the Minster. Sam was being inscrutable, which suited Mira fine. She needed time to think, to plan, to prepare for every possible eventuality. To expect the unexpected. Most of the scenarios she imagined felt like episodes of old sitcoms. She hoped she would be able to stop short of locking Sam in a cupboard.

"Last warning," she said, compulsively smoothing her simple black dress and pushing out a desperate laugh to conceal her anxiety. "You are about to enter 'Mira does history' land. Exports include spectacularly boring displays of public nerdery."

Sam smiled, misinterpreting her nervous energy. "Oh, I think I'll cope. We don't need to wait for Holly if you can't contain yourself any longer."

Of course, since they weren't on the guest list, going without Holly wasn't an option. But the decision over whether to wait or not was settled when a series of irritable exclamations and loud footsteps emerged from behind them.

"Ow, scut. Ow, arse. Ow, bloody bobbins and naffworts, ow."

Mira turned to see Holly tottering towards them before she stopped, raged wordlessly at the heavens, then tore the high heels from her feet and stomped forcefully up to them. She waved the shoes, which were inevitably red, under Mira's nose.

"Why? Tell me why?" she shouted. "It's the daftest thing anyone's ever come up with! And these aren't even the ones with pop-out blades!"

"You have shoes with pop-out blades?" Sam asked.

Mira could only gaze at Holly's head, captivated by what she was seeing.

"Doesn't everyone?" Holly replied before the situation sank in. "And... you're here."

"I hope that's alright," Sam said with the merest degree of polite deference. "Mira said I could tag along."

"Yes, of course, lovely to see you." Holly recovered her wits and smiled warmly. "The more the merrier. Shall we head in?"

"You're wearing a fascinator," said Mira, her eyes still fixed on the glinting artificial peacock feather protruding from Holly's curls.

"I know," Holly replied proudly, her grin growing impossibly larger.

As she led them off, Mira's hand slid into Sam's and squeezed it tightly.

"Are you alright?" he asked, as his fingers tensed under the grip.

"There's a reason you can't expect the unexpected," she sighed. "Which is because it is unexpected."

Holly strode ahead, but as they turned the corner and Treasurer's House entered her field of vision, her pace slowed, until finally she came to a complete stop. Mira drew up alongside her, and noted that uncharacteristic look of dread in her eyes. Her shoes were trembling in her grip, and the fingers of her other hand were compulsively fidgeting with her umbrella.

"Holly?" Mira asked gently. "Are you alright?"

Holly snapped back from wherever she had disappeared to and smiled in their direction.

"Yeah, all good," she said with convincing confidence. "Let's party."

They walked past the staff member on the door unseen, as per usual. Mira feared that Sam would notice something odd, but it passed him by completely. She wondered if his brain was filling in the blanks. Holly was on the guest list; they were her guests.

Another attendant was collecting coats, and Holly made her presence known so she could hand over her umbrella, then shrugged out of her topcoat. Mira's mouth gaped as an off-the-shoulder vintage ballgown in vivid green emerged. Holly struggled to navigate her way back into her shoes, pushing aside mounds of skirt, then yanked at her bodice as she crammed herself back into it with a flounce of puffy sleeves. A monster attacking them would have come as a relief to Mira, but the first sight of the Great Hall provided an alternative distraction.

The historian in Mira longed to scream "this is all wrong!" at the mish-mash of eras, but she couldn't help but revel in the grandeur of it. The diamond patterned floor was crowded with elegantly dressed guests, while a bar had been set up behind the Roman columns that stood in the medieval hall that stood in the reproduction Georgian stately home and weren't bothering Mira in the slightest. A dais had been erected in front of the fireplace, home to a mysterious podium draped in green cloth. Assorted artefacts in glass cases filled a long dark table in front of an enormous painting of Charles I, which was the point where Mira's ability to not be annoyed at historical inaccuracy came juddering to a halt.

"I need a drink," Mira said without a trace of a falsehood.

Sam took the signal, accepted orders for brandy and gin and tonic, and headed in the direction of the makeshift bar.

"What the hell is this?" Holly and Mira both hissed at once as soon as he was out of earshot.

"He was getting suspicious," Mira explained hurriedly. "The police came, he knows about Malcolm being missing. But we're not doing anything weird tonight, so I thought it'd put his mind at rest."

"Why didn't you tell me?"

"Because your phone isn't working! Anyway, you said I should be more open with him!"

"This isn't being open!" Holly said. "This is you lying to him in a public place!"

"It'll be fine. We can work round him," Mira said, trying to convince herself. "We'll find out what we can and compare notes when we get the chance. The more pressing concern, I think, is what the hell are you wearing?"

"I said I were gonna posh up, so I wore a dress."

"I'm wearing a dress," Mira said. "You're wearing a restoration comedy."

"So, it's historical."

"You're not supposed to be one of the exhibits! We're supposed to be nice, normal, boring, academically-minded friends, and instead there's... those."

Holly peered down her own cleavage for an affronted second, then glared at Mira with hands on hips. "Don't you get prudey with me, madam. I remember when they put you in the stocks if a bloke saw your shoes. I never get to wear owt I can't chase a monster round the block in, so if I want to give me paps an airing, I bloody well shall, alright?"

"Sorry, it was just unexpected," Mira said. "I'm a bit on edge."

"Don't fret, nowt bad's gonna happen," Holly said, kindness filling her eyes as she gently took Mira's hand. "Now tell me I look awesome."

"Yeah, you really do," said Mira, and they found themselves both laughing at the ridiculousness of it all.

Holly's grin filled her face, but as she squeezed Mira's fingers tightly, the mask of the smile concealing her fear fell away.

"I'm really glad you're here with me," she said, her voice wavering. "I don't like being in this room."

"Hello. I'm in charge," Delia said with a fixed grin, startling Sam as she approached him at the bar.

"Delia, hi," Sam replied when he'd got over the initial shock. She looked relaxed in his presence, but not as much as she needed to. "How're you doing?"

"Oh, I'm keeping it together," Delia said, nodding vigorously. "Jonathan's left me in charge and I'm hoping nobody notices I have no clue what I'm doing."

"You're doing fine, look," Sam said, gesturing around the room. "Everyone's here, everyone's enjoying the relics, it's all good."

"You think so? Oh, good." She breathed out a sigh of relief. "I've been here all day and I've drunk my weight in coffee. I've had to do all this by myself. And I'm making a speech later.

I don't know how to make a speech. How do you make a speech? You get up and play music in front of big crowds, how does that work?"

"I just concentrate on what I'm doing, I suppose," Sam said once presented with a pause in Delia's gabbling. "I know that's not very helpful."

"No, no, that's good. Concentrate on what you're doing. Yes, yes. I see that." She gazed into the middle distance for a moment, before snapping her attention back to him. "I had no idea you were going to be here; I didn't see you on the guest list."

"Friend of Mira's."

"Well, I am very glad you're here," she said. "You have no idea how good it is to see a friendly face."

"Actually, I think I might."

"Yeah, it's him," Holly said, as she peered into the display case. The steel face of the helmet glared back at her through its gold pince-nez, horns curling above its crown.

"Are you getting anything from it?" Mira asked, and was met with a withering glance.

"I'm not a bloodhound."

"Do you think it's magic though?"

"Dunno. Could be." Holly leant closer until her face was almost brushing the glass. "Maybe we should've brought Gray. But I think he'd probably have to take a hammer to it, and I can't see that going down well."

"Suppose not." Mira nudged Holly as she saw Sam approaching, and not alone. "Company, be normal."

"Mira, hi, good to see you again," Delia said, her desperate grin restating its claim on her face. "I'm in charge."

"Good for you," Mira replied as Holly turned away from the exhibit to receive her drink and face the new addition to the group. "Oh, this is…"

"Oh my God," Delia interrupted, her jaw dropping open as she gestured flappily in Holly's direction. "It's you. You're…. you're you. You with the…"

She made her point with a shakily mimed imitation of punching someone.

"Yep, that's me," Holly said uncomfortably. "I'm Holly. Hullo."

"You're… you're amazing." Delia said with a pattern of slow nods. "Just amazing. You saved my life and it was just… amazing. Really. I could have been… but you saved me."

"Yeah," said Holly, sipping brandy through clenched lips. "Well done me."

"Just, just…" Delia floundered for the next word. "You have a big feather on your head."

Sam sought to jumpstart the conversation while Delia stood dumbfounded in the presence of her new hero. "Delia's had to take charge while Jonathan's in hospital. You were saying, you've got a speech to make?"

"What? Oh, yes," she said, coming back to the world around her. "Never done anything like this, bit nervous."

"You don't say," said Mira under her breath.

"Sam gave me a few pointers, so…" Delia emphasised a confident pause with two raised thumbs. "Good to go!"

"Is that the archbishop?" Mira gestured over to a grey-haired woman in a dark suit with a vivid purple shirt and dog collar, greeting each member of the crowd in turn.

"Oh gosh, archbishop." The wind was sucked out of Delia at the sight of a new challenge.

Holly broadly mimed the word 'gosh' behind her back, earning a swallowed smile from Mira.

"She's coming this way. I have to talk to the archbishop. Right, here we go."

The archbishop was drawing closer now, greeting each person with the same perfectly judged politician's smile and carefully chosen pleasantries. Formal, not cold; approachable, not familiar.

Delia smiled broadly and prepared to introduce herself, when the carefully composed face collapsed in a display of horror.

"Oh, fuck," the archbishop said loudly.

Delia paused frozen where she stood, hand outstretched as the archbishop breezed straight past with her gaze fixed on Holly.

"It's you, isn't it?" the archbishop said, her whole body gripped with tension. "It's you, and you're here."

"Hello to you too," Holly replied.

"Oh, Christ on a bicycle," she continued, shaking gently with fury. "You're here, so something awful is going to happen. This was supposed to be an ordinary boring civic occasion, but instead I've got you to contend with!"

"Boring?" said Delia in a wounded tone that went unheard.

"Fine, just tell me how much time I've got to get to a minimum safe distance before whatever nonsense you're here for comes down on us all."

"No, no, no, you don't understand," Holly said, making placating gestures with both hands. "Nothing doing. It's me night off, that's all. See? Out with friends."

The archbishop fixed her with a quizzical glare. "You have nights off?"

"Well, not many, but yeah, now and again."

"*You* have friends?"

"Yes," said Holly proudly. "I do."

"Good heavens," said the archbishop, her voice shrinking to a surprised whisper as she briskly walked away.

"It's not boring," said Delia to herself.

"What was all that about?" Sam asked once the impromptu ecclesiastical visit had ended.

"Oh, occupational hazard," Holly replied, launching into a freewheeling improvisation with gleeful abandon. "Nobody likes it when writers turn up to a party, you never know when we might, you know, start…"

"Drawing inspiration." Mira dived in as soon as she saw Holly floundering.

"Yeah, that," Holly said, a little too loudly in her gratitude. "I might be having a chat with someone, and think, ooh there's a character, and put them in me next book. Only I might kill them 'cause they're a bit of a twat!"

Holly laughed loudly at her own anecdote, stopping abruptly when Mira gently nudged her with her foot.

"Anyway, shall we have a wander?"

"A whole room full of historical artefacts," Sam whispered. "And you can't stop staring at this one."

Mira turned to smile at him, and took the opportunity to mark Holly's position. She was taking advantage of her unlikely invisibility to listen in on one group or another, dipping in and out of the room like she was panning for gold. Mira turned back to the helmet, the reflection of Sam's face in the glass overlaying the grimacing steel features.

"Isn't it fascinating?" Mira said with a tremor of excitement.

"It's ugly, I'll give it that."

"I'd love to know what they were thinking," she continued. "Someone had to give this to a man who might behead you if he was having a bad day! Can you imagine going up to Henry VIII and saying, here you go, Your Majesty, we thought you'd look good in this?"

Sam's smile broadened as he wrapped an arm gently around Mira's shoulder. She relaxed into the embrace and tilted her head into him.

"You know, doing your Master's is still a possibility," Sam said. "If you wanted to go back. We'd figure it out."

Across the room, academics were engaged in serious discussions, while objects from days gone by flaunted their mysteries. The new priorities that had consumed Mira since she met Holly fell away, and a smile worked its way across her face as she saw it. Something in herself that Sam had seen, and she hadn't. Knowing what this helmet was would help Holly, and save a man's life. But she also wanted to know because she wanted to know.

"Now, I'm here," she said with a breathless whisper. "But I'd never be able to afford it."

"We'd find a way, if it's what you want."

Mira stretched up and kissed him. "Thank you. Okay,

we're looking at everything now. And I'm theorising. And contextualising. And you don't get to be bored because you've brought this on yourself."

Mira was interrupted from her train of thought by two figures on the edge of the room, both of whom she recognised. One was not pleased with the other. Mira scanned the hall for Holly, but could not see her.

"But first, could you get me another drink?" she asked.

Holly had floated through the party, invisibly lurking on the edge of conversations and resisting the urge to correct misconceptions about periods of history she had lived through. There had been nothing of any relevance, and not enough to distract her from the cold sensation that had crept steadily over her from the moment she'd stepped away from the safety of Mira's side.

You're here, I know you're here, I don't want to see you.

The room spun in Holly's head, the exchanges she'd been picking at whirling into a babble, then into a roar. Faces blurred across her vision, all of them becoming one. Everything felt too close, too loud, too tight, too overwhelming, too...

Please don't make me see you. I'm sorry, I just can't.

Her breathing quickened as it all ground to a halt, and for a moment the thing she had dreaded was there. She stumbled back a few uncomfortable steps as the world resumed spinning faster than before, the party exploding in on her, consuming her, but not enough to block out...

"It's my fault!"

"Um, don't worry, I'm fine."

Holly realised after a moment that she had backed into Delia with some force. The archaeologist was looking up at her with genuine concern visible behind her thick glasses. Holly recovered enough of her wits enough to explain her clumsiness.

"Dress. Shoes."

"You look nice," Delia said, focusing her gaze on a foot poking out beneath Holly's gown. "But I'd probably be falling over too. Do you want to sit down?"

"Yes, so much," Holly replied, and followed Delia away from the crowds and out of the hall.

They stopped at the main staircase, and Holly collapsed onto it in an avalanche of skirts, taking the opportunity to slip the heels from her feet. Their only company was a sculpted bronze eagle supporting a shelf before a mirror. The dangling glass tendrils of a chandelier hung above their heads. Delia glanced back to the party before settling down alongside her.

"So, that man," Delia began as Holly caressed her left foot. She held her hands up to her head in imitation of her mysterious attacker. "With the, um, horns. Do you know who he was?"

Holly shook her head as she swapped feet, wiggling her toes as she did.

"Jonathan told the police he was wearing a mask, and I sort of agreed," Delia said, as if admitting a complicity. "I suppose I just didn't want to look stupid. But I'm sure he wasn't, you know."

Holly turned her attention from her feet to the earnest young woman sat beside her.

"Who do you think he was?"

Delia looked around the room with a tiny smirk as if she was about to say something incredibly naughty. She leaned in and the silver deltas of her earrings shimmered.

"I think he was an alien."

Mira drew closer to the two men. Even without whatever magic made her undetectable in Holly's company, she was able to rely on the focus they had on each other. She approached from behind the older, taller and angrier of the two: Marcus Bligh, the dean of the university. The younger man, Richard Rivers, she knew as a journalist. After the series of murders that had brought her and Holly together ended, he had come seeking her personal account. She had seen his smug expression before. It regarded being asked to leave as a sign he was entirely correct in staying.

"I'm just saying, it's a bold move," he said to the dean. "A chance to bury the past, I suppose."

"Ancient history, Mr Rivers," Bligh replied. "And I will not have you digging this up, not after all this time."

"She was one of your professors," Rivers continued. "And here you are, throwing a party, right where it all happened. Bold, as I said. I wonder how people might think that looks."

"For God's sake, that was decades ago! I think we can be permitted to move on!"

"The bodies were never found," Rivers stated dramatically. "And not one of them older than twenty-four. Their families still don't know what happened to them. What would you expect their position to be on the subject of moving on?"

Mira felt herself shudder involuntarily at the mention of their ages. Of her age.

"I think you can leave now, Mr Rivers," Bligh said coldly. "I trust I don't need to call for security."

"You know where to find me if you feel like talking." Rivers smiled through closed lips, as he sauntered in the direction of the exit.

The dean grunted an inaudible curse and turned away. He caught sight of Mira standing behind him and handed her his empty champagne flute before storming off with a curt nod of thanks.

"Maybe I should have worn a ballgown too," she whispered to herself.

"The thing we've found," Delia said, her voice spilling over itself with glee. "Can't be identified. Nothing about it can be linked to any known culture. So, you know what I think? Outer space. It's from outer space. And that man? He's an alien. And he's come to take it back."

"Seems reasonable," said Holly.

"Really?" Delia leaned closer with delighted surprise. "Wow, I thought you were going to tell me I was being ridiculous. Everybody tells me that. You really think I might be right?"

"I'll believe owt, me," Holly replied. "But I reckon you might be onto summat."

"People don't have open minds these days," Delia said.

"Tell me about it," Holly said. "I don't know that he's come to get it though, 'cause he's not tried. What if he were, I dunno, inside it?"

"You mean it's a pocket dimension," Delia said. "Like the TARDIS."

"The what?"

"And he was in suspended animation inside," Delia continued. "And when we dug it up, it revived him and he emerged from the cylinder, and now he's loose on Earth to do who knows what!"

"Sure, why not?" Holly said after a moment to take the theory in. "I mean, we're having this chat in a haunted house, so who knows what's out there, right?"

"Yes, absolutely! Haunted house!" Delia said with a snort of laughter that went on longer than it comfortably should have before she sucked it back in. "But, obviously, ghosts aren't real."

A cough came from the doorway, and Delia turned to see a young man in a black waistcoat and bow tie marking him out as staff, looking at her expectantly.

"Oh, it's time!" she said, leaping to her feet. "I have to go and make the presentation, so you'll be able to see the alien artefact! Oh, it's so nice to be able to call it that out loud! Wish me luck!"

"Nice talking to you," Holly said with a grin as Delia scurried away. Her eyes settled on a bundle of small file cards that had scattered down the stairs in Delia's wake. She flicked through them, ascertained that they were in no way a clue, and left them on the mantle. She never saw Delia's face fall as the young man passed on the message he had been given.

The archbishop was drunk. Sam had been uncertain how to address her, or if he even should. But as she requested the latest of what had clearly been several whiskies from a nervous barman, he decided that all rules of social decorum were off and he should go where the encounter took him.

"Ah, it's you," she said. "Her man."

"Are you feeling alright?" Sam ventured.

116

"Oh, bloody marvellous." She slugged back the whisky and requested an urgent replacement. "I'm the bloody archbishop of this godforsaken city."

"I guess that must be stressful," Sam said, leaning on the bar and flashing a supportive smile to the anxious young man on the other side, who looked barely old enough to sample his own wares and was fighting back waves of terror at his first intoxicated public figure.

"You have no idea," the archbishop said mournfully with a shake of her head. "No idea. I had such plans. They felt so important. But then you get the job, and they tell you everything. Well, you know all about that, I suppose."

"I suppose," said Sam, humouring her as she pressed on in a voice heavy with disappointment.

"There I was, first woman to make archbishop, and I was going to make my mark, I'll tell you. And then they say, guess what? It's a bloody ghost town. Here's your sealed orders in the event of impending doom. And underneath it all there's… her. Holly bloody Trinity and her nonsense. Not her fault, I suppose, but it's hard not to resent her for it."

Sam lapsed into silence. The drunken ramblings made enough sense to be troubling.

"Listen, you look like a decent, upright sort of chap," said the archbishop, as she lurched from the bar to grip his arm. "So let me give you a bit of advice. If you and your friends are in thick with Holly Trinity, don't expect any special treatment, alright? Whatever trouble you get yourselves into, you can get yourselves out of it."

An aide had appeared almost imperceptibly at the archbishop's elbow and led her away in the hope of avoiding a scene, but she broke away to deliver one last parting shot.

"And you can tell her from me, it'd better not be bloody zombies again! We can't keep passing it off as an extra race day!"

She left as Dean Bligh appeared on stage, leaving Sam full of ideas about the many ways that things could be very bad indeed. None of which involved what happened next.

Delia realised she had lost her notes, but somehow it didn't matter. She already had no idea what she was going to say at all, now she knew that the object she finally felt brave enough to refer to as the alien artefact had been taken back to the university for further analysis.

Dean Bligh was still introducing her, but all the sound had been sucked out of the room. It took her a moment to notice him gesturing to her and people applauding. She shuffled forward, scanning the crowd and finding Sam, Mira and Holly clustered close to the front. Feeling supported, she turned to the microphone, which was level with her forehead. After a futile attempt to adjust it, she settled for stretching up as far as she could.

"Hello. Professor Fortune apologises for his absence. I am here on his behalf..."

The dean leaned over and turned a key on the side of the microphone stand, bringing it shooting down to a more comfortable height.

"Thank you, Mr Dean," she continued. "I am here on his behalf. Not your behalf, obviously, since you're... here. But on behalf of Professor Fortune, who is... not here. And, in fact, the artefact that I was intending to share with you..."

"Did I just become the eloquent one?" Mira whispered to Sam as Delia tailed off.

"The ali... that is the art... that is, our discovery..." She drifted momentarily into silence, as nervous chatter bubbled across the room. "It's just, I'm terribly sorry..."

The hubbub of murmuring across the entire hall rose in volume, and Delia realised that all eyes had turned thankfully away from her and towards the display cases.

The case that had contained the helmet stood empty.

Police officers were working the room methodically, questioning everyone present. Mira had been among the first to be interrogated, and as she and Holly waited for Sam to complete his interview, they took the chance to conspire quietly. Holly, of course, had not been noticed by the police at all.

"I went back to it so many times," Mira said, desperately dredging her memory. "I just can't remember the last time I saw it."

Mira had hoped Caroline would be part of the investigating team, which would have made things easier, but she was nowhere to be seen. Delia sat alone on the bottom step of the staircase, engaged in some serious self-blaming. The police were done with Sam, who immediately moved to check on her.

"There was a journalist who got thrown out," Mira suggested, trying to blot out her jealousy by managing their suspects list. "And the archbishop left in a hurry. Nobody would suspect her."

"They would if she stole it in front of a crowded room."

Mira's mind wrapped around the mystery. "So it would have to be someone who could move without being noticed – you didn't."

"Yeah, I'm gripping it between me knees right now," said Holly with a tug on her bodice.

"The only other person I can think of who can…" Mira began, feeling an uneasy sensation of creeping dread. "You'd know if she was here, right?"

"I don't know," Holly replied with visible discomfort. "I told you, I don't like being here. And I had a… funny moment. Anything could have happened, and I wouldn't have known."

Mira decided not to press the matter, quietly filing the unresolved question for future reference. "Of course, we are being a bit mundane about this. Maybe the house ate it."

Holly glanced at the ceiling for a second before hurriedly making plans as their solitude came to an end.

"Sam," she said, indicating his approach. "You two should go home. I'm gonna hang about, see what I can see. Meet me here tomorrow morning, first thing."

"Here?"

"Yeah, I'll be here."

Mira smiled nervously at Sam as he drew closer and decided to try playing up the ridiculousness of it all. "You, me, police. Must it always end like this?"

Sam took her hand. "It sounds like they've got what they need. They're starting to let people go."

"We should be off," Mira took up Holly's plan. "Thanks for bringing us, Holly. It's been great, sort of."

"Nothing makes a party like the theft of the century," Holly said with a grin. "Take care, you two."

As they headed for the exit, surrounded by other departing guests, Holly's eyes were fixed on the ceiling high above her. The room had virtually emptied, and the last few people in attendance were unaware of her presence. Except for one of them.

"You were right, by the way," said Sam, as they strolled in the direction of home.

"About what?"

"Things just happen when you two are around."

"I know, it's really nothing we're doing!" Mira said with a relieved laugh as she took hold of his arm. "Trouble always follows us."

Sam didn't respond, the archbishop's warning dragged to the front of his mind by the word trouble.

"But I'm glad you don't think Holly is a dastardly master thief," Mira added.

"No, of course I don't," Sam replied, but kept what he did think to himself.

THE MCALLISTER INVESTIGATION V

SOMETIME IN THE 1980s...

"In 1675, the house's owner, George Asalbie, was mortally wounded in a duel and brought back to the house to die. Since that day, mysterious bloodstains have often been reported appearing at the foot of the main staircase."

•

Holly's torchlight zipped back and forth as she crept downstairs. She had heard something moving, but whatever it was, it was always a step ahead of her, leading her away from the Great Hall. A faint clicking noise teetered on the edge of audible, confirming something was down here with her.

She arrived at the room leading to the cellar, and noted with weary inevitability that the door stood open. She knew what she was going to see and that no good would come of it, but checked anyway. The room was empty. Sophie's body was gone.

"Brian," whispered Dylan. "Are you awake?"

"Go to sleep." The reply was flat and empty. Brian lay on his side turned away from Dylan, a dark unreadable mass on the edge of vision.

"I just wanted to check…" Dylan began, fumbling for words in the depths of the night. "Look, I didn't know, alright? Everybody else seems to have known, but I missed it. And I wanted to make sure you…"

"Leave me alone."

"I just didn't notice," Dylan said.

After a drawn-out silence, the words finally came. "Richard told Sophie. I didn't want him to. The professor guessed and didn't say anything until today. You were the only one who kept your nose out. Don't stop now."

"I talked to that girl earlier." Dylan swallowed his trepidation and continued. "I don't know what's going on with her. I didn't know what was going on with you. And I guess I'll never find out what was going on with Sophie. I just feel like I need to be more..."

"Disruptive." Brian cut him short. "Now go to sleep."

If he'd done as he was told, the scream would have woken him anyway.

Holly had followed the noise back to the ground floor, where she skidded to a halt in front of Sophie.

The decidedly upright corpse regarded Holly with a face screwed in concentration. Eyes flicked back and forth behind that face, but not Sophie's. They were a dull bronze colour and glinted metallically in the torchlight. As they shifted, there was no impression of movement in the flesh surrounding them, like her face was a mask, or someone had cut holes in a portrait to spy through the canvas. She turned away as if straining to hear something, glared at Holly, torn between two distractions, then sprinted off, her high heels stabbing down hard into the wooden floor with a quick rhythmical click accompanying each impossibly swift step, while her jewellery rattled around her.

Holly gave chase.

Richard's hand was around Erin's throat, lifting her off the ground. The green stone at his wrist shook back and forth, falling into focus as her vision blurred. He was over a foot taller than she was, which meant she had him right where she wanted him. She kicked out and her foot slammed between his legs with a crunching impact. He dropped her and stumbled back

122

but showed no sign of pain, recovering instantly to grab her left arm and pull hard. She heard the stitching of her blazer sleeve giving way. On the bright side, she would be free of his grasp in a moment. But it was going to hurt. She cried out after hearing the distant clicking and saw Sophie bearing down on her. With one arm being wrenched from her body, Erin used her free hand to seize the knife.

Brian and Dylan jolted upright as the cry rang through the Great Hall. McAllister was already heading for the main staircase.

"Stay here!" shouted Brian, but Dylan had stopped of his own volition. He looked up at the ceiling and saw the lights.

it doesnt stop

The presence in the house drove Sophie's teeth into the soft flesh at Erin's throat, while urging Richard's body to rise from where it lay, face carved open by Erin's blade. Memory of what pain used to be kept him down.

it doesnt stop

Confusion rippled through its consciousness as Erin's blood flowed in great spurts that nothing from this world should have survived. Taking her arm alone should have been enough to end this.

it doesnt stop

Unsure what to do, it continued chewing.

Holly arrived at the foot of the staircase just as McAllister and Brian emerged from the Great Hall, and all three were stopped in their tracks by the grisly scene.

Sophie was down on all fours atop Erin's body, her teeth sunk into the girl's throat. Erin's severed arm lay on the floor next to a huddled, shaggy-haired figure clutching his face. Brian moved closer to the wounded man, and Holly guessed who it was.

"Richard?" Brian asked.

"Keep back!" shouted Holly, as the thing that had been Richard snapped upright.

123

His face showed the same torture of concentration as Sophie's had, his left eye socket containing the same inhuman orb. But the right was merely an ugly, gaping hole behind which a brilliant white light blazed. Erin's knife had found its mark. Richard turned away as his fellow walking corpse let out a piercing keen. Sophie jolted upright, blood smeared on her chin and the same knife protruding from her temple. She leapt into a backflip, landing on her high-heeled feet like a gymnast, and darted off at tremendous speed in a storm of plastic clacks, with Richard shambling after her. Before McAllister and Brian could recover their wits, Erin sat up, spat a mouthful of blood out and shouted after the retreating corpses.

"You'd better bring me that knife back!"

"Oh shit, she's a zombie!" shouted Brian, while Holly gestured for him to stay calm.

"It's alright, nobody panic. She's just like this."

Erin stood up casually, blood streaming from the torn hole where her arm had been and the ragged gash in her throat. She tugged hard on her school tie till it was tight to her neck, and stooped to pick up her rogue limb, waving the dripping end at the aghast scientists.

"You've not got any tape, have you?" she rasped.

"Professor! You need to come and look at this!" shouted Dylan from behind them.

Glad of the excuse to leave, McAllister returned to the Great Hall, but what greeted her was perhaps even stranger. The ceiling was aglow. A layer of thick mist covered the beams, lit from within by pulsating blue light and scurrying trails of electricity. The fog started at the edges of the room and rolled in like waves, crashing and dispersing around a tight circular point in the centre.

"Now what?" she whispered.

CHAPTER 13

There were a few hours to burn between sunrise and Mira having to start work. Time enough to maintain her growing collection of mysteries as the last day of her twenty-third year began. A year that she could say with absolute confidence had been like no other.

As she stood alone outside Treasurer's House waiting for Holly, she pondered the medley of disconnected elements surrounding this house. Jonathan had unearthed an artefact. At that exact moment, a grim warning had been sent to the whole city. Three days later, a mechanical device possessed a man. The words 'of unknown origin' were way more applicable to all these things than she would have liked. And now the theft of the helmet was thrown into the mix.

Then there was this house. The Horned Man had tried to come here. The helmet was stolen here. And Holly, for whatever reason, was afraid to be here. Mira was sure of only one thing – anything Holly was afraid of was a reason to be *really* scared.

And on top of that, there was the conversation between the dean and Rivers. The events they'd alluded to were long past, but she knew from experience that didn't matter. If something bad had *ever* happened in this house, it had a nasty possibility of being relevant. Mira decided to do the one thing she could right now. She would phone a friend.

"I should start charging you by the minute," Caroline said on the other end of the line.

"Sorry, is this really early?" Mira asked.

"Crime never sleeps," Caroline yawned. "Which is handy, since Kenny's none too keen on it either. What can I do you for?"

Mira breezed past the unfamiliar name, sensing small talk was not on the cards. She was reminded that she knew nothing about Caroline's private life.

"Could you look up an old case for me? I'm afraid I don't know much about it. Something happened at Treasurer's House, a long time ago, but still living memory. Could you look through the archives? Do you have archives?"

"What am I looking for?"

"All I know is it involved a professor from the university," Mira explained. "And some young people, students, I suppose. And their bodies were never found."

"Their bodies were never found?" said Caroline. "I'm so glad I know you."

"I don't know what happened to the professor," Mira continued. "Maybe she's still around, might be either way. I don't know."

"I'll see what I can find. Try not to kidnap anyone today."

"Goodbye, Caroline," Mira said, as she spotted a figure furtively emerging from the side door of the house. Mira had never seen her with her hair down before, so it took a moment to realise who it was.

"Delia!" she called out.

"Oh. Mira. Hello," she said, looking like she'd been caught doing something wrong. "Are you alright? Sorry about last night. It's all just... Sorry."

Mira noted last night's dress poking out under Delia's coat, and that her hair wasn't just down, but actively dishevelled.

"Delia, have you been here all night?" she asked.

"Yes," Delia replied, then realised that alone was not an explanation. "There was just so much to do with the police, making sure nothing else had been taken, and tidying up. I've just not stopped. So that's what I should do now. I'm going home and going to bed. To sleep. Goodbye."

And with that, she all but sprinted away before Mira could get another word in. She had left the door standing open. Further robbery wouldn't stand, Mira decided, so she set the latch free and pulled the door firmly closed. It immediately fell open again.

Holly had the power to make doors open for her at a whim. Her sister did too. Mira looked back in the direction that Delia had gone and formed worrying thoughts. She had been there when the artefact was found, and when Jonathan was attacked. The helmet had been stolen from her event. The thief has to be someone who can do what Holly does, Mira thought, as she nudged the door open.

What can you do, Delia?

It was quiet and empty in the entrance hall, where Holly had handed over her coat and umbrella last night. Even though the house was deserted, there they still were.

"Holly?" whispered Mira as she tiptoed in the direction of the Great Hall.

Delia had been telling the truth about the place being cleaned up overnight. All trace of the party was gone, the hall restored to its perfect ahistorical beauty. Almost as if by magic, Mira reflected. There was only one remaining sign of the previous night's activities. A single, bright red high heeled shoe lay discarded in the middle of the floor, its twin lying at the bottom of the stairs. Mira picked the shoe up and rolled it around in her hand.

"Holly, are you here?" she called out, dropping the shoe and heading upwards. The steps creaked under her, and as she reached the turn of the staircase, something tickled her ankle. She looked down to see Holly's peacock feather fascinator by her feet.

"Oh, this is not good," Mira breathed. "Holly, can you hear me?"

As she entered the small gallery at the top of the stairs, the next thing she saw made her heart beat all the faster. Draped across the floor like a snake's discarded skin was Holly's dress. Mira scooped it up and clutched it to her chest. She noticed a door standing half open and crept forward, steeling herself for what she would find.

It was a bedroom, decorated in a sixteenth century style, with brocaded crimson curtains hanging around the head of the bed, while the foot was surrounded by a disregarded velvet rope. Holly lay on her side, thick quilted covers wrapped around her, drooling

127

contentedly onto a faithful reproduction of a period pillow. Enough relief swept over Mira for her historian's brain to kick in and feel outraged at the make-up smears on the fabric. Mira tossed the dress onto the bed as Holly drew in a snort of breath and opened one bleary grey eye.

"Hail the King in the Mountain," Mira said with an exaggerated parody of Angie's greeting.

"Mira," Holly slurred, not rising from her sleeping position. "Is it morning?"

"Yes."

"You just got here?"

"Yes."

"Where is she?"

"Gone home."

"Okay," said Holly, and rolled over, pulling the covers tighter around herself. "Wait in the hall. I'll be down in a bit."

Mira backed slowly out of the room, then ran down the stairs to the Great Hall. Only then did she allow everything building up inside her to erupt.

"Oh. My. God!" she shouted, then covered her face to mask her echoing laughter. "Oh my God, the National Trust will go spare."

She allowed the moment of hilarity to pass over her, and felt suitably recovered by the time she heard the slapping of Holly's bare feet on the wooden steps. She came down in her creased dress with the most spectacular display of bed hair Mira had ever seen.

"Morning," she said, ruffling her hands through her curls, although whether this made things better or worse was hard to judge. "Okay, first thing we need to do…"

Holly trailed away into a yawn, so Mira immediately took up the slack. "The helmet, yes. I've been thinking about how someone could have got to it. Could they have turned themselves invisible or stopped time? Do we need to be thinking about magic?"

"Possibly, doubtful, and yes as a rule," Holly responded to the three questions in turn. "But before we worry about that…"

"Ghosts," said Mira, snapping a finger in Holly's direction as an idea struck her. "This is the most haunted house in the city, right? Maybe a ghost took it. Or maybe one of them saw who did. Could we talk to some of the ghosts?"

"Erm, maybe," Holly replied, looking uncomfortable with the suggestion. "Look, Mira…"

"Or what if there's a portal?" Mira was on fire now, so much so that she didn't notice how the word made Holly visibly flinch. "Could there be something like that here?"

"Mira?"

"Yes, Holly?" Mira took in the steely glare and knew whatever was said next would be of paramount importance.

"My knickers are somewhere in this room, and I honestly can't remember where."

Mira turned to look from one side of the hall to the other.

"Oh," she said after her initial sweep.

"I think we should probably find them before this place opens," Holly said slowly and precisely. "And then we can get back to battling the forces of evil."

Mira gave the hall another quick assessment. It felt impossibly large.

"Yes, of course, right," she said and hurried off to the gallery beneath the stairs. She had barely made it a few steps before she felt obliged to spin on her heels and satisfy her curiosity.

"Okay, now you have to tell me everything!" she shouted.

"About what?" Holly replied, as she shunted chairs about.

"You slept with Delia!"

"Yeah, I know. I were there."

"You slept with Delia," Mira continued, punctuating her statement with excited hand flaps. "In a Grade One Listed building!"

"Well, I could hardly take her back to my place, could I?" Holly retorted. "That'd be a bit weird."

"But what happened?" Mira said with delirious confusion. "How did you…? I can't believe you slept with Delia!"

"We were just chatting and we got on," Holly explained. "You must have noticed she fancied me."

"So, she likes women?" Mira asked, feeling a weight lift.

"S'pose," Holly said. "I mean, we'd need to shove a bloke as cool as me her way to know exactly where she stands, but yeah, I should say so."

"Oh, I am such an idiot," Mira said, almost to herself. "I've spent the past week worrying this woman was going to drag Sam away from me, so of course she's a lesbian."

"Well, good for you and good for me an' all," Holly said with a smirk. "And not to blow me own, so to speak, but I suspect the power of good for Delia."

"Are you going to see her again?" Mira asked gleefully, new possibilities opening up in her mind.

"You what? No." Holly looked startled at this line of questioning, as if it was the most absurd suggestion Mira could have made. "I mean, unless she goes around getting herself attacked by monsters every week, I shouldn't think so."

"You could…" Mira began, but Holly's limitations were already lining up in her mind.

"Mira, that's not what this is," Holly explained. "How am I supposed to have a girlfriend? I'd be asleep most of the time and busy when I weren't."

Mira took a breath and proceeded to a tenderer area of Holly's past. "You've done it before though. Had a relationship, I mean."

"That were different. During the…" Holly noted the look in Mira's eyes as she anticipated the words 'civil' and 'war' used in conjunction. "Look, I were awake for five years back then, alright? Got to have a bit more of a life. That's not normal and it hasn't happened since. It's only this past year things have got bad enough I can have a best mate."

"Lucky me, being there when the world was ending," said Mira facetiously.

"The point is, don't go getting any ideas." Holly peered into the grate of the fireplace as she returned to her more immediate problem. "That's not what… look, I just…"

"Just what?" said Mira as Holly slumped against the marble mantle.

"This place is full of bad memories," she said. "And I thought if I had a good one it would, I don't know, balance it out or summat. Daft, I know."

"Did it work?" asked Mira, and felt a chill go through her as she realised Holly was not looking at her, but past her. She turned to where Holly's gaze had settled, but saw nothing there.

"No," Holly whispered. "No, it really didn't."

Mira turned to follow Holly's line of vision again, but there was nothing that might explain the desolate look in her eyes.

"So anyway, you don't have to choose a hat for me great big gay wedding, alright?" Holly said, plastering over her vulnerability with early morning grumpiness as she turned away from whatever had transfixed her. "And I dare say that's the last we'll see of... what?"

Mira's gaze was fixed on the wall, above both their heads. She extended a finger to point at where she was staring. Holly followed its direction to the enormous painting of Charles I. The king was posed elegantly, looking over one shoulder with a supercilious expression, while beside him a groom attended to his horse. The groom's eyes were turned upwards, to the top right-hand corner of the black frame, and the small, bright pink garment incongruously hooked there.

"I am really struggling to decide whether I want to know how they got there," Mira confided.

"I get excited in the heat of the moment sometimes," Holly explained, as she placed one hands on the table in front of the painting, grappling with her skirts with the other.

Mira's eyes widened at her intent, and she gripped Holly's wrist.

"Don't you dare," she said.

"Don't I dare what?"

"Holly, in the time we've known each other, I have seen a lot of strange things," Mira explained. "But I am drawing the line at you standing on a table with no pants. I'll get them."

Mira climbed up and stretched ineffectually to reach the top of the painting. When it proved beyond her height, she took to jumping and flailing an arm above her. After a few combined bounds and flaps, she finally succeeded in dislodging Holly's underwear from its perch and sending it fluttering down to the tabletop.

"Now please put them on and let's get out of here. This table is way too old to be jumped on."

"Take it from me, nothing's ever too old to be jumped on," said Holly as Mira climbed down, looking away and trying not to smile as she heard her friend arranging herself. "Okay, I'm all decent now, shall we get back to having a plan?"

"Yes, we should..." began Mira before a buzzing from her jacket pocket cut her off. She scooped out her phone and noted the number. "Angie. Actually, the first part of the plan is you getting a new phone. I am not your secretary. Hi, Angie."

Mira swiped onto speaker, and the distress instantly echoed around the hall, setting them both on edge.

"Oh, God, Mira, I'm sorry."

"Angie, what's wrong? What's happening?" Mira asked.

"He's gone. I went to check on him and he's gone."

The word landed with a thud as Holly and Mira exchanged a fearful glance.

"I went out and the door was off its hinges and the chains were broken," Angie continued. "He must have got out in the night, I didn't hear anything, but he's gone, and I don't know where he's got to. I'm sorry!"

"It's alright, Angie. We'll handle this," Holly said in a commanding tone as she indicated to Mira to hang up.

"Last time he came here," Mira said. "I'm guessing he's on his way."

"Maybe," said Holly, looking away from her to scan the room. "Unless..."

A scratching noise echoed around the empty space, and they both looked upwards to its source. The Horned Man was squatting on the central rafter, his haunches curled up underneath him as his claws raked the wood. He twisted his neck and leaned his body forward, stretching the muscles to look directly down at them.

"Oh, scut," whispered Mira.

CHAPTER 14

The Horned Man climbed head-first down the chain of the chandelier, hands and feet moving over each other as he drew ever closer to the ground. The glare of Malcolm's lost eyes flicked back and forth between Holly and Mira, sizing up potential prey.

Holly picked up her discarded shoe, testing the weight of it in her hand. She slowly crab-walked around the room in the direction of the other, always keeping her eyes fixed on the creature sliding towards them. Her movement must have made her a more appealing target, and he quickened his descent with malevolent purpose.

"Mira," Holly said. "When you came in, was me brolly still there?"

Mira gave a terrified nod, as Holly scooped up the second shoe, wrapping her fingers around them so the heels came down in front of her knuckles.

"Go and get it. I'll hold him here."

"Will you be alright?" Mira replied.

"Well, this isn't the first outfit I'd pick to fight in, but yeah, I'll be fine. Go." She raised one shoe high above her head while gesturing forward with the other.

"Malcolm, can you hear me in there?" Holly called up to him as he dropped down to the chandelier with a ringing clatter and stretched out among its arms like a spider in its web. His head rocked from side to side in a semblance of understanding, the motion setting the enormous light fitting swaying. He remained focused on Holly with his back to Mira, who took the opportunity to sneak away.

"I don't want to fight you, Malcolm," Holly continued,

her voice soothing despite being loud enough to echo off the walls. "None of this is your fault, and I've just got up, so could do without. Come down and let us help you."

Mira tore through the corridors until she reached the umbrella, snatched it up and headed back as fast as she could. Before she re-entered the Great Hall, the Horned Man reacted to her footsteps, Malcolm's neck twisting far further than should have been possible to stare in her direction before he dropped to the floor.

"I knew I should have worn the ones with pop-out blades," groaned Holly, and leapt forward to meet him, brandishing her improvised weapons.

The Horned Man extended fingers to lash at her head, but she parried with one shoe. The claws tore it to shreds, as she swiftly brought the heel of the other to rake across his chest, ripping through Malcolm's uniform shirt. A wild blow from his arm sent her sprawling across the smooth floor, the shoe skittering from her grip.

"Look out!" shouted Mira from the doorway, the umbrella clutched in her grip.

"Thanks, Mira," Holly sighed, as she wiped the blood from her lip and clambered to her feet. "You're helping."

Mira tossed the umbrella as the Horned Man sprang forward. Holly caught it without looking and in a single motion swung the handle to connect with the Horned Man's head, glancing off the golden circle around his eye and knocking him sideways. She moved in a circle, twirling the umbrella in one hand.

The Horned Man pulled himself upright and mirrored her footwork, claws flexing with a mechanical click.

"Okay, Malcolm," Holly said. "Now I want to fight you."

The Horned Man hissed and lunged forward.

Holly shifted her grip to wield the umbrella by both ends like a staff. Glittering silver talons flashed in the light as they tore through the air, Holly blocking each strike with the closest end of her umbrella. She fought defensively, always aware there was an innocent man locked inside her savage opponent.

The Horned Man's bulk dwarfed her and Mira could sense her friend tiring as blows were exchanged. Her eyes roamed the room, seeking some way to pitch in without getting herself killed. The shoe sprang to mind.

A clawed hand drove forward to seize Holly by the throat and lift her off her feet, which Mira took as her cue. She picked up the shoe and as hard as she could, threw it at the Horned Man's head. It struck with a dull thud, and he turned, spittle oozing between his teeth. With a casual flick of his arm, he tossed Holly aside and bounded in Mira's direction, sinking down on all fours to move in a lolloping gait. Mira stood dumbfounded as he bore down on her, his face a savage mask and an enraged shriek surging from between his lips. Holly leapt up behind him, seized his horns with both hands and pulled him up into a kneeling position.

"Mira, brolly!" she shouted, before he sprang sideways, his body spinning in a circle supported on one palm, tossing her aside with the force of the motion. Before she could regain her balance, claws slashed at her bare shoulder and she cried out in pain.

As he raised his arm for a second blow, Mira rushed over with the umbrella clutched in both hands, memories of school hockey matches flooding her brain as she clouted him across the back of his legs. He flopped backwards onto the marble, while Holly rose, took the umbrella handle from her and worked the controls of the grapple, extending the spike from the tip and bringing out a length of the cable. She pressed the handle into Mira's hand, and it only took one look to share the plan.

As the Horned Man found his feet, they ran in opposite directions on either side of him, Mira clutching the handle and Holly the shaft. The line connecting the two parts of the umbrella circled around him, pinning his arms to his sides. He struggled against the bindings to no avail, as Mira stretched the carabiner to lock onto the handle of the main door. With a roar of effort, Holly drove the spike of her end into the wooden seat in front of the fireplace, before dropping to her knees, clutching her wounded shoulder.

The Horned Man was bound tightly. He howled at the ceiling, screaming his frustration into the void. Unexpectedly, the void answered.

Bright flashes of blue formed around the rafters high above them. Tendrils of smoke swirled around the lights, thickening out of the air. The Horned Man gazed up at the glowing aurora and roared through tortured lips.

"Ver..." he said haltingly, as if struggling to put Malcolm's mouth to its intended purpose. *"Gull... Meer!!!"*

The mechanical components of the creature retracted into themselves, the talons unfolding from his fingers and back into the mask, which finally pulled away from Malcolm's face. The tendrils and curving horns stretched upwards in a spiralling column of glinting metal, straining to reach the storm that was erupting. Soon it was suspended a foot above Malcolm's head, clinging on to his scalp and pulling him up on tiptoes. As his body rose, his restraints were torn from their positions in a shower of wooden splinters, the umbrella clattering to the floor.

"Oh no you don't," Holly said grimly and ran to snatch up the handle, retracting the line and bringing the shaft zipping across the room to snap back into place. She aimed the reformed umbrella at the device and waited until it was completely free of Malcolm, who dropped to his knees once no longer suspended. Holly fired the grapple, sending the shaft speeding into the air. It struck the metal creature dead centre, the spike smashing through the web of delicate parts and tearing them asunder. Holly's thumb danced across the controls, and the umbrella opened. She reeled it back like a trawler net, gathering all the broken pieces into it, slamming closed as it locked back into place. The lights faded as the bulging umbrella clicked shut.

Malcolm stumbled to his feet, apparently unharmed save for some shallow scratches around his face where the mechanism had sat. He squinted around the room, breathing heavily and looking baffled, and let out a shout of pain as his fingers found the lump on the back of his head from the hurled shoe.

They slowly walked towards him, Holly flexing her shoulder

and examining her wound. Blood stained her dress, but the cuts were not deep.

"What's going on?" he said, blinking uncomfortably as if his eyes were adjusting to the light. "Where am I? Who are you people?"

"It's okay, Malcolm, everything's fine," said Mira, waves of relief sweeping over her. "You're safe. We found you here, you looked like you'd had a bit of a shock."

"I'm supposed to be at work," he said, flexing his jaw uncomfortably. "Hang on, is it morning?"

"You're fine now, Malcolm," Mira continued, smiling comfortingly at the bemused man before her. "We'll see you get home, okay?"

"I was doing the crossword," he began, before the explosion of light.

Mira blinked, then blinked again. Her vision was a mess of spots and flashes, like she'd stared at the sun for too long. As her sight slowly returned, it came blurrily, and when it finally cleared, the first things she saw were particles of dust swirling in the light from the windows. Her eyes stung, her throat felt dry and she could feel something tingling against her skin and weighing on her clothes, like she'd been buried in sand. She looked down at herself, and saw a fine, grey dust coating her body. She looked at Holly and stifled a laugh.

Holly's hair was blasted back from her face into a weird halo, and she was covered in the same dust from head to foot, save for tracks of clear skin where her dress had slipped. It was like they'd both climbed out of a giant hoover bag, an image which unfortunately brought the truth rushing into Mira's mind a little quicker than she would have liked.

Mira had a good head for trivia. Pub quiz teams had always been grateful for her presence. And right now, one piece of trivia was consuming her attention. The one about what seventy percent of household dust is actually made of.

"Mira, it's alright…" Holly began, seeing the dread form in

Mira's eyes as she caught sight of the barely perceptible scorch mark where Malcolm had been standing.

"This is Malcolm," Mira said, eyes wide with horror as she beat frantically at her arms and hair. "This is Malcolm! This is Malcolm!"

"I know, I know," Holly said, her voice low and soft. "It's horrible, but…"

"This is Malcolm, it's…" Mira felt her stomach lurch, as she detected the acrid taste at the back of her throat. She hastily spat on the floor. "Oh God, I've got Malcolm in my mouth! I've got Malcolm in my mouth!"

"I'm trying to be helpful here, don't do that to me," pleaded Holly.

Mira slumped to the floor, sending a cloud of Malcolm particles fluttering into the atmosphere. She gazed dejectedly at the dark patch as Holly came to sit beside her, trying her best to clear the dust from her wound through gritted teeth.

"We were supposed to save him," Mira said.

"I know. I think we sort've did."

Holly gestured to the window in front of them, and Mira saw someone standing in the gardens watching them. It was a severe-looking woman in an old-fashioned nurse's uniform, her shoulders covered with a dark blue cape. She acknowledged them with a curt nod but no flicker of emotion, then drifted away. Mira knew what she was seeing. A death collector, one of the strange order that Holly's sister belonged to, who ferried the spirits of the city's dead to wherever they were bound – oblivion, a place to haunt forever more, or something unknowable.

"And that's better, is it?" said Mira, refusing to be comforted.

"There's worse." The reply came in a dark tone that defied drawing out. "Believe you me."

Holly rose to her feet and, with as much respect as she could muster, shook the remains of Malcolm from her dress. "Anyway, if it's any consolation, I think we might have just saved the city."

Mira could only look up at her disbelievingly.

"You were right," Holly explained. "About pretty much all of it. When you said 'portal', well, yeah, there is one here. I've seen it before. That thing were trying to open it and we stopped it – we won."

"Dark road, that," Mira warned as she stood.

"I know," said Holly, her sharp tone not caring for the accusation of callousness. "You don't have to tell me that. Not here."

"I'm sorry, I didn't mean..." Mira began, her voice tailing away. "But is that it? All the warnings of impending doom, and it was all just this?"

"Looks like."

"What about the helmet?" Mira pressed on, trying to make sense of it all. "Who stole it? What for?"

"Dunno," Holly replied dismissively. "Probably just a normal thief. It must be worth a bit."

"He was trying to speak. What was he saying?" Mira felt cheated. The outcome of the situation was oddly underwhelming given that a man had just been disintegrated. "What's a... a vergulmeer? And if he wanted to open the portal, why didn't he just do it instead of fighting you? What does it all mean?"

"It means I'm not gonna be there for your birthday," Holly said. "Sorry. Look, I'm gonna go home while I'm still awake enough to shower. You should go to work, try and have a normal day if you can."

Her eyes settled on the bulging canvas of her umbrella.

"But first things first."

The small bell above the door jingled as Chloe entered the deserted gift shop. Her eyes impatiently scoured the mounds of bric-a-brac, and rolled when they didn't fall on a person.

"Mr Graymalkin!" she shouted. "Are you in here? I've not got long!"

"Out back!" came a muffled shout from the deeper recesses of the shop.

Chloe stepped behind the counter and into the workshop beyond, moving as if this were a significant demand on her time. Graymalkin was sitting at his workbench, fiddling with an array of broken parts, and Mira stood in the corner, patches of dust still clinging to her hair and clothes.

"What happened to you?" Chloe forced the words out through an explosion of childish laughter of the kind Mira had never heard from her before. Her studied teenage sulkiness had evaporated in a heartbeat.

"Street-cleaning van backfired," Mira replied. "Do you believe that?"

"No!"

"Would you have believed that if you weren't you?" Mira asked hopefully.

"Still no!"

"Told you," Graymalkin muttered as he poked at the objects scattered in front of him.

"What's this all about? I've got school," Chloe asked, having recovered her cool exterior.

Mira turned to Graymalkin for confirmation that all was well.

"Whatever it were, it's just bits now," he said, and brushed the parts from the table into a plastic carrier bag. He passed the bundle over to Mira, who held it out to Chloe.

"Here, take this to your grandma to dispose of," she said. "And tell her everything's alright."

Chloe peered deep into the bag with a questing look in her eyes.

"Wasn't there a bloke attached to this?"

"Yeah, it's fine," Mira said quickly.

"Oh." Chloe gave Mira a knowing gaze, making it clear that it would be fruitless to protect her from any ugly truths.

"You don't have to tell her that part if it'll upset her," Mira said. "But there's nothing else to worry about, we've taken care of everything. So, off you go, you'd better get to school."

"You're not that much older than me, you know. You don't need to talk like a history teacher."

"Yeah, well I'll be twenty-four tomorrow, so I'd better get the practice in. Now run along." Mira couldn't help but give the girl's self-assurance an admiring smile.

"Is there going to be a party?" Chloe asked.

"Yes, as it happens," Mira said. "Since, as you pointed out, I'm not that old just yet."

"Can I come?"

"Go on then," Mira said, wishing she'd been as pushy at Chloe's age. "Clifford's on Swinegate, tomorrow night, and if anyone asks, you're Holly's niece. She won't be there, so any lie you tell, she'll have to live with. Use this power responsibly."

"Yes, Ms Chaudhri," said Chloe mockingly. "And twenty-four is quite old, actually."

"And everyone will believe your cover story if they think cheeky cow runs in the family," Mira finished. "Now go, learn things."

Chloe left the shop and took all the joy Mira had momentarily felt with her. She returned to the bench and slumped down in front of Graymalkin. The chairs and work table in the room were perfectly proportioned for their owner and Mira's knees approached her chin when she sat down.

"I've got a shop to open," he said, looking at her as an obstacle in his otherwise smooth-running day. "And so have you."

"Hmmm," mumbled Mira absently. She idly picked up a discarded screwdriver from the bench and ran it through her fingers. "Do you know what happened the day I met Holly?"

"I have an idea," Graymalkin replied as he tidied the rest of his tools.

"A man was killed," Mira sighed. "Right outside the shop, just killed for no reason, because he was in the wrong place at the wrong time. I saw four people killed that week, and when there was a reason for it, it was stupid and petty and mean."

"And you're reminiscing about all this because...?" Graymalkin asked, his voice devoid of sentiment.

"I told myself back then," Mira said as she turned the rough, scratched surface of the orange plastic handle against her fingers. "That whatever happened, I wouldn't forget them. That no matter how much I got caught up in all of this, I wouldn't forget how I got here. I know I moan all the time, but of course I love

141

doing this, I wouldn't be here otherwise. Neither would you. But I promised myself it wouldn't become a game. That I'd always remember what happens if we fail. But we haven't failed since, so of course I forgot. Until today."

"Doesn't sound like you failed," Graymalkin said, turning from his clutter and allowing his gruff demeanour to fade.

"I know, apocalypse cancelled until further notice, I get that," Mira said, flinging a dust sheet over the big picture. "But someone was waiting for Malcolm to come home. I didn't want to know who. And now they're going to wait forever. I don't know what we could have done differently, I know we had no clue what we were dealing with. But now I have five people to remember."

"Good," said Graymalkin, and Mira was shocked by the harshness of his tone. "Look, when it's my head on the block, I don't want you thinking 'what's one less short-arse in the world?' Congratulations, you care. I should bloody well hope so."

"I guess you're right," said Mira, as she handed over the screwdriver and rose from her seat.

"Of course I am. Now sod off and sell someone some books," Graymalkin said, a smile creasing his whiskers in spite of himself. "And stop feeling sorry for yourself, you saved the city this morning."

"Yeah," said Mira as she turned to go. "Happy birthday to me."

THE PLAIN OF DEVASTATION

The blow sent him flying through space until the ground came to meet him and exploded in a shower of bubbles that washed around his body in waves until they reformed and reconnected to the plain. He experienced his pain and tried to right himself in time to fend off the next assault.

She came at him sideways, her body drifting through the colours of the world with terrible grace. He raised a limb to defend himself, but her long digits sank deep into his amorphous flesh and ripped it into a spray of hard gobbets that floated in front of her, then gradually reformed.

we really cant go on like this

New shapes emerged from his being, while she remained the same. They were close to the great maw now, where her shapetakers went. She had watched the things on the other side through their vision, felt them make those creatures their own, and modelled herself in the image of what she had learned. She had abandoned their kind's constant cycle of changing shapes for a single form that stood upright on long limbs, with dextrous hands and a head held high. A shape called 'human'.

Although this human head was crowned in horns.

The form suited her extremely well. She countered every attack until she could finally tear him in half. Once again, the two halves reformed and he wafted back to her, his body undulating as it propelled him through the swirl of their ever-changing world.

i cant beat you you cant kill me

She raised an arm above her head, and others began spiralling through the surface of the plain, twisting its shape into new forms with their very presence. They were her, all of them were her. Some she had made, others had seen the wisdom of her new form and copied it. They were smaller and weaker, but so many. And there would be more. They did not attack, merely held him. He beat great wings, hurling them aside, but they swam back in an instant. As his body shifted, some of them were cast off or broken under the force, but there were always more. More of the demi-things, imitations of the creatures from the place beyond the great maw.

i dont need to kill you

He was learning to understand the language of a single shape through his continual struggles with her. She gestured to the one stationary part of the landscape, the maw, a block of darkness hanging in the colour, wispy forms of shapetakers clustering around its edges probing for weak points.

He tensed for a second, pulling back into a single blocky form before exploding into a succession of shapes, none strong enough to resist the crush of the beings sweeping down upon him, driving him back until the maw consumed him once and for all. And then he was gone.

His victorious nemesis had not only learned shape, but time as well. And as time passed, she felt his presence alive beyond the darkness, heard his expressions echoing across the plain. She sent her swarm forth, in a desperate surge to ensure his final doom.

More of this strange time passed and her forces returned in defeat, their forms spilling over each other in frenzy as they fled from what they had encountered. From the things that had stood against them, as they had never experienced before.

Still, he was gone from the plain. That was enough. Nevertheless, she watched and waited.

The maw flexed and grew. An expression came across the plain, but not of it.

"I see you, oh my God, I can see you."

i see you too, thought the horned beast.

CHAPTER 15

Mira Chaudhri stood in front of the dusty windows of a second-hand book shop in a small side street by York Minster. She was twenty-four, which is not old at all by any reasonable measurement, and this was not the beginning. But it was a similar set of circumstances.

"I don't know," Mira said into her phone, as she peered expectantly into the gathering evening. "Grace didn't say how long he'd take to get here."

"I could come over…" Sam began.

"No, one of us should be there, it is our party after all," Mira said. "And he can't be much longer. Have fun without me. And tell the guys I want at least three songs off the list I gave you."

"Are you sure?" he asked, a concern greater than the possibility that she would miss her own birthday party detectable.

"Well, I'll settle for one, but you know which one."

"Are you sure you don't want me to wait with you?"

"Why, because last time I had to wait at work for an electrician he turned up dead?" She was still trying to brush off the memories that had been troubling her since the technical hitch had emerged. "I'm not saying this isn't really creepy. But I've gone to work every week since that night, and I've been fine. I'm sure I can handle this. Call it therapy."

"I'll stay on the line."

"No, you won't, go to your girlfriend's birthday party," Mira ordered. "I love you."

"I love you too," he said. "But we're not playing that."

"Oh, go on, you know you want to see Dave do it," she

mock-pleaded, as a knock came at the door. "Anyway, that'll be him now, so I shouldn't be long."

Mira gave a contented smile to the image on the phone's screen, an obnoxiously silly-faced selfie of them both, which disappeared as the call ended. She took a second to enjoy the reflection of her dress in the window before going to the front door, expecting to see an electrician who would, if she was lucky, complete his task as quickly as possible.

"Happy birthday!" chorused Jonathan and Delia.

"What are you doing here?" asked Mira, welcoming her unexpected guests into the shop. Of course Delia knew it was her birthday. Mira had clasped her new acquaintance to her social media bosom yesterday for an assortment of reasons, both practical and otherwise. Right now, she felt genuinely glad to see her.

"Just came from the Minster library," said Jonathan, looking hale and hearty despite his recent attack. "Passed the shop, and there you were."

"You're back to work already?" Mira asked. "Are you alright?"

"I'm fine, and there's no sense in hanging about, I've wasted enough time as it is," he replied, dismissive of any infirmity.

Delia was roaming the cramped shop, peering up the stairwell and down into the basement.

"This place is amazing!" she said excitedly. "I had no idea how big it was! It looks so tiny from the front!"

"This is how you choose to celebrate your birthday, is it?" Jonathan asked. "Sitting in a book shop on your own in the dark?"

"In a pretty dress, at least, but no. Observe." Mira found her way to the light switch and waggled it to no apparent effect. "Lights have gone, again. It's an old building, it keeps happening. Someone's supposed to be coming to fix them and I'm the only one in today."

"You should leave it like this, it's really atmospheric," said Delia as she continued to explore. "But I suppose you wouldn't be able to read."

"Anyway, somewhere in the city, my friends are having a party on my behalf."

"Is Holly there?" Delia asked as casually as she could, which was not very.

Mira took advantage of the shadows to conceal her smile.

"Out of town for a while," she replied and studied Delia's unspoken response through the gloom. It was hard to judge whether she was relieved or disappointed, but Mira felt certain that Holly had provided context to a lot of the background radiation of her subconscious.

"So how's the great discovery coming on? Sorry to miss it at the big do." Mira couldn't shake the feeling that Holly was wrong to consider things settled – and the more she thought about Malcolm's death, the more convinced she was that the creature had merely been opening the portal to escape from them.

"Yeah, sorry about that," said Jonathan. "Inspiration struck, and I needed it back in the lab pronto. Nothing came of it, alas. The world always expects a bit of effort."

Delia had drifted back to the stairway, and Mira clocked her almost reflexively looking at the skylight and the stars beyond.

"Very philosophical," Mira said.

"Words of wisdom an old friend once gave me," Jonathan said. "But you can have them in lieu of a card. Sorry, Delia only just told me."

"Oh, don't worry, someone gave me three extra hours at work, so I'm quite spoiled."

"The greatest gift is to be more than you were the year before," Jonathan said, rhythmically sweeping through the rhyme with a time-honed sense of universal truth. "I didn't come up with that and it sounds like fortune cookie bollocks, but nevertheless, words to live by."

"In that case, this is the best birthday ever. Excuse me." Mira heard her phone buzzing and snatched it up. "Hi, Grace."

She listened for a moment, her face sinking as she did.

"Thanks for letting me know. No, don't worry, it's fine. I'm alright. No, I'm really alright. No, really, I mean it. No, I'm not repressing. Thanks. Bye. Bye." Mira switched off the phone and stared at it in silent contemplation.

"The electrician can't come," she said, her voice tinged with melancholy. "I don't know whether I'm disappointed or not."

"That would be the effort I was talking about."

"Which has been rewarded," Mira said, pushing her doubts aside and enjoying her freedom. "Do you want to come to a party?"

They wended their way down a close side street, following the music. It was emerging from a tiny courtyard buried some way back from the front of the buildings on either side, and grew as they crossed to the bar beyond it. Clifford's was spread across several levels, and they pushed through the crowded downstairs bar to the spiral staircase leading to the first floor, where Pre-Cool Systems were playing a private function for the birthday girl.

As Mira ascended the staircase, she stopped in her tracks and focused on the singing. It didn't sound like Dave. The voice she could make out was higher. Sometimes a lot higher. It danced over a vocal range she felt certain he could only reach with the aid of a cattle prod, throaty and fluting and strangely familiar.

"Don't push your foot on the heartbrake," Jonathan said behind her, noting her baffled pause.

She turned to him, even more confused until he provided context.

"Kate Bush, 1978," he explained.

Mira's face lit up at the name and she ran up the remaining stairs.

"Come on, I have got to see this!"

They bundled into the room where the band was in full flow, albeit with a surprise guest vocalist. Holly was making a spirited tribute to her heroine, cramming as much energetic dancing as she could into the tiny space available. Sam was a still presence at her side, his fingers precisely flexing as his mind focused on his guitar. They were so perfect together, complementing each other with their differences, and Mira gazed in complete joy at the two halves of her life, jamming together.

Holly brought the song to a screaming crescendo, earning

delighted cheers from the room. She curtsied with a theatrical flourish and hopped off the stage. While Dave was detaining Sam, keen to reclaim his territory, she and a delighted Mira made a beeline for each other and fell into a close hug. Mira's hand rested on Holly's shoulder, and could feel where the claw marks were healing. She moved her hand further down Holly's back as she brushed intrusive thoughts aside.

"I'm so glad you're here," she said, then broke contact to give Holly a suspicious look. "But why are you here? I didn't ask for any monsters."

"No, no monsters, just me," said Holly. "I didn't go back to sleep, so I came here. No idea why I'm still up, but I am not about to question it. Maybe the world decided it owed me a night out."

"The world always expects a bit of effort," Mira replied.

Holly's brows creased at the statement.

"Anyway, I'm here," Holly said, the moment passing. "And so, apparently, is my niece."

"She wanted to come," Mira explained. "It seemed like the closest thing to the truth."

"Yeah, but now it's my job to make sure she doesn't get hammered," Holly said. "Thanks a bunch for that."

"You've looked after a city for centuries, I think you can handle a teenager for one night," Mira said, mischief bubbling inside her. "Anyway, I've got another surprise for you."

Mira took a look around the room and pointed out Delia, standing with Jonathan at the top of the stairs. Holly's eyes widened at the discovery, then shrank into a disapproving glare.

"Ooh, you evil little minx, Chaudhri," she said. "Here's me looking for me arch enemy, and it were you all along."

"You should go and talk to her," said Mira with a barely convincing veneer of innocence. "I mean, she doesn't know anyone here and you do get on."

"You are so lucky it's your birthday right now."

"Aren't I just?" Mira said as she saw Sam approaching, and bounded forward to kiss him. "That was brilliant. You guys should definitely do more Kate Bush."

"I think it'd be easier to convince Dave to do your playlist," Sam said, turning to bring Holly into the conversation. "Of course, we could always replace him, if you're up for it."

"Careful what you wish for," she said. "You could find yourselves doing the whole of 'Sky of Honey'. In sequence, with the birdsong and laughing like a mad bint."

"Maybe not. But you're always welcome up there." Sam noticed he was being summoned by the rest of the band. "Which is where I'm supposed to be. Dave feels like a challenge has been made."

Mira watched him resume his place on the stage, noting for the first time Abi, sitting alone in the corner and watching her intently.

"You sang a song with Sam," Mira said, amazed at how perfectly the evening was going already. "And everything was alright?"

"Yeah, I thought it'd help. Come into his world a bit, find a common ground. Worked like a charm."

"Thank you," Mira nodded, her delight spreading as she saw two figures approaching. "Holly, you remember Delia, and this is Jonathan."

Holly spun on the spot to regard the archaeologists. Delia's face was a rictus grin, but Holly barely noticed her. Her gaze settled on Jonathan, whom she regarded with a strange curiosity.

"Hullo," she said. "Professor Fortune?"

"That's me," he replied. "I believe I owe you one, and that was bloody marvellous by the way. Love the early stuff, haven't heard that one in a while."

"Yeah, oldie but a goodie," Holly said, her voice drifting. "Sorry, me head's a shed right now, bit of a rush, that. I'm getting a drink to steady meself, but I shall catch you anon."

She stumbled in the direction of the bar, leaving a perplexed Mira behind. Delia breathed a sigh of relief and Jonathan smiled knowingly.

"So that's who saved my life," he mused. "Always good to know who to thank."

"Hello."

Holly had downed a shot of rum in one while a pint of dark porter was pulled on her behalf, when the loud greeting interrupted her. She turned to look at a dark-haired young woman staring at her through bleary, somewhat intoxicated eyes. An elaborate cocktail was clutched between black nailed fingers and there was a visible wobble in her stance. The face looked vaguely familiar and Holly took a moment to place it.

"Sam's sister?" she said finally, allowing the familiar shape of the girl's pierced nose to guide her.

"Abi," she said, extending her empty hand forcefully with a ferociously closed smile, her lipstick dark and hard against her pale face. "We met at Christmas."

"Yeah, of course, right," Holly said, accepting her drink and trying to push back the troubles forming in her head. "So… how have you been?"

"Oh good, really good, yeah," Abi said. "Sorry, straight down to business, quick question. Are you shagging my brother's girlfriend?"

Beer dribbled over the edge of the glass as it stopped far short of Holly's mouth.

"Beg pardon?"

"You. Mira. Great big gay sex. Are you?" Abi said, spreading her hands wide. Her smile was still fixed and had become actively aggressive.

"Well, it was nice seeing you again," Holly replied and moved away, with Abi in pursuit.

"Look, I want you to know this is not a homophobic thing," Abi said, her voice far too loud for Holly's liking and starting to turn heads. "And I say that as someone who snogged Danielle Michaels on GCSE results day and it didn't do anything for me, but it doesn't mean I have a problem."

"Please stop talking now," Holly said weakly.

"I'm just saying that if this is what Mira needs, it's what Mira needs and I respect that," Abi continued, before roughly turning the retreating Holly to face her with a vice-like grip on her shoulder. Her voice grew harder and angrier. "I get that, and I understand that. But Sam doesn't need this. He doesn't need to be put through all this again. He doesn't need another lying bitchface to hurt him, and I won't have it. I won't let you hurt my brother."

She squared directly up to Holly. The woman who had faced down all the horrors of the netherworld for centuries instinctively pulled back.

"I'm watching you, alright?"

Mira tumbled from the room in an explosion of laughter, with Sam following, looking generally pleased with himself.

"I cannot believe you just did that!" she cackled, collapsing against the nearest wall for support. "Oh God, Dave singing that and trying to look cool!"

They were standing at the bottom of a straight flight of stairs. Vintage movie posters decorated the close, windowless walls on either side, one of which Mira leant back on as Sam moved to stand over her, his hand stroking her shoulder.

"It's your birthday," he said. "So just this once, we're going to pretend you have taste."

"That was just beautiful," Mira said, with a hand on her heart and adoration in her eyes. "And I know you hate that song so much, so thank you. You are wonderful."

"You deserve wonderful."

"Yes, I do," she said, gently touching the side of his face.

"Yes, you do," he said, voicing his agreement before they kissed briefly.

As they parted, she glanced over his shoulder. The cast of *Ghostbusters* looked back at her from a poster with text in Spanish, and it made her smile at the thought of herself. She felt brave, and her eyes flicked to the door standing ajar at the top of the stairs.

"What's that?" she asked, and decided not to wait.

"It's a little cinema, believe it or not," he replied. "For about twenty people. Should be locked."

"Hmmm," Mira said, a mischievous smile spreading across her

face, as she touched the end of his nose with an extended finger. "Follow me."

She quickly scampered up the steps before he could protest, and disappeared through the doorway. The room beyond was dark and low ceilinged, filled with rows of chunky fake leather armchairs facing a small screen. Mira satisfied herself they were alone and felt a shiver of excitement at her surroundings. Yes, she definitely couldn't wait.

If Holly can do this, so can I.

Dave held up the piece of paper with the words 'Mira's playlist' at the top, studied it for a moment with a gnawing sense of shame, and decisively tore it into a succession of smaller pieces.

"That's it," he said. "No more of this, and we never speak of it again."

"We did a good deed today, enjoy the karma," Carl said drily with a swig from a bottle of water.

"I need cleansing," Dave said melodramatically. "I feel like I've lost my identity. I need something real. Something with feeling, you know?"

Carl pondered the situation for a moment. The others always depended on him to come up with the perfect answer in times of crisis, and he rarely disappointed.

"You need an angry break-up song," he said after a moment's contemplation. "Nothing better for clearing the head."

"Right," Dave nodded. "We'd better get Nathan back over here. Where's he got to?"

Carl waved a drumstick across the room, indicating Nathan in animated conversation with a bearded older man. From the positions of his hands, guitars were clearly the passionate subject of the exchange.

"Who's the Dude?" Dave asked.

"Some professor. Turned up with Mira," Carl explained.

"Speaking of Mira, where's Sam gone and all," Dave said, realising he had managed to misplace a full half of his band.

"It's his girlfriend's birthday," Carl said with flat-voiced sarcasm. "I suspect he's being rightly rewarded for that display of romantic affection in the traditional manner of good-looking lead guitarists since time immemorial."

"Lucky bastard," sneered Dave enviously as they headed in the direction of Nathan. "Carl, do you reckon I've got a chance with Mira's weird mate?"

"Well, Lev Shestov did put forward the position that all things are possible," Carl explained. "So, if nothing else, you could disprove an entire movement of existentialism."

"Nathan, you're up," Dave called out, ignoring the wisecrack he hadn't entirely understood.

"Cool," Nathan replied. "This is Jonathan. He plays."

"You any good?" Dave asked.

"Our lead guitarist is spiritually unavailable right now," Carl explained.

"Well, maybe I can help you boys out," Jonathan said with a wry smile. "What did you have in mind?"

"Something with feeling. And possibly an angry break-up," Dave said.

Jonathan's gaze flicked back and forth between the three younger men, finally settling on Nathan.

"'The Chain'," he said.

"Now you're talking," Nathan replied with a wild grin. "Step into our office."

Holly's unsettled feeling had not faded, but the encounter with Abi had trampled all over it for now, pressing in a way that actual danger wasn't. She stumbled alone through a gallery of strange faces, and found herself looking at one of the few she knew.

"I'm looking for Mira," Delia said.

"Yeah, me too," Holly replied.

"Oh," said Delia, and paused to study her shoes before completing the thought. "I can't talk now."

And with that she was gone, leaving Holly alone with her worries. The band were coming back, with Jonathan taking up

154

Sam's place. As he hefted the guitar, Holly felt that something was not right.

Everything was right, and nothing else mattered.

The world, whether it was ending or in imminent danger, or casually spinning as usual, had dropped away. Sam's concerns about where Mira went and Mira's about what Sam knew didn't matter anymore. They had each other, they had an empty room and they were going to enjoy it, all night if they chose, party or no.

At least, that was the plan.

"Mira, I really need to talk to you... oh golly gosh!"

Sam and Mira broke from each other in an instant and began the time-honoured ritual of the interrupted lover, hastily ensuring everything was where it should be. Delia stood and flapped apologetically, trying to focus on the far corner of the room.

"Oh dear, I'm so sorry," she babbled. "I didn't mean to, and then you were, and oh gosh, didn't mean to see that and I should go."

"Delia, it's fine," Mira said, arranging herself. She could sense they were only responsible for the most recently formed layer of her distress. "We got a bit carried away. Sort of forget there were people here. Sit down, everything's alright."

Delia nodded, but ignored the invitation. Instead, she paced back and forth in front of the screen with them as an audience to her performance, Sam sat with legs uncomfortably folded.

"Something happened the night of the unveiling," Delia began. "And I have needed to tell someone so much, but I just couldn't because, well, I don't really have any friends in this city. And tonight it was just building and building and bursting inside me and I just didn't know how."

"It's alright, Delia," said Mira gently. "I know what happened. I was supposed to meet Holly that morning I saw you."

"You know?" Delia asked, looking to Sam.

"Actually, no," he admitted. "What's going on? No, sorry, don't say if it's none of my business."

Mira glanced at Delia, acquiring her unspoken permission to proceed. "Delia slept with Holly the other night."

"Oh," said Sam, with a little too much surprise in his tone. "Oh, right."

"It's just, I had no idea. I had no idea I was." Delia paused to make a shaky gesture with laced fingers. "And then this happens, and you start looking back and it all starts to make a kind of sense, and I realised of course I am... I've always been..."

She repeated the same gesture every time she was required to define herself, and Mira had to stifle a smile.

"Delia, can I give you a word of advice?" she asked.

"Oh yes, please do. I would like that very much."

"You should probably get used to saying the word out loud, because this," Mira repeated the gesture as she spoke. "It doesn't really mean anything."

"Yes. Yes, I see. So, it turns out I'm a..." Delia resumed her pacing, holding her arms by her side through sheer willpower. "Lesbian, totally a lesbian. And suddenly everything's so clear, all the things I didn't understand, and things from school, and why the first time I kissed a boy was so rubbish, and all those dreams with Amy Pond and Starbuck..."

"I'm going to have to ask you to stop there for both our sakes," Mira said.

"The point I'm making is," Delia said, standing still for the first time in her disconnected revelation. "I know who I am. I know the truth. I'm a lesbian, and aliens are real. I saw one. I'm a lesbian who met an alien."

"Well, that's good," said Sam. "I mean, the first part. I'm not sure about aliens. Can we put that to one side for now? But focusing on you, and learning that about yourself, that has to be a good thing. Isn't it?"

"Yes, it should be, it's just..." Delia's shoulders slumping in an abject pose. "It's Holly."

"Oh, Delia," said Mira, her voice genuinely pained, as she rose to comfort the troubled woman in front of her. "You're in love with Holly, aren't you?"

"No, actually. At least I don't think so," Delia replied, pushing her glasses up her nose. "I wondered if you could help me break it to her gently."

Holly had heard this song before.

She couldn't remember where, but felt certain that she had. She felt like the song was trying to tell her something, which was ridiculous, but she knew it was important. She focused on the lyrics, but they just reminded her of Erin.

And she had heard it before.

Layers of unrest were building up now. Something was not right at Treasurer's House. Something was not right in this room. The stab of pain every time Erin's face swam into her memory and the other face that was swimming alongside her.

And then there was Abi, making things complicated in ways she hadn't had to think about in so long. Her heart jumped when she saw Abi talking to Chloe, the two youngest people in the room gravitating towards each other while she, the oldest by a couple of centuries, felt completely alone. She sidled closer, wanting to hear what they were talking about, but at the same time not. The last thing she needed was Chloe being dragged into whatever Abi was up to.

"My dad listens to this," said Chloe, as if this was the most damning indictment she could come up with.

"Mine too," sighed Abi sorrowfully.

One worry fell away for the time being, but the others continued to bubble. The song was building, growing faster, louder, stronger, and Holly felt every word in Erin's voice, not Dave's. Why was Erin in her head? Why now? This had nothing to do with her.

Because of the other face that dogged her vision. For a heartbeat, she thought she caught a glimpse of it, but there was nothing but the memory.

She watched the band, watched the man Mira had introduced as Jonathan. Watched his hands dance over the strings, watched his eyes. And there it was, right in front of her. There hadn't been a guitar in those hands when she had seen them move like that, saw those eyes, heard this song and watched a man delight in it. Just like he was now.

After the tiniest silence, Nathan began a deep and ominous bass solo.

"What are you doing here?" whispered Holly.

"Don't worry, everything will be fine," Mira said. "I really don't think you're going to break Holly's heart."

"I just feel a bit beholden, that's all," Delia mumbled. "All of this came out of that night and it was so huge. I don't want her to feel… irrelevant, or a means to an end, or something like that."

"I don't think Holly is capable of feeling irrelevant," Mira confided. "But you're where you are, of course it's a big deal. Holly's… further down the road, you might say. It doesn't mean you don't matter, but I'm sure Holly wasn't looking for anything long term."

"Right, good. I see that now," Delia said, regaining a degree of composure. "I'm so glad you're both here, I don't know what I would have done."

"Any time," Mira said, before remembering how this encounter had begun. "Well, not quite any time, I think we'd all be more comfortable with at least one boundary. Anyway, we should go back downstairs. People will be wondering, and, Sam, the guys will be wanting you back on stage."

"I don't know, it sounds like someone's taken over," Sam said, as he opened the door a crack, letting music filter up the stairs. "They can do the rest of the night."

The music abruptly stopped, replaced by muffled shouting.

"Or maybe not," Sam added.

They ran back downstairs to discover the source of the commotion. Holly had stormed the stage mid-set, and had Jonathan up against the wall, to the shock of all present. Dave looked deeply put out, but too stunned to come to Jonathan's aid.

"What are you doing here, Dylan?" Holly snapped.

"Hello, Holly," Jonathan replied casually. "Long time no see."

CHAPTER 16

The door of the screening room crashed open and Holly drove Jonathan inside, with Mira, Sam, Delia and Chloe spilling in after her in a confused mass. Holly caught a glimpse of Abi bringing up the rear and moved to intercept, slamming the door in her face as she reached the top step.

"Not you, Sunshine," she said, turning the catch. "Sling your hook."

Jonathan had settled himself on an armchair in the middle of the front row. Holly caught Mira's eye, and knew she was supported. Everyone else was confused, and on edge.

"What are you playing at, Dylan?" Holly asked.

"'The Chain'," Jonathan replied in a throwaway manner. "Fleetwood Mac, 1977. Before I was so rudely interrupted."

"Have you been to Treasurer's House yet?" Holly pressed on, her frustration building. "'cause I was there yesterday, and guess what? It's happening again! Don't tell me that's a coincidence!"

"That must have been very distressing." He met Holly's furious gaze with the same kindly eyes Mira and Sam had come to know. "I'm sorry."

"Why do you keep calling him Dylan?" Mira felt the need to chip in, sensing the brewing ugliness in the room.

"It's the name she knew me by back then," Jonathan explained. "It's just a nickname my mates gave me."

"No," said Holly. "If you're gonna answer her questions, you're gonna answer mine. Why would you ever come back here? I warned you, Dylan. She will kill you if she ever sees you again."

"Will she now? We'll see." There was, as always, a quiet peace to Jonathan. The more Holly raged, the more serene he became.

Mira recalled how at ease she had instantly felt in his company. But now there was something infuriating to his aura of guru-like calm.

"I've been in this city long enough to rip up a car park, make a find of enormous historical importance and get stabbed. All documented by the press. I'm practically a local celebrity at this point, and I've not seen hide nor hair of Erin. I've even spent the last few days in hospital. You'd think that was on her rounds."

Holly bristled at the display of knowledge.

"I've had a lifetime to figure it all out, Holly," he said. "It took a lot of digging, but I know all about you and Erin and what that house really is."

"And you're not afraid of what she might do?"

"It was a long time ago, I'm sure she's forgotten all about me."

"She doesn't forget!" Holly screamed as she dragged Jonathan to his feet. "She never forgets!"

"Okay, okay, but maybe she has," Mira said, desperate to keep the exchange from actual violence. "I mean, look at me, she hates me but she's not tried to kill me since…"

Silence descended as Holly and Mira both realised what had been said. Mira could feel a gate slowly closing behind her.

"Who tried to kill you?" Sam asked, the question soft with fear.

"Sam, I can't really explain this now."

"You just said someone tried to kill you!" His voice rose, and Mira could feel that unfamiliar edge that came with his suspicions. "When did that happen?"

"Sam, please, Holly and I just need to…"

"No, Mira!" Sam snapped, his voice growing higher as the tension in the room overtook him. "You can't just say something like that! What happened? What are you doing where you nearly get killed?"

"Oh, yes, let's please do this now," whispered Holly sarcastically.

Jonathan resumed his seat, and Holly had a nasty suspicion that he was enjoying the show.

"Sam, please, it's alright." Mira tried to come up with something, anything that would calm things down. "I told you, I saw the man who killed all those people last year."

"Yeah, the man," Sam said. "You all just said she. This is like Holly's girlfriend or boyfriend again!"

"You have a girlfriend?" Delia piped up, before realising this was hardly the time.

Holly's exasperated reaction lingered long enough for Sam to grasp its relevance.

"She doesn't have a girlfriend, does she?" Sam asked, visibly stung by the betrayal. "You made that up. So what's really going on, Mira? Who's trying to kill you now? Who is Erin?"

"I didn't know how to explain, but everything's fine, you don't have to worry, please, I just didn't know where to…"

"Oh, will you just stop!" said Holly forcefully.

Mira was snapped from her desperation by her friend's strident tone. She looked from Sam to Holly and felt a worrying sense that she had no allies in the room.

"Holly, please don't do this," she muttered fearfully, but could already see control of the situation being taken away from her.

"I'm sorry, Mira. He needs to know," Holly said with a resigned look, then turned to face Sam directly as she rattled off the facts of her life at speed. "Okay, Sam, this is how it is. I protect this city from ghosts and monsters and demons and the stuff of scutting nightmares, and your girlfriend helps me because, as I'm sure you know, she is brave and kind and the best bloody mate I have had in over four hundred years!"

"Who tried to kill you?" Sam repeated the question to Mira, ignoring every word of Holly's explanation, but she merely cowered on the edge of the screen, worlds exploding in her head.

"Ghosts and monsters and demons, assorted," Holly stepped in. "But right now, we're talking about my sister. You met her once, little thing, butter wouldn't melt, but she's death itself in a bobble hat and she knows where you live. Dylan met her too, and the pair of you better bloody hope you never see her again."

"Her sister tried to kill you?" Sam said to Mira, his voice utterly lost. His gaze roamed the room until it settled on Chloe, who had

161

taken up a position on the back row even before that became a tactically wise choice. "Your mum tried to kill Mira?"

"No, she didn't, because Chloe's not really my niece because that was another lie!"

Holly's outburst was the last straw, and a sob exploded from Mira's lips. Sam crossed the room to where she stood and looked into her flooded eyes.

"Mira, please tell me what's going on?" he asked, reigning in some of his frustration.

Mira struggled with the words as she tried to force past the tears.

"Sam, just listen to me…" Holly began, but that was as far as she got.

"No!" Sam shouted furiously, striding the room, gesturing accusingly at each of them in turn. "I'm not asking you, I'm asking her! I'm not listening to you and your ghosts, or you and your aliens, or you and… Who are you? Why are you even here?"

"Don't look at me," said Chloe defensively. "I'm just the cleaner."

"Sam."

Mira was stumbling from her exile in the depths of the room, still shaken. She dragged a trembling wrist across her eyes, and struggled to regain control of herself. They stood before each other in front of the bare white screen as everything changed.

"Mira, just tell me the truth."

"Sam, I'm sorry," she said, grappling for the answer. "But it's true, like she said, it's all true, Sam, please…"

"No," he said, his voice turned cold and uncompromising.

"Sam?"

"No," he repeated, and turned from the room. He yanked the door open, and Abi tumbled in with a startled shriek. Sam helped his sister up and herded her down the stairs and away from it all.

"Sam!" sobbed Mira and immediately gave chase.

Holly could only watch her go as Jonathan rose to stand beside her, placing what should have been a comforting hand on her shoulder.

"It's good to see you again, Holly," he said with a natural warmth to his tone. "I genuinely mean that. And, not to sound like your dad or anything, but I'm pleased you've got friends now. It's good for you, you should have friends. But if you don't mind me saying, I'm not sure you've quite got the knack for it."

"I will find out what you're up to," Holly said, duty overtaking everything else. "And if I don't like it, it don't happen. You know I'll stop you."

"Good, that should be interesting," he said with a smile as he left the room, stopping in the doorway to look back. "Delia?"

"Holly, I'm sorry, I…" Delia stumbled as she followed him out. "I should."

The room had all but cleared, leaving Holly staring at the empty doorway that had taken so much.

"So, if it's all the same, I probably won't ask you to my sixteenth…"

"Shut up, Chloe!" bellowed Holly, hurling herself onto the nearest chair and tossing her head back to study the low ceiling furiously.

Chloe slouched down from her vantage point to stand before her.

"You alright?" she asked.

"Well, let's see," Holly began. "I've scutted up me best mate's relationship on her birthday. I saw a bloke get turned to dust yesterday. I keep remembering summat horrible and I'm gonna be spending a lot of time where it happened. The bloke who were there with me is back and up to no good. And the world just might be ending. So no, Chloe, I'm not in the best of moods right now."

"They'll be alright," Chloe said, with a naïve confidence. "Like you said, he had to find out sooner or later. They'll sort themselves out, and you'll handle the rest. You always do."

"Yeah, I know, I'm Holly Trinity." She waved her arms above her in a mockery of the traditional greeting. "Hail the King in the Mountain, she'll save us all, except her friends of course, and her sister, and any poor sod who gets in the way. 'cause when you

163

get right down to it, she still don't have a scutting clue what she's doing after all this time. God, why am I even talking to you?"

"Because nobody knows you better," Chloe replied with a calm assuredness which prompted Holly to finally regard her.

"Do you still have a scar here?" Chloe traced a finger under her left ribcage.

"Erm, I think so," Holly replied, feeling around to check. "It's only a few years old, so it's probably still there. They start to fade after a bit."

"It's ten years old," Chloe clarified. "I helped Nan stitch that one up. I was five. There was a stone arrowhead in there, and I had little fingers so, you know. Who shot you with an arrow?"

"Night hobs," said Holly. "Little sods love their crossbows."

"I've spent my whole life looking after you," Chloe said. "I see what it costs. And Nan's seen loads more than me. We know what you go through, but you always make it back to us, and you always will. Come on, none of us would have even been born if you properly sucked."

"I suppose," Holly said, her mood shifting. "You do all that for me?"

"I also buy your make-up. I've got a good eye for what suits your colouring," she added. "Ms Grantley says I should think about the fashion business."

"Oh, right, thanks," Holly said, feeling exposed. "I appreciate that."

"Do you want to get chips?" Chloe asked with an air of finality.

"Yeah, alright," said Holly. "May as well treat meself before the sky falls."

THE McALLISTER INVESTIGATION VI
SOMETIME IN THE 1980s...

"On several occasions, visitors to the house have reported turning around to see the grey lady stood directly behind them, a finger to her lips as if to demand silence."

•

"Bloody hell, it's a portal," grumbled Holly. "I might have known it'd be a scutting portal."

"A portal to where?" McAllister asked, trying to ignore the sticky scraping and tearing noise from the corner of the room, where Erin had found a roll of electrical tape and was attempting to reattach her arm. She finished counting under her breath as the latest wave of fog reached the centre and undulated out again. "Five seconds, it's a consistent movement. And it never goes all the way, look. There's always a gap of about four feet in the middle."

"Which probably means it's opening," Holly said. "No one's seen this before?"

Three upward turned heads shook.

"It started up when Sophie went walkies," Holly continued. "Maybe things have ramped up a bit. Where was the last place anyone saw Richard?"

"Sophie said she saw him in the kitchen," McAllister began.

"He weren't him by then. Before that."

"I saw him here, then I sent him to get coffee." McAllister swiftly retraced her mental steps. "Which was strange because…"

"You thought he was in another part of the house," Holly guessed and pointed up into the eye of the storm. "That is a way out. Somewhere in this house, I reckon Richard found a way in. And summat in there came through with him. Hollowed him out and wore him like a pair of old tights. You didn't notice owt weird, sent him for coffee. By the time he got to the kitchen, Richard weren't Richard no more."

"So what…" Brian stumbled on the sentence, then gathered his resolve. "What's up there?"

"I don't know. But we're up against summat that kills people and possesses their bodies to be down here, so I don't much fancy meeting its mates."

"I said I didn't know where the others went," Erin added with a hoarse whisper and a squeal of tape. "I think we do now."

"You're saying Richard's soul went through that?" Brian asked as Erin ambled across the room to stand precisely under the centre of the storm. Her left arm hung limply by her side with a mess of black and silver tape cocooning her shoulder and circling her neck. The front of her white shirt was bright red, and her pale face was speckled with dried gore.

"Sophie too."

"Can they come back?" Brian let his gaze drop from the swirling fog to study the strange girl. Her face was lit an eerie blue by the light above and she giggled at a bright flash like she was watching fireworks.

"Nah, it just eats," she said and did not look at the blow she had landed.

"Alright, let's try and put this lot together." Holly tugged on the ends of her curls as she thought. "Richard goes in, this thing possesses him, opens this portal to come out. Just a bit, but it's started. Powerful enough to cut us off. It kills Sophie, portal opens a bit more. It takes Sophie's body over, bit more. Open enough for us to see it now. It goes for someone else, but gets

Erin, who can't die so it can't do owt with her. So it runs off to figure out what's going on."

"That's what I would've said if I could be bothered," Erin wheezed. Her eyes had not left the gap in the clouds. "Have you figured out how we stop it yet? 'Cause that bit's gonna be fun."

"It's cut this house off from the world and the spirit world," Holly continued reluctantly. "Because that's what it needs to keep the wound open."

"Like we're in quarantine," McAllister said, trying to apply as much science as the situation could take. "So what happens if something from outside gets in?"

"Right now, if we die, the portal eats us and opens even wider. You'll see the movements get faster and the gap get bigger. But if we didn't go into that thing, if we go somewhere else, that creates a lifeline to our world and it can't be doing with that."

"Then the process shuts down." McAllister completed the thought. "But even setting aside the theological implications of the human soul, you're talking about exerting an influence on its location…"

"Doing that professionally since the 1600s," Erin croaked.

"What are you proposing?" McAllister sized up to the girl with a look that demanded to be impressed. "We let these things kill one of us, then try and catch their soul?"

"No, she's not," Holly said in a barely perceptible voice.

"The zombies kill you and take your soul in one gulp," Erin explained, noting Brian's clenched fists but not letting them influence her tone. "We need to get there first."

McAllister swallowed hard on the realisation. "You're talking about murdering one of us."

Dylan let out a gasp of shock as Erin cast a glance across the disturbed ceiling, for all the world like a contractor making a survey. "It's not looking good up there, ready to come down any second, I should think. It's an easy fix, won't take long, all back to normal. What do you reckon, Holly?"

The three scientists instinctively gathered in a tight group.

McAllister turned to where Holly stood, apart from everyone with her gaze locked on the floor before her.

"I mean, we can do it any way you like," Erin continued. "We can draw straws, but the amount of bottling up Brian's been doing, he'd probably be glad to go."

Brian dived forward, lashing out with a clumsy blow that Erin easily sidestepped. The disturbance above them roared, and a flash of electricity burst across the room. They all felt a tingle of static through their skin and hair. The screens of the monitors flared and went blank.

"Make your mind up time," Erin said. "How do you fancy doing this, Holly?"

CHAPTER 17

"We need to talk."

The words sounded out through the churchyard at Holy Trinity, stopping Holly in her tracks. She relaxed as Mira followed her through the gate.

"Am I the one you need to be talking to?" Holly asked.

"I don't think there's anything I can say right now that would help," Mira replied, slouching out of the shadows.

She looked calm and glum, the make-up around her eyes an ugly smear.

"S'pose not. Sorry, I didn't handle that very well." Holly waved the bundle of paper clutched in her left hand. "Do you want the rest of me chips?"

Mira responded to the question by raising her right arm, and displaying the bottle in her grip.

"Better," Holly agreed.

Abi hurled the assorted clutter from the sofa into one corner or another of the tiny front room, items mostly landing with soft sounds on the dusty carpet. Sam merely stood by the door; his face consumed with intense thought.

"You can sleep here, I'll sort some bedding out in a bit," Abi explained. "Emily usually gets up early to do her yoga, so don't expect a lie-in."

Sam still hadn't said a word. Outside of communicating with the taxi driver, he hadn't said a word since they had left Clifford's.

"I'll stick the kettle on," Abi said. "We need to talk."

Jonathan returned to the house he had rented for his time in York. It was dark inside, but he knew the place well enough to move without the presence of light. As he closed the front door behind him, he heard the music, drifting into the air from the small downstairs room he used as a study.

He slowly pushed the door open, and peered inside. The lamp on his desk was switched on, casting a dull yellow from under its green shell. The chair was turned away from him, but he could make out a small figure seated there. A vinyl record spun on the vintage player, the very same album he had shared with her all those years ago. Fleetwood Mac.

"Hullo, Dylan," said the girl in the bobble hat. "We need to talk."

CHAPTER 18

"So, tough love," Mira said, collapsing into the hen hole's chaise longue with the bag of chips in one hand and the bottle in the other. "You said you were good at that."

Holly dismissed the conversation before it could begin as she lit every available candle in the shadowy crypt. "I'm not flagellating you, I'm not that kinky. You did what you did, I made it worse, nowt to be done now. We'll just have to sort it out in the morning."

"Fine," said Mira, as Holly flopped down beside her, and took a swig from the bottle. "Take my mind off it, we'll talk business. Who is Jonathan?"

"I don't know." Holly's voice was heavy with failure. "I only met him once, a lifetime ago. I don't know who he is now."

"You met him at Treasurer's House, and Erin was there," Mira pressed on. "Is that why it's bad?"

Holly nodded weakly.

"Okay," Mira interpreted her reaction. "We don't have to talk about that either."

They sat side by side in silence, the candlelight casting flickering shadows across the room. Mira raised the bottle to her lips, creating a swirling grey vortex on the wall beside her, and gasped at the acrid taste, which somehow still helped. Holly extracted a chip from the paper and rolled the cold and greasy surface between her fingers.

"I've seen Erin do terrible things," she said. "And every time, there's the little voice in me head that says, see that, you made that, you did. When I met Dylan, I saw the worst of what she can be, and I made her worse still. *I* was worse still. So I don't want him here. I'm scared what she'll do to him. But I'm more scared what he'll do to us all."

"You really think he's planning something bad?"

"I don't think it's a coincidence and nowt good comes from that house," Holly said gloomily, and bit into the chip. "These tasted nicer ten minutes ago."

"Erin isn't your fault." Mira grasped Holly's hand. "She made her own choices."

"Yeah, yeah, chaotic evil like D&D," Holly said. "What is D&D anyway?"

"It's short for Dungeons & Dragons."

"Never heard it called that before." Holly shrugged, taking another hit from the bottle.

"No, it's not…"

"Well, the imagery's a bit specific…"

"Can we move on from this?" Mira said. "This bottle is not empty enough to talk about my sex life just yet."

"Then drink some more."

Mira studied the bottle, took a heavy swig, and checked how much of the contents had gone down while her throat burned.

"Sam and I were all over each other at the party," she said with a grin as the headrush kicked in. "It was all going so well until it wasn't. If Delia hadn't come in to come out, we'd probably have left the rest of you and… played Dungeons & Dragons."

"You're allowed to go a bit mad on your birthday."

"With all my friends having a party downstairs?" Mira said, not quite able to believe what she had done. "Anyone could have walked in! What am I saying? Somebody did! That's not me. I don't do things like that, you do things like that!"

"So what? I've turned you into a mad thrill-seeker, is that it?" Holly said.

"But I'm not, not really," sighed Mira. "It isn't exciting, it's just embarrassing. And then it hurt so much. You said the person Sam gets won't be me one day. Well, who did he get tonight?"

"Don't overthink it." Holly dismissed the worry. "You wanted a quick bit of tillage, nowt wrong with that."

"With the man I love," said Mira, pouring another mouthful into the crack in her voice. "I love him, Holly. I really do. And I know what that means, I should have trusted him with the truth, but I couldn't find a way. I just couldn't, could I?"

"Eat some chips, you'll feel better." Holly looked away as she sidestepped the question.

"Could I?" Mira repeated. "Tough love, Holly."

"You could have told him," Holly said bluntly. "I don't think you wanted to. Now eat some chips."

Mira helped herself to a chip and grimaced as she chewed. "These are really cold now. And I don't even like this, why did I buy it? Are we just punishing ourselves for all our mistakes, is that what this is?"

"Do you know why I became the King in the Mountain?" Holly asked.

"Yeah, you told me that one." Mira took another hit and pulled another face, before slipping into a garbled stab at Holly's accent. "This is your city, and your family's city, and you wanted it safe."

"Bit neat, though, innit? You know, I try to keep me family safe from bad things, and the only family I've got left becomes the bad thing?"

"It is textbook dramatic irony," Mira nodded.

"But life don't work like that," Holly mused. "And it's so long ago now, honestly, Mira, I can't even remember why I thought this were a good idea. I mean, it's not like I had much of a life. Don't get me wrong, I had mates. I loved me dad. I loved me mum and all the rest, as long as I had them. And when they were gone, there were Erin, who I loved even though she drove me up the wall. But all the same, there weren't much to look forward to. You'd have bloody hated the sixteenth century, I tell you. Not a lot of opportunities for a lass with ideas. So I've got to wonder, when they says we need a volunteer, was I just looking for a way out?"

"Does it matter?" Mira asked, feeling sobered by her friend's existential angst. "I mean, whatever you did it for, you still did it."

"Come on, though," Holly said. "All me daft talk about the

evil bastard of all bastards who's responsible for it all. Nobody believes me. Not even you. So what if he's not out there? What if it's just a story I tell meself 'cause if there's a villain, I must be a hero? Maybe all I do is tidy up. I'm a glorified maid, that's me."

"You're a bit more than a maid," Mira suggested.

"Well, I feel like a maid sometimes," she grumbled. "A crap maid, who breaks stuff and spills tea all over the rug."

"You shouldn't... I mean..." Mira began, but a tremor of laughter emerged from beneath her concern and engulfed her. "Sorry, I just had an image of you in a mobcap," she said, as she tried to gather herself through the tears of laughter, but it was no use. A second wave overtook her. "And the frilly apron!"

"Well, I'm glad I've managed to cheer you up at least."

"See?" said Mira, wiping her eyes and settling herself down. "You can be a hero. And I told myself I'd never call you that to your face, King in the Mountain."

"Erin thinks I became this to get away from her," Holly admitted. "I couldn't look her in the eye and tell her she's wrong."

"You loved her," Mira said, trying her best to be reassuring. "You still remember that. You wouldn't have done that to her."

"Imagine you're fourteen and the world ends," Holly said quietly. "Like, proper ends, rain of fire, eternal darkness, real biblical stuff. Loads of people die, and there's nowt you can do. But there's somebody who loves you, more than anything, and she protects you, and makes you feel brave and strong and like you can get through all this, and then you do. You live, you see the light on the other side. Because someone were there for you."

Mira nodded. In her few terrifying encounters with Erin, she had heard this same story. She knew what was coming next and felt a pang of sadness at how similar Holly's words were to those of someone who hated her more than anything. She closed her eyes in readiness for it.

"And then imagine she scuts off and leaves you," Holly concluded. "That's what I do. I help people, but I always let them down in the end. Erin, Dorothy, McAl... everyone. And now it's your turn."

"I've failed someone I love too," Mira pointed out. "So right there with you. Maybe sometimes life is that neat. I guess we just need to decide what to do about it."

"You should go back to Sam," Holly said dejectedly. "Put yourself first for a bit. I don't want to be the thing that splits you up."

"Maybe." Mira could see the wisdom of the suggestion, even as she knew she had no intention of listening to it. "But if this is the big one, what's the point of me sorting things out with Sam if the world ends the next day?"

She fixed Holly with a fond smile, which was immediately returned.

"Righty-ho then. Time to break out the big guns." Holly rose from the chaise, crossed to a cupboard, and withdrew a vinyl record from an assortment within. After studying the back of the sleeve for a second, she flicked through the others, selected a second, and stood defiantly with them held in each hand.

"I'm gonna play me music," she declared. "And I'm gonna sing along so loud they hear me on the other side of that portal, and they'll know who's waiting for 'em. Are you with me?"

Mira checked the contents of the bottle, and bit into a particularly grim chip.

"I'm in."

CHAPTER 19

"So then," said Erin, spinning the chair and bringing her feet up to rest on the desk. "You surprised to see me?"

"Not especially," Jonathan replied, not betraying any sign that he was put out by the intrusion into his home, or the heavy boots on his furniture. "I thought you'd turn up sooner or later. Your sister thinks you've got it into your head to kill me."

"But you think differently."

"The possibility crossed my mind when I decided to come here," he admitted as he pulled up a chair opposite her. "But it was worth the risk, and when you didn't come after me right away, I knew you wouldn't be a problem."

"I might be here to kill you tonight."

"You're not."

"Don't get too cocky," Erin scolded. "I'm gonna see where this conversation takes us, and then decide whether to kill you."

"That sounds fair," Jonathan said. "What shall we talk about?"

"Dunno really, the price of fish, the meaning of life, the things that shape the development of the human psyche, anything you like." Erin spoke in a disconnected sing-song voice. "But I think we'll start with your evil plan."

"Evil is a word for children," Jonathan chided.

"Yeah well, I still think boys smell and farting's hilarious, so I'll stick with it," Erin countered. "The portal. You're going to open it."

"I am."

"Do you have any clue what's up there?" Erin asked.

"Some," he replied. "I've done my research. The bit I don't know, well, isn't that the whole point?"

"You're going to blow a bloody big hole in the universe, right here in this city," Erin said. "And somebody is coming through that hole, and when they get here, it will be worse than a couple of your mates turning into zombies. Hell itself is coming to Yorkshire."

"And if you disapproved, you'd have killed me. I think you want me to pull it off."

"Oh, Dylan," Erin said with a sly smile. "You didn't half turn out well."

"I heard most of it," Abi admitted as she sipped her camomile tea. "But I still don't have a clue what's going on. Who was that old bloke?"

"He's an archaeologist in charge of a dig in the city," Sam explained. "And I guess he has a history with Holly, because she really doesn't want him here."

"And did somebody really try to kill Mira?" Abi barely sounded like herself. The swagger floundered in uncharted territory. Sam was used to her finding the punchline in any statement with annoying ease, but now she wasn't even looking for them.

"I don't know," Sam said, his fingers folding tightly around his mug. "It was like they all knew it had happened."

"But they talked like it was just one of those things." Abi completed the thought. "Oh, I had a nightmare day, laddered my tights, got a parking ticket, someone tried to murder me. Who thinks like that?"

"When I spoke to the archbishop…" Sam began.

"The archbishop?" Abi interrupted.

"Yeah, she said…"

"You spoke to the archbishop?" Abi added in disbelief. "I hope you told mum. It'll be the highlight of her year."

"She said Holly was behind everything." Sam grappled with the memory. "Or underneath it all. Something like that. I don't know, she was really drunk. There were things people didn't know about that she was having to deal with, and it was all to do with Holly."

"The archbishop was pissed out of her head?" Abi gasped, relishing the image. "I'd have got her to sign off on something. I'll send you a link to an anti-fracking protest. You two go on another bender, get her on board."

"Abi, this is serious." Sam pushed her back on track, his voice taking on a harder tone. "There's something bad going on, and Holly is behind it."

"So what are you saying, Holly's a gangster?" Abi said. "She's like the godmother of the Yorkshire underworld?"

"I don't know what she is," Sam continued. "But it's not just Holly. She said she had a sister, she said her sister tried to kill Mira."

"Holly says a lot of things," Abi interrupted, trying desperately to keep him calm. She glanced to the ceiling, half expecting the creaking footsteps of a roused housemate. "Holly's a lying bitch. Never forget that. You can't believe anything she says."

"And what if Mira says it?"

"I can't tell you how to feel about that," Abi said with helpless sympathy. "But Mira believes Holly. Maybe the sister is something Holly makes up to keep people in line. Like, my sister's a right psycho, but I'll keep you safe from her. This archaeologist saw through it and was able to break free. And that would explain all the bollocks about... was it ghosts? Like, she's got Mira believing there's a constant threat out there, which only she can protect her from. She uses the delusion to trap people in a dependant relationship."

Sam stared bewildered at Abi's theory. "Where did all that come from?"

"I know a bloke doing a psychology masters," she explained. "There is some no-strings sex involved."

Abi waited for a reaction to her announcement, but none came.

Sam was focused entirely on the facts before him with a clarity that made her nervous.

"But it's not a delusion, people have died. Those murders last year. That bloke who went missing at the museum, and Holly and Mira are always there when it happens."

"You think Holly killed those people," Abi said, trying the thought on for size and recoiling from the implication. "Sam, I know this is going to undermine every anti-establishment rant I've ever made in my life, but do you not think this is one of those things we should go to the police about?"

"What if the police are involved?" Sam whispered, as if the door might be kicked in at any moment. "You said it yourself. There was a bloke arrested for those murders, but he was killed by the police. You're right, that sounds so much like a cover-up."

"Okay, before I get some tinfoil from the kitchen and make us cool matching hats, let's get this straight." Abi breathed out. "Holly is a serial killer, who is gaslighting Mira into believing in the bogeyman. The Church of England knows about this, and is covering for her between bake sales. The police go around fitting people up for crimes Holly has committed, then make sure they die in custody."

"Fine, I'm a paranoid nutter," Sam grumbled. "Better for all of you if I was."

"A few days ago, you were worried Mira was cheating on you," Abi said. "I'm just saying this has escalated really quickly."

"Yeah, well, I think we can discount jealous boyfriend syndrome after tonight," Sam pleaded. "I need to know, Abi. Mira could be in real danger."

"I still vote for police," Abi said. "If we get disappeared, you can say I told you so. But on second thoughts, maybe we don't tell mum."

"So if you're here to help," Jonathan said. "I imagine you've brought some sign of good faith. To encourage me to trust you."

"I suppose so," Erin replied. "And in return, you would of course let me in on the finer details of your little apocalypse. And we'd both pretend that trust had been established. Very civilised and proper grown-up."

"Fair enough," Jonathan said. "Shall we proceed?"

"I'll show you mine if you show me yours."

"Don't be disgusting," he said, his demeanour unsettled

for the first time in the exchange. "I'm old enough to be your grandfather."

"I think we both know you're not."

"I think we both know I am," he said, shunting her feet from the desk as he stooped to unlock the drawer. He reached inside and produced a length of leather with a simple green stone dangling from the end, glimmering in the shadows as it had when worn on Richard's wrist.

"Long time no see," whispered Erin with a wistful smile. "You've had this all that time?"

"My first clue," he said. "And I spent enough time listening to Richard talk about his travels to know where to look next. The rest took time and…"

"Sacrifice?" Erin interrupted.

Jonathan flinched slightly at her choice of words, as he got up from the desk and crossed to a cabinet in the corner of the room.

"Determination," he countered, throwing Erin a glance as he opened the cabinet he knew she had already unlocked. Inside sat a sturdy metal safe, and Jonathan swiftly turned the dials to open it, revealing the artefact within. His fingers slipped across the stone in his hand, stroking the same unknown material as his discovery.

"Richard made a door by chance," he said, adrift in the memories. "I knew someone must have made one on purpose. Should have known it would have found its way back here."

"Funny thing about doors," Erin said. "They open both ways. So something from up there can get down here, after a fashion. Course you found that out the hard way, hence keeping this thing locked up. Reckon whoever made it did and all. Arses will get themselves bit."

Erin reached forward to lay fingers on the smooth surface, and detected a barely audible grinding and whirring in the depths of the artefact. She clasped her hands together and adopted a parodic expression of delight.

"It's a boy!" she shouted. "Where are your kids, Jonathan?"

Jonathan ignored the query, and slammed the safe shut. "In

any case, it appears I have everything I need. Almost feels a waste of time you coming here."

"Well, I still might kill you, so there's that."

"Maybe I'll kill you," Jonathan said as he returned to his chair, idly studying the green stone.

"Oh dear, are we going a bit daft in our old age?" Erin mocked. "Do you remember the bit where I'm indestructible?"

"You've never encountered anything that can harm you permanently," Jonathan explained in a teacher's tone. "That doesn't make you indestructible. You might find that out one day."

"And I suppose in your travels, you found the one thing in all of creation that can kill me," Erin laughed. "Don't be daft."

Jonathan merely sat in silence, staring implacably at her.

"Don't be daft," Erin repeated, drawing only further icy silence. "Stop being daft, Dylan, it's not funny!"

"Well, maybe it won't come to that," Jonathan said, the genial warmth of his demeanour returning. "Consider that a sign of good faith. Now, do you have something for me?"

"Yeah, a word of warning," Erin grouched. "She ain't gonna let you do this. And don't think because you're all human and normal she won't kill you if she has to. Now since we're trying to bond and that, I wanna know what your plan was for dealing with my sister."

"She didn't even know I was here until tonight," Jonathan said, a regretful tone in his voice. "Like you said, I'm human and normal, so off her radar. A creature coming out of the artefact was bound to wake her, and I had hoped she and it would keep each other busy. But it proved a little... hard to manage."

"This evil plot's a bit rubbish, isn't it?" Erin said. "Honestly, Dylan, you're a bloody amateur."

"You promised a sign of good faith. I know what you took."

Erin flicked a thumb into the corner of the room, where a bulky canvas bag sat on the floor. Jonathan stepped forward, and carefully pulled it open, his fingers sensing the shape of the familiar object within. His hands settled on the cool surface of ram's horns in iron, and he lifted the helmet of Henry VIII clear from the bag.

"The man who made this thought he could control chaos," Jonathan said, his face filled with rapturous glee.

"And you're gonna do better?" Erin scoffed.

"I never said that," Jonathan corrected with a raised finger. "Remember what I told you about chaos all those years ago. It breeds creativity. But this will be useful in the short term. Yes, I think we can work together on this project."

"You just need a host ready for when your door opens on its own again," said Erin, spinning in her chair. "And this is where you need me. Because you're still that soppy little kid with his records. Now me, I know people. I know where they live. If you want my sister and her puppy out of your hair, you go to where they live."

"I came to the same conclusion," Jonathan said regretfully, collapsing heavily back into his chair. "And after tonight, I think it'll be easy enough. He's looking for answers. He'll be looking for you."

"Well, speaking as a conveyer of spirits to the netherworlds beyond," Erin said with sarcastic distaste. "I never like to keep people waiting."

The flat was empty when Mira stumbled home. It felt cold and lonely without Sam, wherever he was, although she didn't feel ready to engage in a make-or-break conversation. What she needed right now was sleep. They'd sung until she was hoarse and she could feel the night's multiple strains catching up with her.

She felt like she'd left all her confidence in Holly's crypt.

Without turning on any lights, she made her way to their bed and collapsed on it fully dressed, the weight of the evening dragging her down, carrying her off into a deep and gloomy sleep.

The last thing Mira remembered before drifting off was the duvet gently moving across the bed on its own to wrap her in comfort.

"One last thing before I go," said Erin. "Your little mate with the glasses and the self-esteem issues."

"Delia."

"She's had knowledge of my sister, hasn't she?" Erin asked ominously.

"I couldn't say for sure," Jonathan replied. "But it wouldn't surprise me."

"I have a policy on that sort of thing," Erin explained. "But since we'll be wanting three little helpers, that should work out nicely."

"No."

"You what?"

"No," Jonathan repeated. "Not Delia."

"You sound like her," Erin said with disbelief. "You know people are gonna die when this all kicks off, don't you? Oh, wait, of course you do, Daddy. You're not saving Delia, you're just too weak to kill her yourself."

"You may have a point," Jonathan said calmly. "But those are my conditions. You let your sister keep me, you will let me keep Delia."

"Whatever," Erin said, rolling her eyes. "Not Delia. But when your big day dawns, you might wish she hadn't lived to see it."

"We'll see," Jonathan replied. "Anyway, it's academic, I've made all the arrangements for the endgame. Three young men on my dig. Nasty pieces of work, the lot of them. All selfish, misogynistic, entitled bullies without a shred of empathy between them, and I suspect Mr French may have a history of unreported sexual assault. The world won't miss them."

"Do you know why I do all this?" Erin asked.

"I've always known," Jonathan replied.

"Elaborate."

"You're a twisted sadist who gets sick pleasure from causing your sister pain," Jonathan said.

Erin clasped a hand over her heart and gasped theatrically.

"Dylan! Are we connecting here?" Erin said joyously as she rose from behind the desk. "I'm touched, not everyone gets me.

It's all about the look on her face when everything she's worked so hard on goes to buggery. I live for those moments. They make me feel loved. So, if you want to perform a human sacrifice on my turf, I get casting approval, and it'll be people she'll miss. And I am not gonna settle for a pack of daft lads just because they made poor widdle Delia cwy."

Jonathan remained silent under her unflinching gaze.

"I know people," Erin said, towering over him with a triumphant smile. "I know you. And I know exactly why you want Delia to live, and I promise you, it won't change what you did."

"You want me to kill Mira. I know you too."

"I do," Erin admitted. "I promised I wouldn't hurt her, you see, and I always keep my promises. Most of them, anyway. But if someone else got it into their head to do her harm… well, I couldn't do anything about that, could I?"

"Mira then."

"And two more," Erin said, pressing her advantage. "And not the bunch of twats you've rounded up. I want to know who else you'll chuck under the bus to save poor widdle Delia."

"Sam's friends," he began.

"Boooring," Erin sneered.

"His sister." A desperation was overtaking him and she could taste it.

"Better. I like that," Erin said with a delighted grin. "Good-oh, Mira and Sam's sister. Now can you come up with someone else before I can say Deeeeee…"

"There was a girl," Jonathan blurted out.

"A girl?" Erin took a step back.

"She's about your age, she was there tonight," Jonathan explained hurriedly. "They said she was Holly's niece, but obviously that's a lie."

"Oh right, I see," said Erin, her triumphant mood switching in a heartbeat to disappointment, then nervousness. "Who do you think she is?"

"I imagine she's one of the followers of the King in the Mountain," Jonathan replied, regathering his composure as hers slipped.

"And what do you think that involves?" Erin asked. "Is it like a bloke in a big watchtower? Or a bunch of virgin priestesses simpering in white robes and regretting their life choices? What do you imagine they do, right here in the twenty-first century?"

"Tell me."

"They do her laundry," Erin laughed. "They mend her clothes, or buy her new ones. They clean her up and do first aid. I've seen them taking a hoover down into that crypt. Where do you think she gets her money from? Why do you think she's not still wandering around in a red kirtle covered in pig shit? It's them, they do all the stuff she can't do for herself."

"Your point being?"

"The point is, I have to spend eternity with this woman!" Erin snapped. "It's alright for you, you're gonna die soon. We're stuck with each other, forever. I have to see her. I have to smell her. I don't mess with that girl and her family, because if anything happens to them, she'll end up wearing the same pair of knickers for two hundred years! I need someone to keep her vaguely human or she'll start forgetting what everything is!"

"But you don't want her having friends."

"Friends isn't just human, it's happy."

"Fair enough," said Jonathan. "But it seems to me, that once we're done, human might be something we can afford to be a bit vaguer on."

Erin turned away from him, her fists balled in frustration as she pondered the choice before her.

"And if Holly is so dead set on stopping this," he pressed on. "Maybe it's time for you to let go. I wonder if you can do that."

"She's what? Fifteen, going on sixteen," Erin protested, but her voice was fading fast. "And you say you're not evil."

"I was under the impression that was your department."

"Chloe," Erin said after a lengthy silence. "I think she's called Chloe."

"Right then," said Jonathan. "We have a winner. Chloe, Sam's sister and Mira."

CHAPTER 20

Caroline walked briskly into the noisy tumult of the police station's public reception. It had been a long night, and another babysitter was in line for a generous bonus. She had opted to encourage the legend that they would be paid triple if she died in the line of duty.

The room was packed with fine upstanding citizens in varying degrees of unhappiness, with the occasional uniformed officer visibly trying their best in the midst of it all. A young man with an intense demeanour was talking to a nonplussed desk sergeant, while a woman lurked uncomfortably at his elbow. As she drew closer, Caroline saw his face and the recognition drew a grimace of irritation from her. Whatever this was about, she had a feeling it was on her turf and wasn't going to end well.

"It's alright, Sanjay, I'll handle this one," she said, leading them away from the desk so Sanjay could face the next onslaught in line.

"Ma'am," Sanjay nodded, and, not for the first time in her recent career, Caroline mourned being 'sarge'. The price of advancement was being addressed like minor royalty.

"Hello, Mr Nesbitt. What brings you to my manor?"

"Inspector James, thank God!" Sam blurted out after a moment's fumbling for the memory. "You're just who I need to talk to!"

"Alright, follow me, we'll find somewhere a bit quieter. Are you with him?"

"I'm his carer," the girl replied. "Abi."

Caroline led them back the way she had come, finding a vacant interview room and discreetly drawing them inside.

"It's about Holly Trinity," Sam said, before Caroline could even ask. "You asked me about her last year, when you were investigating those murders. You know she might be dangerous."

"That case is closed now," Caroline said. "The culprit was apprehended."

"He wasn't apprehended, he was killed!" Sam shouted, before being reined in by a glance from the silent girl. "Sorry, it's just... I think you might have got the wrong man. I think Holly might be..."

"Mr Nesbitt, I was the arresting officer on that case," Caroline said with an immaculate poker face. "I can assure you we know that Peter MacMillan killed those people."

"Arresting officer?" Abi piped up, making it clear she knew the exact implications of the phrase. "You mean you killed him?"

"Yes," Caroline lied. "Mr MacMillan resisted arrest and made an attempt on my life. In the course of defending myself, I was left with no choice but to use lethal force. Which, off the record, was one of the most traumatic experiences of my life, and not one I particularly feel like reliving tonight. Now is there anything else?"

"I think Holly Trinity has killed the missing museum guard," Sam said, shaking with barely controlled adrenaline. "She's got my girlfriend, she's making her believe impossible things, I don't know what she's going to do to her, you have to help me."

"Sam," said Abi quietly.

Caroline maintained her icy composure. "This is a very serious accusation, Mr Nesbitt. What makes you think that?"

"They're always there when it happens!" Sam shouted. "Last year, and it's happening again! Why are you asking me this, you know!"

"Sam," Abi repeated, tugging on his jacket.

"You were looking for her last year!" Sam continued, his voice rising in pitch. "You knew she was killing those people. Why aren't you listening now?"

"I *suspected* Ms Trinity might be involved," Caroline explained. "But as I said, we later found the man responsible..."

"And killed him!"

"Sam, we need to go," Abi said in a measured tone.

"Mr Nesbitt," Caroline said, bringing the full weight of her authority to bear on him. "I think you should go home. You need to calm down, and I say that as someone who can arrest you if you don't."

"Come on, Sam," Abi said, and led him gently away.

Caroline followed them to the door, and watched them wend their way out of the reception.

"Oh, God, Mira," she sighed. "Why do you do this to yourself?"

The night air was cold, and Abi hugged her arms to her body as she watched Sam storm angrily around the car park.

"She knew!" he shouted. "Last year, she knew and now…"

"Sam, stop and think," Abi said, silencing his rage in an instant. "She killed the bloke they pinned the murders on. She's in on it! She probably wasn't looking for Holly last year, I bet she was trying to find out how much you knew!"

"You think?" Sam asked, fear dousing his anger.

"I'm starting to convince myself, yeah," Abi said, fishing an e-cigarette from her bag and drawing a puff. "Come on, the copper who killed that bloke just happens to turn up, that's well dodgy. Holly probably rang ahead, warned her you were going off on one."

"I'm going to see the archbishop."

"Sam, for God's sake!" Abi pleaded. "It's, like, stupid o'clock! We haven't slept! Come home with me, get some kip, and then you can harass a public figure! I mean, we'll know just where to find her because it's Sunday!"

"Go home if you like," he said quietly, and disappeared into the darkness.

"Sam!" she shouted. "I'm not following you! Do what you like, I don't care!"

She inhaled hard and spat out a cloud of sweet-smelling vapour.

"Sod you, I tried to help," she grumbled to herself.

The noises from inside the police station provided a deadened backdrop to her irritation. The door opened with an explosion of sound, and she half-expected to see Inspector James advancing stony-faced with a silenced pistol. Instead, two shaken-looking women in matching hen night T-shirts supported each other as they skulked away. Abi stood alone, feeling unsafe and in need of an idea. As it happened, she had a good one.

"Right then, Abigail Jessica Nesbitt," she said to herself in a determined tone. "Let's go see what we can dig up."

CHAPTER 21

The first important thing that happened on the day after Mira's birthday was Delia's phone failing to play Jerry Goldsmith's opening theme to *Star Trek: The Next Generation* at the time she could have sworn she set it to do so. She twitched briefly as if aware something was wrong and continued sleeping through a troubled dream. In the days to come, she would wonder what might have happened differently if the alarm had gone off.

The day continued with a round of applause. Work at the dig had not been due to occur today, but since Jonathan was ready to get back into the swing of things, everyone had agreed to give up their Sunday. They clapped appreciatively as he walked through the earthworks, greeting individual colleagues as he did, and casually acknowledging the massed show of support.

"Thank you, everyone. I've missed you too," he declared, silencing the applause with raised hands. "I'm not going to make a speech; we've got far too much to be getting on with. So, ladies and gentlemen, on your marks, get set, dig."

As the archaeologists resumed their work, Jonathan heard a voice, yelling stridently to attract his attention.

"Oi, Professor!" it said. "I need to talk to you, Professor! Oh bloody hell, what was your name, oh yeah, Dylan!"

Jonathan spun around at the use of his old nickname, and caught sight of a young woman standing on the edge of the dig. It only took a moment to realise he had seen her at the party last night, and another to guess her identity.

"Can I help you?" he asked, as he walked over to the intruder.

"Hi, you know my brother," she said. "Look, I kind of spied on the barney in the pub last night. I'm Abi."

"Jonathan," he said, extending a hand. "Nobody's called me Dylan in years. Well, nearly nobody."

"Yeah, that's what I need to talk to you about," she said with a degree of trepidation that did not suit her. "You know about Holly Trinity, don't you?"

"I do."

"My brother's going off his head," Abi explained. "He thinks his girlfriend's in danger. We need help, we need to talk to someone about Holly."

"I think I can help you," he said with a kind smile. "Don't worry, everything will be alright. But we can't talk here. Come to my office."

"Oh no no no no noooo!" shouted Delia, as she realised how much time had elapsed since her alarm failed to go off.

If Mira had been awake, she might have seen Jonathan and Abi leaving the dig together from her window, but she was still in the last vestiges of sleep. Some distant noises and a nascent headache were working to rouse her. The beef fat smell of the chips lingered on her vegetarian fingers. Her eyes drifted open and she briefly saw the face of a young man in a flat cap, smiling at her with unforced kindness in his brown eyes. She blinked and he was gone, but the noises stayed. Someone else was in the flat. She pushed herself upright, remembering that she had slept in her clothes, tumbled out of bed, and pushed open the door to the living room.

Sam looked dreadful. He was still wearing last night's clothes as well, and his face betrayed that he had not got much, if any sleep. She tried to shake the fuzzy feeling from her head, as he caught sight of her through dark ringed eyes. They faced each other across the room, both waiting for the other to go first.

"Are you alright?" she said eventually.

"Really not sure," he said in a faraway voice.

"I'm sorry," she began. "And I know I said that last night, a lot…"

"Mira," he said, and she knew in an instant that every word would count today. "Do you love me?"

"Of course I do," she replied, swallowing a rush of fear. There weren't many reasons for asking that question, and none of them felt good.

"I don't know what to do." Sam's voice was helpless and lost. "I don't understand what's going on, and I can't take it anymore. I know I promised that you didn't have to tell me everything, I keep going back to it. I tried. Mira, I'm sorry, but it can't be like that anymore. I need to know; I need to know everything. I need to know you trust me."

"I do trust you," Mira said, the words feeling like a useless attempt to back pedal. "No, that's not fair because I haven't. I've kept things from you, I know I have. But I won't anymore."

"Just tell me the truth," he said, taking a step towards her. "That's all I need from you."

"I know this is going to be hard to accept," she said, with a deep breath. "But you have to believe me. It's all true. Everything Holly was saying last night is true. There are ghosts. There are creatures. She's hundreds of years old. There are wonderful and terrible things and that's what we've been doing, and I knew you could never believe it."

"Mira, stop," Sam pulled back a step, his voice frosting over. "Not this, tell me what's really going on."

"No, this is it, Sam," Mira protested. "I really have seen ghosts and fought monsters and all of it. I'm not making this up, I couldn't if I tried, believe me."

"Please, just don't," Sam said, moving close and grabbing her shoulders. "This isn't real, Mira. This is some sick game of Holly's, trying to make you believe in all this. I need you to tell me what you've really been doing."

"No, it's…" Mira began, as a thought struck her. "I'll prove it."

"How?"

"This flat is haunted," she said, excitement at the solution overwhelming her. "There's a ghost, in this flat, a nice one though.

He's called Joe, he worked here in the 1920s, he died here. A box fell on his head and now he haunts this flat."

"Mira, please don't do this," Sam's voice cracked as a manic energy overcame her. He backed away, terrified of what she was saying.

"He's here in the room with us," she continued, her gaze drifting past his and her eyes wide with wonder. "Oh my God, I can see him. I've never been able to see him before, Sam, please look behind you."

"Mira, stop it."

"He's right there," Mira gasped, a delighted laugh forcing itself out. "He's wearing a flat cap and a waistcoat, the most stereotypical Yorkshireman ever! He's smiling. Look at him, Sam. Please just look at Joe! It's all real and he's here and I need you to see him! Please look at Joe!"

"Mira, enough!" shouted Sam.

Mira was shaken by the loudness of his voice, and her concentration wavered. When she looked again, Joe was gone. A loud buzzing from the table shattered the mood further, as Mira's phone burst into life.

"You couldn't, could you?" His shoulders slumped and his eyes cast downwards as he moved past the table, past the glow of the phone's screen, and the name of the caller displayed there.

Caroline.

The previous year, Sam had stood on the edge of a crime scene and met a woman who had told him her full name. They didn't know any other Carolines. He snatched up the phone, set it to speaker and took the call, his eyes remaining fixed on Mira as he did.

"Mira, I've been trying to reach you all morning. Where the…?" came the familiar voice before Sam hurled the phone into the far corner of the room.

Mira instinctively recoiled from the uncharacteristic violence of the gesture.

"You're all part of it!" he yelled, the rage consuming him now. "All of you!"

"Sam, wait…" Mira began, but he was already gone, slamming the door behind him as he left. The crash of the door broke whatever was holding Mira together, and she stood and cried helplessly in the middle of the room.

Sam had made it all the way out of the building and was heading back into town before he noticed his phone was ringing as well. He tore it from his pocket, and grudgingly accepted the call.

"Have we calmed down yet?" Abi asked.

"Yes," he snapped.

"Yeah, I'm feeling the waves of tranquillity coming off you back here," Abi replied. "Come to King's Manor, I've found your archaeologist. Where have you been, did you sleep somewhere?"

"I'm on my way."

"Oh bloody hell," she muttered. "Tell me you didn't talk to Mira."

"I'll see you in a minute."

"Sam, listen…" she began, but he had already silenced the phone as he tore off through the increasingly terrifying city.

Mira had crawled into the corner, huddled in a ball of tears and confusion. The phone had survived its journey, a fact she would have been grateful for under normal circumstances. And it was ringing.

"Mira, are you alright?" Caroline said the second she answered. "I've had your boyfriend down at the station in a hell of a state asking about Holly. I don't know what's going on, but…"

"He's…" Mira snuffled. "He was here. Just now."

"Oh, God," said Caroline. "Did he hurt you?"

"What? No!" wailed Mira. "He wouldn't."

"Look, when I saw him, he was completely out of control," Caroline continued. "I don't know Sam, but I wouldn't trust what he would or wouldn't do right now."

Mira tried to reply, but could only keen uselessly and resented herself for it.

"Oh, Mira," said Caroline. "He doesn't know, does he?"

"I didn't…" she finally managed to begin. "I couldn't. And now he doesn't believe me."

"I'm sorry, Mira," Caroline said. "Listen, this probably isn't the time, but I think I might have something for you. About Treasurer's House. We can talk when you're feeling up to it."

"No, no, I can do this," Mira rubbed at her eyes, her capable side taking over. "Tell me."

"Better if we meet. I've got some stuff to give you. But it can wait."

"No, it can't!" Mira shouted. "It's important, it might be the end of the world, and I can't follow him and I can't stay here so I need to do this instead!"

"Fine," said Caroline after taking a moment to assess the situation. "God, you're probably going to go to Treasurer's House like this, aren't you?"

"Most likely."

"Well then, you'd best meet me in the Minster Gardens," Caroline said, with a grim laugh. "I promised someone we'd go to the park today."

CHAPTER 22

Delia ran as fast as she could through the city, her breath failing her burst by burst. She'd got to the dig, not as late as she had expected, only to be told that Jonathan had moved on to the office. Her ankle twinged with every step, still not fully recovered from her recent fall. It was another thing that Delia would come to think could have changed everything.

Abi tried to assess Sam's mood as he strode across the cobbled courtyard of King's Manor. He looked calmer than he had last night, but that could have been tiredness catching up with him. Jonathan stepped forward to greet him with a paternal smile, and shook his hand vigorously. For some reason, Abi recalled the day her father had insisted on dropping Sam off at uni in a rare moment of interest, and shuddered at the memory.

"Thank you for coming," the professor said with a quiet reassurance. "We can talk in my office."

They walked through ancient stone corridors and Jonathan flourished his pass at the security guard, leading them into the archaeology department's inner sanctum.

"Company now," Abi hissed at her brother as they headed upwards. "But if you've ballsed things up with Mira, I will give you such a twatting."

"You know Holly?" Sam asked, ignoring the threat of sibling violence.

"Oh, yes, from way back," Jonathan replied. "She's older than she looks."

Jonathan's office was on the second floor, the back wall all windows overlooking the courtyard below. It was a small room endlessly cluttered with papers, boxes and jars; all the outpouring of the dig funnelled into this one inadequate space. In the centre of the desk sat a flyer bearing an image of the horned helmet.

"Mira was looking at that," Sam whispered, transfixed by the hideous steel face. "She wanted to know why anyone would make it look like that."

"Yeah, it's always fascinated me too," Jonathan said, idly wiping his glasses with a cloth. "Not because of what it looks like, I figured that out, but what it's for. I even had a go at making my own once. Didn't exactly work out."

He flourished the spectacles in his hand, and dropped them to the desk as if this illustrated a point.

"Tell me about Holly," Sam said urgently. Something felt amiss, but he pushed the concern from his mind.

"I met her in the eighties," Jonathan explained. "I was eighteen and she was, as I said, older than she looks. And, I'm sorry, Sam, I really am. But when I met her, I was the only one who made it out alive."

"Oh my God," Sam said. "What happened?"

"You see, the thing about Holly," Jonathan explained, settling himself down behind his desk. "She doesn't care about people as much as she claims. She'll pick someone up, because it's fun to show off to them, but when something bad happens, and it usually does, deep down, she doesn't really mind."

"What did she do?" Sam asked. For the first time since he left Mira, he was more afraid than angry.

Jonathan's phone buzzed in his pocket, and he fished it out with an apologetic smile. Sam waited on tenterhooks as Jonathan read the message through a squint.

"Delia, running late," he explained, then a glimmer of recognition passed over his face. "Oh, look, do you remember this? From the day we met?"

He held up his phone for them to see the words 'Gjallarhorn is sounded' on the screen.

"Everyone forgot about it, didn't they?" he chuckled. "The way of the world, I suppose. You keep throwing new things at people, they can't process it all, and before you know it, everyone's missed something important. Do you know what it means?"

"Yeah, it's a Viking thing," Sam said impatiently. "What about Holly?"

"That's right, of course you know that." Jonathan smiled as if he hadn't heard the question. "You live in Viking country, of course you know. I used to love those stories when I was a kid. Never got the point of the warning though. Ragnarök is a prophecy, it's a done deal. The world is ending. So why do you need to warn everyone it's going to happen? I was your age by the time I figured it out."

"I don't care, what can you tell me about Holly?"

"It's all relevant, I promise," Jonathan explained. "After I met Holly, well, then the world went a bit mad. Nuclear bombs at twenty paces. May as well have had dead men's ships and a wolf swallowing the sun. Did you know they said we'd get a four-minute warning if it all kicked off? What are you supposed to do in four minutes? But I knew, because of what Holly showed me. I knew the truth."

"Which is?" Abi asked, not actually wanting to know.

"You don't get a warning so you can save yourself," Jonathan said. "It's to tell you that you can't."

Delia stormed through King's Manor in a flurry of dropped backpack and hurriedly located pass card, charged up the stairs and fumbled her way into the offices before she stopped to catch her breath. Her foot wasn't happy with her. She limped to Jonathan's office, and had barely opened the door when she caught sight of Sam inside and thought better of going in. She didn't feel like involving herself in a repeat of last night's confrontation, so held back, watching through the crack she had left open.

"So were you planning on being helpful at all?" Abi asked. "Or are we just doing random scary shit?"

"I told you, it's all relevant," Jonathan said with a placatory hand gesture. "Humour me, for a moment. Norse mythology, you see. It all comes back to that. The Vikings believed in three wells, in the roots of the world tree. You could get to other places through these wells, other worlds. When I met Holly, I actually saw one of these wells up close. It's right here, in this city."

"Oh, that's great, problem solved," Abi said, tugging at Sam's sleeve. "Well, thanks for your help, but we've got to be off now, places to go, people to see who... aren't nutters."

"Odin gave one of his eyes to the well to gain wisdom," Jonathan said with a melancholy smile. "I'm afraid I intend to give it a bit more than that. You can come out now."

"How do," came a shrill voice from behind them.

Shocked, they spun in the direction of the voice to see a ginger-haired teenage girl in a stripy bobble hat standing in the corner of the room.

"How long has she been there?" Abi asked, trying to remember if she had caught a single glimpse of the girl before now.

"Ages," the girl replied. "I nodded off a bit in the middle, he don't half go on. Hullo again, Sam. Long time, no see. I believe you're looking for my sister."

"Oh great," said Abi. "So there really is a psycho sister, but she's about twelve."

"She doesn't get it, does she?" the girl said with an amused smirk as she positioned herself between them and the door. "That's hilarious. I mean, does he have to say 'we're going to kill you' very slowly? Or do we need to break out the diagrams?"

Sam turned to Jonathan, and was taken aback to see he was now wearing the stolen helmet. His eyes could be glimpsed through the golden frames as he nodded ominously, the horns dipping low. Sam felt the trap closing on him as Abi moved for the door. She made it one step before the girl pushed her aside. Her head struck the wall and she dropped to the floor. The girl was so small, but Sam could feel the power in her, the strength. In her spare hand was the cylinder Jonathan had unearthed. Everything was spiralling back to where it all began.

"Gjallarhorn is sounded," he breathed helplessly.

"And it's playing your song." The girl's face was all wicked grin. Her arm stabbed forward and something emerged from the tube, a blurred web that struck his face before he could tell what was happening.

He felt metal against his skin, cold and sharp and digging in. It pulled him, dragging at the edges of his mouth. There was crushing pressure on the sides of his head as icy, rough-edged wire crept from his face, under his clothes and across his body, constricting him, pinching his flesh. He felt his arms and legs flexing against their will as the wires drew in tightly and painfully. He tried to look to Abi, but the web covering his body wouldn't let him. He thought of Mira as golden rims descended over his eyes driving him deeper and deeper and further down...

Delia could only watch. Terror rooted her to the spot and she dared not even breathe in case she was discovered. Sam screamed in agony and it was all she could do not to join in. It felt like forever before there was silence. The girl and Jonathan both watched Sam intently, the professor's bizarre mask contrasting surreally with his mundane work clothes. Abi moved forward, and placed a hand on her brother's shoulder, gently turning his body to face her.

Sam's arm struck out in a heartbeat and a hand was around Abi's throat, the fingers wrapped in rough wire and capped with sharp points. He rose to his feet in one single fluid movement, lifting her into the air as he did, and she stared in horror at a face surmounted with horns and criss-crossed by lines of metal, pulled into a pained snarl. Eyes scared and desperate and not remotely in control glared through rings of gold. He swung her through the air, then released his grip with a violent push forward.

Delia saw Abi smash into the shattering window. Her eyes and mouth were wide, but she disappeared from view before she even had a chance to know what was happening. Sam turned to face Jonathan, the two horned figures sizing each other up. Delia had seen those faces before. Her aliens were here.

Slowly, Sam sank down to one knee, allowing Jonathan to place a hand on his obedient head. The strange girl moved to the broken window, and looked through the jagged gap to the courtyard below.

"Bugger," she said. "We needed her. Oh well, guess we'd better kill Delia after all."

The mention of her name gave Delia the use of her legs back and she ran as fast as she could.

CHAPTER 23

A shower and a change of clothes hadn't made Mira feel better, but was enough to get her moving at least. There was a slight chill in the air, but it was otherwise a fine day. Children were playing on the fresh-mown and welcomingly verdant grass of the Minster Gardens, and a short walk beyond them was the place she would need to return to. Not better. Not at all.

She found Caroline on a bench near a noisy cluster of small children. Two cups sat in a cardboard container beside her, and she lifted it at the sight of Mira.

"I didn't get much sleep last night," Caroline explained. "And I thought you could do with propping up."

"I'm a bit hungover and I've had two critical level fights with my boyfriend, so I came prepared," Mira said, her voice acquiring a croaky edge, whether from crying, drinking or singing she wasn't sure. She hefted her own cardboard container and the two mochas it contained. "The other one's an apology, for dragging you into this."

They sat together and sipped from their cups, grimaced, then swapped and were happier. Mira wistfully watched the children darting about without a care in the world, as Caroline dug around in her bag and produced a battered cardboard file. Inside was a sheaf of old documents, with a black and white photograph paper-clipped to the front. A sharp-featured middle-aged woman looked at Mira through oval spectacles, and made it quite clear that she was not to be trifled with.

"Meet Professor Eilidh McAllister," said Caroline. "Born in Inverness, studied in Manhattan, doctorate in parapsychology from Edinburgh University, became head of the Parapsychology Department at York University, and died right over there."

Mira didn't have to look to see she was gesturing in the direction of Treasurer's House. She hurriedly flicked through the documents.

"Professor McAllister led a research party to Treasurer's House to study strange phenomena," Mira read aloud. "Ghost hunting?"

"Ghost hunting," Caroline confirmed. "Two weeks after her team moved in, a National Trust volunteer came to check on them. He found Professor McAllister's body in the Great Hall, no trace of the others. Like you said, the bodies were never found."

"What happened?" Mira asked.

"The investigation concluded that McAllister killed them all, disposed of their bodies somehow and then killed herself," Caroline said. "And apart from a godawful ITV drama based on the story, case closed."

"And nobody's looked at it since?"

"McAllister was a fifty-two-year-old spinster with no kids and a spooky job," Caroline said. "As far as my illustrious predecessors were concerned, murder-suicide was her alternative to loads of cats. The families were satisfied with the verdict, but not being able to bury their kids hurt, as you'd expect. The police dug the garden up and searched all over the house, but found nothing. It could be there are bones under the floorboards in there somewhere, but where would you start? It's a huge house and it's listed. You're not going to get permission to tear the place apart on the off chance."

"Mummy, look!" came a high-pitched shout from across the park. A small blond-haired white boy was tumbling across the grass towards them in a series of clumsy cartwheels.

Caroline's face exploded into a broad grin and she hopped from the bench, moving towards the child in a crouching shuffle before grabbing him and sweeping him into the air, winning a burst of delighted, uncontrollable giggles.

Mira was taken aback by the affectionate display, and wondered if she should check Caroline for signs of possession as she returned to the bench, clutching the child in her arms.

"Kenny, this is Mira." Caroline's voice practically rose an octave. The boy looked up at her with icy blue eyes before shyly burying his head into her shoulder. She pressed her lips to his fair hair before settling him down on the grass and watching him shamble off to his friends.

"No," she said, as she took notice of Mira's stunned expression. "I did not personally give birth to my son."

"Yeah, I spotted that," said Mira, the surprise passing over her. "It just… never occurred to me that you had kids."

"I'm good at compartmentalising," Caroline explained. "God knows I have to be. There's no way I could bring work into my own home, even if I didn't have him."

"I get that," Mira said with a wistful smile as she watched Kenny and his friends bounce happily around the lawn. "But sometimes it follows you there anyway."

"Kenechukwu James," Caroline said with a loving smile. "I named him after my dad. He was practically a newborn when he came to me, not exactly under normal circumstances. No one else had a chance to call him anything, so I chose. Helped me feel like he was really mine. But yes, I've probably painted a target on his head with that one."

Mira returned her attention to the file, finding more pictures, shots of four young people. None older than her, she reminded herself. There was one woman, smiling earnestly under a titanic hairdo, and three men. One was shaggy haired and knew how handsome he was. The second was heavier set, with piercing eyes. It was the last that seized Mira's attention. She stared intently at that boyish face, noticeably younger than the others, and placed a thumb to cover his chin. The eyes were the ones she knew.

"That would be Jonathan Kitson," Caroline explained. "Just eighteen. Also known as Dylan. The other three were post-grads, McAllister's usual crew, but he was a first year. She'd do that from time to time, take a student along if they looked promising. Didn't usually pick them that young though. But according to her notes, Kitson was quite the golden boy, although a bit of a dreamer."

"I've seen this man. Caroline, he's here."

"Are you saying you've met his ghost?" Caroline asked, audibly intrigued at the prospect.

"I'm saying he's still alive," Mira replied. "He's here in this city right now. He's not calling himself Kitson anymore. He's Jonathan Fortune, a professor of archaeology. He runs the dig by the river, he was the man Holly saved."

"Jesus," Caroline whispered. "Are you sure? He's been declared dead."

"It's him," Mira nodded. "I know it is. And I'll tell you something else that's not in your file. Holly was there when this happened. And her sister. God, she's been skittish about that place all week, this is why. She knows what happened to these people."

"I always let them down in the end. Erin, Dorothy, McAl... everyone." Oh no, Holly.

"Maybe we should ask her," said Caroline, nodding into the distance.

Mira turned to see a fiery-headed figure in purple marching towards Treasurer's House.

"How is it you can always see her?" Mira asked.

"I don't know, I suppose I just look for trouble," Caroline replied. "Now the question is, what am I going to regret more? Taking my son in there or letting you go on your own?"

"You should stay here," Mira said. "I'll be fine."

Caroline considered her options for a moment, then walked over to Kenny and the other children, singling out one little girl from the crowd.

"Hello, Poppy," she said, her voice rising again and swinging into sing-song pitch. "Where's your mummy, sweetheart? I need to have a talk with her."

The girl waved one chubby arm in the direction of a woman obtaining coffee from a street vendor. Caroline waved to get her attention, then turned to Mira, her face all business.

"I speak mum," she shrugged.

CHAPTER 24

The door to Treasurer's House pushed open in an instant at Holly's command. The house was closed to the public today and would be deserted. Not that that made a difference, she could have slipped through a busy tour party unnoticed, but it suited her to be alone.

She headed below stairs to the room where she had found Sophie's body, moving as quickly as she could, not daring to linger where her memories lurked. The door to the cellar was no less ominous with the sun streaming down the white walls from the lightwells above. She headed in, and stood alone in the gloomy chamber. From a pocket she produced the hide tube she had found here all those years ago, placed it in her mouth and blew, a sharp, piercing note echoing off the rounded walls.

"I am a daughter of Cartimandua," she proclaimed loudly. "I am a protector of the great city of Eboracum. Men know me as King in the Mountain. I seek the soldiers of the Ninth."

She closed her eyes and heard the crunching footsteps, the slap of the leather armour, the whinnying of the horses. The distant rumble of one repeated word. Intruder. When her eyes opened, the room was filled with Romans standing shoulder to shoulder, unblinking eyes regarding her from lined faces that had seen much.

"Hi, fellas. Got time for a chat?"

INTRUDER.

"Yeah, I remember," she replied. "I were here once, long ago. Well, not so long from your point of view. Or mine, come to think."

INTRUDER. Hands went to swords across the circle.

"Alright, alright," Holly said hurriedly. "When I were here last, I thought you meant I was intruding in your basement. But you didn't, did you? This is about summat else. You know summat bad's coming."

IT RETURNS. WE FOUGHT IT BEFORE, BUT NOW IT IS COME AGAIN.

No one figure was speaking, but it was as if a single voice reverberated across the crowd. Occasionally, a soldier's lips would twitch in time with the words.

"That's why you're down here, isn't it? To guard the portal, forever."

YOUR PEOPLE HAD DRUIDS. MEN WHO DID NOT DIE. MEN WHO FERRIED THE DEAD TO THE NEXT WORLD.

"I might have scutting well known," grumbled Holly. "They're still about. I wonder if the current lot even know they put you here."

WE BUILT EBORACUM. WE DEFEND EBORACUM. WE CAME ACROSS THE SEA TO BUILD OUR HOME HERE. WHEN THE UNDERWORLD MADE WAR ON THIS CITY, WE DROVE THEM BACK INTO THEIR DARK PLACES. YOUR DRUIDS MADE SURE WE COULD DEFEND EBORACUM FOREVER.

"So defend it now," Holly said. "There is a man who would tear down everything you built. He will let loose the underworld, unless I stop him. If the worst comes, I ask you to stand with me."

WHAT FORCES DO YOU HAVE?

Holly answered by pointing at herself with both hands.

YOU ARE ONE WOMAN.

"I may have the body of a weak and feeble woman," Holly countered. "But I have the stomach and constitution of a right mardy bitch."

Holly emerged from below stairs with a nervous sigh and a backwards glance. She leant heavily against the wall and breathed in deeply to settle herself. She had no idea how many ghosts had been in that room, but it was more than even she was used to. So many in such a confined space was a little more of the supernatural than a body could handle. The nausea took a few minutes to fade.

"God, I hope that worked," she gasped.

A clock ticked loudly and ominously from somewhere nearby, but there was no telling which one. The emptiness of the house amplified every little noise to fill the maze of rooms and corridors that Holly moved through. All the clocks in the house could have been ticking perfectly in synch.

And then they stopped.

"Oh no," said Holly. "Please not now."

She felt more than saw the presence. She knew it was behind her and dared not look. She froze, terrified at what she knew she would see if she turned. And then it screamed.

The scream was not audible in any way, but Holly felt it. Felt it in her heart. Her stomach writhed as if punched, lurching in torment at the presence of the thing, as if her body was tearing itself apart in its hurry to get as far away as she could from what she was sensing. Pain surged through her and guilt seized her mind. Faces flashed before her eyes and she howled in anguish.

She ran, charging blindly and pointlessly away from it. But it was here in the house, it was everywhere. She couldn't not see it. Not anymore. She realised she was in the Great Hall now; her body had brought her here almost instinctively. To where it happened. To where blame waited for her, had been waiting all these years. She saw what she was running from and everything overwhelmed her at once. She collapsed to her knees and shrank into the fireplace, concealing herself from the memory that had come for her at last.

"Holly?" said a voice.

Holly lowered her hands from her face, to see Mira and Caroline standing over her. There was concern in their eyes, but dread as well.

"Help her," she pleaded.

THE McALLISTER
INVESTIGATION VII
SOMETIME IN THE 1980s...

"This concludes our tour of Treasurer's House. Please feel free to leave any comments you have in the visitor's book."

•

"Make your mind up time," Erin said. "How do you fancy doing this, Holly?"

Holly looked up, catching McAllister's eyes.

"Do what you must," the professor said.

Dylan keened, tears in his eyes. Holly nodded, stepped forward and placed a hand on her sister's good shoulder.

"We'll find another way."

Erin snorted derisively. "Don't be daft, you know we won't."

"We'll find another way."

"There is no other way!" Erin growled, with a gurgling inward breath. "And even if there were, it wouldn't matter! This is a nice, easy fix. Stop being difficult!"

"I won't let you hurt these people," Holly said, an old and implacable resolve growing in her voice. "We will stop this, but not by killing anyone."

"But they'll die anyway, you know, like people do!" Erin said, her eyes wide and pleading. "Holly, I thought we were past this! We're all we've got, remember?"

"They don't have to die today, and they won't if I can help it."

"So when, then?" Erin roamed the room in a lopsided stomp. "When her heart gives out, or she gets poisoned by her own tits? They die, it's how it is."

"Shut up, Erin, you don't know what's gonna happen."

"I'm there when people die, I know."

"Imminent death, Erin, your lot predict imminent death!"

"Erm, zombies?" Erin gestured to the nearest exit. "Looking pretty bloody imminent right now."

The storm was intensifying above them, tendrils of electricity crawling down the walls. A flash of sparks blossomed around the deer skulls, sending one thudding to the ground to shatter into a cloud of bone fragments. Holly and Erin stood facing each other at the heart of the maelstrom.

"Come on then," Erin said. "I'm waiting for your brilliant plan."

"Richard found a way in," Holly replied. "We find that. Maybe we can send this thing back. Maybe we can go in and fix this from the inside."

"Maybe maybe maybe. That's not a plan. I've got my plan all worked out."

"I don't want to die," wailed Dylan, and collapsed on the floor, shuddering with terror. "I don't want to die."

"I can't do this!" Brian shouted, all the pent-up energy exploding out of him as he stormed towards the nearest exit.

A chorus of voices shouted at him to stop, but it was too late.

Richard stood before him in the doorway and Brian was frozen by the sight. The dead man grabbed his head with both hands and twisted. Brian's body jerked and dropped, but Richard did not look. He was already lumbering towards them, gathering speed with each step, light blazing from his ruined eye.

"Erin?" said Holly, as her sister scurried off.

"Doing it," she replied and stamped hard on the remains of the fallen skull until the left antler was completely clear. She tossed it across the room and Holly caught it one-handed, just in time to swing it in a wide arc and strike Richard across the jaw, sending him sprawling.

Holly heard the frantic patter of clicking heels before she saw Sophie, her legs pumping rhythmically as she ran at full pelt. She leapt forward, wrapping all four limbs around Holly and driving her to the ground. Erin's knife still protruded from her temple, and as hands closed around her throat, Holly reached up and tore it free, a thin beam of light emerging from the wound. The movement made Sophie release her grip long enough for Holly to push her flat on her back, snatch up the antler and bring it down hard into the dead face with both hands, the old horn smashing into the floor with a crack as both it and Sophie's skull gave way.

But there was no respite. Richard had already pulled himself upright, with a dull glow surrounding the rents in his face where the prongs had torn his flesh, but not a drop of blood visible. Brian had joined his former lover in undeath, his head lolling on one side.

"Stairs!" shouted Holly, snatching up the other antler to replace her broken weapon. McAllister dragged Dylan to the bottom of the staircase, joined by Erin. Holly stood in front of them, wielding the antler and Erin's knife defensively as the zombies drew closer. Sophie was standing too now, her hands tearing the collapsed remains of her own head free, a shaft of light blazing upwards into the roaring tumult from her ragged neck. Holly positioned herself at the foot of the stairs, between them and the others, sweeping her weapons back and forth as her enemies drew closer.

The storm was raging now, intensified by Brian's death. The waves came quicker and the hole in the centre was growing. Curling shadowy shapes danced across the visible ceiling behind the mist. Blasts of lightning came striking down, followed by curtains of static that set their teeth on edge. One bolt hit the bannister beside Holly, causing it to explode in a hail of broken wood.

The others had reached the top, and Dylan's gaze was locked on the howling storms overhead, his eyes entranced. Erin leaned over the bannister, watching her sister eagerly as she drove each attacker in turn down the steps only for the next to follow. Holly was visibly tiring, the zombies' attacks connecting more and more often. Brian landed a blow to her shoulder and grabbed for her throat, but she shoved the antler up hard into his chest and sent him tumbling back down the stairs, smashing the others out of the way as he did. She found her feet, breathing hard, and seized a length of shattered wood as a substitute weapon.

McAllister grabbed Erin by the shoulders and turned the girl to face her.

"Would you survive this fall?" she shouted above the thunder.

"You what?"

"Would you survive falling down there?"

"Of course I would. What...?" Erin began as McAllister strained to force her over the edge of the stairs, sending her tumbling out of sight.

The professor gazed down at the floor, where Erin looked up accusingly, her ankle at a painful angle and the words 'I hate you' visible on her lips.

Dylan stared into the swirling mass of light and movement that blazed in the rafters. Everything else had slipped away. He didn't hear the fighting or notice the others. There were just the shapes in the storm, slipping sinuously in and out of form, as they writhed and curled and waited, waited, waited...

"I see you. Oh my God, I can see you," he whispered.

McAllister ran through the minstrel's gallery and found the nearest stairs, heading higher and higher until she reached the upper gallery a floor above. She pushed the single small window open. At this height, she was so close to the light, she could almost touch it. This was what she had come looking for, she realised. She'd wanted things this huge and ridiculous to be real. But it rankled that she'd never get to understand them. Or if she did, it would be the way dull men in black smocks had told her you were supposed to.

"This isn't a leap of faith," she said to herself. "It's an experiment."

She squeezed through the tiny window to stand with the balls of her feet resting on the tiny lip underneath, her hands clutching the window frame tightly for support. A dumbstruck Holly broke from the struggle to look up at her and McAllister smiled before releasing her grip. Her arms spread wide as she plummeted through the air to land with a crunch on the floor below.

Erin crawled to where McAllister lay, breath rattling out of her broken body. She stroked her face gently as her life ebbed away.

"You're so gonna regret this," she whispered.

In an instant, the storm clouds rolled back from the central spot. The zombies ceased their attack, their bodies jerking as the light from within tore through cracks opening in their skin before each in turn exploded into a shower of ash. Blinding golden yellow drove away the cold blue as the sun blazed triumphantly through windows that had resumed their rightful place. Holly stumbled down the stairs through blurred vision, to where Erin knelt beside McAllister's body. The girl's mouth was upturned in an arc of dark glee.

"What did you do?" Holly asked reproachfully.

"My job," Erin replied. "And it's sorted all this out into the bargain. Turned out nice again."

"Don't play games with me," Holly snarled.

"It's not like I killed her or owt," Erin replied, stretching out her leg and examining the shattered ankle. "She jumped; I just saw she didn't get portalled."

"So where is she now?" Holly asked with growing dread. "Where have you put her?"

"Right here. She'll stay right here," Erin said innocently as she cracked her foot back into place with a wince, supporting herself with her one good arm as she stood. "You can come and visit her, whenever you like."

"Erin, what have you done?"

"My worst," Erin said with a taunting smirk.

Holly caught movement out of the corner of her eye and turned to face the full horror revealed. A shadowy, transparent figure floated a foot off the ground in front of her. Its body convulsed, the limbs twitching and the fingers curling painfully. She could make out the face of McAllister, contorted in suffering.

Holly reached out to touch her, her fingers passing unnoticed through the apparition.

"She's a scream in the dark now," Erin said, her voice gravelly and cold. "All the pain, the fear, the misery, the loss, everything she ever felt that hurt her, she'll feel them all at once. She'll keep on suffering her woes and reliving them again and again until the seas boil and the sky falls. Eternal torment, you might call it. Or what life's really like when you get right down to it. My special present."

"Why?" Holly choked, flinching away from the ghost's pained expression to look down at McAllister's peaceful face and empty eyes.

"To teach you a lesson," Erin said, something oddly sympathetic in her tone. "You keep getting attached to them, and it's no good for you. You're gonna feel so guilty about her, when you shouldn't have even known her name. So now, every time you think about making a little friend, you can come down here and remember what happens to them. And then you can tell yourself that it's all fine. You don't need them. You've got your sister."

"You are not my sister," Holly whispered.

Erin blinked, her mouth dropping open ever so slightly. She bit down hard on something, and gestured with her good arm to Dylan almost falling down the stairs. Whether he could see McAllister's spectre was impossible to judge.

"I let you keep one. Say thank you Erin."

Holly knelt beside McAllister and gently closed her eyes, her free hand gripping cold fingers. Dylan stumbled over and dropped down beside her, his face overwhelmed.

"I'll show meself out, shall I?" Erin said as she tossed the double doors open, sunlight erasing her in an instant from their vision.

Holly stepped out into the tranquil garden. It was a glorious day, the sun beating down on the lush lawn. She clenched a fist which itched where wooden splinters had dug in, and walked away with a quick and heavy tread.

Dylan scurried after her.

"Wait. Where are you going?" he asked. "You can't just leave!"

"It's all done. I'm off to bed," she replied, trudging dejectedly towards the gate.

"But how am I going to explain all this?" Dylan shouted, and she turned to face him, weighing the choices in his red eyes and helpless demeanour. He was clutching one of his records like a security blanket. Only a few years older than Erin was supposed to be.

"Leave," Holly said. "Leave the city. Don't ever come back. She won't forget you, and if you stay, one day she'll come for you, just for spite. So leave."

Dylan nodded. He held out the album, unable to even look at her. She could see how foolish the gesture was making him feel. "You liked this. I thought..."

Holly took a step forward and gazed once again at the great golden eye and the carefree woman soaring on her kite. She felt a pang of jealousy at the sense of freedom in the image, but accepted the gift nonetheless.

"Thank you. Now run, Dylan, run as fast as you can."

"That's not actually my name," he said, with a broken laugh. "They just called me that at uni because I was playing his songs all the time..."

"Well, goodbye, whoever you are," Holly said, and left without a hint of attachment.

CHAPTER 25

"And I never looked back," Holly said, her terrible story finished. "Like I said, the worst thing Erin ever did. And I made it worse."

"You didn't," Mira began. "Holly, none of this is your fault."

"Isn't it? I brought Erin with me because I wanted to be more like her. Because I couldn't be bothered to care anymore. Because I thought there were no point in thinking of people as people. You have no idea how hard it is to be me and be a person at the same time."

"Actually, I think I do," Mira responded.

"So I thought I'd stop," Holly said, staring into the empty fireplace. "Just be the King in the Mountain and nowt else. Then Erin showed me what living like that really means. And I couldn't. I'm not a god, I'm just a lass. I swore that day I would care what happened to every one of you, no matter how hard it got."

"And you have," Mira said. "Haven't you?"

"Yeah," Holly admitted. "But I shouldn't have had to learn me lesson like that."

"Is she still here?" asked Caroline.

"Yeah, she's over there," Holly jerked a thumb into the corner of the room, but kept her eyes turned away from it.

Caroline and Mira both looked and saw nothing.

"I don't think anyone but me can see her," Holly explained, noting their confusion. "If they could, it'd be the ghost story to end all ghost stories. Be grateful you can't. But Erin wanted me to see her."

"The last one was clever, she said," whispered Mira, recalling words Erin had once taunted her with. "She offered to show me where she put what's left of her."

"Your sister is a piece of work," Caroline said.

"You are not my sister, I said." Holly mocked herself with her tone. "I raised that girl after our mother died. I loved her so much, and I said that to her. And that's me when I'm trying to be human, trying to be good, and I come out with the cruellest thing I could think of. I wonder sometimes how many people those words have killed."

"Zero," Caroline said firmly. "That's all on her."

"We'll find a way to help her," Mira said. "We've laid spirits to rest before, there must be something we can do."

"Never found a way to crack this one though. So I stopped trying. I don't often get time for side projects, as you know."

"Well, I do," Mira said. "You asked me to help her. I'll do what I can."

"Your phone's going." Holly turned away to sit dejectedly in front of the grate.

Mira saw the picture from happier times flashing before her.

"It's Sam," she said, holding the phone to her ear. "I need to take this."

"Hello, Mira," came an unexpected voice down the line that made her flinch. Jonathan was being supportive and friendly, like this was a normal day. "I just wanted to say I'm sorry about last night. How are you doing?"

"What have you done with Sam?" Mira demanded, setting the phone on speaker to draw her friends in. Holly was pulled out of her self-pity in an instant.

"He came to see me this morning," Jonathan explained. "He's worried about you. He thinks Holly might be getting you into some sort of trouble."

"Oh, I am, Dylan," Holly chipped in. "I'm good at that. But I'm good at getting people out as well, which is why you're still around."

Caroline joined the fray in full official tone. "This is DI Caroline James, North Yorkshire Police. I assume I'm speaking to the late Mr Jonathan Kitson?"

"It's Fortune now, if you don't mind," Jonathan corrected.

"I've called myself a lot of things, but in the end, I took my late wife's name. Always the forward thinker, that's me."

"So what direction are we thinking in today? Another jam session, a bit of digging, opening up a portal to bring the world crashing down on us all?" As Holly spoke, her eyes rose to the ceiling, and Caroline grasped instantly where the portal was.

"You can call it that," Jonathan replied. "I prefer the mythological term myself. The wells of Yggdrasil. Makes sense one of them would be right here in old Jorvik. The most Viking city in England gets its own bit of the saga."

"Are either of you understanding this?" Caroline whispered.

"There are three springs." Jonathan had heard the hushed question, and spoke to them as if giving a lecture. "They lie in the roots of the great tree that binds the universe together. Their names are Mimisbrunnr, Urðarbrunnr and Hvergelmir."

"Hvergelmir?" said Mira, the last words of the Horned Man flashing through her mind. "Did you say Hvergelmir?"

"Where broods of serpents spew their venom, and the great dragon Níðhöggr gnaws on the roots of creation," Jonathan said with awe. "Wouldn't have been my first choice, but should be interesting."

"Dragon?" said Caroline, her gaze fixed on the ceiling. "There's a dragon up there?"

"Well, it's a generally used term for any kind of monster, but yes, for argument's sake, let's call it a dragon," Jonathan added pedantically.

"Why are you telling us all this?" Mira asked. "What do you want?"

"Oh, I just got chatting and, well, it's a bit of a passion of mine," Jonathan admitted. "But I really wanted to talk to you, Mira. Sam came to see me, and we've come to an arrangement, you might say. I thought I should let you know before you see him. And I wanted to tell you how sorry I am."

"What have you done?" she asked, her voice trembling with horror.

The call ended abruptly, as an ominous creak sounded from

the staircase. Mira knew what she was going to see. She forced herself to turn as Sam walked slowly towards her, his head bound in the mechanism of the Horned Man.

"Sam, no…" she said, and moved up the stairs towards him. "Sam, please listen to me."

He moved so quickly, striking her with an open hand that sent her spinning down the steps, then leapt over the bannister. Holly brandished her umbrella, and with a flick of her wrist, Caroline produced a collapsible baton from the depths of her coat. The thing that had been Sam moved quickly, slapping their weapons away and pushing them aside with a series of swift blows. He hissed loudly before he turned and ran, leaping at the nearest window and smashing his way through it to vanish into the gardens.

Caroline was winded, but recovering rapidly. "Why is he running away?"

"Because he wants us to follow him," Holly replied grimly.

"My son's in the park," Caroline said with unshaken resolve. "I need to… oh shit."

"What? What is it?" Holly asked.

"When Sam came to the station last night, there was a girl with him. Where is she now?"

"Sam left the party with his sister," said Holly. "Bugger it."

"You don't think…?" Caroline began.

"I don't know, but we need to find out," Holly crouched down to where Mira sat. Her eyes were wide with shock and she was shaking. "Mira? Mira, have you got Abi's number? We need to make sure she's safe."

Mira wasn't answering, utterly lost in the horror of it all. Holly snatched up the phone from where it had fallen and stared baffled at the screen. Her fingers punched and scrabbled at the unfamiliar technology until she called up a list of names, and found what she was looking for under A. It rang for an unbearably long time before a voice came.

"Oh, Mira, thank goodness it's you," Delia gabbled. "You need to get here now, something awful's happened."

CHAPTER 26

For the duration of their acquaintance, Maggie Dawkins had always known not to ask Caroline about her job. Not just because she didn't like to talk about it, but because whatever was said would be a guaranteed conversation stopper. Finding a common experience was never a likely outcome.

For her part, Caroline did not consider Maggie a close friend, but took comfort in the fact that she had never knowingly committed a crime. She and her husband hadn't done any of the involuntary flinches that Caroline was used to seeing when she told people what she did for a living. Not the recreational drugs flinch, the financial irregularities flinch, and certainly not the getting away with something far worse flinch. That made their children's friendship manageable. It also made the current situation helpfully free of questions.

"Thank you, Maggie. I am so sorry," Caroline said. "I don't know how long this is going to take."

"Don't worry, I completely understand," Maggie replied, indicating that she did not understand, and would rather carry on doing so. "Always happy to have him."

Caroline crouched down to her son, and wished he couldn't sense that something was up.

"You're going to go home with Poppy, sweetheart," she said, giving the child-wrangling voice her all. "That'll be fun, won't it? Mummy's got to go to work, but I'll come and get you later, alright?"

The boy nodded, and Caroline held him close for a moment.

"I love you," she smiled. "Go on now, and be good for Poppy's mummy."

Caroline watched Maggie walk away, a child's hand in each of her own. She was ready to wave if Kenny looked back. Once she was sure he wouldn't, the parent faded and the police officer emerged.

Tubes ran from where Abi lay unconscious to an assortment of machines, the function of which Mira had the unpleasant opportunity to wonder at. A heavy plastic brace sat beneath her chin, while the covers of the hospital bed concealed what damage had been done, as well as the steps being taken to repair it.

"Thank you." It was all Mira felt able to say to Delia.

"I'm sorry I didn't call sooner," she replied. "I completely forgot I picked up her phone until it started ringing."

"Delia, stop apologising," said Mira. "You rang an ambulance for someone you barely know when you were scared out of your mind. Feel good about yourself for a bit."

"Right, yes, I'll try. I can barely believe any of this, you know. I mean I was just talking to you about meeting aliens last night, and now I find my boss and your boyfriend are the aliens! It's just… I don't know how to think about all this."

"They're not aliens," Mira corrected her. "Or maybe they are, I don't know. It's from somewhere else, so yes, call it an alien. I can't really care right now."

"You sound like you're used to this sort of thing."

Mira gave a hollow laugh. "That probably means I'm holding it together somehow, because this might be the worst day of my life."

"Mira." Delia looked aware she was making an imposition, but pressed on regardless. "Would it take your mind off all this, if you were to explain to me exactly what's going on?"

They sat together in the hospital room and Mira told her everything. The King in the Mountain, the supernatural, the Horned Man, the portal. Delia took it remarkably well, although whether that was because her own theories were even more outlandish was hard to say.

"Wow," she said when Mira was done. "So, Holly's not just a bit brave, she's…"

"Yeah, she is," Mira said. "But don't say it to her face. You'll never hear the end of it."

"She's…"

"Seriously, don't."

"Buffy," said Delia. "She's gay ginger northern Buffy."

"Definitely don't say that," said Mira, and allowed herself to relax for a moment. Which as it happened was all she got.

"Oh my God! Is everything alright? I came as soon as I heard," came an unwelcome voice in a breathless parody of concern.

They both leapt to their feet to see Erin lurking in the doorway, a paper bag in her grip. Delia froze in fear, while Mira moved protectively forward to stand at the foot of the bed.

"Grape?" Erin asked.

"Get out," snarled Mira. "I won't let you touch her."

"Not gonna," said Erin sarcastically, pulling her top lip into a moody grimace. "She's not gonna die, I promise. And you know if I say that, it's twice as true. She's gonna be fine. In fact, she'll be better than fine, 'cause the next pair of shoes she buys? I bet they'll last a really long time."

All the frustration and fear and pain of the last few days erupted in Mira, and she lashed out clumsily to punch Erin in the face. The girl staggered back a couple of steps and collided with the wall, giggling loudly, a trail of blood running from her lip.

"Sorry, it's just…" she began, as she tried to rein her laughter in. "Have you ever actually punched anyone before?"

Mira grabbed Erin by the shoulders and shoved her hard into the wall, which only earned another laugh. Her golden eyes locked with Mira's as she calmly brushed the restraining arms aside.

"Don't get cross with me. This is all your fault," Erin sneered. "You decided to become my sister's puppy. You kept it a secret from people you think you love. And when I warned you what happens when you get too close to Holly, you didn't listen. You made dinner, I just peeled some spuds."

Mira's shoulders tensed as she moved to hit her again, but Erin raised both hands in a submissive gesture.

"There's a copper at the end of the corridor!" she said hurriedly. "So if you're gonna do... whatever that was, I might just make myself visible and run crying into his arms. What do you think? If I said you were screaming at me in Urdu d'you think he'd take the bait?"

"Not likely." Caroline strolled into the room, gently guiding Mira aside and positioning herself between them. "His wife's Bengali and he knows a bullshit artist when he sees one."

"Oh, it's Greg's mate!" said Erin gleefully. "Hullo, Greg's mate! It's been ages. How you doing, must catch up. Greg still dead, is he?"

Caroline smiled thinly, one arm stretching over Erin's shoulder to lay a palm flat on the wall beside her head. She leaned forward, and Erin looked all of her five foot nothing in height before Caroline's commanding presence.

"I know you," she said, then gestured to Mira and Delia. "What do you see over there?"

"Numpties," Erin replied in a flash.

"Maybe." Caroline wasn't letting her guard down for a second. "I see good kids, happy middle-class Asian families. Life's given them some shit already, because life's like that, but not so much that you can't play the scary monster."

Erin snorted nastily and opened her mouth for a comeback, when Caroline slapped her palm hard against the wall and leaned closer still.

"I'm not them," she smiled menacingly. "And I'm not your sister either. I deal with things every day that your little troll brain couldn't imagine. I've seen you and I've been under your bridge and I know everything you're capable of. And you don't scare me."

Mira saw the glint of silver in Erin's hand and was moments from shouting a warning when Caroline grabbed the girl's wrist, and expertly extracted the knife from her fingers.

"Thank you, we've been talking about an amnesty," Caroline said advertising her triumph with mundane procedure. "There will be an officer on the door of this room. He will know how to look for you. Just like me. I can always see you. Think on that while you're pissing off."

Caroline took a step back, leaving Erin uncharacteristically chastened. She made a great show of rearranging her jacket, before stomping out of the room.

"Are you alright, Mira?" Caroline asked, then turned to Delia. "And you are…?"

"Really quite turned on at the moment," Delia gasped in reply. "But also Delia."

"We'll look after her," Caroline assured them both, then lifted her phone up for Mira to see. "Got a text from your phone. It's the bat signal."

Caroline parked her car alongside Treasurer's House, flashing her warrant card to a visibly unimpressed curate heading for the Minster. Chloe was waiting for them in the doorway with an umbrella in each hand, one green and one red.

"Are we expecting rain?" asked Caroline.

"As a rule," she replied, and led them to the Great Hall, where five chairs had been arranged in a circle. In the dramatic surroundings, it was as if some secret society were gathering. Holly stood in front of the fireplace, hands folded over the handle of her own umbrella.

"Right then, ladies," she said. "Shall we get started?"

"I'll help you fight monsters," Caroline whispered in Mira's ear. "I am not doing the charity calendar."

The first order of business was learning exactly what had happened to Sam. They listened while Delia explained everything she had seen in Jonathan's office. Holly's eyes remained fixed on Mira throughout. Her hands shook as she fought to stay in control of herself.

"The helmet lets you control him," Holly said, tapping the end of her chin thoughtfully. "That's why Sam ran away, it's what he were told to do. His job is to keep me busy so I'm not doing owt about all this. He picked Sam to hit us where it hurts."

Mira closed her eyes at the image.

"It's funny, but with the other man with the… horns, it was like Professor Fortune was trying to communicate," Delia said. "But then he just attacked him."

"Right, hence the helmet," Holly replied. "Whatever he were using don't work, so now he's gone tried and tested."

"If we get this helmet, we can control it," Mira said, hope flaring in her eyes. "We can make it leave Sam."

"We have a witness who's seen Fortune in possession of stolen goods," Caroline said, nodding to Delia. "That means I can arrest him. But he's not worried about that, which says short time frame."

"Yeah, whatever's happening, it's happening now and right here," said Holly, looking into the rafters.

Caroline followed her gaze. "Right. The dragon."

"There's a dragon? Wow!" said Delia excitedly, then noted the more serious expressions around the circle. "But obviously dreadful as well."

"Sam has to be our priority," Holly said. "We are not going down that road, not here. So, jobs for the girls. Where would Jonathan hide summat like this helmet. King's Manor'll be crawling with police, so where's safe?"

"His home? He has an office at the main campus, as well," Delia guessed. "I can get us in. I've got a pass."

"Good," Holly said. "You and Mira get the university. Copper, you take his house. Call me on Mira's phone if you find owt. If I don't answer, get back here."

"Right," said Delia, a shiver of excitement overtaking her. "We have a mission."

"You can catch the bus outside the art gallery," Caroline added sardonically.

"Chloe, you're on surveillance," Holly continued. "You watch this house, and that's it. You see owt funny, you ring me, but you don't get involved. You got that?"

Chloe nodded.

"I'm hitting the streets and looking for Sam," Holly moved

across the circle to kneel where Mira sat in silence, and gripped both her hands. "And I promise, I will bring him back to you."

Mira smiled weakly, but with trust in her eyes. Holly moved out of the circle, scooped up the three umbrellas from the floor and placed them on her chair.

"Now, brollies," she said, trying to restrain her new-toy excitement in light of the circumstances. "Mira, you take the black one. The good old grappling brolly. You remember how it works?"

Mira nodded and reached out to grip the umbrella by its shaft. Holly held on to the handle for a second as their eyes met, then released her grip. She picked up the red umbrella and passed it across the circle to Chloe. A pattern of black ivy was visible across the crimson material, and for a second, it appeared to move.

"This is the big gun," she explained, fingers stroking the silver ring on her right hand. "It's no good for me going after Sam, but I want it here in case it all goes tits up. Keep it safe for me. And I get the non-lethal green one."

She snatched up the final umbrella, twirled it through the air, and pulled back the edge of the canopy.

Caroline's eyebrows rose at the sight of a taser built into the straight round handle.

"Why don't you just have a taser?" she asked.

"But then it wouldn't be a brolly," Holly replied, as if she were not entirely sure why that was a question. "I don't have one for you, sorry."

"I've got a collapsible baton and some pepper spray," Caroline replied aloofly, feeling this battle on behalf of reality had been decisively lost. "I'll be fine as long as it doesn't rain."

"Okay then, let's get cracking." The strength was growing in Holly now. "This is our city, and we will protect it. This is not Ragnarök; this is one sick old man who'll let us all go to the wall to satisfy his daft fantasy. It ain't happening. Not while there's us."

They stood one by one, and without a word, Caroline and Chloe headed to their tasks. Mira turned to Holly before following them.

"Save him," she said. It wasn't a request or an instruction, merely a statement of trust.

"You bet I will," she replied. "That's why I'm here."

CHAPTER 27

Holly thought she'd done quite well playing the leader, all things considered. Of course, now came the real challenge. Not actually knowing what she was doing.

Not knowing what she was doing was part of Holly's routine and she worked around it. But Delia and Caroline didn't know that, they expected her to be in control. Mira knew how it was, but this time, she needed things to be different. So Holly had sent them unto the breech, and now she was wandering about looking for a demonically possessed guitarist with no clue where to begin.

"It's all gone a bit wrong, innit?" said the voice she didn't need right now.

"Give me one good reason why I shouldn't decapitate you again," Holly snarled, as she turned to see Erin standing at her elbow, an innocent smile on her face and a red and white striped stick of rock clutched in her fingers.

"Don't be like that. I'm here to help," Erin said, taking a suck of her treat. "And you look like you could do with some. So where do we think Sam-I-Am has got to? If someone were to ask me nicely, I might be nice back."

"Don't play games," Holly scowled. "We know you and Dylan are palling up. You had to come and have a gloat, didn't you?"

"You will keep dragging people into this," Erin chided. Holly was moving away from her now, and she jogged to keep up. "And now you've got your super-duper girl band. The Hollettes. Can't wait for the hit single."

"We're working on it. What rhymes with decapitated?"

"You are so touchy when I hurt your friends," Erin said. "Honestly, it's just a bit petty."

"Erin, why are you doing this?" Holly turned to face her sister in mounting fury. "Dylan is going to destroy everything. Why would you want that? Is this him? Does he want Jonathan to do his dirty work, is that it?"

"I keep telling you, there's no him," Erin said bluntly. "I'm bored and you're happy, so it's time to shake things up a bit, that's all. If you hadn't been awkward and let me kill Mira last year, it might not have come to this. Anyway, nobody's destroying the world. It'll just be a bit different. Funnier."

"Piss off, Erin," Holly said and strode away at a pace. "I haven't got time for you."

"I know where Sam is," she called out, stopping Holly in her tracks. "I'll take you to him."

"Oh right, I see." Holly sighed at the weary inevitability of it all. "So this is a trap, is it?"

"Couldn't say." Erin dismissively reeled off Holly's options as if they were too tiresome a cliché to recount. "But then, it doesn't matter, does it? You need to find Sam. I know where he is. It might be a trap, it might not, but either way you'll find Sam, and if it is a trap, you might get out or you might not."

"Don't play the trickster with me," Holly reprimanded her. "I used to wipe your bum."

"Come on," Erin said. "I'll show you where the trap is."

Caroline parked outside the house Professor Fortune was renting. As soon as she was clear of the car, she pulled out the baton. A wrist slap for excessive use of force felt preferable to the alternative right now. She was already contemplating the best way to wrap this up, but Delia was going to have to lie to the police, and that was not a scenario she trusted.

The door was not locked, but the house stood deserted.

The last time she had got dragged into Holly's world, she had been completely out of her depth. This time there were more familiar elements to the landscape, but that didn't make it any less treacherous. Fortune was human, which put him in her wheelhouse, but his worst actions were off the books. She wasn't going to be charging anyone with aiding and abetting a demonic possession.

She wondered how often Holly had to deal with human enemies. More troublingly, she wondered exactly what Holly did with her human enemies when she had them.

"So, yeah, it is a trap," Erin said. "But more of a moral one. Sorry."

They stood at the bottom of a steep-sided round hill topped by a squat cylindrical tower of pale stone. It rose incongruously at the edge of the city centre, the crenelated ramparts providing a vantage point to look over the surrounding area. A staircase was cut into the grassy hillside, leading up to the tall dark gates.

"Not having this conversation again," Holly said.

"I think you need to," Erin said. "Now, why is Clifford's Tower important?"

"You know why. Stop wasting me time."

"This is important, Holly, you haven't learned." Erin wagged her finger at her sister. "What happened here? Long ago, before our time? Do you remember?"

"They killed all the Jews. Are we done?" Holly snapped impatiently.

"All of them," Erin said, a dark look settling on her face. "One hundred and fifty people herded into that thing, and not one of them made it out. Them's that weren't killed did for themselves because they knew there were nothing left to hope for. It can't happen here, they say, well it can. It did. Now, speaking as an expert on the subject, it seems to me that people don't half hate each other. And you're here to protect them."

"What do you want me to say?" Holly asked wearily.

"What would you have done about it?"

"I weren't born!"

"If there had been a King in the Mountain, what would he have done?" Erin pressed on.

"Nothing," Holly admitted. "He wouldn't have woken up."

"Exactly," Erin said. "And if it happened again tomorrow,

neither would you. This whole world could devour itself in hate and you wouldn't even stir."

"Alright, Erin, I get it!" Holly shouted. "You're right, I'm not a hero! I'm not a protector or a saviour or any of those things! I'm just a... a tool! I just tidy things away for people who don't even care because none of it matters! There's no point, no reason, it's all just stuff happening and that's all I am too! You happy now?"

Erin breathed in for a moment, a contented smile spreading across her face.

"Thank you, Holly," she said, her voice calm and satisfied. She gestured to the tower as she strolled away. "He's in there."

"What, that's it, is it?" Holly asked.

"Yeah, pretty much, that's all I wanted out of this," Erin replied. "Anyway, gotta run. There's an old bloke in that hotel over there who's about to choke on a fish bone and I hate keeping the elderly waiting. Ta-ra for a bit."

Holly watched as Erin sauntered into the distance, then climbed the stairs to the tower's black door.

At Treasurer's House, nothing was happening. Nothing had happened since everyone had dispersed to their allotted tasks. Chloe had positioned herself under a conveniently located tree with a good view of the grounds and the side entrance, and waited for the dastardly plot to get underway.

It hadn't, and she was bored.

To be fair, this was more interesting than her usual duties. But she hadn't expected frontline action to involve this much waiting, especially after Holly had planted a ticking clock in her brain. Whatever was happening was supposed to happen soon. She had now progressed to soon-ish.

Chloe was not used to the supernatural. Beyond the controlled rituals her grandmother was teaching her, she'd never had to deal with anything directly. She could be as oblivious as anyone else unless she had reason to know that something was there.

Which meant she never noticed Erin until she was struck from behind.

It was like standing at the bottom of a vast white barrel. The cylindrical walls of Clifford's Tower rose up above Holly, dotted with arched entrances and criss-crossed with walkways, stairs and dark metal safety rails. A gift shop stood to her right while plaques on raised platforms dotted the floor, revealing fascinating facts about the history of the structure, but neglecting to mention any genocide. There did not appear to be anyone else here.

"Sam?" she called into the echoey space. "Sam, can you hear me?"

The silence did not answer, and Holly clutched her umbrella tightly with both hands, finding the trigger with her thumb in readiness.

"Sam, come out. I know you're here. If you can understand me, let me help you. If you can't, well, let's get on with it."

A movement and the scraping of footsteps high up on the wall drew her attention. In a tiny arched window, she saw the silhouette of curling horns.

"Sam, I'm sorry," she said. "I know I helped put you here. Let me make it right. Mira's waiting, Sam. Come back to her."

The figure in the window stood, and Holly immediately saw the trap beginning to spring. This was not the smooth predatory movements of the Horned Men. It was a man, his face concealed in the helmet of Henry VIII.

"Dylan," she called up to him. "Where's Sam?"

"Where do all young people go?" he replied, his voice muffled by the steel but still audible. "To find what they most desire."

"Mira." Before Holly could run, the figure in the window produced a rifle from his vantage point, and raised it to a firing position in one swift move. The sound of the shot was soft and low.

Holly felt a sting, and looked down to see a metal dart protruding from below her collar bone, its blunt end tipped with a fluffy ball of bright orange padding. She stared bewildered at the unknown object that had struck her.

"What the sc…" she began before crashing to the floor.

CHAPTER 28

Delia poked a fearful head around the door of Jonathan's office, and waved Mira in with a twitchy hand. It was deserted, which did not calm her in the slightest. Mira placed what should have been a reassuring hand on her shoulder, but all she got for her troubles was a leap and a high-pitched cry. Delia slapped a hand over her mouth to silence her outburst.

"Delia, it's fine," said Mira. "There's no one here. Let's see what we can find."

It occurred to Mira how strangely at ease she was when she had to go it alone. It was as if she had to be Holly when Holly wasn't around. Which made Delia the new her. She hoped she was a little less jumpy.

"Where do we start?" said Delia.

If Jonathan's office at King's Manor was cluttered, this was a dragon's hoard of dusty academia and recovered relics. Nevertheless, there were still a finite number of places you could hide something the size of a human head.

"Try that cupboard," Mira indicated, as she crossed to behind Jonathan's desk, noting the room's only personal affectation, a framed photograph of three grinning girls. She yanked open the large bottom drawer, but found only more papers, and a pair of broken gold-rimmed glasses. They glinted as they caught the light from the windows, shining as if brand new, and something fascinated Mira about them. They looked so different from the chunky black pair she was used to seeing Jonathan in. A delicate engraved texture marked the edge of the frames, like minute lettering in some unknown language.

"Delia," Mira asked. "You said you thought Jonathan was

trying to communicate with the man who attacked you. What happened?"

"He sort of made eye contact with him," Delia explained, as she rifled through the bottom of the cupboard. "They looked at each other for a bit, and it was almost like he was listening, but then he just went for us."

"Was Jonathan wearing these?" Mira settled back in the swivel chair as a theory took shape.

"Yes, yes, he was," Delia said. "He started wearing those when the dig began. I honestly didn't recognise him the first time I saw him in them, they make his whole face look…"

"Delia, I think this is what he was using," Mira cut her off, the idea building in her mind. "The helmet has those gold glasses… what if there's something in them that lets you control the Horned Men, and this is Jonathan's attempt to replicate it?"

"I suppose that makes sense," Delia said, completing her search. "It doesn't help, though. I mean, they don't work. He couldn't control the other one."

"But if we can figure out what it is," Mira said, her fingers rubbing the metal excitedly. "Holly has this friend, he makes magic weapons, maybe he could reverse engineer it for us. Maybe we can save Sam with these."

Delia nodded slowly, her eyes staring fixedly at the window behind Mira. "Yes, good, now, go there."

Mira spun the chair to face where Delia was looking, and there was Sam, on the other side of the glass. His hands stretched above his head, gripping the wall, while the toes of his feet rested on the ledge. His body was arched out backwards and his head leaned in close in its cruel mask, rolling languidly on tensed shoulders. His eyes locked with Mira's, unblinking, unrelenting, only barely recognisable as himself.

Mira rose from her seat slowly, the glasses still clenched in one hand. She scooped up the umbrella with the other and backed away from the window with a careful pace, as if there were a sleeping baby in the room that she did not wish to disturb. Or a wild animal that she dared not provoke.

Sam released his grip on the wall, grabbing the window frame with one hand and scraping twisted claws down the pane with another. His head lowered, and she could see the drive to attack building in him, as it had in Malcolm. Staying put had ceased to be an option.

"Run!" she shouted, grabbing Delia's hand and dragging her from the room. As they sprinted down the corridor, they heard glass shattering behind them.

Mira risked a glance backwards as she fled. Delia was a few paces behind her. Sam was bounding from floor to wall to ceiling, jumping forward and gaining on them with each leap. He crashed into a light fitting and it exploded into a shower of sparks, the gold rims around his eyes flashing with the glow as he pounced.

Mira ducked into the nearest door and slammed it shut as soon as Delia had followed, wedging a chair underneath the handle. They were safe, apart from being in a small fourth floor meeting room with no other doors and only a pot plant and some tasteful furniture to fend off further attack. Something crashed hard into the door.

"Oh God, oh God, he's coming," gasped Delia.

"Good. If he's still coming after us, he isn't hurting anyone else," Mira said with such a strong tone that Delia had to gaze in surprise at the woman she thought she had known.

Sam's fingers burst through the door, tearing out four ragged rents.

Mira looked to the tall windows across the far wall, and the building opposite that was visible beyond. She opened the catch and slid the pane aside, poking a head through before stepping up onto the ledge.

"Mira, we're four storeys up!" Delia cried, as another blow struck the door. A frenzied eye was visible through the gap.

"It's okay, I think I know what I'm doing," Mira raised the umbrella and fired, sending the shaft streaking through the air to drive into the nearest wall. As Mira attached the carabiner to her belt, Delia tore off her backpack and rummaged around in it.

"Come on!" Mira shouted as Delia produced her cycle helmet

and crammed it on to her head. "Grab hold of me and don't let go!"

The door smashed off its hinges as Sam leapt forward, landing on all fours and straining his neck forward to roar at them, but they were already gone.

Mira stepped from the ledge with Delia's arms wrapped tightly around her waist and they swung through the air, the brick wall of the building opposite zooming towards them.

How do you stop? was the only thought in Mira's brain.

They collided with a window, startling a young man with the look of an impending deadline, and both felt their grips loosen for a moment before the survival instinct kicked in all the stronger. Mira fed the line out and lowered them to the ground, feeling Delia's head resting on her shoulder and deep, nervous breaths pumping against her back.

"Are you alright back there?" she asked.

"Where does she get those wonderful toys?" came a breathless reply.

Mira pulled the umbrella in as soon as she felt concrete beneath her soles, then heard a noise from above. Sam had followed them through the window and was leaping impossibly across the gap between the two buildings. He caught the wall with his claws and climbed headfirst down the sheer surface, arms reaching ahead of him in long, aggressive strikes. Mira clicked the umbrella back into place, grabbed Delia's hand and they ran again. Losing the backpack had not made Delia any quicker. She was exhausted, and wasn't ready to run on her ankle. But she was also terrified, which helped. They just needed somewhere to run to.

Mira checked for the glasses in her coat pocket. They felt reassuringly solid under her fingers. But even if she was right about what they were, her plan to get them to Graymalkin was desperately untenable. She was holding on to something that didn't work, so the only option was to make it work herself.

Why don't they work? she thought as they charged through a quad, leaving the functional grey buildings behind as the lake at the heart of the campus loomed closer.

I don't know... because it's bloody magic was the unhelpful answer.

The metal was presumably the same, the method was presumably the same because Jonathan does his homework. What was different? Assuming her guess was right, which was a leap in itself, what was the difference between these glasses and the helmet?

A creak echoed behind them. She looked back and saw Sam crouched in the branches of a nearby tree. He pounced forward, covering the distance quickly to descend right down on to them.

Delia pulled the helmet off her head, swung it, and struck him in the midriff. The momentum carried him across the lawn, but he landed on all fours, perfectly balanced and ready to resume the chase. They kept running. Banks of trees ringed the lake, and they darted between the dense foliage, seeking any cover they could find.

A channel cut away from the lake in the midst of the trees, with a small wooden footbridge across it. Mira grabbed Delia's hand and stepped off the path into the knee-deep waters alongside. They splashed hurriedly to the bridge and huddled underneath, waiting for a sign they were still being pursued. She placed a finger to her lips, and Delia nodded, holding her breath in terror.

Something heavy struck the bridge above their head, and a shower of debris scattered into the water. A creaking of wood and the same hissing breath she had heard from Malcolm echoed all around them. Sam was up there, and they'd helpfully herded themselves into an enclosed space. The question was how he was hunting them.

If he can hear us, we're dead. If he can smell us, we're dead. If he's got any other senses normal people don't have, we're really, really *dead.*

A few more groans emerged from the timbers, the loudest of which was followed by silence, then a distant scrabbling. After a moment, Mira poked a head from her hiding place, and gestured for Delia to follow.

"He's gone. He didn't see us," Mira whispered. "So he didn't find us. That... actually that might be really helpful. Delia, I think I've got a plan."

Mira looked around to get her bearings. It hadn't been that long since she had come to this place every day, and the familiar sights slotted into place.

"Alright, you see that building over there?" Delia looked in the direction she was pointing, and nodded. "I need you to go to lecture room 11A, on the second floor. Do you know how to work a projector?"

"I think so," Delia said, forcing herself to concentrate. "I've made presentations. Yes, of course I can, yes."

Mira stepped back onto the bank, and looked all around her, making sure there was no sign of Sam.

"You go there now and get the projector working," she said. "You can set it to project an image you find online. Look for pictures of the helmet. I'll join you there as soon as I can."

"Where are you going?" Delia asked.

"I'm going to find a boy that I like," Mira replied. "And I'm going to get him to chase me."

CHAPTER 29

The lights of lecture hall 11A flickered into life, illuminating tiered rows of seats with a central aisle of steps, a rough and hairy olive-green carpet, and sheer white walls, the windows on one side concealed by long black drapes.

Delia leant up against the door for a moment, her heart racing and her helmet still clutched in her grip. She could see the projector and its control desk at the back of the room, and took a few wobbly steps in its direction.

After her first adventure with Holly, Mira had joined a running group. Not for the first time, she felt that it was probably the smartest decision of her life.

She sprinted as fast as she could, the building she had sent Delia to looming closer, although slower than she would have liked. She could feel Sam behind her. She knew he might leap on her at any moment. But the building was getting closer.

She dived through the wooden door and shoved it shut behind her, briefly catching a glimpse of Sam through the panel of safety glass as he slammed into it. His tormented face snarled at her through the grid. She backed away slowly toward the stairs, deliberately letting him see where she was going, then took them three at a time as she heard it forced from its hinges.

Delia's attention was completely taken up by the gallery of images on the computer screen in front of her, and she took an involuntary leap into the corner when she heard the door slam. She calmed at the sight of a breathless Mira coming up the central aisle.

"He's right behind me. Is it ready?" she gasped, pushing in alongside Delia in front of the computer. She looked at the montage of pictures of the helmet on the screen, and her finger stabbed at one looking face-on.

"That one," she instructed, and Delia set about downloading the image and relaying it to the bulky projector that stood alongside the desk.

"What happens now?" whispered Delia, trying to keep focused on the task.

"I've been thinking about this ever since I fought that skeleton. Long story." Mira spoke quickly, her eyes darting from the door to the screen. "It's all about how creatures perceive the world. Sam is looking for us."

"I know, that's why I'm scared."

"No, *looking*," Mira clarified. "Not listening for us or smelling us or sensing our presence. If he were, we wouldn't have been able to hide under the bridge."

"Primary sense is sight," Delia said, grateful for some science.

"Right," said Mira, and put on Jonathan's glasses. The left lens was splintered and the arms were bent, leaving them wonky and diagonal on her face, barely covering her eyes. Her manic grin suited the overall look. "They don't look like the helmet. That's why it doesn't work. But we're going to make them look like it."

"How?" asked Delia as Mira ran to the front of the hall, switched off the lights and positioned herself flat against the opposite wall.

"When he comes in, project the image onto my face."

"What if you're wrong?" said Delia, moving the projector into position. "Those might just be normal glasses!"

"If I'm wrong, we run away again," Mira replied, and held her breath. She glanced sideways at the door, waiting for the sound of footsteps, of hard breathing, of claws scratching on wood. None of it came.

Instead, a window on the left-hand wall exploded, the heavy black curtain falling to the ground in a wave as Sam's body tumbled over it.

"Delia, now!"

The projector's light blazed into Mira's eyes and she squeezed them shut. The flaw in her plan was now apparent. She was in a room with a monster and couldn't see a thing.

"Delia, what is he doing?" she shouted. She could hear the hissing breath the thing was forcing from Sam's lungs, just a few short feet from where she stood. Close enough to reach her. But she couldn't see and she couldn't move.

"Nothing, he's just standing there!"

"Okay, so working, good," whispered Mira in breathless terror. She balled her fists and forced out the loudest, strongest voice she could muster. "You obey me now! I control you! And I order you to leave this man's body! Right now! And no exploding!"

Through a forced squint she saw the horned head thrashing from side to side against the light.

"You will leave this man and he will not be harmed!" Mira shouted. "Now give me back my boyfriend!"

"Mira?" She heard her name, croaking and distorted but recognisably him, and a gasp of relief exploded from her lips.

"Sam, it's me, I'm here, now come back to me!" she called out. "I love you and I am going to make this right! Please come back to me!"

"You couldn't, could you…" he whispered, his voice trailing away.

"I know, I couldn't tell you. I should have!" she called out. "I know I kept secrets from you, and I know I wanted to, and it did this to us! Sam, please listen to me, just come back now!"

"Can't be like that…"

"Oh, Sam," she cried, tears oozing from the corners of her tightly shut eyes. "You don't have to come back for me, but come back! I don't care if you never want to see me again, just be here, be here again!"

A savage, grating roar exploded into the room, and Mira roared back.

"Let him go!"

A clatter of metal was followed by silence.

Mira inched forward, shielding her eyes against the light. Sam had collapsed backwards onto the stairs. The horns fell away from his head, lying in a tangled pile of components as the slivers of metal left his body. Delia stumbled down the stairs, and slammed her helmet down over the remains of the creature.

Sam was breathing, slow and even and alive. His face and hands were criss-crossed with tiny, shallow cuts, but he did not seem badly hurt.

Mira sank to his side as his eyes began to open.

"Mira?" he slurred.

"Please don't explode," she said desperately.

"I wasn't planning on…" he said, glancing around the unfamiliar room.

Mira hurled her arms around him, clutching him to her as close as she could as they sprawled on the steps. Sam reciprocated, gently stroking her back, while visibly wincing.

"Ow," he said, dislodging her tight grip as a thousand tiny pains struck at once. "God, I'm sore all over. What's going on? How did we get here?"

"You were possessed," Mira said, without any fear of how he would react. "But it's okay now. Delia and I saved you. Because that's what I do, I save people from monsters. And I honestly don't mind if you believe me or not, as long as you're safe."

"Delia?" said Sam, noticing her for the first time.

"Hello," she said with a nervous wave. "Actually, I'd quite like a hug too if that's alright."

Mira laughed in relief, bounded up to her and wrapped arms around her shoulders.

"Thank you for so much," Mira said. "You could not be more brilliant."

"Really? Gosh," said Delia with an embarrassed smile, as she shunted her glasses up her nose. "Should we maybe leave before somebody notices that?"

Mira looked at the shattered window, and clocked Sam's questioning expression. Everything was too big for him right now.

"Yeah, you might have jumped through that," Mira explained,

helping him to his feet. "In fact, you may have jumped through a couple of other windows too. I'm not surprised you're feeling it. Possessed You was limber."

"Oh, no," said Delia, and Mira turned to see her standing frozen in place in the middle of the steps.

"I put my helmet down on top of... it, and now it's sort of... not here."

"Okay, we'll help you look for it," Sam began, but Mira gestured for him to listen.

"Sam, I'm going to say something important, and I don't have time for you to not believe it," Mira said. "Because we are in a lot of trouble right now."

Sam nodded his understanding.

"There is a monster in this room."

CHAPTER 30

"It might have gone out the window," Delia hoped aloud as Mira ran to the door, followed by a clicking noise she did not wish to hear. "Sorry, did you lock us in with it?"

"Yes, I did," Mira replied unapologetically. "I'm not having that thing running loose out there. Now if it wants to get out, it'll have to go back the way it came, so Delia, would you stand in front of the window just in case? Sam, I need you to help me look for it."

As Sam checked each row of chairs, he realised he wasn't questioning any of this. Mira's absolute conviction pulled him along, but he knew there was something else behind his acceptance of the situation. And he had a feeling he wasn't going to like whatever it was. Somewhere in the room, something rattled metallically.

"It's metal, looks like a double-ended corkscrew," Mira explained, wielding her umbrella like a baseball bat. "And don't freak out when I say this, but it will try and jump on your face."

The projector stand toppled forward with a sudden crash, sending the machine smashing to the floor. A chorus of skittering followed the impact. Mira gestured for the others to stay put and advanced up the centre aisle. The casing of the projector was hopelessly smashed, and fragments of glass from the lens littered the step. There was no sign of the creature.

Mira shook her head as she retreated, while Sam continued his search. A round, dark object underneath one seat made his heart jump, but he relaxed as he recognised the shape.

"I've found Delia's helmet at least," he said. As his fingers touched the smooth plastic surface, he felt a sharp scratching across the back of his hand. He withdrew his arm instinctively and stood, watching awestruck at what was happening.

Six slim jointed metal armatures emerged from the openings in the top of the helmet like insect legs, flexed and flipped it over. The rear of the helmet was now facing him in an upside-down position, the three holes on the back staring at him like the eyes and nose of a skull. Curling horns unfolded from within the empty shell. There was something familiar in the image that tortured his memory before it sprang at him, the twitching limbs driving towards his chest. He caught the helmet in mid-air and strained to hold it back, the arms scratching and flailing as he swung it across the room, sending it flying into the shadows with a thud.

"What the hell was that?" he shouted, as Mira ran to check where it had landed. It had already scuttled off. "Did I just get attacked by a cycle helmet?"

"Yeah, I've seen this before," Mira explained. "It needs a body. If it can't get a person, it'll settle for a thing."

"We're fighting a possessed cycle helmet?" Sam asked, shaken but incredulous.

"Yes, but last time it was a sabre-toothed tiger skeleton, so call that an upside."

Mira moved along the far wall, poking the curtains with her umbrella. She could see Delia was spotting something terrible in every shadow.

"Mira, behind you!" she shouted.

Mira felt the sharp needles of the thing's limbs against her back before she could process the warning. It was crawling over her now, digging in hard as it scurried towards her shoulders. An appendage lashed round to press tightly across her throat. She choked for breath and pulled hard against the constricting metal. Delia ran to her aid, gripping the helmet and dragging it away. She tossed it to the floor and it landed on all six feet, rattling its body as it prepared to strike again. Which was right when Sam brought the fire extinguisher crashing down on it. The helmet broke in two, legs splintering under the weight of the blow.

Sam lifted the extinguisher and they peered into the broken helmet. It was as if someone had tipped the workings of a broken clock into it. Mira poked the fragments with her umbrella and nothing moved. She looked up at Sam and saw a determined expression vanish from his face to be replaced with complete bafflement.

"So, closure?" she suggested, but he still looked lost.

"Are you going to be alright?" Mira asked Sam as she supported him on the way back to the lobby. He looked exhausted and she could see him struggling to process everything that had happened. Delia followed at a discreet distance with the umbrella beneath her arm, anxiously checking her phone for some word from Holly.

"I don't know, it's a lot. I don't really remember any of it, I'm not sure I want to. And this is your life now?"

"Well, I've never fought a bicycle helmet before," Mira clarified as they entered a gallery leading to the steps down to the entrance hall. "And usually Holly's here, so I don't have to be in charge quite so much, but, yeah, this is what it's like. Is it okay?"

Before he could answer, they saw a figure in the lobby below them. He wore a long black raincoat that bulged over something concealed underneath, and his face was covered by the helmet of Henry VIII. Mira could feel Sam flinch with terror at the sight of him.

"Back with us, I see," came Jonathan's muffled voice. "I suppose that means I can take this off, but I don't know, I'm quite liking it. Face to face with history, you might say."

"It's over, Jonathan," Mira replied. "We've killed your little pet. Drop this before anyone else gets hurt."

"Yeah, I'm sorry it had to go down like that, Sam," he said, a forlorn tone barely detectable under the mask.

"What are you...?" Sam began, and Mira saw the memories starting to coalesce in his expression. "Where's Abi?"

"You mustn't blame yourself," Jonathan continued, his calm demeanour visibly shaking Sam. "You weren't in control, and I wasn't fast enough to stop you, I'm sorry."

"Sam, she's going to be fine." Mira felt the situation slipping from her grasp. "Delia was there, she took care of her."

The anger was simmering in him now. "Did... did you make me hurt Abi?"

"I didn't make you do anything," said Jonathan.

Sam was poised to charge down the stairs when Jonathan pulled back his coat and raised a rifle from underneath. Mira protectively shoved Sam to one side as with a dull pop, a dart struck the wall beside them. She herded them both back up the stairs while Jonathan advanced, carefully reloading.

Mira flung open a door to see another threat advancing towards them. Erin was wearing Holly's coat, which trailed on the floor behind her. The sleeves were bunched up around her elbows and she clutched an umbrella in each hand. One red, one green. Mira gestured to the others to head in the opposite direction and they fled through the corridors.

"What's happened to Abi, Mira?" said Sam as they ran. "Where is she?"

"She's in hospital, she's going to be alright," Mira replied. "She went through a window, but Delia got to her..."

"Went through a window?" Sam had stopped moving. He grabbed Mira's arm and turned her to face him. "Mira, tell me the truth. Did I hurt Abi?"

"Sam, we don't have time for you to deal with this now!"

"Did I hurt her?" he shouted.

"You pushed her through a window, but..."

He looked utterly devastated, and she saw that he could not, would not forgive himself for this. Suddenly, his body tensed, then spasmed wildly. He dropped to his knees and fell forward, revealing Erin standing behind him. The green umbrella was cocked under her arm and silver wires stretched from the handle to Sam's back, the sound of a crackling current passing between them. As Mira ran forward to him, Erin dropped the umbrella and snatched up its red twin from the floor, swinging it by the tip and striking Mira on the side of the head with the handle. She collapsed unconscious and Delia was left alone.

Delia scurried to the nearest room, finding herself in a small study hall with no other exits. Erin followed, and Delia let out a cry at the sight of the knife in her hands. She waved the black umbrella uselessly to fend off her amused-looking attacker.

"It's funny," said Erin. "With blokes, she's got a definite type. But when she goes tufthunting, you never know what you're gonna get."

Delia's back was to the wall now, and Erin was right in front of her. The umbrella was gently pulled from her grip while the knife was pressed to her throat and everything felt so much more real than it had when monsters were lurking in the dark.

"In my day, we had a saying. The herder dies after telling his tale," Erin explained, stretching upwards until their faces almost touched. "There's a saying from your day that's a bit apt right now. Bury your gays."

Mira lurched awake as she heard the scream. Her head rang, like she'd been hit much harder than she had been. If they made it through this, she'd have to find out what the red umbrella actually did. Sam was still out cold. Mira stumbled into the study hall to see Erin theatrically draping Holly's coat over Delia's prone body. She looked like a small child proudly displaying her finger painting. There were spots of blood on the floor.

"It's alright," Erin said. "You won't have to miss her for long."

Mira backed out of the room to where Sam lay. She hooked her hands under his arms and tried to haul him down the corridor, but it was no use. He was too heavy, and she was out of time. Jonathan was advancing towards them, the rifle lying casually in his arms as Erin stepped out of the study hall, gripping the black umbrella, the spike extended.

"I'm sorry, Mira," Jonathan rasped. "You need to come with me now. Where's Delia?"

"She killed her!" Mira shouted. She saw Jonathan's shoulders slump and desperately grasped for the only hope she had left. "Jonathan, she killed Delia. Do you really want to be part of all this?"

"I thought we had an understanding," Jonathan said, his grip on the rifle tensing.

"Be fair, she came at me with this!" Erin protested, waving the umbrella in the air. "She's a bit tougher than she looked, I can see what Holly saw in her. And she was in with them, she'd only have tried to stop us!"

"She didn't have to kill her!" Mira pressed on, rising shakily to her feet to stand protectively over Sam's prone body. "You can still walk away from this, Jonathan. You haven't killed anyone!"

"Oh, Mira," Erin said gently. "You don't know Dylan half as well as you think you do."

Mira turned to look at her, sickened by the satisfied smile on her face. In that second, she felt a second blow to her head and fell forward. The last thing she saw as she lost consciousness was the grimacing face of Jonathan's mask.

Between them, Erin and Jonathan dragged their unconscious captives down the corridor in grim silence. Once they were safely gone, a terrified voice came from the study hall.

"Oh, gosh. I really hope I'm not a ghost now."

CHAPTER 31

Mira woke to the feel of something cold, hard and sharp, pulling her hands together. She was enclosed on each side by a press of bodies, like she'd been crammed into a crowded elevator, or a tube train or…

She shook her head until she woke fully. Or the middle of the back seat of a car. That was it.

Sam was passed out on her right, his head resting on the window. Holly was on her left. All three of them had their wrists restrained in heavy manacles of sharp-edged black metal. A length of rope bound her and Sam to the seat, but not Holly. It took Mira a moment to realise why she did not need to be restrained. Here she would be no threat.

Holly was awake, but looked terrible. She leant forward in her seat, breathing hard. Sweat dripped from her face and her hands shook uncontrollably. She was too weak to even speak, but Mira could see she was in absolute terror for her life.

They had pulled over by the side of a tree-lined road, currently deserted, that stretched on ahead of her as far as she could see. A tall crimson sign stood a short distance ahead.

YOU ARE NOW LEAVING YORK.

"What happens if you do?"

"I don't know, I never tried. It was impressed upon me very firmly not to."

Holly had never left the city. The condition of her immortality was to stay there, forever. Nobody knew what would happen to her if she crossed the line just a few feet ahead of them.

There was a knock on the window beside Holly's head. Erin stood by the car, waving at them with a broad grin on her face.

Beyond, Mira could see the masked figure of Jonathan by the roadside. Erin made a mocking hand gesture asking them to wind down the window, before she opened the door.

"Erin, what…?" Holly made the effort to speak. "What is this?"

"The end of the road," Erin replied. "Well, I suppose the beginning, actually. It goes quite far, can you see? Not that we'd ever know."

"Erin, you've got to take her back to the city!" Mira pleaded. "Look at her, she shouldn't be this far out, you know that! Do what you like to me, but she's your sister!"

"Do you mind? This is family time," Erin said, crouching down to stand level with Holly's face. "I've been thinking about what you were saying, Hol. We've been playing this game for so long, where I cause trouble and you sort it out and nothing ever changes between us. I don't think it's good for me. I need to move on. So, if the offer's still open, I'd like to kill you now, if that's alright."

Holly gave an exhausted snort. "Don't believe you."

Erin leaned in and kissed her on the temple, her head resting against Holly's for a moment. When she pulled back, her face was a deathly mask. Mira saw the knife in her hand.

"No!" she screamed, straining uselessly against her bonds as she saw the blade drive into Holly's side. A stream of blood oozed over her waistcoat as it was pulled clear. She was struggling to get her hands to the wound in their manacles, so Mira did what she could, the ropes holding her tight as she felt the warm liquid slipping between her fingers.

"All yours, Dylan," Erin called out, and the professor returned to the car. "He's sulking 'cause of Delia. Anyway, thanks, all of you, I'm feeling a real sense of closure. But before you go, there's one thing I've always wanted to know."

Jonathan climbed into the driver's seat and started the engine. Mira looked from Holly's terrified face to Erin's delighted grin.

"You must have wondered what happens if you leave the city," Erin said. "And if we don't find out now, we never will, so here we go. It's exciting!"

She slammed the door shut and waved at them as the car gathered speed.

Holly looked up from the blood pooling in her lap to Mira's terrified face. Slick fingers closed on each other as the sign passed them. Holly closed her eyes and let out a cry of pain.

It was like a thousand tiny fireworks were going off. Small pin-prick flashes of brilliant light dotted Holly's face and hair, followed by bursts of thin smoke. Her hair became like trails of mist, empty and insubstantial. Looking at her was like staring into the sun. Mira felt like she was seeing two things at once, a version of the world where Holly sat beside her and one where she did not, and never would. She blinked once and that was enough. She heard the manacles fall to the floor.

A pile of blood-soaked clothes sat on the seat; two empty boots flopped on the floor in front of them. It was as if she had never been there at all. Jonathan turned the car round and drove back to where Erin was standing. The girl peered through the window and nodded, her curiosity apparently satisfied.

"So that's what it does," she mused. "Good-oh. Well, I suppose you'll want to be getting on with your big show now, won't you?"

"Yes, I will," Jonathan replied curtly. "And I never want to see you again."

"Everyone's so precious about their mates these days." Erin returned to the rear window. She pulled the door open a crack to smile down at Mira's distraught face. "Ta-ra, Mira. It's been fun getting to know you and all that, but time you were going. Say goodbye to Sam for me if he ever wakes up."

"I was right about you," said Mira, holding back her pain. She would not give Erin the satisfaction of seeing it. "You are just evil. There's nothing else left."

"I said you were clever," said Erin. "Any chance I can grab a lift back to town?"

The car roared into life and sped away, leaving Erin stood by the roadside.

"Be like that then," she said, pulling a face.

Mira knew where this would end, and it would not end well. They would return to Treasurer's House. Jonathan would try to open the portal. And she had a pretty good idea why he might need a couple of hostages to do it.

And Holly was dead.

CHAPTER 32

As the car headed through the city, the pile of clothes on the seat taunted Mira mercilessly, daring her to be brave now it was all up to her. She couldn't. She had acted on Holly's behalf because she knew Holly was there. It was quite another thing to go it alone.

And then there was Delia. Poor, shy, well-meaning Delia, who had risked everything to help them, lying alone in an empty classroom. Maybe she would haunt the university. If she did, it brought Mira no comfort. Her list of names was growing. Delia had trusted her, and she had failed her utterly.

Sam was coming round. He rattled the manacles he had discovered were binding him, and looked to Mira for an explanation.

"Sam, don't panic. It's..." Mira couldn't maintain the brave face a moment longer. "Holly's dead, Sam. And Delia. And I think we're going to die too."

In the driver's mirror, Jonathan's eyes flicked in her direction from behind their golden rims, silently confirming her prediction with neither joy nor regret.

Jonathan parked alongside Treasurer's House, right where Caroline had earlier today. He had not said a word during the journey, and Mira had not felt able to challenge him. Not with a pool of Holly's blood sitting beside her. He climbed out, opened the passenger door, and held the umbrella to the rope binding them. The spike extended and tore through it, and they both drew in deep gasps of breath as the severed cord hung loose.

"Get out," Jonathan said, gesturing with the umbrella.

Mira's eyes explored the alley and found nobody. The car was tucked between two buildings, positioned carefully out of sight. But there were still options. They could run, they could shout for help, they could even fight. Erin wasn't here, and Jonathan was just a man. She looked to Sam and saw the same thought. Jonathan was a lot older than him, smaller too. One man with a silly trick umbrella.

A silly trick umbrella. Oh, Holly.

"I'd rather you didn't do anything foolish," Jonathan said, placing the spike under Sam's chin. "I know this is going to sound a bit rubbish, but I don't actually want to hurt either of you."

The spike lingered close to Sam's throat.

Mira wondered if she could still get the drop on Jonathan. She could hit him from behind. He'd helpfully clamped a lump of metal to her hands. She could knock him down and they could run. But the spike was so close to Sam's throat.

A familiar metallic scraping filled the car. A cool needle-thin pressure was driven into her skin at both her temples, just light enough not to draw blood. She strained her vision as hard as she could, and knew what she would see there.

A gasp from Sam confirmed it.

She looked to him, and saw another of the Horned Man mechanisms poised at the back of his head, ready to take him again. His eyes told her he was seeing the same thing.

"I'd rather you came willingly," Jonathan said. "I don't need another pair of hands right now. But I won't turn one down."

They stepped from the car and walked slowly through the house, not daring to make a sound or move more than one foot in front of the other, feeling the mechanisms on their heads flexing, the pointed arms digging in, restrained from their purpose only by the will of their master.

In the Great Hall, a bizarre centrepiece had been erected. A wheel of twisted metal sat on a dais in the middle of the room, at its centre the relic from the dig. Two lengths of chain extended from it to lie on the marble floor.

Jonathan nudged Mira into position with the umbrella, and attached the end of a chain to her manacles, before doing the same to Sam. The chains were just the right length to keep them from reaching each other.

Only once they were securely bound did the terrible apparatus on their heads drop to the floor. The metal creatures wheeled to Jonathan's feet, and squeaked back and forth as he looked down at them from behind his helmet. Apparently granted their instructions, they spun around and trundled from the hall. Only then did he remove his mask, to look on them with the same kindly eyes she knew so well.

Mira heard a low sobbing, and saw a third chain coming off the far side of the machine. At the end of it was Chloe, huddled in a ball and scared out of her mind.

"Mira, I'm sorry!" she cried as soon as she saw them. "She made me tell her where you were!"

"It's alright, Chloe, it's not your fault," Mira said as Sam tugged on his restraints in an attempt to reach the terrified girl. It was no use. The roots of the chains were equidistant around the wheel. Jonathan had designed it to separate them utterly.

The flashes of blue light that had accompanied Malcolm's demise were already visible in the rafters. As Mira glanced from the concern in Sam's eyes to the guilt and fear in Chloe's, she knew she couldn't afford to be helpless. She would do the other thing instead. She would be brave for them.

"So this is what it's all about, is it?" she said.

Jonathan appeared calm but was noticeably keeping his distance.

"You open the portal, this dragon comes out, and since you're the winner of the silly hat contest, it does as you say?" She felt impressed with herself. Despite everything, that sounded like Holly. Maybe because of everything.

"Well, you're right up to a point," Jonathan replied. "The helmet only gives me power over the creatures in their mechanical form. I'm not planning to control whatever's up there. I'm not that presumptuous."

"Then what do you want? Please, do a monologue or something, we've got time, and I think you'll enjoy it."

"What makes you say that?" he asked, a curious look in his eye.

"You're not like Erin," Mira replied. "Or any of the other things I've had to face. You're human. And that means you want to be understood."

"Very good." He conceded her point with an impressed smile. "Honestly, I just want to know. I got a glimpse of all this, and away it went. I've spent a lifetime watching people I care about die, watching people try to destroy themselves, or everything else, and nothing has ever made sense of it all. Nothing. I mean, look at that."

He gestured towards the windows, where the outline of the Minster was visible. "All that effort to build it. Do you think God lives there?"

"Atheist lapsed Hindu," Mira said. "Wouldn't know."

Jonathan smiled. "In my twenties, I dabbled in all sorts of mysticism like the worst kind of bloody hipster. I didn't find a point anywhere. One day I realised, I didn't have to look for something greater, I knew where it was!"

"So why do you need us?" Sam asked. He was getting into the swing of this a little, Mira realised, but not enough. That should have been a lawyer's question, but she feared he hadn't figured out their role in the grand scheme of things.

"The relic lets the creatures from their world come to ours, after a fashion," Jonathan explained. "I want to open the door from this side. But I need a key and, well, blood is the great materialising agent."

Chloe sobbed at the realisation, and Mira reshuffled her priorities. "You've got plenty of blood with me and Sam, you don't need Chloe. She's just a kid, Jonathan, and I don't think you want to be what that means. Let Chloe go."

"I'm afraid I do need her," Jonathan said. "The ritual requires three sacrifices. The first opens the portal here in this room. The second and it should encompass the city."

"And the third?" asked Sam, and this time he knew the answer before he asked.

"Everywhere," Jonathan said with a beatific smile.

On the far side of the park from Treasurer's House, people had filled the Minster to hear the archbishop give a sermon. It had been a long one. And while the majority were still spiritually enraptured by her words, a few feet had gone to sleep and at least one watch had been surreptitiously glanced at. But what happened next caught everyone's attention. It began with a rush of wind, although from where no one could say. Candles guttered across the immense vaulted space. A flash of brilliant light shone off every surface for a fraction of a second, then was gone.

And a naked woman was standing in the middle of the church.

She felt along her side as if looking for something and not finding it, and looked around the room, rapidly getting her bearings.

"Wait, I just end up back here?" she called out to no one in particular. "That's it? I mean, glad not to be dead an' all, but they might have scutting told me. I've been scared of nowt for centuries."

She noticed the chorus of murmuring and the huge number of eyes turning in her direction, as well as those trying not to and failing. A woman three rows back slapped the arm of the distracted man alongside her, while a boy directly in front of her stared open-mouthed. She turned on the spot to look up at the disapproving face above the lectern.

"Un-fucking-believable," the archbishop sighed.

"How do, Your Grace," Holly said. "Long story. I'll be on me way, and you can pick up wherever you'd got to."

"Holly!"

At the back of the church, she saw Delia, clutching her purple topcoat and red umbrella. Holly ran down the central aisle, the gabble of the congregation growing as she passed each row. Delia handed over the coat which she quickly wrapped about herself.

"I met your sister. She did this to me," Delia indicated her left leg, where a bandage was visible through a dark-edged tear in her trousers. "She told me you'd be here and I had to give you this. Sorry, whose side is she on again?"

"I ask meself that a lot," replied Holly, gratefully accepting the umbrella.

This time Delia was even more sure she could see the ivy pattern moving.

"And she said you'd need this… it was very important." Delia handed over Holly's ring, which she quickly slipped on. The ivy writhed once again as she did, the pattern running along the handle as well, although it hadn't been there before.

Holly took in Delia's bewildered expression and flourished the ring finger in front of her.

"This makes the thing in the brolly work," she said by way of a limited explanation. "It's a bit handier than what I usually use. Now we need to get out of here."

"Where are we going?" Delia asked as she limped after a rapidly departing Holly.

"Treasurer's House, fast as we can," Holly replied. "You know what? Mira's right."

"About what?" Delia asked.

"This is totally summat I would do."

"So you're going to kill us," Mira said. "Well, I'm not planning on lying back and accepting my fate. What about you, Sam?"

"Not a chance," Sam replied. There was bravado there. That was good. Hopefully.

"I wouldn't have expected anything else. I did hope to be civilised about all this." Jonathan reached into his coat pocket and produced a revolver.

Mira's heart leapt. She had faced all kinds of monsters, but nobody had ever pointed a gun at her before.

Sam moved around the circle to get as close to her as his chains would allow.

"What did you think I was going to do?" Jonathan asked. "Cut out your heart with a ceremonial dagger while chanting to my heathen gods? Blood's blood… it doesn't matter how it gets there, it just has to find its way."

He turned on the spot, training the gun on Mira, then Sam,

and finally settling on Chloe. She scrambled backwards until her chains would let her go no further.

"Jonathan, please, don't do this," Mira pleaded.

"I'm sorry. I don't have another way."

"Mira?" Chloe was begging with her eyes; demanding Mira find a way to save her.

"You said you have daughters, Jonathan!" Mira shouted. "You couldn't do this to them, you can't do this to Chloe! Imagine your children, Jonathan! What would you do if it was them?"

"I am," he said, and Mira caught a glimpse of a tear in the corner of his eye. "I need this or they died for nothing. And no, that doesn't make it any easier."

Mira strained as hard as she could on the chains. She saw Sam moving in the other direction around the circle, trying to get to Chloe, shield her, do something to stop this. None of it was enough. Nevertheless, she pulled on the chains until her shoulders ached. Whatever it took, she had to get free. She had let down Greg, and Susan, and Peter, and Malcolm. She had let down Holly and Delia.

"Mira, please," whimpered Chloe. "Nan…"

A shot rang out, echoing into the empty space of the hall.

Her teacher was showing her college prospectuses. Her nan was baking a cake. There was a book, with all the secrets she would have to learn. She was four years old when she found out magic was real. The princess was sleeping and needed her help. She excitedly showed her dad the stone arrowhead, and did not see it made him unhappy. She was twelve and magic had become a job. She could see it made her dad unhappy. She wanted to tell her friends but knew she mustn't. She knew who she fancied but they mustn't know that either. Nobody must know everything. Keep you for you. Be cool. She wanted chips.

Mira slumped to her knees as she let down Chloe.

Holly smashed the window of Jonathan's car with the handle of her umbrella, opened the door and gathered up her discarded clothes.

"That's more like it," she said. "Not that I don't appreciate the coat, but I think I'm gonna need a bit more on where I'm going."

She turned to the side door of the house, and pushed it open with an ominous creak. Voices were vaguely audible.

"Right, I have no idea what's going on in there," Holly said. "But it's nowt good, so you need to get yourself gone. Get as far away as you can."

"Okay," said Delia.

"Don't argue with me, it's… Wait, hang on, you're not arguing with me, are you?"

"No, I've just been stabbed and I'm absolutely terrified."

"Well… good," said Holly, feeling derailed by Delia's compliance. "Look, thank you for this, and all your help and… ooh scut."

She bundled her clothing under one arm, pulled Delia close with the other and kissed her.

"Now run," she said, and slammed the door between her and the quietly befuddled woman shunting her glasses up her nose. Once inside, she pulled a face as the door closed behind her.

"If the world don't end, I am so gonna regret that."

CHAPTER 33

The blood should not have been doing that.

Chloe's body lay sprawled across the marble, blood flowing from the neat hole in her forehead, but not forming a puddle. It moved purposefully, as if it were still a living thing. It rippled across the floor in a stream, until it reached the centre of the hall, directly below the artefact.

As soon as it did, a burst of brilliant red light erupted from the cylinder, blasting up into the rolling clouds in the rafters, which turned from pale blue to a deep and foreboding crimson. The dense mist spread further, electricity crackling through the vapour. The room grew darker as the doors and windows disappeared from the walls.

Jonathan levelled the revolver in Sam's direction, then turned to Mira with a look of bizarre tenderness on his face.

"I was going to save you until last," he explained. "It'd be nice to have someone who understands to share this with. But if you'd rather go next, it's your choice."

"I have nothing to say to you," Mira replied coldly. "You don't get to be nice. Not after what you just did."

Jonathan nodded, and levelled the gun at her head. Mira saw Sam yanking on his chains, roaring in fury as he failed to tear them loose from their moorings.

She closed her eyes and waited.

"Hello, again," came a familiar husky brogue from behind her. "Whoever you are."

Mira spun in the direction of the voice, while Sam ceased his struggle and Jonathan stared open-mouthed. Holly sauntered into the room, twirling her red umbrella nonchalantly.

"It's not possible," Jonathan muttered. "I saw you die."

"Oh, Dylan. You didn't listen to what I told you all those years ago, did you? Don't ever trust my sister."

Jonathan was visibly losing control as the storm intensified, while Holly poked idly at the blood caked on her clothes.

"She didn't even kill Delia. I think she might be growing as a person," Holly explained, provoking a cry of relief from Mira. She shoved a probing finger through the tear in her waistcoat left by Erin's knife. "Although I wish she hadn't done this…"

Her mood shifted in a heartbeat at the sight of Chloe. She looked on Dylan with rage, but also disappointment.

"And I really wish you hadn't done that."

All Jonathan's justifications unravelled in the face of the woman he had stood with in this place, when he was little more than a boy. Mira could see more than a little of that boy in his eyes now.

"She was necessary…"

"She was fifteen," Holly said, a stark fury in the words.

"Be that as it may," Jonathan protested. "The well is opening. A new world is coming."

"Well done you," Holly spat, and glanced over into an empty corner of the hall. "If she could see you now."

Jonathan turned to look into the same spot, and Mira knew who stood there. Somehow, Jonathan was also able to see McAllister's ghost, but the terrible sight clearly held no fear for him.

"I'm sure she can," he said. "I hope she'd have understood in the end. That this house was built to bring them forth. It can't be stopped."

"S'pose not. Reckon I'll give it a bloody good go, mind." Holly yanked on her umbrella. She tossed the canopy aside to reveal a short, slim blade marked with the same ivy pattern as her ring, like the magic sword Mira had seen her use in the past. It made the same ringing noise as it arced through the air, but higher and sharper.

Her thumb flipped a catch on the handle and it was not one blade but two. Holly swung one in each hand to slice at the chains holding Mira and Sam. The links struck by the blades shattered.

Each other link in turn went the same way until the path of destruction reached their manacles, which burst open.

They ran towards each other as soon as they were free, holding close for a moment before forming up behind Holly.

"You're all done, Dylan," Holly said, the swords raised before her. "No puppets, no Erin. Just you and us."

The clouds rolled back. When they looked up, it was like seeing the sea from the air, a rolling mass of liquid gently washing across the ceiling. The waters looked dark and deep and something was stirring in them. A shape was looming closer.

"Oh, and the dragon," Holly added.

CHAPTER 34

Mira looked around the room and found it was all wrong.

A long, shimmering limb the colour of bronze descended from the pool in the ceiling. Fingers, or possibly toes, or some other prehensile digit, spread out like the roots of a tree. Mira felt the floor shift beneath her feet, and looked around to see the room expanding, the walls towering higher and higher while the floor stretched outwards as it grew to accommodate what was coming.

A second limb descended next to the first before the rest of it landed, curled up in a great metallic ball. The walls vibrated frenetically as it stretched out, long arms reaching upwards above curling horns sprouting from a smooth head.

Sam groaned, and clutched his head in pain. He was far from used to the otherworldly, and this was definitely going in at the deep end.

Jonathan dropped to his knees in almost religious awe, gazing adoringly at what he had brought forth. Holly clutched her swords.

It was a humanoid figure. Or rather she was, that was immediately impressed upon Mira by the shape, which looked like it was carved from bronze. She stood some twenty feet tall on impossibly long and slender legs, like one of Dali's elephants in human form. Her torso was disproportionately small, the waist cinched like an insect's, and its long, powerful arms terminated in sharp talons. The face gazed down at them, and it was the face of the helmet, of the Horned Men, all pale imitations of the horror before them. Teeth jutted from a lipless mouth and no eyes sat above them, merely thin circular patterns decorating the gleaming surface. The Horned Beast had come at last.

"Níðhöggr," whispered Jonathan.

The great horned head swayed from side to side, and Mira instinctively looked away as it turned in her direction. She felt vibrations through her body as the creature analysed the tiny people before her.

where is he

The question reverberated in Mira's mind. She had not heard it spoken but it was there in her head nonetheless. A quick glance around the room told her that they had all heard it.

"Who's he when he's at home?" Holly replied, and gestured to Jonathan with a sword. "That's the bugbear what brought you here, if that's what you mean. If he's wasted your time, take him and clear off."

where is he
the one i sent here
i would face him

"I don't know," Holly protested. "Please tell me there's not more to this. I thought we'd figured it all out."

where is he
where is

Níðhöggr paused for a moment and twitched irritably, like she was looking for the right word.

prospero

Holly looked to Mira for an answer, but they were both equally confused.

"We don't understand," said Mira. "We don't know who that is."

your word

"Fine, you have our word, we don't know any Prospero," Holly said.

your word

"Our word." Mira was starting to understand. "Not giving our word, our word for something. She's trying to communicate; she's chosen a word from our minds that she thinks we'll understand. Prospero. She's looking for someone that word describes, someone like the Shakespeare character. Am I right?"

that is your word for what he is
bring him here now

"Okay, so Prospero," Mira said, feeling every day of six years out from English lit A-level. "Help me out here, Holly, you're the Tudor in the room."

"Isn't he from the last one?" Holly asked. "Brave new world, that one. I know a bit of me stuff, but be fair, I were long gone by the time that came out."

"Prospero was a sorcerer," Sam chipped in, delving through his memory as quickly as he could. "He was exiled to an island, he has a daughter, and a monster and a fairy servant, he wants revenge on his brother I think."

"It's Jonathan," Mira realised. "He's an exile, a father, he made a monster and does magic. It's him she wants."

Níðhöggr turned to regard Jonathan closer, her torso bent in a crescent shape and pivoting impossibly at the waist while her legs remained firmly positioned on pointed toes. It was like she had no internal structure, or someone had skim-read human anatomy to create her. Dissatisfied, she stood and flexed her claws in irritation.

not him
bring me prospero
he will die before me

As she spoke, it was like somebody was shaking the world, and they felt every vibration.

"Wait a mo. Exile," Holly said, recovering quickly as a disturbing realisation came to her. "Are you the one what exiled him? Is there another one of you knocking about my city?"

this one knows
she has his touch on her
where is he

"Oh, pumpernickel," Holly grumbled. "Look, I am a bit different from this lot as you've probably clocked, and if this is a family thing like Sam were saying… well, I know a thing or two about that, but I promise you, I've never seen owt like you in all me puff."

he is here

we sent him here

"Well, he's not here now, so wasted trip!"

then it is safe for us

"Safe for who?" asked Sam.

"Yeah, may have just made things worse. Sorry," Holly explained as the words came louder than ever.

i watched this place and saw wonder

i made myself in your image

i could not end him so i bound him here where he would be gone from the plain but i still wanted more

to walk among you as the gods you worship to make this place mine

i would build a new plain of devastation upon which to battle among your dark satanic mills and end my brother while he slumbered in the earth

"But the Romans kicked your arse back through that portal, didn't they?" Holly asked, daring to mock the towering figure.

they were strong none are strong now

"I am not just strong," Holly said. "I am mickle, and so's me mate. And her fella's holding up pretty good so far, considering. And I'll tell you summat else. He's wrong – this house weren't built to bring you here. It were made to stop you going one step further."

what are you to stand against me

"I am the King in the Mountain," Holly replied with absolute confidence. "My life has been longer and stranger than you can possibly imagine. The world has grown and changed around me, becoming nothing I could foresee, and I learned to live in it. I hold a light against the shadows and I do not fear them. I have been alone but I am not anymore."

She snatched a glance at Mira and Sam, before turning her gaze back to the creature.

"And I know why."

Níðhöggr rose up, lifting her claws above her head. Her arms stretched to impossible lengths and the ceiling retreated from them, as if the world hoped to escape what she might do to it.

Her talons sank into the clouds and pulled them aside. Shapes were moving through the pool. Lots of shapes.

"Holly, plan?" Mira asked, as shimmering bronze bodies emerged from the liquid.

"Yeah, hold this a mo?" said Holly, handing her a sword as she plucked something from her pocket. It was a small tube, which she placed to her lips and blew. The noise that emerged was like a thousand great horns reverberating through the house.

Mira gave a cry of surprise to find a Roman soldier standing right next to her.

The great hall was full of Romans. They stood shoulder to shoulder across the floor, shields formed in a wall ahead of them and spears gripped ready for battle. But they weren't just on the floor. Ranks of soldiers stood on every wall like it was flat level ground and all eyes were fixed on the slippery, sinuous creatures emerging from the undulating waters of the portal. A single voice, low and whispery, yet proud, echoed across the great hall and beyond.

LEGIONNAIRES. WE FIGHT FOR THE RIGHT MARDY BITCH.

"Guys, c'mon!" protested Holly, as she snatched her sword back from Mira. "Oh, never mind. Righty-ho, dragon lady. What do you make of me brave new world now?"

Níðhöggr roared her defiance and swept claws across one wall.

A rank of Romans scattered and quickly reformed. The creatures from the portal were dropping into the hall to stand by their mistress.

"War it is, then," Holly said grimly.

CHAPTER 35

A creature like a smaller version of Niohggr dropped to the ground in front of them. It stood six feet tall, but in a hunched, animalistic posture. Glittering silvery fluid oozed between its teeth as it lashed out at Holly with a claw, but she parried its blow with one sword while circling to slice its head clean off with the other.

The severed skull exploded into a cloud of shimmering metallic bubbles, while the body liquefied into the same metallic substance.

"Mercury?" said Sam.

"Venom-spewing serpents," Mira countered.

More of the monsters descended from the portal, and the Romans stood fast in their ranks, pushing forward as one to drive them back.

Jonathan scrambled to his feet and made for the exit.

"Get after him!" Holly shouted, as she took on another of Níðhöggr's army.

"Where's he going?" Mira called back.

"I don't know but I doubt it's good!" Holly swung both swords in front of her, neatly bisecting her opponent. "And don't freak out, but it's gonna get weird in here!"

Mira grabbed Sam's hand and they fled, her mind reeling at her surroundings. The walls of the great hall had expanded outwards, branching at every conceivable angle. The surfaces drifted like icebergs, disappearing and reappearing as they moved against each other. A group of Romans stepped from the highest point of the far wall and marched onto the floor that was simultaneously a great distance below and right next to them.

And in the midst of it all stood the titanic figure of Níðhöggr, revelling in the mayhem she had unleashed.

"Weird," Mira said. "Good to know."

Everything was peaceful as Caroline ran across the Minster Gardens, which worried her far more than if the sky was falling. A familiar figure stood in the park, looking at Treasurer's House through dazed and uncertain eyes.

"Delia!" she shouted. "What's going on? I can't get hold of anyone!"

"He took Sam and Mira in there," Delia said falteringly. "Holly's gone in to save them. She said that something terrible's going to happen so I should stay out here."

"And that's the plan, is it?" Caroline asked. She could see Delia contemplating the options. As soon as the wheel spun round to the appropriate place, she brought out the baton.

"Right then. In we go."

Jonathan ran up the stairs, with Mira and Sam in pursuit. They'd have caught him easily under normal circumstances. But the stairs weren't behaving right now.

It started with getting bigger, the steps growing wider and more numerous beneath their skittering feet, stretching up and up ahead of them, with Jonathan disappearing into the distance. A rift tore through the middle of the floor, and Mira and Sam clutched each other to stay on the same side. Now there were two staircases, but they weren't lying flat. They curled around each other like a double helix spiralling on and on forever. The walls smoothed out into a cylindrical tube that spun around them… although Mira was struggling to tell if it was spinning or they were or both. None of which was the strangest part.

As the two staircases drew closer together, another Sam and Mira became visible on the other path, keeping perfect pace with them. They stared open-mouthed at each other for a moment.

"Stop gawping at us and get after him!" said Mira, but she

wasn't sure if she'd said it to Sam, or to the other Mira, or if the other Mira had said it to her. Had she heard it or said it? She didn't know, but decided to listen anyway.

There was still only one Jonathan, who only became visible when the staircases crossed each other. He turned and fired, the bullet splitting into two to travel along both routes at once.

Mira pushed Sam out of the path of the weirdly slow-moving projectile, but out of the corner of her eye, saw the other Sam doing the same for the other her. Carl would have a field day with the philosophical implications if they lived long enough to tell him.

They came to the top of the stairs, and reality snapped back into place. Sam and Mira collided with Mira and Sam and two figures fell in a heap on the perfectly normal landing. Sam looked around nervously for his doppelganger.

"Where did we go?" he asked.

"I'm not sure they were ever real," Mira guessed, and hoped it was true.

A blow sent Holly reeling and her swords clattered from her grip just as a rolling motion swept across the floor, carrying them away. Disarmed, she settled for grabbing her attacker's horns with both hands and bringing its head down sharply onto her knee until the neck bent backwards.

Most of the Romans were maintaining their traditional blocky formations with rigid discipline, driving the creatures back. However, a few had dropped from the ranks to join her, tackling the foes that broke through the lines one on one, while cavalry circled the room to contain the fighting.

Níðhöggr was getting personally involved now, lashing out with her claws and sending Romans flying in every direction. The legionnaires were tough and already dead, but Holly could see some of them fading to nothing when struck down.

A horseman rode past and she made a grab for the back of his armour, hauling herself up behind him and galloping across the battleground. As they drew close to her swords, she swung herself down to grab them, and slashed out at the serpents as they rode on.

Caroline gently pushed open the side door and stepped through with Delia following close behind. They could hear a clamour of shouting in the distance. The young archaeologist noted the presence of the great sculpted metal eagle she had seen before.

"Oh gosh," she whispered.

"What is it?" Caroline asked.

Delia was frozen to the spot, watching the statue with rapt attention.

"Three things. First, you'd really think I'd have a reflection in that mirror, but I don't at the moment. Second, this room was definitely on the other side of the house last time I was here."

"And the third thing?" Caroline asked, and was answered by a scraping of metal on metal.

Horns rose from behind the eagle's wings, as its head turned to look at her.

"I think this statue might be coming to life," Delia squeaked.

"I can't explain what just happened," Mira said as they crept through the oddly silent corridors. "At a guess, I'd say the rules of wherever those things come from apply to the house now."

"Right, so local by-laws of physics," Sam said, trying to ease his fear with a joke. "And the paintings moving?"

Mira looked up at the portraits lining the walls, and noted the faces turning to follow them. A plump-faced Regency gentleman in a mighty wig bowed his head and she automatically returned the gesture.

"Memories of the house asserting themselves," Mira replied.

"Did you make that up?"

"Yes, I did," Mira admitted. "But it made me feel better at any rate."

They turned the next corner to be greeted by four deafening bursts of noise as Jonathan emptied the gun in their direction. Sam grabbed Mira and pushed her aside, then flung himself to the ground. A series of dull clicks followed and Sam looked up to see Jonathan running into the distance. The portly subject of the portrait was now bleeding from four wounds to his chest, but looked remarkably calm about it.

Mira was nowhere to be seen.

The eagle tore itself from the wall in a shower of plaster and lunged towards Caroline and Delia. It couldn't fly – the mechanism wasn't about to fight the weight of solid metal. It used its wings like forelimbs to stalk forward, while Caroline struck at it uselessly with her baton. Delia retreated up the stairs, and as she did, noticed that the paintings on the walls were moving. The woman in the portrait closest to her was pointing directly up, and Delia's eyes followed the gesture to the chandelier above her head, with arms made of slim glass tubes in curling shapes. It looked like an octopus, a comparison she instantly regretted as she spotted another mechanism lurking in its branches. The fixture swooped down, the smooth arms writhing and wrapping around her as it lifted her into the air.

A smell of salt filled Mira's nostrils as she found herself in another room. On the table in the centre sat a large display case of wood and glass, with a model ship inside. She looked back the way she had come and detected a faint ripple on the wall.

"Cool. Let's see what else we can find," she said to herself, and walked through it.

this is good

Níðhöggr's creatures were dying and the spirits of the defenders were fading and it was all as one. All was chaos and destruction. The spectacle of time thrilled her as it passed.

when this is done, i will seek him out and finish our fight, make this whole world into this battle

She yanked the chandelier from the ceiling and swung it hard into the floor, which exploded into a shower of fragments. The broken floorboards reformed into an uneven structure of sharp angles.

Holly looked up at Níðhöggr, and knew that battling her minions was getting them nowhere. More serpents were slipping through the gap between worlds every moment. She would have to go for the head of the snake. She noted a rank of Romans striding at a right angle to her along the wall nearest Níðhöggr, and gave a sharp whistle.

"Guys! Steps!" she shouted and they arranged themselves precisely into a diagonal line.

They held their shields out flat over their heads so she could hop from one to the next, rising higher and higher up her improvised staircase until she was level with Níðhöggr's face. She jumped and struck with both blades, sending a rain of seething metallic fluid across the hall. Momentum carried her forward and gravity kept its nose out – but her freefall did not take her out of the monster's reach, and she was snatched from the air.

"Mira?" Sam whispered as he pushed open the door, when he was struck hard across the shoulder by a heavy length of wood and fell to the floor.

He looked up to see Jonathan standing over him, a pike clutched in his hands. Before Sam could move, the point was at his throat. Behind the wild-eyed professor, he could see a clock sliding slowly down the wall, and a woman in a grey dress with a finger poised at her lips. He hadn't the strength to question any of it.

"You won't stop me," Jonathan said. "It's here somewhere, I know it is. There's a way in, and I'm going to find it."

Sam wasn't listening. He was distracted by the movement behind Jonathan, as the tapestry dominating one side of the room bulged and swayed. Fingers forced their way through the threads and tore an opening through which Mira emerged. Behind her, the wooden wall rippled like water. She grabbed a lamp from a small table, and brought it crashing down on the back of Jonathan's head. He slumped unconscious at her feet.

The grey lady smiled knowingly as she faded from view.

Níðhöggr's hand pressed Holly down into the floor, which shuddered under the impact. Beneath her back, the tiles dug in, rearranging themselves to grip her more tightly. The monster raised her free hand high above her horns, and Holly heard the terrible voice in her mind as everything shook violently around her.

this is the world now

the shadows don't care if you fear them or not

you foresaw nothing so see no more

The claw descended and Holly's vision exploded into a blinding white.

CHAPTER 36

"There's a room downstairs and everything in the house leads there," Mira explained. "Like it's the heart of the place. Maybe Holly's right – the house is helping us somehow."

"I'm not going to pretend to understand, I'm just glad you got here. What do we do now?" Sam was binding the unconscious Jonathan to a table leg with strips of the ruined tapestry. Mira had winced each time he'd torn a piece off.

"Well, Holly's leading a Roman legion into battle against an army of aliens and the house is going all Escher," Mira said. "I'm thinking maybe we need to find a way out."

"That's it?" Sam said, looking surprised at her answer. "You want to run away?"

"Quite a lot of the time, actually." Mira could tell he was struggling, but knew what they had to do. "Sam, this is really dangerous. Even by my standards, this is really dangerous."

"Then we'd better look out for each other," he said, picking up the pike Jonathan had wielded from the carpet and passing it to her, before lifting its twin down from the wall.

"Don't say I didn't warn you," Mira said, and turned to the rippling surface where the tapestry had hung. "Run at the wall."

Holly felt Níðhöggr's grip relaxing, and scrambled blindly away. Her vision was clearing and she could make out Romans stabbing at the monster's arm with their short swords. Rough hands pulled her to her feet. The right side of her face burned as she focused on the face of the ghostly soldier before her.

DAUGHTER OF CARTIMANDUA. came the voice of the legion. *YOU SHOULD LEAVE THIS PLACE.*

"Hold up your hand," said Holly, bringing bloody fingers away from her cheek.

The soldier obeyed without question.

"Five," said Holly. "That means I'm still good for a bit more."

Sam and Mira emerged from the house's rippling gaps and fell flat on the floor of the court room. Somewhere in the distance, wood creaked.

"This is the room I was talking about," she said, inspecting the model ship as she picked herself up. "It all leads here."

"Mira, can you hear birds?" Sam asked, and she found that she could. The creaking was growing louder and there was a pungent smell of salt and fish.

"You said memories of the house were making the paintings move," Sam ventured.

"I told you, I made that up."

"Yes, but now we're in a room with a model ship, and I can hear the sea," Sam explained. "Give yourself a bit more credit on this one."

Water was trickling down the walls in one corner.

"I don't want to be right about this," Mira said. "I want to get out of this room and go and fight an army of monsters. Now stop thinking about the sea."

They turned to the door and the creaking intensified.

It was too late and the tide engulfed them.

The problem with striking at the head of the snake is that everyone else gets the same idea.

Holly stood back-to-back with Mr Five Fingers, fighting off the serpents surrounding them. She wanted to find out his actual name, if they had them anymore. Níðhöggr's minions came on in waves no matter how many they destroyed. New foes crawled over the melting bodies of their forerunners.

Holly felt claws shred through the back of her waistcoat. She turned to see a serpent had thrust an arm right through Mr Five Fingers' body, and he was slowly fading from existence. With no one at her back, they came from all sides, engulfing her with their shimmering, twisting mass. One sword slipped from her grip so she tightened her hold on the other and lashed out blindly, her free hand groping for its twin.

Her fingers found something, an umbrella handle, but not the one she had expected. She glanced over and saw the black grappling umbrella she had given to Mira. She raised her arm and fired blind, then as soon as she felt the impact reeled herself in the direction of the ceiling, casting aside her attackers. She halted the reel to get her bearings and found herself dangling at right angles to the world.

The room had gone, and Mira was deep underwater. She forced her eyes open and could see nothing. Just water, all around her, spreading out forever. If it had a surface, she couldn't make it out, but kicked her way upwards all the same. Even if she couldn't make it into the open air, she didn't want to sink. She looked down, and there was no bottom either. Her legs were tiring, and despite her best effort she began to drift slowly down into the depths.

There were voices in the water, a multitude of distant soft voices, each repeating its single phrase over and over again.

Oh, dear, I fear I've killed us both.

It occurred to Mira as she sank that Sam had got this wrong. The room hadn't become a sea because there was a ship here. Someone had placed the ship in the room because, subconsciously, they knew there was a sea here. The room *was* a sea, it was a place between places.

She felt pleased with her intuition as she sank into the sea of voices, when she was distracted by something new, louder and more urgent than the rest.

Don't you dare, it said, and familiar rough fingers gripped her wrist.

The sea dropped away the second they were together. There was a door in front of them and it fell open, a torrent of water carrying them into the corridor beyond. Gasping, Mira forced herself to her feet, leaning on the pike that had fallen alongside

279

her. Sam lay slumped against the doorway, and she tilted his head to look at her.

"Sam, I know you've been through a lot today," she said, resting her forehead against his. "But if you make me give you mouth-to-mouth and we end up kissing, I will impale you."

"Wouldn't dream of it," he whispered, and she kissed him anyway.

"Caroline, help!" choked Delia, as she clutched at the glass tentacles engulfing her, her hands gliding uselessly over the smooth surface. Caroline was retreating up the stairs, trying to keep the eagle at bay with ineffectual blows from her baton.

"Bit busy right now!" she snapped.

The bird's wingtips sliced into the fraying carpet as its beak pecked forward.

Caroline looked up, catching sight of where the fitting for the chandelier was screwed into the ceiling. It didn't look that strong. Maybe not the weight of two people strong.

She wrapped her arms around Delia's waist and pushed them away from the stairs, sending the whole fixture swaying. They were swinging in space, a few feet off the ground, and the fitting was grinding perilously. She felt something give way above them, and they went flying to land in a heap alongside the staircase. The chandelier's momentum sent it back the other way to crash into the wall of the stairwell, the remains landing with a shattering cacophony on top of the eagle.

Caroline helped Delia to her feet. She wasn't hurt, but the wound in her leg had not enjoyed the experience.

"Come on, we need to find…" Caroline began, then turned to follow Delia's awestruck gaze in the direction of the stairs.

A glassy tendril was draped over the bannister and a bent brass beak was poking around the edge, solid eyes locking on to them.

"I think we just made an octobird," Delia said.

The Great Hall was even more twisted than when Mira and Sam had left it. The Romans had abandoned their ranks, or been forced out of formation. Individual soldiers were scattered about, engaged in brutal one-on-one struggles with the serpents. Níðhöggr stooped languidly to scoop Romans from the ground. And on the far side of the room, the ghosts of two small boys were playing marbles without a care in the world. Mira was no expert on warfare, but she had a sense that things were not going well.

Her eyes roamed the chaos for a glimpse of Holly, finally catching her standing on a sheer wall, one side of her face coated with blood. She had lost one of her swords, and replaced it with the grappling brolly.

"Holly!" she shouted, catching her friend's attention as she struck down another creature, whose body exploded into sparks. "Give me the whistle!"

Holly passed her sword to her other hand to rummage in a waistcoat pocket, and flung an object through the air. Mira ran forward into the mayhem with Sam following, and snatched the hide tube Holly had summoned the Romans with. She placed it to her lips and blew.

"Legionnaires! Form ranks!" she shouted, looking to Sam as he awaited instructions. "Follow my lead. It's like rugby, but with spears."

They gripped their pikes as Romans formed up alongside and behind them, shields braced together into a solid wall at the front, and a ranked mass of soldiers at their back. They marched forward as one, pushing the rolling mass of serpents aside. The Romans at the front produced swords to stab at their enemies, while those behind extended spears to thrust through the gaps. Níðhöggr's legs stood before them, and Mira drove the formation forward.

High above, Holly could see what Mira was thinking. Slipping her sword into her belt, she raised the umbrella and fired a line at a suitable wall. As Mira's troops slammed into the monster's shins, she ran and leapt, swinging herself through the air with both hands on the umbrella handle, and extending her braced legs to crash feet first into Níðhöggr's face. The monster was thrown off balance, toppling slowly to the ground. As she fell, a sweeping hand struck Holly. She lost her grip on the handle and was sent flying, then vanished through another burst of ripples.

Holly slammed into a huge expanse of white cloth which she clung to as tightly as she could. The space around her was dark and shadowy, her grip was faltering, and wherever she was, gravity was behaving itself. She released one hand to draw her sword, slashed into the fabric and let go, the slicing of her blade through the cloth slowing her descent until she hit solid ground. It was only then that she realised she was on the deck of a ship, towering masts rising above her head.

But something didn't feel right. The planks she stood on weren't individual boards. As her fingers roamed its surface, she realised it wasn't wood either. It was bone, a solid piece of whale bone sculpted to look like a deck. Her vision grew accustomed to the shadowy surroundings, until she could see the glass display case around her and the court room beyond that.

She was standing on the deck of the model ship. And she was not alone. Serpents were popping into existence high above her and tumbling downwards through the air. She gripped her sword and prepared to repel boarders.

The Romans weren't about to give Níðhöggr the opportunity to find her feet again and swarmed over the prone monster, stabbing at her with swords and spears. Sam and Mira were left to fend off the serpents coming to their mistress' aid, striking out with all too mundane pikes that did little damage, but at least kept the creatures at bay. There was no time to think about where Holly had gone.

"Oh, great. You." Mira saw Jonathan stumble into the room. He walked through the battle not caring, making determinedly for the fallen Níðhöggr. As he placed a hand upon her horn, a look of rapture covered his face.

A deep roar rang out, as Níðhöggr beat her fists upon the shattered ground. Jonathan hastily backed away as Romans were thrown in all directions. The creature flipped upwards, bending impossibly at the ankles to rise to her full, terrible height. She bellowed with apocalyptic rage.

im very angry, Mira heard in her head.

Caroline and Delia ran, the mess of tentacles and twisted metal shambling in their footsteps. The tendrils of the chandelier wormed their way through the broken parts of the statue, criss-crossed with fine cracks as they bent into new, aggressive shapes. It dragged the brazen bulk forward, leaving a trail of shards behind.

Delia slammed the door of a small room shut behind her, while Caroline looked for something to brace it with. There was little furniture, aside from a wooden-framed display case on a central table. Inside was a model ship, which Caroline stopped and stared at with a look of utter disbelief on her face.

Delia leaned in close until she could see what had caught her attention. On the deck of the ship stood the miniature figure of Holly, wielding a sword as she fought off a succession of horned creatures.

"Holly?" said Delia. "Why are you tiny?"

Holly turned to look at the source of the sound and was momentarily taken aback by the gigantic figures towering over her. She kicked out at a serpent and sent it tumbling overboard, where it burst like a tiny firework on the tabletop.

"Throw the ship at the wall!" Holly shouted, cupping her hands around her mouth. She threw in a frenetic mime of picking something up and tossing it, then pointing in the direction she intended. The next boarder lunged at her, and she struck at its throat with her sword.

"I don't..." Delia began, then looked in the direction Holly was gesturing. The wallpaper was rippling gently, as if something were moving beneath it.

Caroline grasped the instruction, and took her baton to the display case, smashing the glass and splintering the wood into fragments. She tore the wreckage away as Holly dispensed with her last foe and ran to the prow of the ship.

"I think this might be really valuable," said Delia as she and Caroline scooped up the large model between them. "We're not going to get in trouble, are we?"

Caroline threw her a sideways look before they tossed the ship in the direction of the motion in the wall. In the instant it struck, the model vanished from sight.

"Where did it go?" asked Delia, right before the door burst off its hinges and the flailing octobird leapt onto her.

finite mortal alive things
   experience time as it runs out
Níðhöggr swept her talons slowly and gracefully, not decisively.
   playthings
Mira and Sam jabbed at her ineffectually with their pikes, to no avail. With a sudden burst of speed, her claws sank into ground that shattered beneath their feet. The floor crumbled to dust and they were drifting downwards into a quicksand of ground marble. The fragments compacted in around them, holding them fast no matter how much they struggled. Níðhöggr stood over them, looking pleased with herself.

   this is what your world will be now a world crushed a world made impossible
Mira forced her hand through the dust and into Sam's, gripping it tightly as they sank further, the powdered stone engulfing them on all sides as their fingers tried with all their strength to stay together.

   a world without saviours a world without
A great creaking and groaning echoed around the warped walls. It was coming from above, where the portal churned and frothed like never before. Mira gazed up into it with wonder at what she was seeing.

It was a ship. A vast tall ship, sails billowing from its towering masts, descending at great speed from the ceiling to fill the hall with its bulk. Expanded to life size, it was instantly noticeable to Mira that the hull was crafted from bone. Holly stood in the prow, clinging to a rope from the sails with one hand and brandishing her sword with the other, terrible purpose blazing in her one good eye.

"The dead man's ship…" breathed a stunned Jonathan as Mira heard Níðhöggr's borrowed words in her head one last time.

what the scut

The ship crashed hard into Níðhöggr's torso, smashing her to the ground under its weight. The prow was caved in by the impact but the rest of it kept coming. As the bone beneath her feet shattered, Holly jumped clear, gripped her sword above her head in both hands and brought the point slamming down hard into the centre of Níðhöggr's forehead, before rolling to the floor.

Rising to her feet, she pulled the sword clear and struck at the ground in a series of clumsy, brutal strokes, then stooped to lift Níðhöggr's severed head with both hands. The serpents were fleeing to the upper recesses of the ceiling, and gathered in clusters around the edges of the portal to witness their leader's destruction.

"As for you lot," shouted Holly into the rafters. "Sling your hook and don't come back."

She swung the head round by its horns and hurled it upwards. Once clear of her grasp, it moved on its own, as if the portal had a gravitational pull sucking it in. The serpents followed it into the breach, which pulled itself shut behind them with a clap of thunder. The clouds dispersed and the lights from above faded, before a more natural illumination took their place. Imperceptibly, the dimensions of the house resumed their natural shape. Mira found she and Sam were lying side by side on the floor, and stopped herself struggling against quicksand that was no longer there. Beside them sat the broken remains of the model ship, returned to its natural size, the fallen chandelier, and the remains of Jonathan's apparatus. At the edge of the hall, lay Chloe's body.

The octobird stopped moving. Delia looked up at the beak hovering an inch from her face, and felt the stabbing pain in her wrist where the statue had smashed down hard on her. Caroline hauled the unmoving heap of metal and glass off her, the parts of it that were chandelier grinding into sparkling dust under its own weight.

"I think we might have won," Delia winced. "In which case, I'd quite like an ambulance."

It was over, but something felt wrong to Mira. Holly stood silent and still. She had recovered her second sword, and both blades tensed in her grip. There was something primitive and ancient in her appearance. Her clothes were shredded and stained with both her own blood and the metallic fluids of the serpents. Her right eye was a ragged mess and dried gore caked her cheek. Mira could see Holly's true age, and more than that, a heritage. It frightened her more terribly than anything she had seen today.

"Bring forth the traitor," she ordered in a voice utterly unlike her own. She advanced on Jonathan, transferring both blades to one hand so she could drag him struggling to the centre of the room and hurl him to the floor.

Mira saw the blades shudder gently as her grip tightened.

"Holly, what are you doing?" Mira asked in horror.

Caroline was coming into the hall now, supporting an injured Delia. All eyes were fixed on the terrible figure before them.

"I will protect the city," Holly said, raising the swords above her head. "Against all threats."

"Right, so we're going to cut his head off and stick it up on Micklegate Bar, is that it?" Mira asked.

Jonathan looked to her in desperation.

"He brought this upon us," Holly continued. "He aided our enemies. This is my city. I will keep it safe. It will always be safe."

"No, this is *our* city," Mira insisted, fixing Holly's single fierce eye with her gaze. "All of us. And I'm telling you we don't do this anymore. You have protected the city. Now rest."

Mira noticed Holly was looking past her, to where Chloe lay, and beyond that. Mira could sense McAllister standing in that empty space. She caught a glimpse of movement out of the

286

restored window and saw the nurse who had come for Malcolm, waiting expectantly for the inevitable to take Jonathan.

"Holly, I know," Mira said. "But this isn't you. You said you remembered how to be a person right here. Don't make this the place where you forget."

Holly's hands trembled for a moment, and her eye closed. She turned the blades point down and handed them to Mira. Caroline stepped forward at Mira's invitation, leaving Sam to attend to Delia.

"Jonathan Fortune," said Caroline, producing handcuffs from her coat pocket. "I am arresting you on suspicion of murder, kidnapping and grand theft. You do not have to say anything, and frankly, anything you do say will sound batshit insane, so maybe keep it to yourself."

And the battle was won.

CHAPTER 37

First the police came, listening to Caroline's half-truths and explanations before taking Jonathan away. Paramedics followed, attending to Delia's broken wrist and gently ushering her from the house, while Chloe's body was carefully and respectfully loaded onto a stretcher. Nobody noticed the three figures seated in front of the fireplace, or the many more who waited on the edges of the Great Hall, their spears raised proudly.

When it was quiet, Holly stepped forward, wrapping her recovered greatcoat tightly around her. A single legionnaire came to meet her in the centre of the hall.

"We're done," Holly said with a pained smile. "Thank you. All of you. Now, you'd best be off. Nowt to worry about now."

UNTIL WE MEET AGAIN.

"You're done, fellas, really. The war's over. Be at peace."

EBORACUM WILL ALWAYS NEED US. WE WILL WAIT FOR THE DAY.

"Well, I hope you're wrong," Holly replied. "But I will be glad to have you lot about if you're not."

FAREWELL, DAUGHTER OF CARTIMANDUA. chorused the voices of the legion as one by one they faded from view. *FAREWELL, RIGHT MARDY BITCH.*

And then there were three. Mira and Sam took each other's hands and moved to where Holly knelt beside the wreckage of Jonathan's contraption, deep in her own thoughts. The relic that had brought so much pain lay shattered into fragments.

"I need to sleep for a week. And just eat chocolate all day

Sunday." Mira winced at Holly's wounded face. "Holly, you really look awful. You should get that seen to."

"It'll sort itself out," said Holly dismissively. "And if not, Angie and… well, it'll sort itself out. But right now, I'm wide awake, and there's one more job needs doing. And I'm gonna need you two with me."

One look told her they were on her side for whatever was coming.

"We'll start by putting that boat back where I found it."

Mira delicately placed the tangled wreckage of the model ship on the table. Its masts were snapped, the sails torn and the hull a crushed mass of fragments. She was sure there was an important history attached to it, and finding out would only upset her, so she resolved not to ask.

"There," said Holly, pointing with the black umbrella into the corner of the room.

Once again, Mira detected a faint ripple in the wallpaper.

"The hall's a portal out of their world. I always knew there were a way into it," Holly said with a melancholy smile. "And right where I met her an' all."

"That's what Jonathan was looking for," Sam realised. "I think he wanted to go to their world."

"But it doesn't just lead there. The whole house is connected through this room," Mira added. "And I think it takes you where you want to go. You wanted to get back to the battle, I wanted to find Sam."

"And Richard blundered in, and went somewhere far, far away," Holly said. "Well, I know where I need to go."

She triggered the spike on the umbrella and slammed it down hard into the floor, connected the handle to her belt and shrugged out of her coat.

"I'm going to find her, and I need you two to bring me back. You hold onto that brolly with all you've got, alright?"

"We'll be here," Mira promised. "Be careful."

"Wish me luck," she said with a broad grin, ran full pelt into the wall and vanished from view. The umbrella tilted after her and they both lunged to grip it, holding it upright. The line seamlessly disappeared into the wall.

At first it was dark. Then she was falling at tremendous speed, and then she was drowning, pressure driving the air from her lungs. And finally, she was sitting in a scratchy armchair. She opened both eyes, to her surprise, so blinked since she could.

She was in a small white room, and in front of her was a desk. Behind the desk was a man in a neatly pressed uniform.

"Just a moment, Miss," said Malcolm. "I'll see if she's ready for you yet."

"Oh, right. Thank you... Malcolm," Holly said, as the security guard picked up the telephone on his desk, spoke quietly into it, and returned it to the cradle.

"Professor McAllister will see you now, Miss," he said with a warm smile.

"Right, thank you, good," mumbled Holly, as she turned to the only door in the room. Her hand paused above the handle before curiosity and concern pulled her back. "Are you doing alright here, Malcolm?"

"Oh, yes, Miss," he said. "Couldn't be happier."

Holly pushed the door open, and all the screaming began.

The noise filled her mind, a constant babble of a thousand voices, all in anguish. A rain of blows and fire and cold swept through her body until she could feel nothing else and knew it would never end. Memories she could not remember and all of them bitter. But then as quickly as it had begun, it was replaced by soft music.

"I'll be right with you, take a seat."

Professor McAllister sat behind a desk in a wood-panelled office, her attention focused on the documents in front of her, which she furiously transcribed with a pen. A black umbrella occupied a coat stand by the door, and a record player sat in one corner, the sleeve of the album playing propped up against it. Kate was riding her kite in front of the yellow eye and all was well.

Holly pulled up a chair which seemed purposefully designed to sit much lower than the desk and waited.

There was another door to her right, which was pushed open by a girl in an oddly Victorian maid's dress. She carried a tray, and carefully placed two teacups and a small plate of biscuits on the desk.

"Thank you, Chloe," said McAllister, and Holly snapped to attention, catching a glimpse of the girl's face as she closed the door behind her.

"Hang on, Chloe and Malcolm – they're both here with you?" Holly asked hopefully.

"No, your subconscious put them here to make you feel better about their deaths," McAllister said matter-of-factly. "Sorry, I never was one to sugar-coat things, even before I spent decades in eternal torment. Do help yourself to a biscuit."

Holly picked up a hard, pale biscuit and noted the thin layer of clear crystals coating the rounded upper surface.

"These are sugar-coated," she pointed out.

"Yes, ironic, isn't it?" McAllister finally laid down her pen to look directly at Holly. "Chloe, I fear, was devoured by the portal. I couldn't speak to Malcolm's whereabouts; I imagine you'd have to talk to your sister's friends."

"And this is all a bit good for eternal torment," Holly added as she dunked her sugary biscuit in her tea and chomped down hard on the sweet crumbly surface.

"Eternal torment isn't every moment. Just any moment."

Holly leaned forward to look deep into her eyes. On the glossy surface of her irises, she fancied she could see some of the images that had greeted her in the scream. McAllister's sad smile confirmed what she was thinking.

"One learns to have good moments," she explained. "And in those moments, you learn to convince yourself it's over. And therein lies the trap because the wolf is never far from the door. But in those moments, I can at least be useful."

Holly looked to the coat rack as the realisation struck her. "The umbrella, during the battle, right where I needed it – that were you?"

McAllister smiled as she rose and walked to the door Chloe had emerged from.

"Come along. We've not got long, and there's a lot to get through."

Holly felt a twitching at her hip as she stood. The umbrella handle sat there, with no sign of the line coming from it. McAllister stepped through the door and Holly followed, the scream engulfing her in darkness once more.

The umbrella lurched, the line pulling at it and producing a creaking from the floorboards. Sam and Mira tightened their grip, their hands folding over each other as they did. They looked at each other and kept their promise to hold on as long as it took.

"What the scut?" shouted Holly as the bright yellow car sped past, nearly knocking her off her feet. She stood by the side of a busy road stretching impossibly far in both directions. Vast buildings, bigger than anything she had ever seen, towered on either side like the walls of a canyon, while lights flashed from the immense billboards mounted on them. More cars were speeding through the great concrete crevasse, and she was deafened by the noisy and frantic sounds of life.

"Oh my God, what is this place?" she shouted in terror at McAllister.

"You've lived in York all your life, haven't you?" she asked, earning a desperate nod in reply. "Welcome to the new one."

"Why did you bring me here? I'm supposed to be getting you out..." Holly asked, but the professor only pointed.

Far down the long, straight road stood two people. The tiny figure of Erin was instantly familiar to Holly, and beside her stood a man she could barely make out. It was like he was surrounded by a motion blur, vibrating softly.

A distant droning sounded overhead, and Holly felt the ground shake beneath her feet. Blossoming clouds of smoke were rising in the distance, and high above, she could see the outlines of dark shapes moving through the overcast sky. Balls of fire erupted from the shadows overhead, streaking through the air to strike the buildings, blasting them to dust and fragments. The screams began and did not stop.

"I wouldn't take this too literally, I think it's my subconscious this time," McAllister explained casually as the city was shattered to ash around them. "The blitz never quite reached Inverness, but I heard enough about it to have bad dreams when I was a girl. It's still my mind's go-to place when it needs a cataclysm, even now."

A ball of fire erupted beside Holly, and she was flung to the ground. She fell hard onto the pavement and felt a rain of hot dust sizzling on her back. When she looked up, McAllister was already walking away.

"Quickly now, still more to see," she said.

Holly picked herself up and dusted herself off, which was when she noticed the umbrella handle had gone.

Splinters tore from the floorboards as the umbrella vibrated in Sam and Mira's tight grip. With a grinding whistle, the line whipped away from the wall, swinging across the room in an arc to lie uselessly on the floor. It has been sheered clean through at one end. There were no more ripples on the wall.

"No!" shouted Mira, and ran to the corner, desperately feeling the wallpaper for any sign of movement. "Holly, come back! Holly, can you hear me?"

She turned back aghast to where Sam sat beside the umbrella, his face deep in thought.

"She's gone, Sam," Mira whispered.

"Do you have your phone on you?" he asked by way of reply, and Mira could sense a purpose in his request.

"No, I gave it to Holly... coat." They leapt to where Holly's greatcoat lay crumpled on the floor and Sam rummaged through the pockets for the familiar oblong shape. Once he had it, he was already moving from the room, and Mira could only trail confused in his wake.

"What are you doing? We can't phone another dimension!"

she protested as Sam came to the Great Hall, thumbing at the device purposefully.

"Holly said that was the way in, and here was the way out," Sam explained, his voice quick with newfound assurance. "If she's going to come back on her own, this is where she'll do it. Let's give her something we know she'll come towards."

"Like what?" Mira asked, then saw Sam was looking at her music and understood.

"Oh, you are wonderful," she said, and kissed his cheek before pointing at the track list for *Hounds of Love*. "That one."

Sam tapped the play symbol and held the phone high above his head. When the first words were heard, he began to sing 'Cloudbusting'.

The house looked small and old-fashioned amid the towering modernity of the new York, and had remained untouched by the bombardment. Holly could see McAllister in the doorway and ran to keep up as she stepped inside.

Beyond the door, a set of ancient, hand-carved stone steps headed downwards, with bare concrete walls on either side. Hearing the distant thump of explosions, Holly took a breath and stepped into the dark. The steps went straight down, and Holly could make out a crude doorway at the bottom through which a pale light emerged. When she looked to her feet, she saw spots of blood on each step. She thought she could hear a baby crying.

She stepped out into a square chamber of white marble. There were no windows or lights, but it was bright and gleaming inside. Plinths sat at the four corners of the room, with piles of broken stone sitting in front of each of them, where statues had been toppled.

"I know this place," Holly said warily. "How do I know this place?"

"I have no idea," McAllister replied. "I've never been here before. I just know this is where something terrible will to be set in motion."

"By who? There's no one here," Holly asked.

The baby let out one last piercing shriek before its voice faded to nothing. McAllister's scream replaced it in a split-second, pummelling Holly with its devastating power.

"You know. You've always known." McAllister looked quizzically at Holly with her head cocked on one side. "Actually, I'm curious. Why have you always assumed your enemy is a man? I'm not saying you're wrong, but it's clearly a He in your mind."

"I suppose that's me and Erin," Holly shrugged. "Daddy's girls at heart."

"We are all the sum of our parts, even your sister," McAllister said, before the scream blossomed forth again, leaving them both gasping. "It's dark where I am, and it's pulling me back, but I think I understand. A long time ago, something was put here, in this city. And it has waited a very long time. It's nearly ready now. And when it has everything it needs, it will start here, in your little corner of England. And from there, it will break the world."

"Tell me what it is," Holly demanded, fear creeping into her voice.

"I don't know," McAllister replied with a stifled tear. "I'm just a scream in the dark."

"If it's happening now, I need to get back."

"I said soon, Holly." McAllister gathered enough of herself to sound disappointed, as if a prize student had made an obvious error. "You of all people know that soon is a relative term. It's not happening now, and it won't happen tomorrow or the day after. You can rest easy."

Holly nodded her understanding as McAllister leaned in with serious intent in her haunted eyes.

"But your friends will live to see it."

"Great, so what do I do?"

"Well, that's up to you," McAllister sighed, leaning hard against Holly as she pushed the agony back down. "I mean, if you were just a function, a cog in a machine, you could view this as the machine's natural obsolescence. But if you're not, if you're capable of more than that, than how about stopping it."

"No pressure, then," Holly said, as the scream overcame them both again, driving them to the floor. "Look at me, I thought I could save you! No plan, I thought I'd just come up with summat when I got here, same as always! And I'm gonna stop the end of everything, am I?"

"Why do you think I ended up like this?" McAllister asked.

"Erin…" Holly sighed.

"Then why come here, if it's all her doing?"

Holly looked up and caught the understanding in her eyes.

"Because she did it to spite me."

"And that's the key to it," McAllister said, gently catching the tear on Holly's cheek. "That's why you can see me, that's why this whole stupid thing works. Did I strike you as someone who'd end up with this kind of afterlife? Someone racked with inner torment?"

Holly shook her head sadly.

"You've always known how to set me free, because you know how she works. You know what she would give you as a way out. It just never occurred to her it might be good for you. So just bloody well say it. Then get out of here fast, or you're going down with me."

"How am I supposed to do that?" Holly asked, scraping a fist across her cheek.

"You gave yourself a lifeline."

"Yeah, and I lost it in all the exploding."

"Not now, back then. You'll figure it out," McAllister said with an indulgent smile.

Holly felt the weight of what was to come looming. "I never said thank you. Not just for the brolly and the cryptic pep talk or for sacrificing yourself to save the world. But for listening to me. I were getting lost, and you set me right. All this talk of saving the city, or the world, but when I needed saving there were you."

McAllister shook her head, but smiled all the same. She plunged a hand into her coat pocket, produced her hip flask and took a swig.

"Are you ready?" she asked, and received a nod in response. "Now say what needs to be said."

Holly squeezed her eyes shut and forced the words out one at a time.

"It's. Not. My. Fault."

A trickling noise filled the chamber. When she opened her eyes, water was flowing down the steps and oozing from between the bricks on every wall. It slowly spread out to encompass the space. A deep and ominous groaning came from somewhere far away.

"Oh, that's not good," she whispered.

McAllister grabbed her hand as the room crumbled and the great sea engulfed them.

Mira only knew a handful of the words to 'Cloudbusting', and as it played, she realised how few of them she understood. Seriously, how was a yo-yo supposed to be dangerous? Sam was more confident, singing out in a haunting tenor alongside the recording.

But Mira knew the chorus, and when it came around, she pitched in with everything she had. She sank all the hope she had into those words, like a prayer or a summoning or a mantra. It would bring Holly back to them. She believed it. She had to.

Holly and McAllister floated in the deep, hearing the distant rumble of voices. A disconnected repetition of ghostly memories, most of them no longer empowered to consciousness. The Romans were in there somewhere, saluting their fallen brethren. They drifted down, pulled further and deeper into the white noise.

But Holly could hear something different. A rhythm in the midst of it all, thumping drums driving onwards like a great machine, and above it a voice this place had given her. Wrapped around that voice were two more. Real voices, her voices, voices that told her to be human, to love. Holly looked into McAllister's eyes, saw her smile as she drifted peacefully in the great sea, far away from the screaming. Then she kicked down with all her might.

The song was drawing to an end and Mira felt a rush of dread, that if this didn't work now, it never would. Nevertheless, she swore she'd do the whole damn discography if she had to.

A droplet landed on her head.

Mira looked up and saw that it was raining, raining indoors. There were no clouds, but water was falling on them all the same. A burst of white filled their vision, as the shower became a waterfall, drowning the hall in a great cascade. Mira was lost in the icy flood, separated from Sam as she struggled to keep her balance. They stumbled chilly and shaken towards each other as the deluge came to a sudden end, leaving only a few puddles on the marble floor. The temperature returned to normal in an instant, and steam drifted in the air.

Holly lay spread-eagled at their feet in a growing puddle. She pushed aside the curls that trailed across her face like seaweed, wincing as she touched her wounded eye.

"Did it work?" asked Mira, as she hauled Holly to her feet.

Holly pushed back her wet hair and peered into the ceiling. She turned to look at them with a smile, even though it hurt.

"You know what? I think it did," Holly said. "And that were brilliant, by the way, calling me home like that! She's a clever one. You see how lucky you are, Sam?"

"Yes, he does," Mira said with a smirk, and squeezed Sam's hand.

"Aw, me favourite couple, come here the pair of you!" Holly shouted and wrapped an arm around both necks and held tight. "You've got each other, and I've got the pair of you."

She took a step back and danced through the puddles as she took in everything.

"I don't know what happens next, but I reckon it's gonna be magic."

CHAPTER 38

1604

"You will be the King in the Mountain. Your life will be longer and stranger than you can possibly imagine. The world will grow and change around you, becoming something none of us can foresee, but you will learn to live in it. You will hold a light against the shadows and you will not fear them. And you will be alone. But you must know why. If you are to be strong enough, you must know why."

She gave a nod to indicate her understanding of the stranger's point, and she told them her reasons. When she was done, she looked hopefully into the stranger's kind eyes.

"Is that alright? Is that good enough?"

"Yes, my dear," The stranger said with an encouraging tone. "I think that will do very well."

CHAPTER 39

A thin sliver of light shone through the small window at the top of the bare cell. Jonathan lay back on the block of a bed and watched it shrink.

He'd had another glimpse, and it wasn't enough.

This time there had been more. He'd seen what lay beyond, touched them, watched them, walked in their footsteps. He had experienced what their world could be. When he closed his eyes, he saw the face of Níðhöggr. But he still wanted more.

The door opened, and he flinched at the realisation that he had not heard anyone unlock it. A man stood in the doorway, wearing an immaculate police uniform and peaked cap, decorated with badges of rank. His face was old and hawkish, and his eyes glittered in the fading light.

"Professor Fortune," he said amicably as he closed the door behind him. "I am so glad I had this chance to meet you."

"I've got nothing to say to you," Jonathan sighed, and turned back to the vanishing light.

"I rather think you have a great deal to say to the right person," said the policeman. "But who would believe what you have seen?"

"Don't humour me. I'm not mad."

"No, indeed. That is rather impressive of you," the visitor continued. "The Plain of Devastation is a sight few of your kind are equipped to process. And to have been in her presence and lived to tell the tale is truly remarkable."

Jonathan shuffled up to a sitting position and stared at the twinkling eyes of the quietly satisfied stranger he was sure was not a policeman.

"Who are you?" Jonathan asked.

you know who i am replied a voice in his head and he cried out in pain.

"I must apologise, I've not had to do that in quite some time," the man said.

"You're the other one," Jonathan gasped, leaping to his feet in joyful fascination. "You're the one she talked about, the one she sent here. You're Prospero."

"I do enjoy names," the man said, as he sat imperiously upon the bed. "I've grown greedy over time; I've answered to so many. But of them all, I prefer Lankin."

"There's so much…" Jonathan said, his mind fizzing with questions. "I don't know where to begin."

"I'm sure you don't, but I'm afraid I don't have much time," Lankin said. "I just wanted to take this opportunity to congratulate you. You have served my purpose marvellously."

"Your purpose?"

"Do you know the best way to manipulate someone?" Lankin asked. "You don't make them do things. You don't deceive them. You simply work out what they are going to do anyway, and make that serve your own needs. Take our current situation. You came here seeking knowledge, and found it. Holly Trinity and her friends came as protectors, and they saved the entire world from horror beyond reckoning. You all accomplished your own goals so perfectly, that you never noticed you were also accomplishing mine."

"What are your goals?" Jonathan asked, his excitement shifting into dread.

"You see, you did know where to begin," Lankin replied. "Let us just say that my sister was a loose end. I couldn't have her threatening the sanctity of this world with her witless brand of mayhem. Not while I have my own plans for it."

"I just wanted to know," Jonathan said. "To know everything, about you, about where you come from. About what else is out there. Tell me. Tell me everything."

"I wish I could," Lankin said apologetically. "I have so few opportunities to share my thoughts. But I am truly sorry,

Professor. You are also a loose end. And that is why our mutual associate will be visiting you tonight."

Panic flared in Jonathan's eyes and he bolted to the door. It was firmly locked. He hammered hard against the metal and shouted, to no avail.

Lankin moved to stand beside him, a small bottle held between his thumb and forefinger.

"I can't tell you what's going to happen when she gets here," he said coldly. "I tend to give her a degree of creative freedom, I'm sure as a teacher you will understand. But she did like the thought of dispensing with you, so I expect what she has in mind will be unpleasant. And, as a child murderer, I can't imagine anyone will come to your aid or mourn you."

He held out the bottle to Jonathan, and it sounded as if there was not one voice but two, the genial tones of the old man chiming alongside something darker and uglier.

"If you would like to depart quickly before she gets here, this will help," he said, palming the vial as soon as Jonathan reached for it. "But you must answer a question for me first."

Jonathan nodded his assent to the deal.

"You led Erin to believe you had come into certain knowledge," Lankin whispered. "She thought you were bluffing, of course. But you're not, are you?"

Jonathan flinched from his gaze, and Lankin knew it was true.

"Tell me how to kill her."

CHAPTER 40

Mira rolled over in the bed a little further than she had expected to. She forced open sleepy eyes to find herself alone. It was just before five. The sun had barely started to rise.

She pushed herself upright then flopped from the empty bed, wrapped herself in her dressing gown and headed to the living room. The lights were out, and Sam sat in the gloom, hands clasped before him as he wrestled with something intangible.

"How long have you been up?" she asked.

"A while," he replied.

She noticed that he was dressed. He'd clearly had no intention of returning to bed.

"I didn't want to disturb you; you were completely gone."

"We have had a very busy day," she ventured as she crossed the room to sit beside him.

"You remember that bloke I worked with who used to be in the army?" Sam asked. "He always used to say you sleep when you get the chance. You can go through all this, and go to sleep like nothing happened."

"I'm not a soldier," Mira countered, but when she looked in his eyes, she could see herself leading the ninth legion across the field of battle.

"No, you're a superhero," he said lovingly.

"That might just be the nicest thing anyone's ever said to me." Her heart soared, but she could already see him sinking low again.

"When we first got together, you used to have those nightmares." Sam's fingers slowly orbited each other as he spoke. "I knew that was normal. You'd seen people die, that wouldn't just go away. But then you slept fine again. It's stupid, but I felt proud of myself. Like I'd helped you get through it."

"You did help, Sam," Mira butted in. "I wouldn't have been able to cope with all this if I didn't have something to come home to. There were no monsters here, just you."

She could see Sam holding something back. "I don't know, Mira. I think you just got used to it. This is normal to you now."

"Sam, this was a bad one," Mira said. "This was bigger than anything I've seen. You shouldn't have had this as your first experience, nobody should. And I know that's my fault. Next time will be different, I promise. And, yeah, you get used to it."

"I don't know that anyone should be used to this." Sam's voice was cracking under the strain of it all. "I don't know that I want to be."

"I'm not saying I don't care," Mira said. "He murdered Chloe right in front of us, and nothing will ever make that right. I've failed to save people and I will always wonder what I could have done differently. That part never stops being hard. But you will get used to the monsters and ghosts, I promise. They're just things, like anything else."

"Mira, this isn't about that."

She saw his fingers tracing the lines on his hand where the claws had sat.

"You say there's no monsters here, just me, but I'm really not seeing that distinction right now." He turned to look at her, and the thin light of dawn caught the marks on his face. "I couldn't sleep, because I'm remembering."

"Oh God, Sam..." She pulled him close to her, wrapping an arm around his shoulder and interceding her free hand between his troubled fingers, which gripped hers tightly.

"I don't know what was a dream, and what was memory," Sam said, his voice wavering.

Mira could feel his body shaking softly against hers as she held him.

"But it all felt so real. I was in there, and I could see it all, and

304

I couldn't stop. I wanted to kill everything. I wanted to kill you. I saw what I did to Abi. And she was so scared…"

"It wasn't you…"

"Did I hit you?" Sam asked, pulling away as his voice tensed. "Because I dreamed that I did that, and it felt so real."

"It wasn't you, Sam," Mira repeated, and saw that it wouldn't be enough.

He rose from the sofa and stalked the room, all nervous energy, never turning back to look at her.

"Yes, when that thing was controlling you, it *made* you hit me," she said with a calm, measured tone. "But I'm not hurt, and I don't blame you, not for any of this. Abi won't either."

"Abi doesn't even remember. As far as she knows, Jonathan pushed her."

"As far as I'm concerned, she's right," Mira stated firmly. "Please don't blame yourself, Sam. You didn't know."

"But you did," he said, and a terrible thought process overcame him. "Mira, if you'd told me… No, that's not fair, I'm sorry…"

"I don't know, and I asked myself that a lot yesterday," Mira replied. "I think Jonathan would have come after you anyway. He wanted to get to Holly, through you, through me."

He turned to look at her and she saw the resignation in his eyes. She made Abi a target, and they both knew it.

"God, that's not better, is it?" Mira admitted. "It's so much worse."

"Look, I need to get out of here for a bit. Clear my head. Is that okay?"

"Yeah, sure, of course," Mira nodded. "I'll be here when you get back."

"I might go and see Abi when it's a bit more… today."

Mira waited for the suggestion that she join him at the hospital, or meet somewhere and go together, or that he would text her to make arrangements. None of them came.

"Listen," Sam said. "When I was talking to the archbishop at Delia's party, she said something about sealed orders, to do with Holly. Like she had some kind of secret documents telling her what to do if things got bad. She was pretty drunk, but I think it might be important."

"Thank you," she said, and walked over to where he stood. "I'll see you later."

He took her hand and squeezed it tightly, leaned in and kissed her once before he left. Mira knew that he had told her the story about the archbishop now in case he didn't come back.

Later that day, Sam was seated by his sister's bedside, watching her sleep. He had walked, and thought, and remembered, until a practical hour dawned. He had glimpsed the front page of the *York Press* declaring that Professor Jonathan Fortune had assaulted Abigail Jessica Nesbitt, 19, and murdered Chloe Mosby, 15. That was all anyone would ever know.

He had talked to a kindly doctor about things that were even harder to think about than the memories. He had tried not to look distressed at the mention of paralysis. And when all was done, he had sat here. Her eyes were drifting open, and he gently pulled his chair closer.

"Hey bro," she slurred through a jaw compressed by supportive bracing.

"Hey you," he said, gazing at her with complete love.

"Thinking about when we were kids," she said. "Remember when I fell off that wall and broke my arm?"

Sam nodded at the memory, as Abi's face tensed. She was trying to lift her head and look at her own legs, but was prevented from moving.

"I think this time it might be a bit worse."

She looked up at him, and knitted her brows in disapproval at the expression on his face. "Stop that. You pity me like that, there'll be trouble. When I'm on the Paralympics, I'll tell all the interviewers you never believed in me. Especially her on Channel 4 who you fancy."

Sam laughed despite himself, and took her permission to take comfort in humour. "I don't think they do drinking games at the Paralympics."

"S'pose not," she said. "That'd be the Paralytics, wouldn't it?"

They exchanged a look and couldn't laugh any more.

"I will be alright," she declared, and failed to keep from crying. "I will make it my business to be alright."

"I know you will," he said. "And I'll be here."

Sam took hold of her hand, and she gratefully accepted the small comfort.

"And don't worry, this time I won't let Mum think you pushed me."

Sam said nothing, and his silence felt like a lie.

CHAPTER 41

The branches of the willow tree hung low in front of the house, and Delia took a moment to appreciate them. Something simple and natural and not terrifying. Her leg hurt where the wound was healing, and emphatically told the rest of her there was no point in further prevarication. She headed up the garden path to the bungalow, and rang the doorbell.

After a few moments, the door opened a crack, and her heart leapt into her throat as a double-barrelled shotgun was thrust through the gap.

"No, no, no, please don't shoot me, I won't hurt you," she gabbled. "I'm looking for Angie, Mira sent me. I'm Delia, and please, please don't shoot me."

The gun was retracted and after much rattling of locks, the door opened to reveal a stout elderly lady staring at her through careworn eyes behind horn-rimmed glasses.

"Sorry, love, can't be too careful these days," she said. "I'm Angie. You'd best come in."

Delia stepped over a pile of unopened post and followed Angie to the sitting room. The old woman slumped dejectedly into a faded armchair. A children's book, careworn from generations of stories told, sat open on the arm of the chair, the time-honoured image of a sleeping princess on the cover.

"Sit yourself down, dear. Sorry about the mess," she said, indicating the near immaculate state of the room. "I've not had much company lately. My son's not really talking to me right now."

"I'm sorry about what happened," Delia said, taking a seat. "I only met Chloe briefly, but she seemed nice."

"Thank you, dear," Angie said, not looking in Delia's direction. "She was."

"Mira says she's sorry she hasn't called round," Delia explained. "She promises to come and see you, but things are all a bit fraught at the moment."

"I hope they don't think I blame them," Angie said, her voice all concern for others. "I know they did their best. You look like you've been in the wars yourself."

Delia's eyes turned to the support binding her wrist. "Oh yes, that. There was an octobird."

"Oh my."

"It was so scary," Delia said breathlessly. "I only came here for an archaeological dig, and suddenly I'm getting chased around by monsters. I've not been sleeping well at all since and... I'm sorry. Wittering on about me."

"I understand, dear," Angie said, a trace of a smile settling alongside her mournful eyes, as she picked up the book. "I was only little when my mum told me. I've been thinking about her a lot. How she never let me get too close to it all. When I was Chloe's age, I begged to be allowed to go and have adventures with the King in the Mountain. She wouldn't have it. But I've always been a soft touch."

Her eyes squeezed closed and her mouth hardened as she clutched the slim volume.

"Sleeping Beauty. My mum read this to me, and I read this to Chloe, so when they're ready, you've got somewhere to begin. The princess is sleeping, and she needs our help. I never thought... I should've kept her here. But it's hard to resist when you're young, isn't it?"

"Oh, I'm resisting," said Delia. "I'm resisting like mad. I don't know how Mira does it. I never asked for all this and I really don't know that I want it. But it's just..."

"Just what, dear?" Angie noted the uncomfortable demeanour that had come over her guest, who was studying her injured wrist.

"I can't not help," said Delia. "I just can't. I know what's at stake and I know what can happen, and to walk away now feels wrong. But I'm so scared. I saw terrible things. I watched a man I trusted do terrible things. I saw people I like get hurt, and I got hurt, and I could have died, and Chloe... I'm not Mira. I'm not ready for this. I don't want to die. But I can't not help."

She looked up at Angie, with nervous expectation in her eyes.

"So, I was wondering, if it would be alright, could I help you?"

"Yes, dear," Angie replied, a motherly smile crinkling her face. "I think that'd be grand."

CHAPTER 42

The trapdoor was flung open with a bang, and Holly ascended into the church. She paused to adjust the string tracing across her cheek before heading toward the door, back to the city where some fresh horror had presented itself. Business as usual.

"Aye aye," a familiar voice punned from behind her.

"Hello, Trouble," she sighed, and turned to see Erin sitting cross-legged on the stone floor in front of the wooden altar.

"Aren't you gonna say thank you?" she asked with a sly grin.

"I wouldn't mean it if I did. Seems like every time you try and help, someone ends up dead."

"Yeah, well, I put you right where you needed to be to save her, so that one's on you," Erin shrugged guiltlessly. "Run faster next time, if you're so set on this caring-about-people bollocks."

"And you wouldn't know about that," Holly said, drawing closer to her sister. "Can't have been easy for you. Betraying Dylan, I mean. I remember when we first met him. I've not seen many put a proper smile on your face since you became what you are."

"Don't get sentimental," chided Erin. "The bloke what came back weren't the boy we knew."

"You were a person that day. Just for a bit. Yeah, must have been hard."

"You're wrong, actually," sneered Erin, defensively avoiding her sister's one-eyed stare. "That's why it was so easy."

"Course it was," Holly said with a knowing half-smile. "And I suppose whatever it is I'm gonna find out there, it's summat you've cooked up to remind me how completely evil and irredeemable you really are."

"Couldn't say," Erin replied with a perfect poker face. "It might be a trap, or it might not."

"Ta very much," said Holly, then strode off with a wave. "Now get your arse out of me church."

"Love you too, Sis."

Mira sat in the window of the coffee shop turning a small plastic fork in a circle, watching the green leaf on the end swirling in its thin oily coating, but failing to muster the energy to eat it. She stared into the unappetising contents of the plastic tray and ignored the rest of the world, until a welcome voice at her shoulder brought her rushing back to it.

"So there's some terrible force for evil at large in the city right now. And I were wondering, d'you think it's that salad?"

Mira turned to the seat beside her and saw a crimson patch concealing where Holly's right eye had been.

"Oh, Holly, I'm sorry," she said.

"'S'alright," Holly said, sadness visible beneath her bravado. "I mean, no, obviously, it's not. I've not lost a big part of meself before, but I'll live. You might have to aim the grappling brolly from now on is all. Me scars usually disappear after a few years, mind, so maybe it'll grow back if I give it long enough. But I kinda think it won't."

"No," Mira said, contemplating her own losses. "I guess not."

"Anyway, Angie got me a load of really cool patches to wear," Holly added with a genuine sunniness. "It's like having lingerie for me face, it's brilliant."

"I'm glad you're okay," Mira said glumly. "I suppose it's not the end of the world."

"No but that's on its way an' all," Holly said. "Having all me mad ideas turn out to be true definitely takes the sting out of this. Officially not going barmy."

"Good for you." Mira shook her head. "An apocalypse must be a hell of an 'I Told You So'."

"It is if you stop it." Holly looked out at the crowded street, taking in the sight of all the people hurrying back and forth. "And

I intend to. Whatever he has planned for this lot, he'll have to go through me first. What I've seen in't happening. Not while there's us."

Mira said nothing, and silently prodded the salad with downcast eyes.

"There is us, isn't there?" Holly asked, fearful of the answer.

"Sam's gone," Mira replied. "He left, and he was right to leave. I put that man through so much, and he actually blames himself. And Chloe… Jonathan would never have even known she existed if it weren't for me. You want me to help you protect people, and I feel like all I do is put them in harm's way."

"Look, Mira," Holly said. "Whatever's coming, that's not today. This is just a normal day at the office, maybe a get well soon card from Erin for me eye. So, if you're not feeling it right now, I'll be alright on me own."

"Sam called me a superhero," Mira said, mocking herself. "I spend half my time clinging on for dear life, and the other half enjoying feeling special, so yeah, maybe that's what I am. Or maybe I'm the one who needs to be smarter, I don't know. I keep thinking about what I could have done differently, and going round and round in circles, with nothing to show for it but a broken heart and an indigestible salad. If I keep this up any longer, I am going to go mad."

She pushed the plastic tray across the counter and turned to Holly with tears in her eyes, but strength behind them.

"I'm a hero, Holly Trinity," she said, and owned it. "And so are you. So that's what I want to do today. We are going to help people, people who might end up like Chloe or Malcolm. But they won't because we'll be there for them. We'll keep all these people safe, and they'll never even know we were there."

"Righty-ho then, Chaudhri." Holly gripped both of her hands and broke into a Cheshire cat smile. "Let's go have ourselves an adventure."

Find out more at www.bensawyerauthor.wordpress.com